Hiding Behind The

No Time Like The Present

by

Debbie McGowan

No Time Like The Present

Second Edition
Published 2016 by Beaten Track Publishing
First published 2012

ISBN: 978 1 78645 088 3

Beaten Track Publishing,
Burscough. Lancashire.
www.beatentrackpublishing.com

For Carl:
words still fail me.

***

This novel is a work of fiction and the characters and events in it exist only in its pages and in the author's imagination.

“My fault, my failure, is not in the passions I have, but in my lack of control of them.”

Jack Kerouac

Table of Contents

Chapter One: Holdings

Not the typical murder scene: no dark, rainy street, with concealed doorways, grim, spooky nooks where dangers lurk, imagined or real. Not even a place devoid of other people, who might witness such grisly events with relish. This, an average office in a busy, multistorey block, in the middle of the day—a bright and unseasonably warm one at that—and the usual staff milling around, mostly temps, armed with reams for photocopying, or otherwise glued to the nothingness of their computer screens. No-one heard, saw, suspected anything out of the ordinary.

The coffee was ghastly, and he'd poured it into the drip tray almost before it registered with his taste buds. Bitterness sensed by the tip of the tongue, cup tossed carelessly into the bin. Would they look there for evidence? Unlikely they would look at all. Yes, ironically the coffee was beyond disgusting today—a perfect day for dealing with the one and only enemy a man ever had. He dragged a towel across his hands, appreciated the possibility that they may find him by this act, and stuffed the towel into his briefcase, along with *The Guardian*, a sheaf of papers, his diary and the seven-inch knife he had taken from the fisherman down by the canal.

***

Alice walked past the machine three times before she recognised the odour. It was becoming increasingly familiar and almost as distasteful as the coffee. The coffee: it pervaded not just her nose, but all her other senses, getting into her clothes, and into her mind, refusing to leave her alone, even when she was safely home at night. It wasn't her job to deal with the blasted thing, nor her pleasure, being as she despised even the most richly, freshly ground variety. In fact, that was quite possibly worse, on account of its delectable yet ultimately deceptive aroma, willing people to sip from the poisoned chalice. She hated coffee, hated the dispensed tea, even the chemically decaffeinated equivalent, all of it so bad for one's health, leaving its grubby little rings everywhere and a stink on the drinker's breath.

Fortunately for the coffee supplier, the vast majority of the workforce didn't share Alice's loathing of vended hot beverages, although it was her duty, if not formalised through a job description, to see to it that the coffee was always fresh. Needless to say, it was rarely her priority. The first thing she did when she arrived in the morning was switch off the air conditioning and open the windows—a futile act, for within ten minutes, the clones would arrive, close the windows, and soon thereafter someone would take it upon themselves to turn the air conditioning on again. Back to the constant drone and the dryness and allegedly temperate conditions for both human and machine to work with perfect efficiency. Yet it never did quite get rid of the stench of the coffee.

Alice noted the drip tray was full to the brim and muttered under her breath—such as she ever bothered to speak any louder—on the waste of time and milk. Why add it in the first place, if only to tip it away? And was there anything to stop them using the sink, other than sheer laziness and lack of consideration for the poor soul who had to tend to the mess it made? A torrent of insipid, brown goo oozed irreverently down the path of its own stain, onto the brushed chrome stand—which was ugly and out of place, but it came with the lease—and eventually the floor. Surely it wasn't difficult to miss? Well, not for Alice.

It was apparent from its syrupy resistance that the culprit on this occasion had positively piled in the sugar. That was another ploy: to hide the taste of something clearly not intended for constant consumption, and now it was drying on her hands, in between her fingers, glueing them together. It was enough to make her vomit, always washing away other people's waste and mess.

A personal assistant to whom? She asked this question of the taps, strangling them in exasperation when they failed to reply and scrubbed her hands, leaving traces of her crime on a rancid, chequered tea towel.

The filter was set and ready to go: just past eleven-thirty and already the fifth pot. She estimated the cost in her head, as she did every day at about this time, when it was always the fifth pot; it would have been closer to the seventh, had she been doing her job properly—the bit that wasn't mentioned at interview and was glossed over at every performance review. If she were to be run over by a bus that very day they'd all notice, because the coffee would go stale. They might even question where 'Thingummy-bob who does the coffee' was. It happened on her last day off: hardly fun, a lengthy wait in a stretch of draughty hospital corridor euphemistically signposted as a waiting room, followed by a swift and insincere apology, something to do with emergencies, and then she was seen, told all was well and sent on her less-than-merry way.

Arriving back at work the following morning, one of the temps—who had been working there long enough to essentially be permanent, but none of them were permanent anymore—noticed Alice's return and intercepted her at the empty coffee machine. No stock had been ordered, Alice explained, so there was nothing she could do. They would have to go without for a day. That was all the evidence required: said temp returned to her seat and all returned to normal, minus the caffeine.

Alice wrinkled her nose, as the trickle of fresh coffee brought her back to the moment, the nauseating aroma filling the space around her and making her feel faint.

***

Upstairs in the boardroom, an interesting meeting was afoot. It was the usual set-up, the boardroom, with a vast oval beech-laminated surface, polished in an ad lib fashion, leaving smears to catch the eye in the right light but on the whole perfectly presentable. Slim-cushioned seats on each of the sixteen chairs around the perimeter provided sufficient comfort for one or two hours' convening. A couple of clip-framed Monet prints adorned three of the magnolia walls; on the fourth was a screen that didn't work the way it should, and the tech people couldn't say why. A hard-wearing beige looped carpet completed the frugal décor.

Standing just behind the closed door, two men were engaged in conversation that to any eavesdropper would have seemed jovial and entirely appropriate to the context: the latest financial news, any chance of sun at the weekend for that round of golf, and so on. It all belied the reality, the build-up of years of envy, months of planning and finally this—not the opportunity he had endeavoured to create, but one which had arrived of its own accord. God knew, the coffee was bad enough to disguise the most obvious poison, but that was not the way it occurred.

The director leaned back against a chair, heaving in deep, gulping breaths, winded by the surprise, a patch of shimmering red radiating outwards from his shoes, across the beige nylon expanse. *How? Why? After so long and so many, it comes to this?* The handle of the knife was there in his thigh and he could not shift his hands from their clutch on his chest to remove it; the pain there far greater. He slid, grasping blindly at the chair, which followed him down,

down, to the floor, while his companion shrugged, smiled and walked away, quietly closing the door behind him.

Muffled conversations, passing the time of day as if all was as it should be. Not one person could he identify by name, all of them relative strangers in this significant, modern building, where each spent two-thirds of their waking hours. Some voices he could match to faces, or to backs, but names? Who needed names in a place like this? Clocking in and out was a thing of the past, now computers logged the arrival and departure of every single member of staff. No more loitering at reception, stealing a few minutes here and there, and it all added up. It shouldn't matter anymore. After all, he was bleeding to death in his own boardroom.

And there were people out there; surely someone would stop when they heard his calls for help? Except he wasn't making any. The words formed in his mouth—he was renowned for his deep, hearty baritone—but left his lips in wisps and wheezes, over and again, until the boardroom faded from view and a flat facsimile of Monet's 'Water Lilies' bloomed, for Alistair Campion, for the last time.

Chapter Two: Limb from Limb

If only she'd tested the lights in the first place, not now, when she was sitting in the midst of a tangled mass of wires of varying thickness, with absolutely no way of determining where one set began and another ended. Brute force only resulted in crackles like static, as yet another piece of cable broke off in her hand, to the accompanying pop and swish of the branches giving way.

It had been so exciting, all those hours ago, operating in the dark, trying to contain the childlike impatience, even daring optimism on occasion. Every bauble carefully placed, each dangling loop of tinsel draped with precision, all ready for the grand turn on. Plug in socket, switch down, sudden swell of glorious illumination, slight fizz of current, enormous bang and instant blackout.

Funny how the tree, as if bestowed with some kind of prior knowledge, had come to life as soon as it was released from its netting, flaying spiky limbs in all directions, one last wild protest at having been scragged from a managed forest somewhere bleak and northerly. Its revenge was to refuse absolutely to relinquish its hold on the broken fairy lights. Each tug sent a further torrent of baubles crashing to the floor—thankfully they were mostly plastic—and if the tinsel hadn't seen better days before this whole saga commenced, it was certainly past utility now, not that tinsel was especially useful in any situation.

There was no other option. Scissors were the way forward, the only chance to save the tree, at the expense of the lights, which no doubt would have pleased it considerably, had it been a living thing, instead of a dying plant, crammed into a drilled-out chunk of tree trunk and ceremoniously dumped in a living room, the carpet of which had been rendered invisible by a thick bed of fallen needles. It was some consolation that the lights hadn't been particularly impressive last Christmas, although all this unnecessary expenditure for, at most, one month of spectacle and a further twelve of digging bits of old pine tree out of the sofa seemed so entirely futile.

Eleanor returned from the kitchen with the scissors: a vast pair of wallpaper shears, with which she hoped to avoid contact with the psychopathic tree. She snipped randomly, wherever she could gain access, cursing under her breath each time she snagged her skin or her jumper. This was not her doing. The room was too small for the tree, or it too big for the room. Perhaps it would have been better, as James had originally suggested, if they had bought a house somewhere, together. It was her own stubbornness, mixed with a sense of losing both control and her independence, that led to the decision to keep the flat. James was 'satisfied' with her decision. Whatever she wanted, whenever she was ready, then that was what they would do.

He said these things and it sounded so wonderful; so caring, thoughtful, ever considerate and infuriatingly indecisive. He passed the buck back to her every time, patiently waiting for her to reason through each suggestion made, all of the possible options and their potential outcomes. The thing with the house, for instance: he had one to sell, so he could more or less buy another property outright. But then, Eleanor explained, if, not that she thought it likely, but *if* their relationship ended, she'd have nowhere to go. That same eventuality had brought her back from Newcastle, after she and Kevin agreed to call it a day, and he'd been in no rush to sell up. Their parting had been amicable, and, she assured him, whenever he got around to it she'd be glad to receive her share of the meagre proceeds, but not to worry too much. She was just pleased to be back with her friends and out of medicine.

So, James said, he would lend her half of the money, and she could pay him back. It was a marginally more attractive proposition and would certainly save a lot on the interest. However, it still meant James would have some kind of hold over her, not that she imagined for one minute he was anything like that. Had it entered her mind at any point in time, she would never have fallen in love with him.

His last-ditch attempt was to suggest getting a mortgage together, whereby he would pay his half up-front as the deposit, leaving them with a fifty percent balance, which, of course, was Eleanor's share. He would pay the bills and help out with other expenditure as and when required. But she wasn't having that, either. So finally, he moved into the flat, leaving his house empty, apart from when he was needed at head office, which was most of his time, hence that was where his house was. Eleanor was implicitly aware of his sacrifice and how selfish she was being, yet somehow she couldn't stop herself.

Her frustrated hacking had turned the fairy lights into dull, stringy lametta that hung in rigid little arches over the now somewhat less feisty branches, apparently satisfied by the slaughter of the lights. Eleanor carefully pulled out each strand of cable and dropped it onto the mounting pile of broken decorations in the centre of the floor. Any second now, James would arrive home, and she had desperately wanted the tree to be ready for his return. The last thing she needed was yet another bout of late-night shopping, but there were no two ways about it. She had destroyed everything. Was it some kind of unconscious ploy to sabotage Christmas? She restarted the music, trying once more to get into the spirit, whilst she shoved the tree's hapless victims into a plastic bag and hummed along to a happy melody. It was almost working.

***

"That's quite possibly the most outlandishly festive décor I have ever come across," George said with a grin as he poked the tiny, battery-operated, fibre-optic tree. It was so small and light that it slipped several inches across the waiting room table, before Josh put out his hand to stop it.

"What do you expect?" he retorted. "Perhaps something like the monstrosity in Trafalgar Square would be more to your tastes?"

"No, no, don't be silly. But as far as therapeutic intervention goes—"

"Christmas is a time for giving all your money to the VAT man," Josh interrupted. "It's tasteful and pleasingly understated." He straightened his little tree, then added, "And it was on special offer in Gadget Heaven."

George tutted knowingly. Getting Josh to buy anything new was a virtually impossible task, unless it involved buying new gadgets, in which case stopping him was a far greater problem. It made his Christmas gifts interminably predictable; whatever the latest fad was, they'd all get one. Last year it had been various wi-fi devices, all courtesy of Gadget Heaven, all received with gritted-teeth gratitude. And it wasn't that the gifts were thoughtless, convenient acquisitions; nothing could be further from the truth. Josh spent hours pondering over his purchases, trying to match items to each of his friends' interests. He'd even found a USB shaver for Dan a couple of years back, which turned out to be one of the most useful things he owned.

"Would you please stop playing with my tree!" Josh slapped the back of George's hand, and he immediately retracted it.

"But it feels so nice."

"Ha! And you said it had no therapeutic value. Anyway, what do you want?"

George grinned again but said nothing. Since he'd started the counselling course, he'd had to ask Josh for more favours than even the strongest friendship could withstand, and it was truly the case that every time they met up he needed something else.

"You know after Christmas? I have to increase to twelve hours of one-to-one, no hand-holding allowed, et cetera?"

"Which you're doing at the hospital."

"Which I *was* doing at the hospital, but there aren't enough places available."

"And?" Josh asked, but went on before George could respond. "You do realise all the goons on your course are my competition?"

"I know, you said already. The thing is that the hospital asked me to ask you if I can do more hours here instead."

"By the hospital, you mean that bloody Tierney idiot again, don't you?"

"Well, Sean suggested it, yes." George flapped the fibres of the tree, and they responded in a little wave of light, bouncing gently up and down for several seconds through their own momentum. He was about to do it again, but Josh was frowning and blowing air out of his nostrils so hard it was a miracle he wasn't snorting. He glared at George, who obediently folded his arms.

The truth was, Josh didn't really mind at all. It would leave him with tons more free time that could more usefully be put to planning lectures for the course. That's what made it a double-edged sword, seeing as he'd avoided teaching at the university for the past ten years and utterly loathed the place, even if it did pay the bills. Then Sean Tierney had started his latest bullying regime, by proxy, because he wouldn't have dared to suggest it to Josh directly.

"I'll get you an apple every single day," George offered, unhelpfully.

"I don't want a damned apple."

George knew the answer was 'yes' and was about to say thank you when the sound of shuffling up the stairs distracted him. Both men stopped dead and held their breath, waiting like hunted-down teenagers in a horror movie, knowing all the while that the rustling of bags, the low-volume grunting, signified one thing: Eleanor was coming, and she was in a very bad mood.

"Festive spirit, my arse," she said, emerging from the staircase, her arms weighed down by plastic carrier bags, spilling their cargo of shiny beads, tinsel and multicoloured, glittery baubles onto the floor. "Don't you say anything," she shouted at George before he even opened his mouth. Instead, he went to the kitchen and filled the kettle. He knew better than to test his fledgling skills on this patient, but he listened in to hear what the latest excursion into life with a live-in partner had done to her.

"Working late again," she stated loudly to no-one in particular. It was an exclamation of her annoyance that, having spent two hours putting the decorations on the tree, she'd had to take them all off again—a further two hours—she was convinced that the scratches on her arms—"Look at the state of them, please!"—would go septic and now it had cost her a small fortune—"Forty-seven pounds eighty? For a box of glass balls and two strings of beads? Are you having a laugh?"—to replace all the stuff that she and the tree had wrecked between them. That tree: her unwitting accomplice and new nemesis.

Josh chuckled and picked twigs and needles out of her hair as she ranted away, pausing only to take in breath. And, Eleanor continued, there was something very wrong with chopping down trees for the sake of Christmas, which, when all was said and done, was about new life and the Saviour of the whole world, which she was pretty sure extended to trees, although the 'living trees', as they liked to call them, cost twice as much again as the half-dead thing now taking up most of her living room, and probably wouldn't look any the better for their roots being intact, come December the twenty-fifth.

Yes, he said he was sorry, but the American MD's plane had been delayed in Ohio, and his meeting had to be postponed. No point, after all, having a video conference with a blank wall, but he'd drive up just as soon as they were done. It would be well after midnight, and he promised not to wake her, would warm his hands before he snuggled up behind her and even go and make the cocoa, should he inadvertently disturb her.

"Doesn't James know you're disturbed enough already?" Josh chanced.

"That's not funny," she snapped, but with a little less venom than her previous onslaught. "I thought I'd do something nice for him for a change, and look where it's got me. I'm wearing more flora than a church done up for a wedding, I'm bleeding, and my carpet is utterly destroyed."

"They're only pine needles, Ellie. They do vacuum up."

"Eventually. By Easter, perhaps, if I'm lucky."

"You know what your problem is?"

"No, what's my problem, Joshua?" She glowered at him.

"George will tell you." Josh turned his attention to his own little tree, just as George placed three cups on the table.

"I'll what?" he asked, too terrified to even contemplate letting on that firstly, he had heard every word—but then the dentist downstairs would have been able to as well, had it not been seven o'clock in the evening—and secondly, he did know precisely what Eleanor's problem was. It had nothing to do with carpets, or Christmas trees, and everything to do with not wanting to share her life and her space with James, or any other person. Too much independence for too long: a hard habit to break, even if she really was willing to give it a try.

Chapter Three:
The Smell of Murder

It was well into the evening before the chairman's body was discovered, slumped part way under the table and framed by a maroon-black, irregular oval. Curiously, in spite of the knife sticking out of his leg, or indeed, because of it, the initial consensus was that the evidence pointed to an accident. After all, it did look very much like her husband's fishing knife, his wife conceded from her long-term deathbed. And he was planning a trip imminently. How imminently? She couldn't quite say, not in her state of health, not with the grief and the shock that he had gone before her.

Alice was quite convinced it was no accident. Her keen olfaction and the synaesthesia left her with little doubt about much of what went on around her. However bad the smell, the colours were worse, and the boardroom, like the coffee room, had the same kind of tint to it: a dirty, bruise-like blue-purple, like the glow of the evening sky in opposition to the setting sun. Most of the darker ones were blue, regardless of their attempts at disguise, always obscuring their colours with the same sorts of cologne; perhaps it was something hormonal. This one was most distinct, but the policeman wasn't interested: there had been a major drugs raid somewhere or other, lots of paperwork, not a priority.

"But a man is dead!" she exclaimed meekly. People smiled and nodded in placation. *Who was he again? Will our jobs be safe?* Then back to the grindstone. Most of them, whether they knew her or not, thought Alice was stark raving mad, always going on about auras, like some psychic off the TV, and the harder she tried to explain that she saw *aromas*, not auras, the more convinced they became of her insanity. She'd long since given up on meaningful relationships with anyone other than her budgie, Albert, who was getting on a bit and starting to look very grey in places, but he didn't smell particularly pungent, so was very welcome in her life. Not once had he betrayed his curious mistress, and he could talk when he wanted. Generally, when the news came on, he would be there chattering away, his favourite line, 'And now the weather', over and over again, until Alice gently placed the floral cage cover over her chirping companion.

She was simply the mad old woman with the talking budgie, who saw things that weren't there, so all of what she had to say about the death of the chairman fell to the floor, along with his steadily congealing blood. The board wrote off the loss and ordered her to book in some fitters at her earliest convenience. Incidentally, they added, some tea and coffee would be nice. And maybe a plate of biscuits, if it wasn't too much trouble. Alice did as she always did and obliged.

The immediacy of their convention was most interesting, for it usually took them weeks to plan an emergency meeting; months, if it wasn't too urgent. Yet, like circling vultures, there they all were, congregated in the boardroom, as if nothing was to do. No-one had sat near the pool of blood, but it may as well have not been there, for all the notice they took of it.

Alice waited patiently while the little machine spat and spluttered, and did her best to avoid its repugnant bloom as she eased the jug out and onto a trolley. She decanted the milk and eyed the fairy cakes at the back of the shelf, uncertain and disinterested in how they'd got there. They carried no tag declaring ownership and would appease the baying wolves, distract them whilst she made her retreat, back to more useful work. At least, she concluded, she could lay them out on a nice plate, with a doily, for the gentlemen upstairs, who perhaps wouldn't care one way or another, but she did.

"Hey, Alice! How's it going?" The familiar voice called her back to reality, rapidly followed by the cascade of colours that signified Dan Jeffries was in the building. These sensory registers always kicked in a couple of moments after her stomach flipped. Silly, really; she was old enough to be his mother.

"Good morning, Dan. I imagine you've heard the news about Mr. Campion?"

"News? No, I've come straight from the airport. I've been in Dubai visiting my brother. What news is this?"

Alice liked to think she was one of those who took no joy from sharing gossip; nor was this an occasion for smug, warm, newsworthy chit-chat.

"He's dead," she said.

Dan reeled slightly, though it wasn't that much of a shock. He waited for more information, and when it wasn't forthcoming he prompted, "A heart attack, presumably?"

"Oh, no. Nothing like that, or at least the doctor who pronounced him dead said that was probably what killed him, due to the excessive blood loss."

"I'm sorry, Alice, but I'm not following. Did Alistair have an accident of some sort?"

Alice nodded solemnly. "Yes, an accident, of some sort." She stopped, as if she had been put on pause, the plate hovering in her hand. Dan frowned.

"I don't think so, no," she said, thoroughly attending to wiping the plate with a paper towel. "He was stabbed." She opened the cakes and carefully placed them, one by one, on top of the perfectly centred doily.

"Pardon? Stabbed, did you say?" Dan shuddered, his scars twingeing, as if uttering the word itself might reopen the wounds that had taken far less time to mend than it was taking to deal with the psychological reasons and consequences of their happening.

Alice nodded again, very slowly this time, hoping the movement of her head would convey the message more clearly. She added the fairy cakes to the loaded trolley and made to manoeuvre past Dan.

"Here, let me help," he said, taking the other end of the trolley and holding the door open with his foot.

"Oh, thank you so much," Alice gushed gratefully, "although I'm sure I can manage from here."

"I have absolutely no doubt of that, Alice, but why should you, when I'm more than happy to lend a hand?" Dan smiled and gave her a wink.

Alice blushed and said no more about it, instead walking along behind the trolley, not really pushing it at all, but with her hands resting on the back of it so she at least had the illusion of doing something. Dan pressed the button for the lift, and they waited.

It wasn't exactly an uncomfortable silence that ensued, because neither wanted to converse with the other especially. They had been dealing with each other long enough for theirs to be a little more than a gracious passing acquaintance, and Dan was far from lacking in confidence when it came to the accomplishment of small talk. Alice, too, could hold her own, if she chose to, but there was little to say, when the sum shared experience of both parties was in arranging appointments with someone who was now dead. Dan chewed his lip while he pondered, enjoying where the thought processes took him sufficiently to not consider asking further of Alice, although he imagined she knew little more than she had already stated.

"It's so kind of you to assist me like this," she said, as the lift doors slid open and Dan pulled the trolley inside with him. She dutifully followed; the visual display caused by his proximity in the enclosed space was both disturbing and beautiful.

"No problem, Alice. I should go and catch up with Bill, anyway." He had picked up on her discomfort and backed away as far as possible. Given that the floor space was no more than five feet square, and the trolley was taking up most of this, it wasn't very far.

The lift trundled up three floors, slowed down and jolted to a stop. The doors opened onto the bright corridor ahead, where the usual people marched back and forth in their usual way, barely stepping aside for them to pass. Alice delivered Dan and the refreshments to the boardroom and darted away, like a frightened mouse, back down the stairs to the safety of her own booth in the main office. Nothing else was amiss.

"Dan, old man, how the devil?" Bill Meyer rose to his feet immediately upon realising that the tea trolley was not unaccompanied, his greeting both cliché and trademark.

"Bill, good to see you," Dan responded, his gaze automatically shifting to the large ruddy patch on the floor. He consciously looked back to the men of varying ages sitting around the table and nodded his greetings and condolences to each in one motion.

"Al's PA has filled you in, I take it?" Bill asked matter-of-factly.

"Mmm? What? Oh yes, well, sort of. She was a little sketchy on the details, to be honest."

"We all are." Bill hesitated long enough for one of the other men to pick up the story, someone Dan hadn't seen before: oldish, quite bald, with a hypertension pallor, not that it made him in any way distinguishable from his associates.

"Al was going fishing at the weekend. I still lay money on it being a cardiac in the middle of preparing his kit," the bald man stated smugly.

Bill shrugged. "The truth is we just don't know what happened, and the police don't seem to be in any rush to find out, either. His GP said Al had been complaining of chest pain and went for an ECG recently. The doctor's pretty certain it was a heart attack. Time will tell if the knife in his leg had anything to do with it. How's the nipper?"

Dan was only mildly surprised by the sudden change of subject mid-conversation. It was another of Bill's little nuances, not quite understanding how to deal with social niceties, especially in an extraordinary situation. Alistair Campion had always been Dan's point of contact; that was whom he had come to see. As the major shareholder, Bill would be stepping right into Alistair's shoes, and it would all go on as before.

Dan offered Bill a congenial smile. "I imagine Adele wouldn't take too kindly to you referring to our daughter as 'the nipper', but she's fine, thanks for asking."

No further questions. Down to business. Dan had spent his time in Dubai doing the groundwork for a new project and was keen to get the ball rolling, so he joined the other men in their remarkable feat of sitting right next to death whilst failing to appreciate that it was staring them right in the face.

***

Alice waited until Dan had cleared the building before she returned to the boardroom, listening at the door to make sure there was no-one inside. The coast clear, she entered quietly and locked herself in. She had her own theory about what had taken place and needed some time alone at the scene of the crime. There was still the rainbow of colours lingering above the table, mingled with pale browns and greys, a perception that entertained her when first she started working with traditional businessmen. They smelled the way they looked—bland and uninteresting—and adorned themselves and their offices accordingly. At some point, someone had suggested that they call in a Feng Shui expert to try and clear the drab, miserable atmosphere at Campion Holdings PLC, but Mr. Campion was having nothing to do with 'that new-age nonsense', and as always she was on his side, in public at least.

There was no more loyal a PA than she. It wasn't her place to disagree with her boss, even though at times she wanted to speak out against some decision or other he had made, and she could have told him why his staff never stayed. It just wouldn't be right to worry him with her suggestions, or warn him about the aggrieved employee in sales who seemed mentally unstable, or mention the number of new contracts he would pull in were he to consider appointing a woman to the board.

Campion Holdings was old-fashioned, making it all the more surprising that people like Dan Jeffries had any dealings with them. The directors' lives consisted of golf and fishing and evenings at the lodge, meaningless affairs and staid business traditions. In short, they were nothing like the young entrepreneurs they dealt with. They were nothing like Dan Jeffries, whose scent had thankfully dissipated sufficiently for her to now concentrate on her investigation.

Her theory went something like this: whenever Mr. Campion had a meeting with anyone, regardless of whether it was business or personal, he'd phone through to ask her to check that the coffee was fresh. It was the only time he did so, and it was for his own benefit, for he trusted her well enough to know that it would already have been dealt with.

"Always at the ready, Alice," Mr. Campion would say, to the extent that it could have been her nickname. And so, that was what had preceded his demise in the boardroom, so she knew he had not been alone. She admonished the place where he had exhaled his last breath for not having real CCTV installed—*In a building filled with paper and people and old computers? What point is there, Alice?* after all.

Looking around the room, there was nothing peculiar. All the chairs had been as they should be, bar the one he fell against. None of the pictures were hanging in a lopsided fashion, contrary to every murder mystery she'd ever watched or read. There was little else to go on. Not a mark on the table, no hairs on the furniture, shoeprints on the carpet nor—if she'd had a dusting kit she'd have readily discovered—a single fingerprint that didn't belong there. But someone had been there. She knew. It was someone who would not seem out of place in the building, or indeed on the directors' floor. Definitely not a director; they were all out at their clubs or working from home. She'd had the forethought to phone wives and girlfriends, and each alibi checked out perfectly. Yet someone had been there.

Dropping to her hands and knees, she bent down low over the blood patch, almost keeling over with the vertigo induced by the onslaught of sensory information it yielded. The carpet had been cleaned, with a foam cleaner by the look of it. It was pointless stuff the cleaners bought from the wholesalers and as likely to remove a bloodstain from a beige, nylon, foam-backed carpet as it was to offer to make the coffee from this point forward.

She crawled a little further under the table, scrunching her eyes up, as if that would make it easier to pick out any small clue missed by the police or the vacuum cleaner. There was nothing there, other than crumbs from the cakes, which stuck to the palms of her hands and would no doubt make a dreadful mess of her tights.

Slowly, she shuffled forward, scanning every inch of the floor under the table, before she emerged from the other side and sat back on her heels, brushing the crumbs from her hands in displeasure. Except that this wasn't a crumb, it was a—

"Alice? What are you doing?"

No time to look now, she picked up the tiny object and pressed it against her palm so as not to lose it.

"I thought you had gone," Alice answered, blushing.

"And you normally resort to kneeling on the floor of the boardroom after I've visited?" Dan's intention was humour, but he could see she was extremely distressed by having been discovered. "So, the cleaners are that bad, are they? Did Al charge you with one last task to get rid of them?" he tried to joke again.

"I was just checking something. Contact lenses, you know the sort of thing."

"Contact lenses? Since when did any of your senses fail you, Miss Marple?" He continued to affect a jocular tone to hide his suspicion, for Alice was quirky, a little eccentric, but not the sort to engage in anything as undignified as crawling around the floor, not without what she believed to be good reason.

"I…I thought I'd locked the door," she stammered, embarrassed and overwhelmed to be caught in such a predicament.

"You did. Maintenance let me in. Your carpet fitters are here." She still looked very much like the best thing that could happen to her right now was to follow her boss into the afterlife. "Tell you what," Dan suggested. "I won't ask any more questions, but if you decide you want to tell someone what you think happened here, then I promise to listen. How about that?"

"Oh, I'm sure there's nothing to worry about." Alice smiled nervously and stood up, still clutching, she hoped, the very small item in her hand.

"And I'm sure there is, otherwise, you wouldn't be here now, doing the whole Agatha Christie routine."

"I shouldn't be concerned with my silliness if I were you."

Dan raised an eyebrow, a motion that confirmed he was sincere in his offer, and that she was off the hook.

"Anyway, I only came back to ask you a small favour," he said, allowing her to pass, before closing the door on the beige boardroom murder scene.

Chapter Four: Gathering Steam

James wasn't late coming home; he didn't come home at all until after the weekend, by which point Eleanor had convinced herself that she liked being on her own far too much and could see little reason to tolerate his lack of consideration any longer. She was GP on-call, dealing with a constant stream of flu cases and not much more to keep her mind occupied. Kevin had assured her, in the unofficial pre-career-return briefing, that it was pretty much par for the course. Being on-call meant spending all day and all night waiting for the phone to ring, and just when she thought it was safe to pop to the loo, somebody somewhere would decide their need was considerably more urgent than hers.

By the end of Sunday, there was nothing Eleanor wanted more than to languish in tatty old pyjamas and a fluffy dressing gown, and as soon as she handed over to her relief, she did just that. She went straight home, changed out of her clothes, made a cup of tea, flopped onto the sofa and closed her eyes. As an afterthought, she turned on the all-new, fully functioning Christmas lights, and her mind was changed in an instant. The tree was no longer the vast, imposing set of ugly spikes she had at first perceived it to be. Her arms hadn't gone septic, and the dropped needles were all but gone. The new glass baubles stayed exactly where she'd hung them, and the star at the top was rather more tasteful than its predecessor: the rotten old angel that looked for all the world like a Barbie doll with a tree stuck up her skirt.

Yes, it is perfect.

She watched the lights twinkling gently, a chasing golden glow, spiralling downwards, like trails from a shooting star. How lovely it would be to share this feeling with James...if he decided to return at some point before Christmas.

It was almost bedtime on Monday before he finally walked through the door, fully expecting to find her sitting with a pile of books and a notepad, for that was all she'd done every night since they'd got together. Instead, she was showered, wearing the same fluffy dressing gown, and curled up on the sofa, watching TV. Without a word, he bent down and kissed her gently on the head. She responded by lifting her face towards his, a cue for him to kiss that, too. He took his bag to the bedroom and then made cocoa for them both—not a word about the Christmas tree, but she'd anticipated as much. He'd get around to it, like he got around to everything eventually. Less haste and less speed was James Brown all over.

Twenty minutes later, he returned, armed with two steaming cups. He handed one to Eleanor before he sat down next to her and took her free hand in his own.

"When you said you'd be late home, James, I did think you meant on the same day."

"Ah, yes. I didn't think of it that way. You are right, of course. It seemed sensible to stay, for I was able to move forward all of my other appointments. I promise that you have my undivided attention for the rest of the week."

"Perhaps you could tell me what you're thinking next time? I'm not a mind reader."

"I disagree. However, I am sorry. I was hoping to clear the decks so that we could prepare for the festive season together. I see you have begun without me."

Eleanor didn't respond. The nagging wife part of her personality was all set to turn it into an unnecessary argument.

"Did you see Oliver over the weekend?" she asked instead.

"Yes. Indeed I did. He is very excited about his visit. I, too, am looking forward to spending time as a family. This is not overly optimistic, I hope?"

Eleanor didn't imagine that she, James and Oliver would ever spend time 'as a family'. OK, so on the other occasion they had been together, it had been quite successful, aside from the usual tantrums that preschool children are prone to when placed in new situations for any length of time.

"It'll be fun," she said, her attention still artificially directed at the TV. James sipped at his cocoa, staring into the tree's chasing lights; the sparkles reflecting off the baubles made his eyes twinkle.

"The scent of a real tree is so wondrously festive. I like it."

"You do? I'm not so sure." Eleanor pushed up her dressing gown sleeve to show off the remnants of her battle wounds.

James examined them carefully. "It fought you all the way, or...did you fight it?" He smiled.

"A little of both, perhaps." She was starting to soften, as always. It didn't take long—it was how she'd ended up here in the first place. "So. You're home for the week? Maybe I'll take some time off, and we can go shopping for Oliver's presents."

"I'd like that very much. Yet—" James sat forward on the sofa, put his cup down and turned to face her. "I sense you are reticent. Are you still worried about how you and Oliver will get along?"

Eleanor shrugged; he held her gaze. She didn't think she was especially troubled by the prospect, but now he'd mentioned it, she became aware of something stopping her from falling into her usual annual over-indulgence in all things Christmas. She loved the build-up: putting up decorations, going shopping, bustling through crowded streets. Evensong was her favourite occupation throughout December, the candles at the altar seeming to glow with an incredible promise of miracles past, present and future. She got completely caught up in the spirituality of it all, and it served to strengthen her faith. What James had picked up on was the feeling that it just wasn't quite right this year, and she didn't know why.

***

"Try it now," Dan shouted from upstairs. George turned the gas tap to the 'on' position and depressed the ignition switch, holding it in for several seconds before the pilot light flickered to life behind the little glass window on the front of the boiler.

"Yep, we are alight," he called back and turned the hot tap, waiting expectantly for the little flame to erupt into a wall of blue fire. Nothing. Warily, he prodded a finger into the slow trickle of water coming from the tap to confirm that it was still icy cold, withdrawing it quickly and chattering his teeth, largely for effect.

"Still no hot water though," he shouted. He heard the sound of a wrench landing hard on the bathroom floor.

"Bollocks." Dan pulled himself up from the cold tiles and returned downstairs, slamming the bathroom door on his way. "I don't know what's wrong with it. I'm sorry," he said, wiping his hands on his jeans and swigging the last drop of whisky from the glass he'd left there an hour previously.

"Want another? Or are you off home?" George asked, retrieving the bottle from the cupboard and topping up his own glass.

"Yeah, why not?" Dan held out the empty tumbler for a refill.

"Thanks for trying, anyway. You must be exhausted. You haven't been home yet."

"No, I still need to do that part. Mind you, it's weird. I'm not that tired—must be the time difference. Admittedly, I don't really get jet lag, but I haven't slept for twenty-four hours, and I feel wide awake. Well, relative to usual."

For all that Dan was a real man's man, he was more than happy to do his fair share of the parenting. It had to be that way, with baby Shaunna being born so prematurely, and the hours he and Adele had spent at the hospital, fretting over minor infections that were always life-threatening to their tiny baby. The worry didn't end when they were finally allowed to take her home, and then came the sleepless nights, which didn't last long, really—not of Shaunna's doing, at any rate. Since she'd started to sleep through, it was Adele getting up every half hour to check on her that kept Dan awake, although that likely wouldn't be a problem tonight.

He sipped at his whisky, frowning thoughtfully at the boiler. "I've no idea what Andy did, but I can't fix it. And it's a cold one tonight. You might want to give Josh a call, see if you can kip there."

George nodded, thinking that would have been a great idea, if he hadn't already asked so many favours of Josh. Still, George didn't mind the cold much, seeing as he'd spent more than enough nights in his shack of a house in the States with no power of any sort, let alone heating. The wood burner was all well and good, but it required him to go outside and chop logs, a skill it had taken him some time to acquire, in order to complete a task which took almost as long again, especially with numb fingers and a blunt axe. Woolly jumpers and blankets had served him well then; there was absolutely no reason why they shouldn't now.

"Right, then, George, I'm off home to my little women for another sleepless night," Dan said, emptying the glass in one go and heading for the door. George smiled sympathetically and followed, watching on as Dan struggled with the lever on the lock. It was stuck solid, no doubt something else he would suggest his brother had 'fixed', which was generally the case in this house. Poor Andy couldn't win either way. The landlord was useless at getting jobs done; Andy had said in all the time he'd lived there—and he'd live there since uni—the landlord had only come out once, to sort out a problem with the roof leaking. The rest Andy had either put up with or sorted out himself. As a general rule, not that Dan would admit to it, there was nothing wrong with Andy's handiwork.

Finally, the door flew open, almost hitting Dan in the face. He cursed under his breath as a blast of cold air whooshed into the already frigid hallway.

"Actually—" he stepped back and slammed the door hard to close it again "—I've just had an idea."

With that, he disappeared back up the stairs, clearing them two at a time. George sighed and waited patiently. He hadn't intended for Dan to come over and try to fix it. He'd only phoned him because there was no-one else he could think of who might know why he had no heating or hot water. Now, the longer Dan stayed, the more guilty George felt—for Adele rather than Dan, because clearly, he was after any excuse to delay going home.

"OK. Try it again."

George obediently returned to the kitchen, checked the pilot light was still glowing, and turned on the hot tap. The boiler chugged, the tap started to trickle, spluttered a couple of times and hot, steam-powered water came exploding out.

"Ouch!" George grabbed the tea towel and wrapped it around his hand to insulate it from the scalding metal. He quickly shut off the tap.

"And?"

"It's definitely hot now," he said, turning on the cold tap and bathing his palm in its flow.

"That's a start." Dan came back downstairs, wrench still in hand. "Perhaps I should just try hitting it with this." He shook the spanner menacingly at the boiler, which was still merrily chugging away and sounding none too healthy.

"I think I might just turn it off until tomorrow," George suggested, more than a little concerned by the increasing tempo of the tuts and clangs coming from the corner of the room.

"Give it a minute. It'll settle down, I'm sure."

"More whisky?"

"Go on then."

Chapter Five:
A Touch of Frost

Alice scraped the ice off her windscreen as if it were there for the sole purpose of offending her, shoving the scraper vigorously up and down, then left, then right, until small heaps like snow were piled all around the front of the car. She didn't like being late for work and never was, but then her idea of late was less than half an hour early, which looked probable this morning.

Climbing inside the chilly car, she started the engine and wondered if the day held any surprises, very much hoping not. Since Mr. Campion's death, she'd had little more to do than refresh the hideous coffee machine. Mr. Meyer was far too busy trying to make sense of the customer database to ask for her help—his loss, seeing as she'd put it together—but being supernumerary was no excuse for tardiness. She slowly pulled away from her reserved parking space, knowing someone would steal it as soon as it was vacated. Fortunately, they were always gone by the time she returned home; she wasn't the sort to fight for it, not even when the entire street was marked 'residents only'.

***

As Josh's weight had failed to stabilise since he had given up smoking again, and because he had given up smoking again, he had taken to walking to the surgery. One of his clients had commended exercise as a marvellous avoidance strategy, not that they were a smoker; nor was it normal for Josh to emulate clients' behaviours, though it had worked to a certain extent, for it was now almost six months since his last cigarette. Only another seven pounds and he'd be back to his previous weight. George had remarked that he looked no different; the next size up in trousers had told another story.

It was a crisp, clear morning, the sun still low in the sky, just starting to show its face over the rooftops on the right. Josh walked on the opposite side to stay out of the shade, enchanted by the white glow of frost encapsulating the branches of trees and holding each blade of grass staunchly upright on the verges. He recalled a fleeting moment, not long after George emigrated, when he'd contemplated leaving England to try out life somewhere else, although not with the intention of being closer to George. It just seemed for a while like a change of scenery might be a good thing, but he'd decided against it, and mornings like this made him remember why. Now, if George were to leave again, it would be an entirely different matter. They were closer than they'd been for a very long time.

As he'd predicted, Eleanor had, by and large, abandoned her friends, only making the effort to visit when James was away. *No, that's mean.* They still saw a lot of her, but then James was also away a lot. *So, therefore, the first assumption is true.* At the same time, Josh was aware that Eleanor's absence from his daily life didn't entirely explain his closeness to George. The counselling course accounted for three months of seeing each other almost every day for some reason or other—either because Josh was giving the lectures, or for the loan of books relevant to the current assignment—and now George's latest request for a placement. There were several clients who would be unlikely to see that as acceptable. After all, they'd chosen Josh as their therapist, not George, even if he was exceptionally good at it.

Josh couldn't deny the dependence was mutual, renewed by George's amateur counselling during Josh's last bout of insomnia. The recurring dream had eventually stopped recurring, although his tendency to leap to the assistance of any and all of his friends on the basis of a single anxious phone call persisted, getting in the way of other things he probably ought to be doing, like coming up with a way to get rid of his responsibilities at the university.

What a shame George couldn't take on that work. It would be highly unethical, seeing as he was one of the student body, but the thought had crossed Josh's mind more than once. He was far too professional to see it through, so he kept on going, every Friday, to the grotty office in a building due for demolition as part of the campus upgrade. It was about time they employed someone full time, particularly as they seemed to have money to throw around on new buildings and leisure facilities. He'd almost single-handedly funded it himself, the amount of coffee he purchased from the canteen and the vending machine on the floor above his office.

The frost had begun to melt and didn't look anywhere near as pretty in the shade, which Josh had been unable to avoid for much of the way. It was still early enough to pop into the local bakery and buy something hot, tasty and containing enough calories to entirely counter the brisk half hour of walking. The smell of bacon toasties got him every morning.

Emerging a few minutes later with three paper bags—two twisted shut, one open, with a nibbled corner of toast sticking out of the top—Josh crossed the road from the bakery and climbed the driveway to the building adjoining his own.

"Morning, Lois," he greeted the young woman booting up her computer at a desk just inside the door. The letters from the etched glass, picked out by the low morning sun created a warped shadow across her face and the wall behind her. It was an intriguing effect.

"Good morning, Joshua." She smiled and, through force of habit, turned her monitor towards her. Josh still cringed when she called him by his full name—Jess and Eleanor were to blame—even though he knew there was nothing meant by it. It was what they called him when he was getting a ticking off, in jest or for real. Lois, who was the niece of someone they had gone to school with, had assumed 'Joshua' was the proper term of address for her employers' associate. She was newly graduated, well-spoken, immaculately dressed and far more classy than her uncle. She was also stunningly beautiful, although her uncle Rob was a good-looking guy, too.

"I've brought bacon—" Josh corrected himself "—toasted bacon sandwiches." He beamed and placed one down on the desk next to Lois.

"Is that for me?" she asked. Josh nodded confirmation that it was. "Thank you, very much," she responded politely, but then noticed there weren't enough left to go round and wondered if she'd jumped the gun. "Who's not having one?"

"Eleanor. She doesn't like bacon toasties."

Lois opened the top of the bag, nibbling delicately at a corner of toast whilst logging in to her computer with her free hand. Josh chuckled and strolled across the reception area, a trail of crumbs marking his path all the way up the stairs to Jess's office.

"Hey!" he called, peering through the open door. Jess glanced over her glasses.

"Hello, you. I bet you've left a mess all over my carpets again."

Josh looked at the floor behind him and bowed his head sheepishly.

"It's getting to be a habit, you know." She leaned over her enormous, dark oak desk to take the last of the three toasted sandwiches from him. "Nearly as bad as smoking."

“Nowhere near.” Josh sat in the large leather seat on his side of the desk. “I’m not stopping, by the way, just thought you’d like one, after the last time I came in and you complained.”

“Because you stank the place out for the day.”

They both munched away quietly at their sandwiches, or as quietly as toast could be consumed, but not quietly enough, for Eleanor sensed she was missing out and appeared a moment later, armed with a water bottle and a pair of coffee mugs.

“What’s this then, the Breakfast Circle?” She shoved Josh over and squeezing into the chair next to him. He nearly choked at the reference to their friendship group as ‘The Circle’; it was a phrase he hadn’t heard for quite a while.

“Well, now we’re working next door to each other, we see each other less than when you worked all hours at the pizza restaurant,” he protested, helping Eleanor to brush away the crumbs he’d catapulted at her a moment earlier.

“That’s quite true,” she agreed. “James got home last night, incidentally.”

“Working really late, then?” Jess observed.

“Don’t start her off again,” Josh warned, but it was too late.

“He just doesn’t think to tell me. It’s so bloody infuriating, because it’s not that he’s being thoughtless. Well, he is, but not intentionally. He’s done his own thing for far too long.”

“Have you thought, though, Ellie, and I’m not saying it makes it right or anything, but maybe you refusing to get somewhere to live together makes him feel as if he’s not really coming home, as such?”

“Yes, Joshua, I have thought. It’s still not an option, not until he shows me some consideration and at least pretends that I’m part of his life now.”

Josh didn't respond, because it was the same old catch, and neither Eleanor nor James was going to budge. Both of them were waiting for the same signal of commitment from the other, and unless one backed down, the other wouldn't.

"Oh, well, must get on." Josh got up carefully and cupped the crumbs in his lap with his sweater. Eleanor glowered at him—an insinuation he was making a quick getaway, which he was—but it only served to make his exit even more hasty, leaving her sitting opposite Jess, who didn't look too happy with it, either.

"See you later," he called and disappeared back downstairs, waving at Lois, as he left the door to their building and unlocked the one to his own.

Eleanor waited a minute or so before moving and then flapped her arms once to indicate her disappointment at the apparent lack of support from her friends.

"It's all right for you," she snapped at Jess. "This arrangement with Andy worked out for the best all round, didn't it?"

"More by luck than judgement, but yes it did. Are you going to begrudge us that, just because James stayed away for a weekend?"

Eleanor opened her mouth and closed it again, flapped her arms once more for effect, and left Jess to wonder if she had been unkind. She had too much work to do to dwell on it for long, plus an early appointment with Angie Sharston, the woman whose husband she'd almost had an affair with more than a year ago, before he'd died in the arms of another gorgeous young lawyer. Lord knows why she'd agreed to deal with the inheritance issue—still pending guilt for her part in the poor woman's problems, maybe? It was more likely out of gratitude: she had much to thank Angie for, because the sordid almost affair had forced her to rethink her situation and was the motivation for finally setting up on her own.

The only problem with offering a 'women only' legal service was that it presented the same old cases over and again. It was interesting enough but not very challenging, and there was a steady supply of work, almost as if they left Josh's therapy with a resolution to tackle their problems and saw the lettering on the next door along as an omen. She felt bad about it, although it wasn't quite so immoral as the antics of the coffin-chaser lawyers she'd had the misfortune to work with in the past. They did lots of work for the hospital and other institutions in the service sector, picking up the individual cases after winning malpractice suits brought about by their future clients, who bizarrely took this as a good sign that they would win their case as convincingly as they had the big guns before them.

She quite liked Angie Sharston, though, now that they met on Jess's terms and territory. That night, when Angie had given her a lift home, had been one of the worst of her life, fuzzy-headed due to alcohol and oxygen deprivation in the cigar-smoke-filled dining room of the Sharstons' considerable property—now the focus of the pending challenge to Charles Sharston's last will and testament from the 'jumped-up little tart who killed him'—Angie's words, not hers. All the pain and suffering Angie had endured and still Charles was not to blame; it was these young women, and he couldn't resist. He was 'just a man'.

That was, and always had been, Angie's only weakness. On a good day, she recognised it as the misplaced loyalty of a past era, when women stayed with their men, regardless of how badly they were treated, but it was something to be admired, not emulated.

Jess had realised that at some point in her life, and convinced herself *she* was using *them* as a career stepping stone, whilst also allowing them to take what they wanted. Angie had put it well and truly into perspective for her, when she challenged her to consider the reality of how she was pursuing her career.

If anything, Eleanor's current quandary made it easier for Jess to appreciate the time she spent on her own, because she was in control of her life, finally, and still before she'd left her mid-thirties. Andy's visits home were regular as clockwork, as he'd promised they would be. Any more frequent may well have been for the worse. As it was, by the time he was due back in Dubai, they'd usually had at least one minor disagreement over something silly, like squeezed-in-the-middle toothpaste tubes or coat hangers hooked the wrong way in the wardrobe—a wardrobe she was proud to say was almost as empty as when he left, taking with him his half of the eBay proceeds from the spoils of her lifelong shopping addiction.

***

Eleanor's morning was less emotionally demanding, with only one or two appointments and no home visits. Patients were gradually transferring to her from one of the larger general practices, and it looked like she was going to be inundated with single old ladies. Not a thought had been given to whether they'd mind leaving the GP they'd been seeing for the past thirty years, who was a single old lady herself, and she was retiring. In the meantime, she was continuing to work part time while slowly but surely persuading her patients to accept their new doctor. It meant Eleanor spending a few mornings at the other surgery, sitting in on consultations that barely met the new codes, yet still provided startlingly good examples of the best in doctor-patient practice.

It was not the glamorous re-entry into the profession that all of Eleanor's friends had imagined, other than Kev, who'd been brutally honest in sharing the mundanities of his experience as a GP. Certainly, Jess had anticipated a much more 'Harley Street' atmosphere, with private patients similar in social status to her own clients, a few of whom had, in fact, transferred to Eleanor. Even so, young, healthy, wealthy women had little cause to consult a general practitioner, so Eleanor's register was in a much fuller state than her appointments diary. Right at that moment, the work would have been a welcome distraction, and she'd more than likely have to apologise to Josh at some point. He was a forgiving friend, even if he did like to have his say in that irritatingly smug 'none of my business but…' way of his. Even now, she wasn't sure whether she'd done anything to offend him, but she had snapped at him. She'd been doing that a lot lately.

"Just popping next door, Lois. I've got my mobile if anything crops up."

"Right you are, Doctor Davenport," Lois acknowledged.

***

Josh was ushering a client into his consultation room and acted with such surprise when he saw Eleanor that the client wouldn't have been out of place in thinking they were long-lost lovers who hadn't seen each other in years.

"I…you're busy. I'll come back," Eleanor mumbled but remained where she was, waiting for Josh to tell her to stay. He almost did, but then he remembered what George had said a couple of weeks ago. Eleanor had gone to Josh's house and found it empty, then on to George's, before finally tracking them down to a restaurant in town, where she stood over them, waiting for an invitation to join them. George concluded it was attention-seeking behaviour, and it needed taking in hand.

"I'll be done in about thirty minutes," Josh responded, not exactly coldly, but without his normal welcoming warmth. It was all an act—she probably knew it. She'd been his best friend for a long time, and he wasn't about to let it go for the sake of a disagreement over how she was messing up a relationship with some apparent prior deliberation.

By the time Eleanor returned to her own building, Jess was occupied with the delectable Mrs. Sharston, so there was nothing for it but to spend a couple of hours moping in her lonely office, the silence punctuated only by the perpetual tapping of Lois's fingernails against the keys of her computer keyboard, and a brief call from James, which only made her feel worse. So much for a week off and his undivided attention.

Chapter Six: Connections

Adele put the phone down and sat back on the sofa, a fluffy, white towel still clutched in her hand. Now, why would the police want to talk to Dan? There hadn't been any recent mishaps, not that he'd mentioned to her, anyway. He said he'd spent half of the evening trying to fix George's boiler, a fact that was backed up by George's text message to say he'd ended up calling out a heating engineer. It was certainly a puzzle. She picked up the phone again and dialled Dan's number, but then thought better of it. He said he was in a meeting all morning, where he could be contacted if it was urgent. Somehow, she doubted this was what he would consider urgent.

It wasn't unusual for Dan to get calls from the police. Most were from friends on the force who thought he might know something about a case they were working on. These days, he rarely had useful information to give them, although a year ago it was a very different situation.

***

Since becoming a dad, Dan had changed, and so had his business dealings, with more of the legitimate variety and less of taking into his own hands matters better addressed by the appropriate authority. The man who had sold him the infected carp that killed his entire collection, for instance, was in prison for importing livestock without a permit, and he would have been stopped a lot sooner, had Dan told someone about it instead of battering the hell out of him.

Those kinds of antics were, mostly, a thing of the past, because the stabbing and the arrival of baby Shaunna had pushed him towards introspection, and he dared not delve too deep, stopping by just long enough to appreciate that life was a fragile gift, and he had been ungrateful. Now it was payback time. It wasn't just about him anymore, if, indeed, it ever had been to begin with. The realisation didn't remove the urge to thump someone, but so far, he had been able to redirect his rage into working with a rehabilitation scheme, where young offenders completed their community service through local businesses. He was no less angry, but at least he felt a bit better about himself.

In fact, it was Alistair Campion who had put him in touch with the scheme. Early on, Campion Holdings had been a small firm, undertaking sub-contract work for cable television companies and the telecommunications industry before and during the technology boom, making Campion's one of the fastest rising companies on the market.

It was at that time that Alistair decided he wanted to do more for his local community, and the company not only took on young offenders, but also provided free laying of cable to help vulnerable people afford telephones. The crossover with Dan's work in telecommunications was significant, and they developed a very productive working relationship, which didn't have to end because of Alistair's death but probably would. It was unlikely that Meyer and the other directors would continue to honour Campion's commitment to community regeneration, when all they seemed interested in was profit, and lots of it.

Dan wondered about Alice's insistence that Alistair's death was suspicious. True enough, Dan would probably have reached the same conclusion himself, given that a knife was involved. However, he could think of no-one with strong enough motive to do it. Al was a decent bloke, and

Alice, whilst an excellent personal assistant who was both discreet and loyal, was prone to reading too much into what she heard and saw, and by her own account, she saw a lot more than the average person. As he had told George the night before, when they had resorted to huffing steamy whisky breath in the freezing kitchen, she'd once described Dan's scent as a hundred minuscule rainbows floating across the blue of a clear sky at midnight.

Dan had no idea what that meant, never having taken the time to fully contemplate the beauty of a rainbow or the sky at night, but George thought it was poetic and quite apt. That was when Dan decided it was time to go home, where he found Adele and the baby fast asleep in the bed, leaving him with the sofa and a sore head in the morning.

The hangover had worn off somewhat, with the help of several large glasses of water and a very interesting proposal from the consortium who had just bought out the local shopping centre. They were set on installing a wireless security system linked to the local police station, and Dan had persuaded them to install a backup cable system for security. The contract was his, if he could give them a decent quotation. It mightn't have been anywhere near as exciting as the kinds of jobs he used to do, but it made as much money and gave him time to spend on pursuing the other things he loved, which still didn't include himself. Goal-oriented, highly motivated go-getter that he was, there was no way he was putting self-discovery on his personal agenda.

He'd always prided himself on being different from his brothers, yet there was no denying the similarities between the three Jeffries boys. Michael, the eldest, had fared least well in the personality stakes, Dan the best. Andy was the most self-confident, even if all three had the looks and the charm that meant they should have been positively oozing with the stuff. Still, Dan had to pretend life came easy to him, when in reality, it was an uphill struggle every day. If it had anything to do with his absent father, then Josh hadn't mentioned it, but it was possible, considering all three of them had the same complex when it came to tying themselves to one place, relationship or vocation.

Andy had seemed quite content working on a large development in Dubai. He was responsible for ordering in the materials, and he complained incessantly about the heat, the problem with keeping staff, ensuring supplies arrived on time, keeping track of shipping and all the other boring little routines that went with the job of site manager—one he hadn't initially been employed to undertake. His commitments back home were keeping him there, because he had promised to be sensible and responsible, first to Jess in helping her set up her all-female law firm, and then to himself, believing that after all those years of living it up, free of responsibility, he owed Shaunna more than money could ever repay.

Longer still had passed since Dan first connected it all together, shards of truth so deeply embedded that it hurt less to leave them where they were. In hindsight, it had been nothing like he imagined, although life with that knowledge was far too dull to take much relief from the knowing. Andy hadn't said as much, but Dan was pretty sure his brother felt the same way. When the dust finally settled, there was only one real victim, and that was Kris. For Dan's best friend, the revelation, and his subsequent mistaken attack, were the beginning of a total mental breakdown from which he was only just emerging, every illusion from which he had constructed his life shattered. Tonight was going to be one of those strained evenings out together, where Shaunna and Adele chattered about children and clothes, while Dan and Kris endeavoured to join in, or talked about football and the like. It was as tedious as it sounded.

Dan pressed the screen of his vibrating mobile phone and held it to his ear.

"Hey, you," he greeted Adele.

"Hiya. How did your meeting go?"

"Fine. Got the contract, I think. I'm just on my way to Campion's to discuss the next stage. Everything all right at home?"

"All OK, yes. Shaunna's making a dreadful mess with a teething rusk, I've done all the ironing, ordered your mum's Christmas present—oh, and the police called for you."

"Really? I wonder why?"

"They didn't say. I'll text you the number." There was a slight pause. "No, sweetie, not that way. Oh, bless. She's chewing the ribbon instead," Adele explained.

"Aww—right, I'll be home before six. See you later. Love you." Dan waited for Adele to respond before hanging up. He put his phone back in his jacket pocket, where it vibrated a moment later to indicate she had sent the number, as promised. He was curious to know what the call was about, but it could wait until later, as he was already in the car park outside Campion Holdings PLC, the building towering formidably, with its large chrome lettering glinting in the chill midday sun.

***

Josh waited a full half an hour before he gave up on being 'cruel to be kind' and went back next door to see Eleanor, knowing exactly what George would have to say about it, should he decide to tell him later.

"Is she in?" he asked Lois, who nodded and said no more, implying she was alone and he could just go through.

"What's up, Doc?" he said warmly as he opened the door to Eleanor's consultation room. It was much brighter and more modern than Jess's room upstairs, with a younger, less formal atmosphere, or would have been, were it not for the pervasive misery emanating from its occupant. She grunted an acknowledgement without looking away from her book.

"What're you reading?" Josh tried again. "*Latest Treatments for Haemorrhoids*?" He turned his head to the side to try to read the cover.

"*A Christmas Carol*," she confessed.

"Any good?" Josh grinned, sensing she was about to relent.

"It's OK, I suppose."

"A new release, is it?"

"Oh, all right. I give in!" Eleanor closed the book and put it down on the desk in front of her, on top of a pile of case notes that Lois had somehow procured from her hastily scribbled observations.

"Sorry about before, by the way," Josh added, with little in the way of sincerity.

"I'm sorry, too," she replied, but she really meant it. Josh nodded once, which she took as an indication of his acceptance and permission for her to elaborate further on her apology. "George is right, of course. I have abandoned you, and him, and everyone else. Sometimes I have no idea why I'm trying to make this work. James and I are so different. I think—"

"Actually, the problem is you're too similar," Josh interrupted. "He wants it all his own way, and so do you. Unless one of you gives in, you're going to be in this stalemate forever, or for as long as your relationship lasts, which won't be very long, the way it's heading. And what do you mean, George is right?"

"He told me you were feeling like I'd ditched you, the way I always do."

"Did he now, the toad. I'll be having a word with him about that."

"Oh, don't be cross, Josh. I pushed for it. I phoned him because I couldn't figure out what I'd done to upset you."

Josh wasn't just cross. He could feel the anger rising within and was doing his best to contain it. He was starting to wonder if George was the one playing the game here, trying to keep him and Eleanor apart, but then, why would he do that? They'd all been friends for long enough to not feel threatened by each other, even when relationships shifted around the group, which they often did. If it weren't for shared professional interests, he'd have been seeing a lot less of George at the present time anyway, particularly as he'd taken to going for a drink with Kris on a regular basis, or so the story went.

"Look, Ellie, can I be honest with you?" Josh asked, but he was primed and ready to go, whatever her response. "I do feel like you've ditched me to a certain extent, and yes, you do it every time you're with someone. And before you protest, I know it's more than ten years since the last time you were with someone, but things haven't changed."

"I'm not in Newcastle this time," Eleanor protested.

Josh ignored her and continued. "I totally get that you're in a relationship. Of course you should spend your time with that person. And from what I've seen of James, I like him." Eleanor looked at him questioningly. "I do. Not that I disliked Kevin—well, to be fair, I didn't really get to know him, either. But you understand what I'm saying. I don't expect us to see as much of each other as we did, but it would be nice if we could still get together sometimes, the way we used to after work."

There was a moment of silence, whilst Eleanor considered what he had said.

"I think it's more to do with the change of job than James and me," she suggested. Josh looked at her ruefully. "Agh, I don't know. Maybe it's a bit of both. It was OK back then, because we always worked late. Nowadays, I'm home before you most nights of the week, and there's nothing to stop you coming over for coffee, you know, regardless of whether James is there. But you don't."

"And nor do you."

"True enough. I suppose I got used to you coming to me all the time. Guess we're gonna have to try a bit harder from now on."

"I guess so," Josh agreed. Eleanor got up from her chair and put her arms around him.

"I do miss our chats," she said.

"Me, too." Josh stroked her hair and kissed her cheek. "But I'm still going to thump George later."

***

Dan watched Alice bustling around her little alcove at the far end of the main office, stopping every now and then to mentally measure some thing or another that had occurred to her. She picked up piles of paper, straightened them, put them back down somewhere else, checked all her desk drawers were locked, checked them again… She stopped dead in her tracks, her eyes slowly following something only she could see, along the length of the room, over the heads of all the temps, who were turning off their computers and sliding into their jackets to head home for the night, until her gaze rested on him. He smiled.

He was so pleased she had agreed to babysit, otherwise the cosy meal for four would have been at their house, interspersed with Adele looking in on the baby every five minutes. He'd double-checked with Kris that he and Shaunna were still up for it and booked a table for seven. That still left an hour and a half to get Alice home so she could feed Albert and be back at the flat for six, traffic allowing.

"Thank you ever so much for waiting, Dan," Alice breathed. "The nice man from the garage said my car should be fixed by tomorrow, but I appreciate it's a terrible inconvenience."

"Not at all," Dan assured her. "You're doing me a favour, when all's said and done. And I'll make sure we're not too late getting back, so you can get your beauty sleep. Not that you need to." He winked and then mentally kicked himself for being cheesy.

Alice didn't notice. She blushed and scurried off ahead of him, anxious to get into *that* car before anyone saw her. Otherwise, they'd have much to say about 'Thingummy-bob and her new toy boy' tomorrow.

Dan pointed the alarm control and pressed the button, sounding a distant beep across the car park, slowly striding so that he kept up with Alice's brisk trot. He still hadn't figured out how he'd talked Adele into leaving baby Shaunna, and so long as Alice didn't do anything too eccentric between arriving home and getting Adele out of the door, all would go according to plan.

"So," he said, climbing into the driver's seat and pausing while Alice rooted around for the seat belt and finally succeeded in fastening it around herself. "Tell me about Alistair's murder."

Chapter Seven: Changes

Andy checked the fax machine one last time and went for his final shower of the day before bed. He'd hoped the confirmation would come through tonight so he could book his flight, but it didn't look likely now. It was early evening in the UK, probably too late for anyone with authority to still be there. Another day wasn't so long to wait.

***

Kris was lively and upbeat, and Dan could hardly hide his relief. Sometimes it was the hardest thing in the world to pretend to be having fun and lie convincingly when cross-examined. Being as Shaunna and Adele had abandoned them for the Ladies' some time ago, it would have been a drag, to say the least, if Kris had been in a down phase. That was how he described the periods when the slow withdrawal from the medication was at its worst, before he became accustomed to having a few more of his faculties come back online. The dosage was still high enough to slur his speech and made him lose track of what he was saying mid-sentence, although on a good day he would laugh at himself, rather than resort to talking about the pointlessness of trying to get his life back. A good memory and clarity of speech were fundamental to a radio actor's career, and Dan could fully appreciate why, at times, Kris felt like he'd lost his identity.

Meanwhile, in the Ladies', Adele's current dilemma was a decision between two shades of dark-pink lipstick, both of the 'stay put' variety, and she'd be stuck with her choice for the rest of the evening. Only Shaunna and she could tell the difference, tease out the subtlety in shading that made one a slightly better match with her cashmere sweater. The process took just under twenty minutes and included a brief conversation about whether Adele had changed her mind on the issue of remarrying—which she hadn't—before the two women returned to their respective partners in the restaurant.

"Oh, and the police called this morning," Adele whispered as they approached the table. "He hasn't said anything about it." Shaunna raised her eyes to indicate her lack of surprise.

"I know I've asked a hundred times before, but what on Earth do you do in there?" Dan enquired, looking Adele over with some appreciation for her lipstick decision, even if he wasn't fully aware of the effort that went into it.

"Things you don't need to know about," she said with a wink at Shaunna, who didn't follow her lead for a moment, but then got it and played along.

"Oh, yeah. All sorts of women's secret things," she said unconvincingly. Dan didn't take the bait.

"We've ordered drinks and starters," he explained, as the waiter arrived with a bottle of house white and poured a little into Dan's glass. He sipped, nodded his affirmation that it was acceptable, and the waiter half-filled all four glasses.

"I'm not sure I want this," Adele said, thinking of the night ahead with wine in her system.

"Oh, come on, I'm not even supposed to drink at all on my pills," Kris cajoled, "but I'm going to. We all need to let go now and then."

His words seemed to do the trick, and she downed the glass in one. Dan filled it for her again, and this time, she sipped more carefully, knowing exactly his intention was to stop her worrying about the baby.

Between them, they polished off four bottles during the course of the evening, and by the end of the last, Adele had no cares whatsoever for whether or not their single, fifty-something, childless spinster babysitter had the patience and experience required to care for a very small child. In her inebriated state, Adele confessed that she herself had not exactly been kitted out for the job at the start, but she'd struggled through, with a lot of guidance from Shaunna on all the things that worried her and always turned out to be entirely normal for a growing baby. She gushed teary thanks at her friend for being there at the birth and hugged her so tight it made Shaunna squeal.

Somehow, Dan had forgotten he was driving and had promised to take Alice home, so he had to use his charm on the restaurant staff to secure his car in their car park until the morning. The car park was located off-road and had significant, iron, lockable gates, although leaving the car there meant he wouldn't be able to get it back until the following afternoon, when the restaurant was getting ready to open up again. It was also going to cost him for taxis home for both Kris and Shaunna and he and Adele, and then another for Alice, but it was worth it for the possibility that Adele would sleep through the night for the first time since the baby came home from the hospital. Perhaps, once he'd had a full night's sleep, he'd feel up to the task of figuring out what had happened to Alistair Campion and be able to follow up the lead Alice had given him.

***

Josh climbed into bed, furious that he'd left it so late again and wondering if he should think about setting some kind of timer on his laptop to stop him from messing around with pointless things on the internet. He'd initially ridiculed George for his love of social networks, and it worried him just how much people gave away about themselves on their profile pages. When he'd created his own profile, he'd been deliberately vague about everything, and still, some of the students from the university had tracked him down and added him as a 'friend'. His response was to neither accept nor reject their invitations, instead leaving the requests to pile up, all the while thinking that whichever he did would give out entirely the wrong signal, because a rejection was a rejection, however it was delivered.

For all of that, he wasn't deterred and spent hours reading comments left on other people's pages and trying to figure out how the commenters were related to the owner. It was all rather pathetic when he considered it. Then there was that whole instant messaging nonsense, to which he had become totally addicted, sitting 'chatting' with people he didn't know outside of the virtual world, whilst his TV chunnered away in the background. Before he realised, it was way past one in the morning, and he'd only himself to blame.

No point reading tonight, he thought, reaching across to turn off the light. As he did so, there was a knock at the door, maybe not so loud as to startle him at any other time, but it did make him jump. With a yell of frustration, he threw the covers off and went back downstairs.

"What on Earth?" he said, opening the door on a wet, windswept, shivering George.

"Heating," he explained, rubbing his hands together and, assuming he had been invited in, stepped into the warmth of the hallway.

"I thought you'd got it fixed."

"So did I, but apparently not, so if you wouldn't mind, can I stay, please? Just for tonight? It's absolutely freezing, and I've had to turn the water off because the boiler was spewing steam into the kitchen, and the hot tap was stuck on, and I had to wait for the tank to empty before it stopped, and—"

"YES!" Josh said, halting his friend mid-flow. "Just shut up and go to bed."

George sighed gratefully, following Josh to the top of the stairs. Josh stopped, pulled a set of sheets and the spare duvet from a cupboard, and shoved them in his direction.

"Good night."

"Good night, and thank you."

Josh grunted and closed his bedroom door, leaving George standing in the dark, groping for the handle of the door to the spare room.

***

"So you think a gold eye shadow would suit me best?" Alice asked Adele. One-thirty in the morning, and they were discussing beauty tips. Adele was too drunk to have noticed the time; Dan wasn't, and he wanted to go to bed but needed to make sure Alice was safely on her way before he did.

"Absolutely, Alice," Adele slurred, lifting strands of Alice's hair, which she had freed from its band for examination. "It would match your complexion perfectly and really accentuate the gold in your hair."

It wasn't something she would have anticipated, but Alice was enjoying all the fuss being afforded her by the lovely young couple: so beautiful on the outside and somehow maintaining the beauty within. She had discerned that Adele was a very straightforward person with nothing to hide, so there was nothing artificial about the way she was talking now—not like those dreadful creatures in the office, all so tied up in their own looks to even notice that other people existed, or, in Mr. Campion's case, ceased to.

"I've never really gone in for cosmetics," Alice said. "I very much think that being natural is more important than being beautiful."

"Oh, but you can be both. There are many natural products available now. This syn-a…this thing of yours."

"Synaesthesia."

"Yes, now how does that work again? You see colours?"

"I see smells. I can smell them a little, too, but mostly I see them."

"Gosh, that's amazing. So you would be able to see what a perfume looks like."

"Yes. For example, your perfume is mostly yellow, but it has edges of pink, like the petals of a rose. Someone else would look different in that perfume, of course."

"Ooh. Like they smell different. My favourite perfume smells awful on me since I had the baby."

Alice and Adele continued as Dan nodded off in the armchair, satisfied his work here was done. OK, so it had taken almost a year of countless introductions, rejections, rows and apologies, but he'd finally found an Adele-approved babysitter. However, his next mission was a little more daunting; he was going to try again to convince her that they should get married.

***

A rare day off: Andy's lie-in was disturbed by the sound of his fax machine churning out several sheets of paper, and he immediately leapt out of bed. It was the confirmation he had been waiting for: the contract was in place, and he could finally resign. He'd still have much explaining to do to Jess and Dan, but for once he'd have the upper hand.

He hated Dubai. The constant heat and humidity drove him crazy, the job was boring and stressful, waiting on deliveries, where the men could do nothing for days, and then taking abuse from the manager, who was usually back in London and didn't have to endure the endless hours of tedium. Andy didn't want the position in the first place, and it was supposed to be temporary, but apparently he was far too good at it for them to put much effort into finding him a replacement.

The development was three months behind schedule and he was powerless to do anything. There was simply no challenge in making calls to irate suppliers with their supplies stuck in customs, if they even got that far. And yet, in spite of his loathing of the job and all that went with it, he had wanted to see it through, always his intention to resign after the completion, because that, at least, would have allowed him to say he'd achieved something.

For the first time since he'd arrived, he sat on his sofa and took a moment to enjoy the glorious air conditioning. There was still time to sleep some more, and he returned to bed, happy that it was all finally going to come to an end.

***

Jess must have sensed something across the thousands of miles, because her thoughts were entirely focused on Andy from the second she awoke, and it was getting in the way of her work. It wasn't like her at all—more the sort of soppiness she expected of him, being such an old romantic at heart. He liked to take her out, not for expensive meals or anything like that, but to the cinema, or bowling or even to play squash. Just the two of them together, out having fun, and at this time of year, he really was great fun to be with. She'd tried to hide her disappointment when he said he didn't think he'd make it back for Christmas or New Year, although he said he'd try. It would be so good to have him around again, even if he did make a terrible mess and refused to do things her way. She could cope with that and was, in truth, a little jealous of Eleanor, for all the trouble she was having with James. At the precise moment she started to question why that was, Eleanor burst into her office in a state of panic.

"James has been arrested!"

Jess gasped. "What?"

"On suspicion of murder."

"Murder? Of whom?"

"I don't know. He's still in Birmingham. The police called to tell me, at James's request. But that was all they said." Eleanor was hyperventilating and Jess had no idea what to do.

"Wait here. I'm going to get Josh," she said, running from the office. She made it as far as the top of the stairs before Eleanor intervened.

"He's not there. I already tried. Jess! What the hell is going on?"

Jess started to panic, too, because she was going to have to deal with it herself. It sounded selfish, but she wasn't good at coping with a crisis, and Eleanor was starting to have trouble breathing.

"I'll ring Josh, then," she replied as calmly as she could, even though she was making it up as she went along. "After that, I'll ring the police station and see what I can find out." She picked up the phone and dialled Josh's house number.

"Hello. Oh. George. I didn't expect you. Is Josh there?"

"He's in bed. Shall I wake him?"

"Yes. No. Actually, don't worry, I'll call him later." Jess said goodbye and hung up.

Luckily, listening in on this brief conversation had led Eleanor to hold her breath, and the palpitations had started to slow as a consequence.

Before Jess got even halfway through explaining, not that there was any need, the phone started to ring. It was Josh: George had obviously woken him immediately after her call, knowing that there would be a good reason for it.

Jess waited quietly while Josh complained, at length, about being awoken first thing in the morning by one friend, after being kept up late by another. In the background, she heard George protest that it wasn't true. Once they were both done, she replied, in full 'lawyer-speak'.

"Eleanor has received a call from the Midlands police to inform her that they have arrested James in relation to a murder inquiry."

The line was suddenly very quiet.

"You are still there, I assume, with your complaints about sleepless nights?"

"Yes, Jess, I am. I apologise for my outburst. I'll come now."

"Right. Well. Good. Then. See you in a while." Jess put the phone down. "He's on his way."

"I got that," Eleanor said, her words deceptively calmer than the thoughts behind them. It didn't please her that she needed Josh, but she felt much better for knowing he would be here.

***

"You're doing it again," George stated, as Josh grabbed his gloves and his car keys. "Running at her beck and call."

"What would you have me do, George? Leave her stranded? James has been arrested for murder, or didn't you hear that bit?"

"Yes. I did, but why do you need to be there? What you gonna do? What *can* you do? Ring the police and be told that he's being questioned as part of their investigation? That's pretty much it."

"And if that's all I can do, then at least she won't be on her own. I'll ask again. What do you think I should do?"

"What you think is right, I guess. Which is to go running to Ellie each and every time she wants you to, whether she gives it back or not."

Josh took a deep breath and blew it out loudly. "Look. I'm going. You can stay here if you like, or come with me, or go home—whatever. We can deal with your wise thoughts on this matter later. If need be, I'll drive her to Birmingham, because that's what friends do, not because they expect it back, but because they care for each other. I thought you, of all people, would understand that."

"That's not fair!" George looked hurt but had nothing further to say. "I'll lock up for you and go home. Maybe see you later?"

"You might," Josh said, flinging the door open and then exiting with a slam.

"Fuck him," George spat and threw the tea towel he had been nursing after the closed door.

Chapter Eight: Unwarranted

When they picked James up, they said it was to help with their inquiries, and he'd had no reason to doubt that—until he indicated he wanted to make a phone call, at which point they formally arrested him. Now, they were in the process of securing a warrant to search his car, his house and Eleanor's apartment. They implied they might go even further and start searching head office and all of the restaurants in the chain. Still, no-one had mentioned precisely what the crime was, nor why he was a suspect.

The company lawyer was en route, but had been away in Devon on business, and it would be a few hours before he arrived. James could do no more than wait out the time with his own thoughts and vain attempts at meditation. The duty officer brought him a sandwich and a cup of tea for breakfast; as far as the police were concerned he was guilty, so that was all he was getting. Four hours: no phone call and no chance to shave or brush his teeth before they dragged him out of bed and brought him in. Still, he reasoned, there must be due cause for all of this.

***

The duty officer had, with great effort, eventually convinced Eleanor that there was little point in her driving down to Birmingham, as they didn't anticipate being able to release Mr. Brown for quite some time yet, not until all the searches had been completed. When she asked what they were searching for, they wouldn't tell her, suggesting instead that she wait at home for the local police to arrive and do what was necessary, because if she wasn't there, they had the authority to force entry.

Josh took Eleanor home and settled her in the living room, where she absent-mindedly flicked on the tree lights, watching through hazy eyes as they twinkled and chased. Josh made her a cup of tea and sat with her, nursing his own coffee, wondering how he was going to deal with George, how long the police would take and, guiltily, how much of his day was going to be spent waiting around and taxi-ing her here, there and everywhere.

It was a ridiculous situation…or was it? Now he came to think about it, none of them really knew James. He seemed a decent man, young and ambitious, but with a generous aspect to his personality. He had stepped out of the way when everything came to a head with the Krissi situation, didn't utter a word about what Kris had done, and he'd covered at the restaurant while Eleanor joined the rest of them in cleaning up the mess afterwards. All of that suggested he was a trustworthy and honest person. But there again, none of them would have guessed at what Kris was capable of, until he almost killed Dan. That was an extreme situation; this was different. No, taking a life is always extreme, but was James really a murderer?

Eleanor appeared to be pursuing the same train of thought and neither of them dared speak it, both desperate to get the search over with for their own reasons. Josh's phone punctuated the silence and startled them out of their stupor.

"Hi, Josh, it's Krissi. Any idea why the police are searching my restaurant? All they'll say is it's in relation to an inquiry involving the managing director."

"Ah. Hey, Krissi. As a matter of fact, I'm with Ellie just now, and we know about as much as you do. They've arrested James. For murder."

"Are you winding me up?"

"I wish I was." Josh listened to the voices at the other end of the phone; they became muffled and indiscernible, and he presumed Krissi had put her hand over the receiver.

"They've gone," she said a short while later.

"Right. That means they're probably headed here next," he reasoned.

Eleanor looked away, dreading the invasion of her home and the turning over of all her things—her private things. She'd have rather been burgled. Well, maybe not.

When Eleanor resigned, and Zak—the manager of the other pizza restaurant—was promoted, Krissi had applied for his job. She didn't get it, but she was offered a position as trainee manager. In any event, the real manager spent so much time off sick that Krissi had essentially been running the place for months, and then the manager had also resigned, but Zak insisted it wasn't his decision to make. James had promised to sort something out officially as soon as he got the opportunity. It looked like it might take a while for that to happen now, if ever. And yet, Eleanor kept reminding herself, wasn't James always true to his word? Didn't he always come through, eventually?

In all her doubting about their future together, she would never have guessed that this might be the next turn of events pushing her towards calling it a day. She loved James more than she'd ever loved anyone, but this was too much. The constant working away, failing to let her know what he was up to—even now she refused to believe that any of it was due to shady dealings, or that he was guilty of the charges against him. That wasn't really what was bothering her; she had given so much of herself already, but to have her home, her possessions, her entire life turned upside down because of something James may or may not have done, was one step beyond what any reasonable person could be expected to tolerate.

With time to fill, the thoughts kept tumbling, going back around the same arguments over and again. The anticipation was making her queasy, and she needed the search to be over. It felt like an eternity passed while they waited for the police to arrive, but when they did, there was no mistaking their knock on the door, and it instantly riled Josh.

"There is a doorbell, you know," he said, stepping to one side to let the four officers enter, the first of whom flashed a piece of paper at him faster than the credits roll on a TV movie, before they all trudged gritty boots across Eleanor's carpets.

"Sorry about that," the last of the four said, making a vague attempt at wiping his feet on the way through. Josh exhaled sharply.

"Miss Davenport?" the second officer asked. She was even gruffer than the first.

"Yes," Eleanor muttered, trembling slightly.

"That's *Doctor* Davenport," Josh pointed out indignantly, his tone betraying how angry he was. The female officer ignored him.

"Stay where you are, and we'll get this over with as quickly as possible."

Eleanor nodded and did as she was told. Josh likewise understood the requirement, said no more, and sat next to Eleanor, whilst three of the officers searched the rest of the flat, before returning to search the living room. All the while, the third, silent officer had been standing by with his eye on the pair of them.

One of the others indicated that they should stand, so they did, and watched as each cushion was upended, followed by the sofa itself. Next, they turned off the fairy lights.

"Ouch." The female officer caught her hand on the tree, which, in its favour, didn't seem to discriminate between those it attacked, making it a far worthier prime suspect. Eleanor stifled a giggle.

"OK. All done," said the officer, sucking her finger where the tree had got her. Josh moved to see them to the door.

"Can you give us any information about what's going on, please?" he asked, addressing his question to the fourth officer—the one who had wiped his feet.

"There has been a recent death under suspicious circumstances in the local area, and we believe that Mr. Brown may have been involved in some way. This is just one of many avenues we are following."

"Thank you, officer."

"Thank you for your cooperation, Mr…?"

"Sandison."

"Miss Davenport," the female officer nodded coldly towards Eleanor and followed her colleagues out of the building. Josh closed the door behind them.

"That's *Doctor* Davenport, you obnoxious cow," he muttered under his breath. He came back into the living room and Eleanor started to laugh, then cry, then a bit of both. Josh hugged her tightly. "I'm going to make us another drink." He left her in the dark of the room. She didn't much feel like turning the lights on again.

***

"Now then, Mr. Brown, or would you prefer James?"

"I don't mind, Detective."

"James, can you please state your full name for the purposes of the recording."

"James Tobias Johnson Brown."

"And your date of birth?"

James gave each piece of information as requested, with no intention of making this any more difficult than it already was. He stumbled slightly when it came to his address and couldn't remember the postcode for Eleanor's apartment, which made the detective ask him to explain why he didn't know his own address, and he dutifully obliged.

"Sounds like an interesting woman. She must be quite something to make you commute to the Midlands on a daily basis."

"She is wonderful. I trust she will be told of what is going on?"

"Miss Davenport has been informed, yes. Right, let's start at the top. You say you were at your head office last Thursday evening. That was the fourth of December."

"Yes, I was."

"And during the day?"

"Travelling from Eleanor's to head office in the morning, then in a meeting all afternoon. After that, I had dinner and a further meeting was scheduled, but cancelled, so I returned to my house."

"What time did you leave to travel here?"

"Around ten-thirty, I recall. I had to resolve a management problem at the local branch before I left. The manager there will confirm this."

"Yes. She has already told us that you left around ten-thirty. However, Miss Johansson is the daughter of one of Miss Davenport's friends."

The officer said no more about it, but the insinuation that Krissi might be lying was clear.

"Can you tell me whether you are familiar with a Mr. Alistair Campion, CEO of Campion Holdings?"

"Yes. I know Alistair very well. I have known him for many years."

"When did you last see Mr. Campion?"

"Over a year ago. We are both very busy men."

"And you haven't seen him since then?"

James thought for a moment before answering. "No. I haven't seen him since."

"You don't seem too sure about that."

"I was trying to recall the date I last visited him. That is all."

"A year is a long time for someone to remember the exact date."

"I have a good memory for dates, but you are correct."

"So when you say over a year, is that closer to one or two years?"

"I would estimate it has been around thirteen months. It was a little before Miss Davenport and I started dating, so it would have been mid-October. Yes—now I remember—he told me it was his wedding anniversary, which I believe falls on the fourteenth."

"Impressive, Mr. Brown. Do you recall anything else you discussed on that occasion?"

"No. I am afraid not. Is he dead?"

"Yes, he is."

James appeared to be shocked by the news, and the officer noted it for the purposes of the audio recording.

"Have you had any reason to meet with Alistair Campion recently? Let's say—in the past month?"

"No. Can you tell me how it happened?"

The police officer completely ignored his question. "So, you don't recall what you discussed with Mr. Campion the last time you saw him?"

"We often speak of the work Alistair is engaged in. I imagine that we also spoke of his wife's state of health. This would be in keeping with our conversations."

"And why would that be, Mr. Brown?"

"As you are undoubtedly aware, Mrs. Campion suffers from multiple sclerosis and has been very ill for some time now."

"Is the state of her health common knowledge?"

"Amongst closer acquaintances, I believe it is."

The detective continued to quiz James on this theme for some time, asking if he had met Mrs. Campion, which he had, on many occasions. The route the questioning took after that somewhat astounded him, as he was asked about the state of Alistair's personal finances and whether the cost of the care was a burden to him. If that were so, then it was certainly not something Alistair had shared with him. Adding it all up, James realised he was essentially being asked if he had killed Alistair at his wife's request, as some kind of insurance scam. For the first time during the interview, he started to lose his composure.

"What you are implying is ridiculous, Officer. Firstly, Mr. and Mrs. Campion have been together for many years. Secondly, I would trust him with my life! After all, I asked him to be my best man."

"For your marriage to your first wife?"

"No."

"And yet you say that haven't seen Alistair Campion since before you started dating Miss Davenport."

James sighed and rubbed his eyes. He was tired and couldn't be sure of the truth of anything he was saying.

"So, I will ask again," the detective said curtly. "When did you last see Mr. Campion?"

"Just a couple of weeks ago. We spent an evening at a jazz club."

"Can you remember what date that was?"

"I cannot recall the date specifically, but it would most likely have been a Thursday."

"So, you know it was a Thursday, and yet you had forgotten you'd seen him?"

"Apparently."

"That strikes me as a little odd, would you agree?" The question was rhetorical, which was fortunate, for James didn't have an answer. "And you haven't seen him since then?"

"No. I am absolutely certain of that. Please, can you tell me how he died? It is very important to me."

The police officer shrugged. It was about time for a break anyway. "It seems that Mr. Campion was attacked by someone that he knew, with a knife taken from a fisherman nearby. The crime occurred around midday, hence we need to be very clear about the time you left to travel to Birmingham on the fourth of December. We are waiting on video taken from the motorway cameras."

"I do not use the motorway to travel. It fatigues me."

"In that case, you will need to jot down the route you took last Thursday for me, please." The officer turned his notepad around and pushed it across the table towards James. As he wrote down the list of roads, he considered the news of Alistair's death. The thought that someone would murder him was most strange. Alistair Campion was a good man.

"Can I ask, why I am a suspect?"

"Yes, Mr. Brown. An eyewitness has testified that you were in the building shortly before the time of Mr. Campion's death." The sergeant checked his watch, stated the time and paused the recording.

Chapter Nine:
Sensational

Dan put the newspaper down and then picked it up again, refusing to believe his eyes. *They must have got it wrong, surely.*

LOCAL MAN ARRESTED IN CONNECTION WITH CAMPION MURDER

A local resident has been arrested and is being held by Midlands police in relation to the death of Alistair Campion, founder of Campion Holdings, PLC and esteemed philanthropist.

Police believe that James Brown, managing director of The Pizza Place chain, who controversially closed one of their local branches last year, took a knife from a fisherman on the canal en route to Campion's office. At some time around midday, Brown is thought to have stabbed Campion and left him to bleed to death. The motive for this attack remains unclear.

Davey Price, aged 42, reported seeing a tall, black man in a suit a short while before he noticed his knife was missing. An employee of Campion Holdings later confirmed that Brown was seen leaving the building a little after midday.

Police have searched the suspect's place of residence - apartment of Doctor Eleanor Davenport, 37 - but have yet to locate any further evidence linking Brown to the murder.

"Adele!" Dan leapt up and strode through to the kitchen, where Adele was trying to push the point of the iron into the corners of the smallest frilly blouse. "Have you seen this?" he asked.

"Have I seen what?"

Dan put the paper down on the ironing board; she snatched it up quickly and scowled. "I'm sure Shaunna will look lovely in a newspaper-print top. Now, what am I looking at?"

Dan prodded at the cover story. Adele adjusted the paper away from her eyes until the words came into focus. He waited while she read, watching her for a reaction, although it was taking so long he was becoming impatient.

"Are you done yet?"

"Hold on," she said and carried on scanning the page.

"Bloody hell, Adele. I know you're a slow reader, but—"

"I'm going through it again, if you don't mind. Wow, so Ellie is famous."

"Oh, for all the right reasons, obviously!" Dan snatched the paper from her in disgust and automatically turned to the back page, while she tried to worm her way out of her silly remark by giggling.

In her defence, it was more of a shock response, because she couldn't quite fathom what she was reading. James Brown a murderer? That couldn't be right.

"Isn't Alistair Campion the one who does the cables and stuff?"

"Yeah. I knew him quite well."

"Did you know he was dead?"

"I did."

"Why didn't you say anything?"

"Why would I? But Alice—you remember Alice?"

"Of course I do. I'm not stupid."

Dan looked at her doubtfully. "She was his personal assistant, but you were too busy discussing how to apply blusher for it to come up in conversation."

Adele accepted his explanation without comment. She folded the tiny blouse and moved on to a pair of socks. Dan raised an eyebrow in disbelief at her ability to continue unperturbed, never mind that she was ironing his socks. He went back through to the living room and sat at the edge of the carp pool, waving his hand gently back and forth through the water, until the fish came to the surface to nose at his fingers. *James Brown: what did he have to do with Alistair Campion and what motive to kill him?*

"Did it say they'd searched Ellie's flat?" Adele called through. "That must've been dreadful. I might give her a call later and see if she's OK."

Dan didn't respond. At times, the simplicity of Adele's view of the world frustrated him to the point where he had to work really hard not to say something cruel and which he would inevitably regret as soon as the words left his mouth. It had been the undoing of them many times before, as Adele gave as good as she got, and neither stopped until they had done everything they could to destroy the other.

***

Adele was right. The thing that had bothered Eleanor most was not that her boyfriend was still being held in custody on a murder charge, but the horrendous invasion of her privacy. The police officers who conducted the search had been courteous enough, and they had put everything back in its place. Nonetheless, Eleanor felt violated, and when she called Krissi to find out whether they'd come across anything in the restaurant, she said she felt the same. It was the thought of having total strangers comb through their personal possessions that had got to them both.

Seventy-two hours and no charges later, The Pizza Place company lawyer had assured the police that there was no problem raising the money for bail, if that was what the problem was. Indeed it didn't even get that far, as the police were all set to release James. He was a respected man who was suitably well known and therefore unlikely to attempt anything as foolish as leaving the country, should more than circumstantial evidence turn up. Then there was Oliver and Eleanor. She was keeping her distance, even though curiosity was threatening to get the better of her. Her sense of control over life relied on knowing what was going on at all times, and she'd often been accused of sticking her nose into things that were none of her business. But this *was* her business—a strange contradiction, considering she was struggling to justify continuing the relationship.

***

Finally, James was allowed to leave the police station, and he returned to his house to shower and change out of the clothes he'd been wearing for three days. He was so exhausted that, as much as he wanted to see Eleanor, there was no way he could safely drive anywhere. Nor could he bring himself to call her for fear of her response. Instead, he ordered a curry to be delivered and ate half of it in bed. The other half fell onto the floor in the middle of the night.

***

Oliver's mother had heard the news. She was in the process of trying to find the number for head office when Eleanor phoned to ask if James had been in touch at all, not knowing whether the former Mrs. Brown was aware of what had gone on. She lived only a couple of miles from James's house but refused absolutely to go and see if he was there. She suggested to Eleanor that calling his office might be a better strategy, seeing as that was always his priority, at the expense of his family, including his wife and son, let there be no illusion there. Eleanor listened silently, with little intention of defending him against the truth.

> *There are times when it is impossible to decide with any certainty on the best course of action to take.*
>
> *Having the news delivered that your live-in partner is a murderer could constitute one such occasion, when you can't be sure one way or the other of their innocence, even though you know you should believe in them.*
>
> *It is an entirely normal reaction, and the best policy is to delay making any decisions one might regret later. Ending the relationship with James was one such decision that should not be made in a hurry.*

So said Josh's email, intended to be a comfort in her hour of confusion. Instead, it enraged her, because he was right. She wanted to believe James was innocent, but where *had* he been? He had left on the Thursday morning and hadn't come home until the Monday, with little by way of explanation. She hadn't questioned it at the time, for he rarely disclosed his activities in detail. Why bother, when they were mostly of the ordinary, administrative variety? Nor was there the slightest indication that anything might be wrong, but then, to have given it would have been to incriminate himself.

The rational explanation was that he had nothing to hide, yet he was as unfathomable to Eleanor now as he had been when he first walked into her life. He was so wonderfully intense and mysterious—it was what she loved about him, and she was missing him dreadfully—but she just couldn't shake the feeling. There had to be more to this, or else why was he the prime suspect for a murder?

There was much about James Brown that she didn't know, and it was absurd. After a year together, three months of sharing the same bed and a whole lot of deep conversations…but they were always about her. Was that her doing? Did she talk about herself all the time and not allow him the opportunity to share a little of his history? It was entirely possible, she realised, because Josh had levelled the same criticism at her in the past. But that was Josh, her best friend for more than twenty years; she was allowed to be self-indulgent with him.

No, if James had wanted to tell her, he could have done so at any time, which, in her mind, implied he was definitely hiding something. It hadn't looked that way before, because she'd had no reason to suspect him of anything untoward, but the saying of 'no smoke without fire' was ringing a million alarm bells in her head. Without thinking what she was doing, she had made four pieces of toast, covered them in blackcurrant jam and eaten them. It was only when she was putting the third pair of bread slices into the toaster that she realised what she had done.

And now he was making her binge. *Just bloody perfect.* He was the first person she'd voluntarily told about her eating disorder—Josh and George didn't count, because they'd figured it out for themselves—however, there was no way she was going to give him the satisfaction of being responsible for a relapse. She succeeded for several moments in convincing herself that she could deal with it. Only four pieces of toast, after all, not exactly a huge binge. She'd not eaten anything else that morning, apart from her breakfast and a banana—she started counting on her fingers—a bar of chocolate, two bags of crisps—*two bags?*—and an entire packet of biscuits.

With that, Eleanor ran for the bathroom, and there she stayed for the next fifteen minutes, alternately retching and screaming at herself for doing so. And right at that moment, it wasn't James she wanted. She needed Josh, more than ever, but it was wrong to call him. She'd have to face this alone. She'd done it before. She knew how.

***

Josh had also seen the newspaper and wanted to phone Ellie to see if she was OK, but George was on his case again, although this time, it was not about him running to her every time she so much as sent him a text message. It was because Sean Tierney had asked for written confirmation that Josh was able to offer George sufficient hours in his surgery in the new year. He was preoccupied and only half listening, so he said yes, told George to type up the letter himself and signed at the bottom without reading it. He really would have to contact her at some point today; he hadn't heard from her, and he was starting to worry she'd done something stupid. It would be the food thing if it was anything at all, but each time he picked up his phone to make the call, George glowered at him. It was easier to wait until he was on his own than engage in another pointless quarrel.

At last, George decided he was going to the library to look up something to do with Carl Rogers, Josh didn't pay attention to what, and may well have been able to help out if he hadn't been so eager for George to leave. He didn't have a problem with Rogers, even if most of what he said was common sense.

As soon as he was alone, Josh tried Eleanor's landline, and then her mobile phone. There was no answer on either, which wasn't a good sign. He decided to pay her a visit—he didn't care what George would have to say about it. Or that's what he kept telling himself.

***

Eleanor dried her face with the towel and cautiously peered in the mirror over the sink. She didn't look *too* bad, she thought. Admittedly, a shower and a good teeth-brushing weren't going to undo the damage, but it was enough for her to feel marginally less appalled by what she had done. It hadn't been this way since...well, for so long she couldn't really remember, but it had to be at least ten years. Of course, there were occasions when she had eaten far too much, but always in the company of friends and with some conscious awareness of what she was doing. At Adele's wedding, for instance, she had stuffed her face and enjoyed it for the most part, because it was a nice day. All right, it wasn't that great a day, and it was still about pushing herself to the limit, as if she had to feel so bloated she could barely move before it counted for anything.

The solitary bingeing, though, she thought she had left that long in the past. The times, as a teenager, she had spent all of her pocket money, filling her school bag with as many chocolate bars and other goodies as she could, locking herself in her room to devour them all, one after the other—*hardly touching the sides*—she'd kept the saying in her head, repeating it over and over as she did it. Then to the bathroom to get rid of the evidence before it attached itself to her body.

She'd never quite figured out why she did it, or even if her parents had known. There were a few times when they'd asked her awkward questions about smoking, which she, Jess and Josh had tried, but she'd kicked the habit before she left high school. It cost too much and left her with little money for the food she craved far more.

In her anxiety to try to push away what she'd done, she didn't think about anybody else or how it might affect them, for this was *her* problem, and it was profoundly selfish. Possibly, she cared about what Josh thought, and even what James thought. But hadn't they both abandoned her, leaving her alone long enough for her to do this? Should she be angry at them? It was *their* fault, because they weren't there to stop her. No. That was nonsense, and now she'd done the dirty deed, she knew it.

Eleanor filled a glass with cold water and sipped at it, trying to ease the burning sensation in her throat. As a child, she'd hated vomiting—nothing unusual there. Who enjoys the sensation of stomach acids tearing up their oesophagus? But her multitude of siblings never seemed to suffer quite so badly whenever they had stomach bugs or anything that involved throwing up, whereas she had dreaded it to the point that it made her cry. So how, in all of this, was it that she coped best with life when she was stuffing herself with food, knowing that once she was done her sole intention was to evacuate her stomach so that not a trace remained?

It had not made sense then, and it wasn't about to start making any, because it wasn't rational. She'd heard it before, so it must be true.

The rapid hammering on the door indicated that now was probably going to be her time to start explaining herself, because she instantly recognised it as Josh's knock.

"I'm thinking of joining a convent," she said, opening the door and letting him pass through.

"Yes, I always thought a habit would suit you. Ah." He stopped just inside the hallway and looked her up and down, the expression on his face showing he could still read his friend like the proverbial book. "But I see you already figured that out for yourself. Oh, Ellie, come here." Josh opened his arms to her, and she readily went into them, grasping desperately and sobbing into his coat.

"So you've seen it, then?" Josh asked gently. Eleanor nodded her head against his shoulder. "Well, it wasn't as bad as it could have been," he consoled. "After all, they didn't mention where you live or anything like that. And remember, he's not been formally charged, has he?"

Eleanor stepped away from him. "I saw your email. Is that what you're talking about?"

"Shit. No, no it's not, Ellie. Come on, let's go and sit down. Would you like a drink of anything?"

"What's happened, Josh? Who didn't mention where I live?"

The minute he'd recognised that look on her face, he'd thought it was because of the newspaper article, but now it seemed it was his email, which had been frank, but not brutal. Now, he felt terribly responsible, because it had evidently been the last straw.

"The local paper has published the story on the front page," he explained, steering her into her own living room and to the sofa. He was preparing for a complete breakdown, thus her reaction took him somewhat by surprise.

"They've done *what*?"

"The paper—I should have brought it with me, because I can't remember what it's called, but the free one, anyway. They've printed the story on the front page. It's only a little corner, though, bottom of the right-hand column," he lied. "I doubt many people will even notice it."

Eleanor was breathing so hard that Josh thought she might explode, and she did, verbally. For several minutes she ranted, starting with the trashy journalist who wrote the story—"not that I even knew or care who it is, but they're cheap and bloody evil, quite honestly"—then the paper—"anything to sell advertising—they'd pimp their own daughters, if they weren't such filthy examples of humanity as to not have any, if they even count as humans at all"—followed by the police and judicial system in general—"letting scum like that into our courtrooms to blight the names of good men, because he is a good man"—at which point she stopped abruptly.

"He is a good man," she repeated and fell apart.

"You're absolutely right, Ellie, they are scum, and he is a good man." Josh waited for her to recompose. "Is there any real news? Has he been released?"

"God knows. I don't. He hasn't been in touch—no calls, text messages or anything—since he was first arrested. I don't even know who he's supposed to have killed, or how."

"The paper says it's the guy who owned Campion's, you know, the big building in town."

"The one where that hideous girlfriend of Dan's worked?"

"Which one?" Josh asked, tongue-in-cheek, because Dan had dated quite a few of the girls who worked at Campion's and other places, all of them pretty hideous, on the inside, at least. By and large, they were stunningly beautiful to look at but wouldn't have been able to come up with one other redeeming quality between them.

"The last one before he and Adele got back together," Eleanor said. "Alison, was it? Something like that."

"Yes, I remember her now. Well, the murder victim was Alistair Campion. He was found dead in his boardroom."

"Never heard of him. I don't remember James mentioning anything about him, either, do you?"

"I can't say I do, but then you've kept him all to yourself. Are you scared of what we'll think of him?"

"No, not at all! It's just been the whole 'new love' thing. And what a nonsense that is! I can't quite get my head around how I ended up in this situation. I've worked so hard to get my life back together. It's bloody medicine, I swear. I mean, the last time I did something this stupid was when I married Kevin. I was all right while I was working at The Pizza Place."

"Yes, you were, but you were so wasted. You just need to learn to meet the challenge head on."

"Hmm. My boyfriend the murderer. Sounds like a challenge I could do without."

Josh shrugged. "Well, you don't know that he is a murderer, and the only way you're going to find out is by asking him. Shall we give him a call and see?"

Chapter Ten: Shades of Guilt

Alice was finally satisfied. She'd known all along that it was no accident. How could it be when a weapon was involved? And as for that fisherman—he was an interesting sort, creating all kinds of strange hexagonal shades of green when he came into the office, rather too keen to visit the scene of the crime involving his knife, and sufficiently potent for the actual sensation of smell to register over the usual array of shapes and colours. It wasn't a bad body odour, just distinctive, and he was evidently enjoying the fame.

The local paper had called Alice too, but she wasn't going to sully Mr. Campion's reputation, nor that of James—whom she hadn't seen for years—not just for the sake of saying 'I told you so'. She wondered how, if it were James, he had accomplished a visit without being seen. Why would he have done it, when Mr. Campion had been so good to him? It didn't add up, but at least the police were on the right tracks, inasmuch as they acknowledged the circumstances were suspicious. Now there was only the funeral to attend, whenever they decided to release the body.

Poor Jenny. How cruel to leave her waiting to bury her husband. Her relapses were often set off by stress, which was why he did not worry her with his troubles. He'd done everything he could for her, and the hopelessness of her illness motivated him to help others. Sadly, it also meant that as her condition deteriorated, she saw less and less of her husband, and the parting had begun long before he was taken from her. It was only temporary, anyway, for if she'd had any reason to fight to survive before his death, then it had died with him.

There were others like her, less fortunate, with no-one to care for them and unable to earn a living when their illness took over. They deserved a little something. He had it to spare, but Jenny had always been his top priority. When she'd wanted to stay at home, he'd found the best live-in carer, a young woman who was happy to work all day and be on-call all night, in return for living in the small house on the outskirts of the old estate. In its day, it had been a glorious, regal property with extensive landscaped grounds, which he had sold off to fund his various projects over the years. Now all that was left of the Campion fortune was a house with a modest garden, twenty percent of Campion Holdings PLC and a refrigerated carcass in the morgue; not the most dignified end for a man of such distinction.

Alice took a packet of antibacterial wipes from her bottom drawer and proceeded to wipe over her monitor, mouse and keyboard. Mr. Meyer had dreadful personal hygiene, by her standards, and had no right to use her computer, but it didn't stop him from doing so. Carefully, she pressed the corner of the small, damp cloth between the keys, having first turned off the power, of course, so as not to type random letters or accidentally delete files. It all looked clean enough, but she just knew it wasn't.

When Mr. Campion had offered her the job, his office was much smaller and located on the other side of town, in an old building, far worse than this one in many ways, making its own dust each time someone closed a door too hard, or opened one of the old sash windows. Yet it was so much nicer to work in, with fewer people leaving their unnecessary clutter on every available surface. The little carrels should have kept each member of staff safely away from others and given ample space for the storage of all the personal artefacts with which they liked to adorn their workstations, from sticky fluffy blobs with ridiculous slogans, to small stuffed bears and photographs of children, wives, husbands and so on.

It displeased Alice to see so much mess in a work environment; there was simply no need, especially not when the average temporary contract lasted less than three months. However, the shorter the time they spent there, the more stuff they appeared to need, like a little home from home. Inappropriate, unattractive and unnecessary. If she were in charge, or at least if they recognised that she was in charge, she would make a rule that all personal effects be removed immediately. She didn't bring Albert in to work with her each day, now did she?

"Good morning, Alice. I have a letter I need typing up straight away." Bill Meyer appeared next to her desk, a kindly expression on his face that didn't match the stern tone of voice he used to deliver his request. He placed a hand-scrawled sheet on Alice's desk. "It's about the change in management and needs sending out to all staff."

"Yes, Mr. Meyer. Should I send it as an electronic memo?"

"Whatever." Mr. Meyer waved his arm dismissively and walked away. "By lunchtime, if you can, please."

Alice picked up the letter and read it, pausing to squint at the occasional word that failed to match any she had in her vocabulary. The letter had obviously been penned by a woman—a young woman, even—resulting in large, rounded letters with short tails and ridiculous little circles standing in for dots and full stops. Surely whoever had taken the dictation could have typed the letter, too?

None of the content surprised her. Mr. Meyer had been elected as the new chair of the board of directors; Jason Meyer, his son, had stepped up as deputy chair. He was a pleasant boy, not long out of university and clearly not enamoured of the job his father had cajoled him into before Mr. Campion's death. Now he'd leapt right to the top of the corporate ladder, and if the police were short on motive for Mr. Campion's demise, then this one stood out proud and above all the rest, but not the boy. He wouldn't have it in him to do such a thing.

The rest of the board had remained as they were, so nothing much had changed. In the real world, it might have an effect on how much charity work the company undertook, but it wasn't going to alter the requirement for administrative staff. That said, considering that a young woman had penned Mr. Meyer's note, it was entirely possible that very soon, Alice would be out of a job herself.

She typed up the letter in a couple of minutes, opened her email programme, and had it around the office in under five—all her usual efficiency. There was mention behind her that the coffee pot was dry, and there was another job to see to, giving her time to wonder whether Dan had uncovered any further information about the arrest and also whether his lovely wife had been able to pick up the eye shadow and blusher she had promised. Alice was babysitting for them again tonight, so she'd find out soon enough.

Thinking back to the day of Mr. Campion's murder, Alice tried to picture herself doing precisely what she was doing now. There had been the familiar smell, most definitely not James. He almost created music, always did, even as the precocious and impulsive lad he was when first he came, holding a bucket in one hand and a soapy sponge that dripped everywhere in the other.

"Miss, please can you tell Mr. Campion I've finished cleaning his car."

"That's splendid, James," Alistair called heartily, emerging from his office.

"What shall I do next, sir?" the boy asked, realising the mess the sponge had made and carefully placing it back in the bucket.

"I think that will be all for today, young man, but I do have something I'd like you to do tomorrow." Alistair beckoned him into his office, and he immediately complied.

Alice sighed and shook her head, as she had done so many years before, when she had no need for the respite that a moment such as this could bring. Back then, there was so much more to the job. It involved real people, visiting places where men were at work, to chase up missing timesheets and check on progress. They had treated her with such respect, yet never as great as that given by the community service boys. Mr. Campion insisted they simply needed a father figure, someone who trusted them and whom they could trust; over and again they proved him right.

"Miss Friar?" Alice was startled back to the present.

"Oh, hello there." She smiled. "I was just thinking about you."

James did not return the smile. "I am sure that the news has given people much to think about." He maintained his serious expression. His stay in police holding cells had supplanted his joy for living with a solemn and desperate requirement to prove his innocence, before he lost both Eleanor and his son.

"How have you been? Did they look after you?"

"Yes, thank you for asking. They were polite and ensured my basic needs were met. The company still continued without me, so in most regards, I have been fortunate."

"Oh, well that's good. The story is much the same here." Alice passed the letter she had just typed to James, and he scanned it slowly, pursing his lips more tightly the further he progressed. He finished reading and handed it back.

"I believe that is where I must start."

"I can save you the time. If you have a few moments to spare, I will tell you what I know."

Chapter Eleven:
Play On

James didn't tell Eleanor he had been released, because he truly believed she wouldn't want anything to do with him. So it was left to Josh to keep her company, until such time as one or the other of them decided to make contact, both utterly mistaken in their assumption about what the other was thinking. Meanwhile, little Oliver Brown was getting very excited, now that he was old enough to understand what Christmas meant. He was also blissfully unaware of what his father was going through, as any three-year-old should be.

After Alistair Campion's funeral, James met with one of the local police detectives to discuss his concerns regarding the inadequacy of his statement to the Midlands police. The inspector was very understanding, implying that he believed it to be a case of mistaken identity. He even let slip that his team was already investigating on James's behalf, but for now, he had to appreciate that he was the main suspect. After all, a witness had identified him in the line-up *and* he had lied about his visit to Campion's just prior to the attack, which was ultimately what had aroused the suspicion of the police in Birmingham.

The first Eleanor heard of James being back in the area was when Dan mentioned it a few nights later, when they were all out for one of their usual meals. Alice was 'more than agreeable' to another evening of babysitting, so Adele was holding the floor, orating a heavily descriptive and overly long account of The Makeover, goods purchased with a sneaky discount from the girls in the department store, where Tom was nowhere to be seen, thankfully. Alice was overjoyed with her makeover, Adele told them.

***

It was a supposition well on its way to becoming fact, borne out by the number of times Alice had trundled restless little Shaunna with her to look in the wall-length mirror at the end of the living room. Only beautiful people dared to possess such a thing and baby Shaunna appeared to have inherited her parents' vanity. She really did love that mirror, bashing her rusk against it, whilst Alice laughed at their reflections and then raced off for a cloth and cleaning fluid to remove the little biscuity fingerprints from the glass.

***

"So," Dan said, "what's happening with that man of yours, Ellie? He was looking very down in the dumps, even considering the circumstances."

"Was he indeed? And when exactly did you see him?"

"Yesterday morning. He was at Campion's funeral."

"Oh really?" Eleanor put down her fork for fear of swallowing it whole.

The entire group went silent; no-one knew what to say. Krissi had been about to speak, but now the news of her friend Jason's promotion pooled on her tongue like swilled mouthwash. His appointment had come about because of Mr. Campion's death and, by extension, was linked to James's arrest, thus also to Eleanor's current dreadful state of mind. Poor Eleanor; she had hardly touched her food. She had barely spoken to anyone all evening and kept wandering off to the bathroom, each time returning with increasingly reddening eyes.

Kris could see Krissi had something to say. She always bounced up and down when she was excited, even as a babe in arms. Now twenty-two, it was still endearing, and however much she tried to contain it, she couldn't.

"Go on, Missy," Kris prompted. She glared at him and shook her head.

"I'll tell you later," she whispered. "Just change the subject before anyone else notices."

"Ah. OK." He turned to the rest of the table and, in his best radio actor's voice, said, "What do we all want from Santa, then? Shaunna and I are off shopping tomorrow, so now's your chance to put in your last requests."

That, too, went down terribly. It seemed however carefully the words were chosen, they held a double meaning linked to what was going on, making it virtually impossible to have anything more than a one or two line conversation, before yet another awkward silence was encountered.

"We've done ours," Adele attempted. "We went up to that huge new shopping mall. It's fantastic. Lovely decorations. We bought some new ones for the house."

"Oh, yes, I saw those. They're lovely, Adele," Krissi said.

"Yes, they are," Shaunna agreed. "Have you put up your tree yet, Ellie?"

Another icy silence.

Eleanor shrieked. "That's it, all of you! Enough, already! You don't have to feel so bloody uncomfortable. Just so you know, I haven't spoken to James since the arrest. Yes, I have put up my tree. No, I haven't done my Christmas shopping, because we were going to do it last week, when he got arrested. And I don't give a damn just now what anyone wants to buy me for Christmas. As I'm sure you can appreciate, I'm not feeling especially festive at the moment."

At another time, the scene around the table would have been hilarious. For a few seconds, everyone remained motionless, paused at various stages of eating or drinking, forks dangling from mouths, wine glasses tipped to lips.

Eleanor pulled her chair in and spooned some rice onto her plate.

"Well said, Ellie." Josh squeezed her hand.

George, for once, had nothing to say, his prior disdain abandoned, as he now understood why Josh stuck by her, not that he especially liked it, but she needed him. After being back from the US for over a year, their mutual dependence was coming to an end. He had his course ahead of him; Josh was coping with life the way he always had, so there was little point in protesting further.

More than that, he realised he was being selfish. It had been a long and difficult year for all of them, and by comparison, his own troubles were relatively minor. It was hard to imagine that Kris, so gentle and even-tempered, and presently engaged in whispered conversation with his stepdaughter, was the same rambling lunatic who had turned up at the house, covered in blood, on the night he stabbed Dan. George watched on, wondering when the mask would slip again. The possibility continued to trouble him, and his promise to help Kris recover was no different than that which Josh had made to Eleanor so long ago.

"That's better, isn't it?" Eleanor said some minutes later, when normal conversing had resumed.

"Yes, it is," George agreed. "Listen. I need to apologise."

"For what?"

"For being a bit of a bastard, actually. I've been trying to stop Josh from seeing you. I thought it was for his own good. The thing is, he was pretty worked up over you spending so little time with him, and I tried to explain that you are—or you were—with James, so he had to accept it. Then all of this kicked off, and I realised I'd made a bit of a boo-boo."

"Hey, you don't need to say sorry for trying to look out for Josh."

"Oh. I do. It didn't really have much to do with that at the end of the day, but I'd convinced myself I was doing it for the right reasons, so I really am sorry. I can see how hard this is for you, and I had no right to get between you."

"All right. I accept, then, if it makes you happy."

"It makes me feel a bit better, yes. Thank you."

"You're still in love with him, aren't you?"

"Need you ask?"

The rest of the meal passed politely, with no further uncomfortable silences, just friends enjoying a night out together. At the end of the evening, Jess volunteered to deal with the bill to save any potential disagreement, and as they all paid their share and left, mostly in pairs, Josh pulled George back, waiting for the others to go. Eleanor had gone to the bathroom.

"James is waiting outside," Josh whispered.

George peered out of the steamy window, and sure enough, there was James, standing with his back to them, stamping his feet in an attempt to stay warm. "Oh, hell. Should we go and intercept, do you think?"

"I don't know."

"Decide, quick!"

"Why me?" Josh asked. "What do *you* think?"

"Let's do it," George said bravely and headed outside. Josh hung back for a second and then followed. The two of them stood in the street, looking to James, then to each other, neither knowing what to say or do.

"You two are useless," Eleanor muttered, bustling up beside them and pulling on her hat and gloves. "You're like a couple of schoolboys waiting to ask the footy captain if you can play on the team."

Josh and George remained where they were and watched Eleanor walk towards James, who was acting as if he hadn't heard her, even though he must have done.

"Hey, you. What you doing loitering around restaurants at closing time?"

"Eleanor, my lovely. How pleased I am to see you, although I am aware my behaviour does not tell the same story."

"You could say that, James Brown." She linked her arm through his. "Shall we walk and talk?"

"If I may invite your very good friends, who I see have been looking after you, as always."

Eleanor looked slightly puzzled but nodded to acknowledge that it was acceptable. Josh and George obediently trailed behind, down the high street and into the little jazz bar. It was full of murmured conversations drifting quietly over low-key live music—not Josh's idea of a good night out, but the ideal place to maintain the current state of cordiality and perhaps uncover what was going on.

James went to the bar and bought the first round, although it was customary for him to refuse all offers from anyone else to buy drinks for the rest of the night. He spent a few moments in quiet discussion with the barman, briefing him on his experiences of the past few days, before returning to the table with their drinks.

"There we are, my friends." James placed the bottled beers in front of George and Josh, who had taken the low armchairs opposite the sofa, where James now joined Eleanor. He took her hand and sat back, allowing the music to drift into his mind and quieten his soul a moment.

"I must tell you I am innocent," he began, "or, should I say, I am innocent of Alistair's murder. He was a fine gentleman and dear friend, who helped me in many times of great need. I am deeply saddened to have lost him and prayed at his funeral that they might find the man responsible for taking his life.

“It is to be expected that you doubt my word, for I have kept myself away from you all, especially you.” He held Eleanor’s gaze, his eyes beseeching forgiveness. She granted it. “Should I succeed in demonstrating my innocence to you this evening, I am hopeful that you will assist me in resolving the matter, for I believe I know who killed Alistair. However, I must keep a low profile, as I am still the lead suspect.

“First, let me explain the connection, and thus the reason why I have been charged with this terrible thing. As a young man, I was wayward—I daresay even offensive—and foolish, often in trouble with my teachers, my neighbours and, on occasion, the police. I mixed with those who could influence me to cast aside my scruples, engaged in many antisocial acts as a means of achieving some status with my acquaintances, and finally excelled in my short and chaotic criminal career at the age of seventeen, when I was caught removing double-glazing units from a manufacturer on the industrial estate not more than a mile from where we sit now.

“I was found guilty and sentenced to serve two hundred hours of community service, working on a scheme to replace old windows in the houses of those who were unable to pay for it, through no fault of their own. I believe that this kind of restorative justice has proved to be most effective in turning many a boy away from the spiral downwards into prison sentences and further crime.

“Yet I was a dreadful glazier and became increasingly frustrated by the work I had to do. Still seeing my so-called friends each and every day was hardly the type of rehabilitation I required. At the time, Mr. Campion was also involved in providing work for adolescents like us: those who had stepped out of virtue. For some reason, although I have yet to fathom it, he appeared to like me and offered me a position working for him instead. I jumped at the opportunity to put some distance between myself and my old associates, who were only partially responsible for what I was becoming, but nonetheless continued to push me in the opposite direction to that which I aspired.

"Alistair set me to work on any and every task. I cleaned offices, delivered letters and wage slips to the staff—he even trusted me to deposit the daily receipts. He turned me around, because, as you know, Eleanor, my father is very distant. I may well have benefitted from his example to a far greater extent, had he been there more to support my mother through those difficult times.

"There are some who did not fair so well in their rehabilitative time with Alistair, less able to accept his trust at face value. His wife suffers a most tragic illness and could not provide him with children. That was all there was to his kindness; no ulterior motive. It is the time spent with untrusting souls that leads us to judge according to our own values. My ability to not take their lead must be credited to my mother.

"I recall one boy, several years younger than I, his life such an ordeal that it failed to sustain in him the more positive traits of human nature. Still, Alistair was prepared to put in the effort, so certain he could turn each and every one of us around. Unfortunately, the boy became a man who has since spent some time contemplating his actions from the confines of a cell. When last we spoke, he assured me he had left it all behind, was faring well in business, and shared my gratitude for Alistair's good works.

"He declared himself to be back on the straight and narrow, ready to repay his debt to his benefactor. And in wanting to see the good in everyone, Alistair allowed us into his life as well as his business, for these have not been separate entities. One imagines a scene where this man speaks as an ally and equal, building a mutual understanding between them, so much so, that Alistair would never suspect he was being deceived, played, hunted."

James paused momentarily, moved as if to say more, but then appeared to be consumed by his thoughts.

His companions waited in silence. Eleanor was wondering whether he had deliberately kept his true identity hidden, or if it were more the case that it simply hadn't come up. She hoped it was the latter and for now chose to invest in that option. Josh didn't really know what to think, seeing as the entirety of his working life was spent listening to people reveal their past indiscretions, which inevitably came back to get them later, however hard they tried to repress or conceal them.

"So," George hedged, "what you're telling us is that you didn't kill what's-his-name and you think you know who did." Put that simply it didn't seem anywhere near as complicated as the whole story James had narrated.

"Yes, George. That is precisely what I am telling you. I promise it is the truth. I have been many things in my life, of which I am not proud. To take the life of another? No. I would not and could not."

Josh picked up his beer. "I wouldn't be so sure," he said, watching the swirling liquid as he allowed the bottle to sway in his hand. "All of us have the capacity to kill if we are faced with no other choice."

"As much as I agree with you, I had a choice." James's tone was as quiet and peaceable as ever. He noticed George and Eleanor had both finished their drinks and went to the bar.

In his absence, the friends could have discussed their thoughts, and it had been his intention to give them time to do just that. Instead, they remained silent, all three satisfied that what they had heard was nothing less than the truth.

By the time James returned with the second round of drinks, Josh and George had individually decided to help him uncover the real killer, as had Eleanor, although whether their relationship could go on any longer was another matter entirely.

Chapter Twelve: Innocent Men

Sean Tierney was one of those dark-haired Irishmen, blessed with cheeky good looks and a sharp sense of humour that appealed to virtually everyone. In spite of his sociable nature, he lived on his own, in a small terraced house on the outskirts of a village just beyond the boundaries of the main town. It was a close-knit community, and the villagers rarely accepted strangers into their fold, but with some carefully measured interaction and just a little Irish cunning, Sean had successfully endeared himself to them, in particular, the leader of the Parish Council—a woman in her early sixties who took a very dim view of everything. Or, it would seem, everything apart from Sean Tierney.

Like him, his house was slightly extraordinary, having been built on an ancient cemetery, making it a site of great interest to local archaeologists. The other residents of the terrace had no intention of letting interfering academics near their property, but Sean gladly granted them access, so long as they wiped their feet on the way in and gave him a mention in their reports. However, even the most patient of souls can only tolerate so much, and the front garden was still a deep trench, with a good twelve inches of rain water stagnating in the bottom, and it had been like that for three months.

As he stepped over the muddy hillock between the pavement and his front door, Sean paused to take in the devastation and chortled to himself. It was always the same with the university: enough money to start a research project, but never enough to see it through to its conclusion. He'd been assured that the matter would be addressed immediately, probably before the end of October, then November, then before Christmas. Now it was scheduled for the very start of the new year. When he asked the dean's secretary if she meant calendar or tax year, she became flustered, tittered nervously and hung up on him. Perhaps it would be easier to tell them to forget it and turn it into a landscaping feature. He wasn't that bothered, really.

Ultimately his major issue, and the reason he kept pestering the dean for something to be done, was Sophie, his girlfriend, who was pretty and liked good clothes and nice shoes. Moreover, she didn't like to get her nice shoes covered in mud, and his suggestion that she should keep a pair of wellies for when she visited was not well received. The other slightly less significant problem—to him, at least—was that if there was heavy rain, the water in the pit overflowed, taking a mini mudslide with it into the road, thereby blocking the drain in the gutter, which only served to infuriate his neighbours further, not to mention the Parish Council, who, needless to say, didn't blame Sean in the slightest. The university's insistence that there would be 'as little inconvenience as possible' had been an under-exaggeration at best, an outright lie in retrospect.

Sean poked around in the dark with his key, eventually felt it come to rest in the keyhole, and gave it a full turn clockwise. Sphinx, his very curious cat, was mewing loudly just the other side of the door, anxiously awaiting the return of his master, or servant, as was the reality of the cat-human relationship. The creature was a real oddment: mostly Siamese, with ears that bent over ever so slightly, and a vast bushy tail like a Persian, hence the name, because he looked like two cats merged into one.

"Hello, Sphinxy, how was your day?" Sean switched on the light in the narrow hallway and bent down to stroke the cat's head, at which it slithered the whole length of its back against his palm.

"Mine was quite the usual sort of day," Sean continued, in response to the cat's greeting. "I had a meeting this morning with the community health team. It went quite well. They still won't give me any more money, which is a shame. Then I went up to the university to try and catch up with Josh, but he wasn't there. Again, it's a pity; I haven't seen him in ages, but I should've phoned him first, d'you think?" The cat continued to parade up and down, pausing occasionally, as if to listen intently.

"Ah, now. I bet you remember Josh. You were a tiny kitty when he came here. And he liked you, so he did. He picked you up and sat you on his knee there. I think you liked him too. OK, so, it's dinner time, I suppose. What shall we have tonight?" Sean scooped up the cat with one hand and continued to stroke him with the other, walking through to the kitchen, turning on lights as he went.

"Hm. I don't remember leaving the tin opener there. Has Sophie been to see you? She didn't say. No matter, saves me looking for it. Ah, here we are. Salmon or tuna, Sphinxy?"

The cat mewed, walked to the back door and then doubled back and hopped onto the cupboard. Sean chose to interpret that as a preference for salmon and proceeded with the tin opener. The cat wandered up and down along the counter, trailing his tail across the top of the tin and generally getting in the way. Sean pushed him to one side, emptied the food into a small ceramic bowl, and placed it on the floor.

"There, Mr. Greedy. How's that?" He stepped back and watched as his beloved pet rapidly devoured the expensive cat food, with apparently little concern for whether it was the gourmet or budget variety. There was no way of telling, as Sphinx had always been a keen eater, not that anyone would know to look at him. He was a very sleek creature and for all of his mismatched body parts, quite an attractive animal. Sean always wanted a Siamese cat, but a pure-bred would have been far more nonchalant and spiteful than Sphinx.

A slight grating sound, nothing much, nor extraordinary, considering next door had more weather vanes and other pointless garden ornaments than the local garden centre. Their tuneless cacophony of whizzes, bumps and grinds used to keep Sean awake; now it was comfortingly normal, whereas the noise he'd heard had caught his attention, because it sounded close by, as if it were inside the house. He held his breath and listened hard; the bowl shuffling across the floor made it all the more difficult.

Nothing further, Sean put it down to his imagination and turned his thoughts to his own culinary requirements. There was no food in, because he hadn't been shopping properly for about a month, so it was looking like takeaway again, and soon—there was only one reason why cat food started to smell appetising to humans. The question was whether to have pizza or Chinese, having had both far too many times of late. Either that or go and buy real food, which he didn't fancy much, considering he'd only just got in, and it was cold and wet outside. He filled the kettle and unwrapped a new box of teabags whilst he pondered his options, and then came to a very rapid decision when he opened the bin and eyed the mass of takeaway containers within.

"Look at all this junk food, Sphinxy. Well, shopping it is," he said, heading back out, with Sphinx following closely behind. He had to be the only cat in the world that liked cars, so they set off for the supermarket together, Sean vowing that for once he would buy healthy rather than easy food, the cat not caring one way or the other.

***

No point lingering, almost caught already. That stupid cat, moulting all over the place…almost managed to stifle the sneeze, but not quite. It would have to wait.

***

Josh finished reading the statement and handed it back to Jess. He hadn't a clue what she was seeing that he couldn't, because there was nothing in there to suggest James had incriminated himself. Throughout the twenty-six pages, he'd clearly denied all knowledge of the murder, and his 'forgetfulness' in relation to when he last saw Alistair Campion was hardly enough to imply guilt, contrary to Eleanor's paranoia regarding the weekend James had stayed away. To Josh's untrained eye, there was nothing there, not even circumstantial evidence.

Jess flipped another page with some force, making it crinkle and almost rip. She sighed again and shook her head despairingly. James shouldn't have made a statement at all, not without his lawyer. She couldn't understand why anyone risked it these days, least of all those who could afford good legal representation. Being certain of one's innocence was insufficient justification for going it alone, because anything said can be and was used as evidence, and James had said far too much. On the plus side, since he'd now told Eleanor more or less everything that was in the statement, there would be no nasty surprises later, when it all came out in court.

"I need to speak to him," Jess said without looking up from her reading. "I have to hear it from him."

"This is *his* statement," Josh pointed out.

"I know that."

"You don't trust him?"

"I'm not sure. You know what the police are like. Much as they claim to be unbiased, their preconceptions always come through. No, I want to ask him some questions directly, to clarify some of the things he said."

"Such as?"

"OK—" Jess flipped back the first few pages "—tell you what. I'll get Lois to photocopy it. Then we can write notes on it." She pressed the buzzer on her desk; her PA appeared a few seconds later.

"Could you make me two copies please, Lois?"

"Certainly." Lois smiled and took the statement from Jess, nodding courteously as she left the room.

Jess took off her glasses. "The bit that worries me is where James explains how a witness claimed to have seen him. Now, the police shouldn't have asked him who he thought it was, but that's by the by. You see, he didn't give any response whatsoever, which strikes me as odd. Normally, when someone is under that sort of duress, they rack their brains and come up with a couple of names in an attempt to focus attention elsewhere. James's reaction is much calmer than that."

Josh frowned as he considered what she'd said. "Yes, I understand what you mean. I've sometimes felt—well, I can't really read James, so I don't know what it is. I put it down to worrying about Ellie falling head over heels again, and when he explained his past the other night, I thought perhaps that was all it was, but it still feels like he's…I'm reluctant to say hiding something, but maybe he does know more than he's letting on."

Josh had been playing with a pen he'd picked up from Jess's desk, unconsciously clicking it on and off. Now she leaned across, snatched it from him and returned it to the pen pot. He smiled guiltily.

Lois returned with the photocopies and handed all three versions across. Jess nodded her thanks and passed one to Josh.

"Will that be all?" Lois asked. It was already way past her official finishing time.

"Yes, thanks, Lois. See you tomorrow." Jess waited for the sound of the door closing before she continued. "Now, let's go through this a page at a time. More coffee?"

"I think I better had. I get the feeling it's going to be a long, long night."

***

Sean locked the cat in the car and collected one of the more shallow trolleys from the nearest bay, thinking it would be less space to fill with impulse buys and also one less for the poor bedraggled trolley man to struggle back to the shop with. A list would have helped, too, because now he was here, Sean had no clue what to buy—a state of play which always led to a cart-load of seemingly random products, with not one combination of items equating to a balanced meal. Now he came to think about it, the last time he came shopping, Sophie basically did it on his behalf, leaving him with only the bill to pay. It wasn't a vast improvement on the usual, although he was at least able to conjure a few meals from the mix-and-match components she had selected.

Alas, Sophie wasn't with him now, and he tried to recall what they'd bought on that occasion, but to little avail. The shop was full of tempting festive treats, and by the time he'd been in there an hour, he'd selected several trays of Christmas snacks, half a dozen mince pies, a Christmas pudding with free sachet of ready-made brandy sauce, two ready meals, a bag of cat snacks shaped like holly leaves, and a large tin of chocolate biscuits—not exactly what he had intended.

Back at home, he heated one of the ready meals, gave Sphinx a cat treat, and retired to the living room for the rest of the evening, still with the same nagging feeling that someone had been in the house. Sophie usually tidied around, plumped up the cushions and whatnot, yet everything was as it should be, other than a sense of unease akin to when one realises one is being watched. Quite why that should be the case he wasn't sure, but there it was.

***

"So then. Page—" Jess checked again "—eleven."

"Got it," Josh replied.

"To the question of whether he'd seen Alistair Campion in the last month, James replied no, but then—well, read the next bit yourself."

Josh scanned the page in question. "We went through this bit already. Given the situation, I'm pretty sure I'd have problems remembering dates, too."

"That's precisely my point. He didn't have any problem remembering the date he *supposedly* last saw Campion. And if Ellie is as important to him as he makes out, there is absolutely no way he would've forgotten. He asked him to be his best man, for goodness' sake."

"Hmm, that's very true. Presumably, he didn't propose, though, or else she would've mentioned it."

And that was the real mystery. James and Eleanor were both adamant the resistance to making a formal commitment lay with the other of them, and in itself, merely pointed to their equally obstinate natures. Given what James had told them two nights ago, it made perfect sense that he should ask Alistair Campion to be his best man, yet there had been no proposal of marriage. Whichever way Josh looked at it, James was lying.

"I'll phone him and ask him outright," he suggested. Jess nodded her approval and waited while he made the call. There was no answer, so Josh left a voicemail.

"Well, there's nothing else we can do tonight," Jess said, turning all of the pages back and laying the statement on her desk.

"No, I guess not. We'll just have to wait and see what he has to say for himself." Josh was kind of pleased, as it was getting late, and he'd been looking forward to a couple of hours of reading for pleasure.

Jess ushered him out of the office and switched off the lights. She was so used to working into the evening, it didn't cross her mind that he was somewhat less familiar with the layout of the building, until there was a series of thumps and bangs.

"Ouch!"

"Josh?"

"I'm fine, just missed my footing," came the breathy reply. "It'd help if I could see where I was going!"

"Hang on." Jess flicked the light switch and illuminated the stairway. "Better?"

"Much."

"I wouldn't mind, but it's exactly the same shape as your building."

"True, but then I don't tend to wander around there in the dark, either," Josh remarked dryly.

He made it to the external door without any further mishaps and waited outside for Jess to set the alarm. Within a second of her locking the door, his phone vibrated. Wearily, he took it out of his pocket and peered, bleary-eyed, at the screen.

"You'd best open up again. He's coming now."

"Then I guess we won't have to wait very long at all."

***

Alice and Albert were enjoying a cosy night in by the fire, with Albert chirruping a noisy commentary of whatever programme was on, wherever he could. It was one of those funny noises, to which Alice was so accustomed that at times she barely noticed it, although on other occasions it was all she could hear.

He was a dear, sweet thing and, as much as a budgerigar was capable of demonstrating love, he did seem to love his mistress. However, at times like this, with Alice attempting to stitch together miniature cardigan sleeves, it was a distraction she could readily do without. Nonetheless, she persevered with the task, because Dan had been so kind, yet again providing her with transport to and from work. This time, leaking brake fluid had been the problem, and she was starting to believe that the mechanic was right about the poor little car being on its 'last legs', so to speak.

It wasn't so much that she had an emotional attachment, for a car wasn't the sort of thing she could get attached to, not with the persistent frosts and its dreadful heater, which failed to blow anything other than dusty cold air. The car was also old enough to not have power steering, although small enough for her to cope without, the thought of Dan's initial reaction to having to hard-steer making her smile. He was a strong, young man, spoilt by his new fandangled motor car and its 'super-reactive controls', as he'd called them.

Alice placed the final stitches in the cuff and cut the wool, giving the tiny garment a shake and holding it at arm's length to admire her work. It had been a while since she'd knitted, and she was rightly proud of herself for still knowing how to read a pattern. It had to be the same principle as riding a bicycle, although the latter wasn't accompanied by the heavy eye strain of precision needlework in subdued tungsten light.

"Definitely time for bed now," she informed Albert. The little bird cooed in response. She covered his cage and took herself off up the stairs, closing and locking all the doors on her way.

In her bedside cabinet was the tiny silver object she had retrieved from the boardroom floor. Every night since she'd brought it home, she had tried, and failed, to forget it was there. She opened the drawer an inch or so, peered inside, and ruefully shook her head. It was a nightly ritual that brought no answers. She quickly closed the drawer and turned off the light. Some things are best kept hidden.

***

"Hot chocolate time, I think, Sphinxy," Sean said, checking there was enough water in the kettle before he turned it on. He knew it was naughty, over-filling and re-boiling the kettle—though not exactly a striking blow to the planet—but it was far easier and boiled quicker the second time, he reasoned, so probably used about the same amount of power overall.

He heaped instant hot chocolate powder into a mug and filled it, his mind on his work for the following day: a lecture on the humanistic approach. He should spend a while planning it, but he'd given it so many times before, there really was little point. The basic principles remained the same. He knew instead he was going to sit and watch bland TV for the next few hours, until it was a suitable time for bed, because that's what he always did when he was bored. He strolled back to the living room with his mug, the cat following in fits and starts, intent on capturing the trailing belt of Sean's dressing gown.

***

James approached the office door and knocked with a level of reticence that was entirely out of character. He inhaled what he hoped would prove to be a calming breath and waited. A moment or so passed before Josh appeared at the base of the staircase and headed across the reception area to let him in.

"Hello, James. Good to see you."

"You too, Josh. How are you?"

"Fine, thank you. Jess's office is just upstairs. Well, you know that already."

James nodded and followed Josh up the stairs, the only light the dull amber glow of street lamps and then a shaft of white across the upper hallway, narrowing at the foot of the open door ahead. The two men entered and Jess glanced up. She waited until they were seated, took off her glasses and placed them on the large, leather-edged blotting pad.

"Good evening," James addressed her. "I take it you have discovered something of interest in my statement?"

"Yes, James, I have. Certainly, I can see how they believe they have enough to charge you."

Jess passed James the copy she had been working through, open at a page that was heavily highlighted in fluorescent yellow ink, with additional pencil markings in the margin and long curvy lines from starred paragraphs to little hand-scrawled notes crammed wherever they would fit. James had to squint to read the notes.

"I can understand what you are saying here," he said, indicating to one particular section. At the time, he hadn't realised his comments about knowing Alistair well enough to recognise his weaknesses could have been construed into meaning he would also take advantage of them, yet his remarks implied that he had done so. Following from this was a section in which, he recalled, he had vehemently denied having any knowledge concerning Alistair's love of fishing, only to find that he was once again caught out when asked if he had ever been invited to go along on a fishing trip. To this, he had agreed that it was possible, because Alistair had invited others at various times.

"This is a terrible thing," James remarked solemnly, passing the statement back to Jess. "I did not believe words could be twisted so, when I am so careful to choose the right ones at all other times."

"Don't beat yourself up about it," Jess consoled. "That's what happens in police interviews, which is why you must always ask for legal representation. Money's not the only reason we advise this, you know."

"I quite agree. However, my other option was to refuse to answer their questions until my lawyer arrived, and at the time, it seemed a far more incriminating course of action to take."

"Well, there's no point worrying about it now. Don't forget—there's no concrete evidence linking you to the scene of the crime. Admittedly, that fame-crazed fisherman will have considerable impact on a jury, but that's the only thing they've got. I'm confident we can work around it and get most of your statement discredited." Jess turned over a few pages. "Josh and I wanted to ask you about this bit, because, well, it, erm…"

"It struck us as being a bit strange," Josh finished off. "You know Ellie is my closest friend, which makes it a little difficult for me, for us, to be objective about this whole situation."

"And that is how it should be," James said reassuringly. "I am quite certain I would be the same. I hope you understand that I love her intensely."

"The thing is, James, you said in your statement you asked Alistair to be your best man."

"Yes, I did. And he accepted."

"Well, it's just that Ellie hasn't mentioned anything about a proposal."

"No. That is because there has been no proposal."

Jess stopped thumbing through the interview transcript and joined Josh in staring, waiting for further elaboration.

"You realise she thinks you're afraid of making a commitment to her?" Jess asked.

"Yes, and she is right, but not for the reasons you might think. I am concerned my offer will be rejected, in which case there will be nothing left for me other than to walk out of her life, which will continue as well without as it does with me."

The silence that followed came from the two recipients of the message being surprised yet again by how inept their straight-talking friend and her equally straight-talking partner could be in communicating their feelings towards each other. Eleanor was terrified of commitment also, but it was because she was certain that it meant something different to James and would ultimately result in a lonely departure from their life together at some point in the not-so-distant future.

"I think you're wrong," Jess said finally, "although I'm curious. When you were asked if you'd seen Alistair recently, you initially said you hadn't, then told them you'd forgotten. Now how could that be? You say you love Ellie. You've told her, and us, that she is the most important thing in your life next to your son. How can you possibly forget asking someone to be your best man?"

"Old habits, I suppose. I have been in that terrible situation before, under pressure to provide the right information. It can be quite an ordeal—"

"I'm sorry, James, but I don't buy it," Jess interjected. "Throughout the transcript, you appear cool and calm—too calm, in fact—and if I can see it, then the prosecution will have absolutely no problem spotting it, either. I'm afraid you're going to have to come up with a much more convincing explanation."

James looked from Jess to Josh and back again. It was only right that they should be suspicious of his motives; they were her best friends, after all. He shrugged. "I was terrified. Not of the police, you understand."

"You're frightened of Ellie," Josh realised with a wry laugh. "Join the club!"

James smiled and continued. "I lied because I thought they would reveal my intentions to her, when I had been too much of a coward to make my proposal."

"I suppose that makes sense," Jess said. "Unfortunately, it really doesn't help much." She threw the statement down onto the desk; Josh jumped at the loud slapping sound it made. James didn't hear it, for he had regressed into his own thoughts.

"And now it is too late," he said sadly.

"You're quite right," Jess agreed, checking her watch by way of deliberate misinterpretation. Josh scowled at her and turned his attention back to James.

"Is that what you want?" he asked gently.

"No, it is not. I love her, but if I leave now it will be easier."

"For her, or for you?"

"For both of us. It is why I came to you two nights ago, to explain all that had passed."

"You said you wanted our help in establishing your innocence."

"Yes, that is so. Tell me, Jess, truthfully, do you think I will be found guilty?"

She was already in her coat and at the door, luckily, as it meant she had her back to them. She crossed her fingers.

"No, I don't."

Josh waited for James to move from his chair, pulled on his jacket and fell in behind him.

"We'll do everything we can," Josh said, catching a glance from Jess. "Just don't go anywhere yet. OK?"

"For the time being, I will stay," James agreed. "If only to prove that your trust in me is not misplaced. And if I am shown to be innocent, then, I promise you, I will propose to your dear friend."

Chapter Thirteen: Scene Kid and Gothboy

"This is super-miserable, even for you."

Krissi reached up through the van window and took the two ice cream cones. She handed one to Jason.

"What d'you mean, 'even for me'?" he grumbled, but he knew exactly what she meant. They walked back to the swings, took their usual positions—arms hooked around the chains, feet just touching the floor—and swayed gently back and forth. If there had been any children around, they'd have relinquished their seats—reluctantly—but it was late afternoon and cold, dark and wet, so other than the occasional dog walker, they were alone. Jason stared absently into a remote copse of bony trees and poked the chocolate flake down inside the cone with his tongue.

"It's not so much that I hate the job," he began, as if there were more to follow. Krissi waited.

"But?" she prompted.

"But…agh." He swivelled in his seat and looked at her. "I really, *really* hate it. You know how much I used to love My Chemical Romance? If you take that number, reverse the scale and multiply it to the power of infinity then add another twenty zeroes or so, that's how much I hate it."

Krissi turned her attention to the distant trees. "That's quite a lot," she said, trying not to smile.

"Oh, it's all right for you," Jason snapped. Again, it was done in jest. "With your little pizza shop and knowing the managing director's girlfriend."

"Hey, that's not fair!" Krissi protested, and she wasn't playing around. She'd already had the same accusation levelled at her by the regional manager. If there had been even a quarter of an ounce of truth in her having been offered the position because Eleanor was a friend of her mum's, she'd have taken the jibes. However, she was convinced she had been held back from promotion for precisely that reason. Mr. Brown—she still couldn't bring herself to call him James—was full of praise and compliments, but now her branch manager had resigned, so why was she still only the 'relief'?

"I'm sorry," Jason said. "I was only joking, but it was out of order. I'm a bit jealous, to be honest."

"Jealous? Of my job? Now you really must be joking!"

"Not of your job, but the fact that you got it on your own merits. Even if I liked mine, which I don't—"

"Really? I'd never have guessed."

He ignored her. "Even if I did like my job, we both know I don't deserve it."

She wanted to tell him he was wrong, that it didn't matter his dad was a director. She didn't say it, though, because it would have been a lie.

"I'm wearing dead man's shoes," Jason complained. He'd reached his previously buried flake and was nibbling away at the surrounding cone.

"I thought that'd be right up your street." She was trying to lighten the mood. He gave her a sideways glance. "Gothboy," she said, pushing him away. He lifted his feet and swung back at her.

"Scene kid." He pushed her in retaliation, and she laughed. It had always been this way between them—the same daft insults that meant nothing—for they were best friends.

***

To an observer, it would have seemed curious that they chose each other as friends. It had been the first day of their penultimate year in high school, and they didn't yet know each other. Krissi had arrived in full, correct school uniform, and sat in the very centre of the room. She'd always done OK: neither a high flyer nor an under-achiever; rarely in trouble; never involved in fights; not the sort of pupil who would give backchat to a teacher. Rather, she preferred to blend in, so that is what she did. For the first ten years of her education, she kept her head down, did her homework and didn't answer back.

Thus, there she was, being inconspicuously on time and well-prepared, sitting with a couple of other girls she'd been 'friends' with throughout high school, all three with new folders open, file paper and pens at the ready, listening carefully to the oddly friendly introduction being given by their business studies teacher, evidently hoping to inspire them to great things over the next couple of years. It was the usual beginning-of-course information overload: exam dates, coursework deadlines, contents of each unit, what they would be doing for the rest of this term and beyond, how to email their work, and so on.

Twenty-five minutes into this address, the classroom door opened. The teacher froze mid-sentence, whiteboard pen poised on the dot of the 'i' in 'Product Li…'. All heads watched, as the apparition in black mumbled his apologetic entrance, slid himself into the nearest seat and pulled down the hood of his black, goth metal band emblazoned hoodie, revealing shoulder-length lank black hair. After as much as a further minute of staring, the teacher finished off '…fe Cycle', brushed non-existent chalk dust of a bygone era from her hands, and turned to, or perhaps, more aptly, turned *on* the late arrival. Her interrogation was public, humiliating and shocking, especially given her prior conviviality, as she demanded confessions on the whereabouts of blazers, and derided the insolence of flouting school rules.

Morning break came an hour later, and the latecomer sat alone in the canteen, his new classmates too afraid or apathetic to attempt befriending. Krissi and her friends queued up to buy drinks, after which the other two made a beeline for the only vacant table. Krissi made a beeline for *The Emo.*

"Anyone sitting here?" she asked.

He shook his head. She could only see his nose and one of his eyes, peeping through his long droopy fringe.

"You OK, after…" Krissi began.

"Yeah, thanks." He pushed his hair back. Two eyes now, of shiny bright hazel, although his mouth was still concealed by the neck of his hoodie.

"I thought what she did was really mean," Krissi said, playing with the twisty lid of her water bottle.

He nodded.

"She didn't even ask why you were late, and it could've been something really serious, like—well, I don't know what."

"It was."

"Oh, no! Really?"

"Nah, not really," he said. She peered under his hair and caught a hint of a smile in the crinkle of his cheeks. "My mum's alarm clock packed up, and we got up late. That's all. I'm Jason, by the way."

Krissi sat back and narrowed her eyes. "You nearly had me there."

"Sorry." He sounded sincere. "And thanks."

"What for?"

"Talking to me."

"Why wouldn't I talk to you?"

"Because I'm a goth."

"I didn't notice." She smirked. "You were in my English class in year eight."

He thought for a moment and shrugged. "I don't remember. I was getting bullied."

"Yeah, well, you do kinda stand out," she observed. "Not that I'm saying it's right to bully someone just because they're…unusual." She blushed. She really didn't mean that at all, not after what Kris had told her about how both he and her mum had been bullied at school, although each for very different reasons. Jason didn't pass comment. "So," she ventured, "are you a goth? Or an emo?"

"I'm neither! I'm just into the music."

"Weird. How come you're doing business studies?"

"My dad said music wasn't a *proper* subject." He air-quoted the word 'proper'.

"Why not?"

"Dunno. He said he'd already *compromised*—" the air quotes again "—by letting me choose art, even though that's not a *proper*—" and again "—subject, either."

Krissi laughed. "I'm doing art too. Kris—my stepdad—did it for one of his A Levels. He said I'd enjoy it." She made a big thing of gesturing air quotes back at him on the word 'it', which made him smile for real.

"What sort of music are you into?" he asked.

"Anything. Nickelback—"

"Ugh."

"What's wrong with Nickelback?"

"Cheesy rock's not my thing."

"What is your thing? No, wait. Let me guess. And You Will Know Us By The Trail Of Dead?"

"You know about emo music then?"

"Nope." She pointed at the front of his hoodie, and he glanced down.

"Oh, yeah. I'd forgotten I was wearing this one. I'm listening to a lot of MCR at the moment."

"MCR?"

"My Chemical Romance."

"Ugh," she repeated his earlier response.

"What's wrong with MCR?"

"Nothing, probably. I've never heard any of their stuff." She grinned. He folded his arms and scowled at her, although it was all an act.

"I like metal, too," Jason said, evidently feeling the need to further justify his music tastes.

"Metal?"

"Yeah. Some of the Old School stuff, like Metallica and Maiden."

"Never heard of either of them."

"And Slipknot. I listen to a lot of Slipknot."

"Ugh. I have heard of them. They're the dudes with masks."

"Yeah. They're really talented musicians, actually."

"If you say so."

Jason ignored her. "Plus, I'm in a death metal band."

"Death metal. Sounds gruesome."

"It's not really."

"What d'you play?"

"Bass and lead guitar, a bit, but I'm not very good yet."

"I won't come and watch you play yet, then," Krissi said, checking her watch: break was nearly over.

"Fine, don't," he said, pretending to sound hurt. She laughed.

"Anyway, gothboy, shall we head back? Oh, and I'm Krissi."

"OK, Krissi, cool."

***

"So, what you gonna do about it?" She climbed down from the swing and put the last of the dry wafer cone in the bin. Jason finished his ice cream, picking every last crumb off his black woolly trench coat.

"I can't leave, if that's what you mean."

"Why not?"

"My dad. He'll go mad. He's still going on at me about doing music at uni instead of economics." He put his chin down on his chest to create the effect of a double chin. "No jobs in the music industry, son," he said in the deep voice he affected whenever he wanted to imitate his father.

Krissi giggled. "He only does it because he cares," she contended.

"Pfft. I doubt that very much. No, that's a bit mean. I'm sure he does care about me. But he cares more about Campion's—as if I wasn't sick to death of hearing about the place already! Now I get to spend all day sitting in his crappy office *and* all night listening to him prattle on about contracts and meetings. And d'you know the worst bit? He wants me to play golf with them. Golf. Me. What the hell?"

Krissi laughed. "Ooh, that really is taking it too far."

"Would you stop taking the piss? This is serious."

"I know, I know. But it's too funny. You're twenty-two, on the board of directors for the biggest firm in town, and you're moaning about golf? I get what you mean, but it still sounds ridiculous. Listen, I've got a plan."

Jason groaned. He had learned from bitter experience that it was best to get some clarification on the details in advance of agreeing to any of Krissi's 'plans'.

"Does it involve roller coasters?"

"Nope."

"Nickelback concerts?"

"Nope."

"Sweaty Greek hotel rooms?"

"No, it doesn't involve any of those things, or underwater breathing apparatus, or snowboards, so shut up a minute and listen."

"I'm all ears."

He lifted his hair away from the side of his head to reveal an earlobe with a very large tunnel stretched into it—an accessory he was forced to remove every morning on the journey to 'the office' and routinely re-inserted every evening. A few years from now, he really would be all ears. Krissi raised an eyebrow and shook her head in disdain.

"I like it," Jason defended.

"Just as well, seeing as you're stuck with it forever more."

"Yeah, shut up. So what's this plan?"

Krissi had been thinking about it for a few months now. Life at home was tough; worse even than when Kris was really sick. Of course, she wouldn't have considered it at all back then, not when she'd already caused so much trouble trying to find her real father. Her parents—her mum and Kris, that is—were hardly on speaking terms, and it was all her fault. They didn't blame her, which was typical of them, but in a way she wished they would. A couple of screaming rows might clear the air, instead of this constant creeping around, saying nothing and keeping it bottled up, terrified that her mum would lose the plot, or Kris would lose it again. So, this seemed like the best solution, and all that was left was to pop the question.

"D'you want to rent somewhere with me? A little flat or something?"

"Oh my god! How selfish am I? I've been going on and on about my shitty job all day and not even asked about—"

"Forget it. It's the same as the last time you asked, and I don't want to talk about it, so just answer the question, gothboy."

"I s'pose."

"You suppose? Well, thanks for your enthusiasm!"

"It'd beat listening to my dad's full-on Campion's love-in all day, every day, day in, day out…"

"No MCR posters, though."

"Not even one?"

"Maybe one. In your bedroom. But definitely no Slipknot."

"Their posters are a bit grim, anyway."

"Posters, music, videos—whatever. It's a Slipknot-free zone."

"I'll trade you on Nickelback."

"Rats. You got me."

"I'll start packing tonight."

Chapter Fourteen: Missing in Action

George glanced up at the clock: 11:24 and the lecture had been due to start at eleven. It was…unusual. Sean was frequently late—by a few minutes or so—but not this late, and there were no notices on the classroom door, nor, according to Sophie, on his office door. She hadn't seen him that morning either, not that she generally shared such information freely, being as their relationship would have meant her travelling thirty miles to the next nearest college offering the counselling diploma course. George checked the clock again, not sure whether he was anticipating that the minutes would pass more quickly because he was looking at it all the time, or to be sure he hadn't misread it to begin with. Sophie did likewise, and he wondered why she didn't just phone Sean, but then thought again about the semi-secret nature of their relationship. She must have read his mind.

"Shall I give him a call, do you think?" she whispered so that none of the other students heard.

"Yeah, I think that would be for the best. He's not the most punctual person in the world, but this is a bit much, even for him."

Sophie nodded her agreement and left the room, taking her phone from her bag on the way. George doodled absent-mindedly on his notepad, trying to listen for any overspill from the conversation, but the new block was well soundproofed, with heavy, self-closing doors, and he couldn't hear a thing. The new classrooms were quite comfortable, with padded chairs, attached to which were small, paint-palette-shaped tables that pivoted on a metal arm so the sitter could move them out of the way when they were ready to leave their chair. They weren't very practical, though, as even with his slim build the table pressed against his stomach.

Some of the other students seemed to have assumed that Sophie had taken the initiative and decided the lecture was cancelled, and they followed suit, leaving George and only two others sitting a couple of rows in front. A few more minutes passed before Sophie returned to the room, staring in George's direction and raising her eyebrows expressively, although what she was trying to convey he wasn't sure. She returned to the seat next to his and swivelled the little table around in front of her—out of habit, apparently, based on what she told him next.

"He's not at home. He's not in his office. No call to the secretary to say he's sick. Nothing. And do you know what she said?" Sophie whispered angrily. "She said to let her know if he doesn't arrive before half past, because they would need to dock his pay. He could be dead, for all she knows!"

George laughed, completely unsurprised by the mercenary response Sophie had received. "What shall we do? Wait here?"

"It's half past now. I'll try his mobile again in a minute," she suggested, as the last two students relented, leaving her free to speak at normal volume. "Shall we go and sit in the café instead?"

"Good idea," George agreed, and they departed, leaving the lights to turn themselves off.

Sophie tried phoning Sean several times on the way but still received no answer. She decided to wait a while before trying again.

“How long have you been together?” George asked once they were settled with their cappuccinos and muffins in a quiet corner of the campus café.

“A couple of years. If you can call it ‘together’. We’ve been friends for about four years, but only started seeing each other about two and a half years ago. He was still married then—separated, of course—so we didn’t properly start anything and haven’t really got around to it since. Plus his cat hates me.”

“Really?” George said. “Sean doesn’t strike me as the sort of person who would have a pet.”

“No. I don’t think he is. That thing of his—Sphinx, it’s called—is more of a sideshow than a pet. It’s got this ridiculous fat tail and a tiny head and body. Not a particularly nice animal at all, but it kind of chose him, so I think that’s why it got to stay.”

“Wait till I tell Josh that Sean’s got a cat called Sphinx. He’ll love that.”

“Why?”

“Oh, err, n-no reason, really.” George blushed, realising that he, too, had confirmed his more than professional connection to Josh, who was, of course, their other lecturer. George bit off half of the large chocolate muffin so as to fill his mouth and stop it running away with him. Sophie pretended not to notice and took the opportunity to try calling Sean again. George stopped chewing and waited. She shook her head and sat back, examining George thoughtfully, her hands casually resting in her jeans pockets, a mischievous twinkle in her eyes.

“So, what about you and Josh? Been together long?”

“What?” George nearly choked on his muffin. “Me and Josh aren’t together!”

“You act like you are. When he gives the lectures, it’s like you’re digesting his every word.”

"Hey, that's not fair. I listen attentively to everything. I love this course, and Sean's a great lecturer."

"That's very true. So is Josh, although sometimes I get the feeling he doesn't want to be there."

"That's because he doesn't," George said, feeling the heat in his cheeks subside slightly.

"I'm sorry I embarrassed you. I just thought you looked like a couple. I've noticed you going to his office a few times and stuff."

"Well, we went to school together," George explained. Sophie gave him one of those looks that pressed for more information. "We are very good friends. Been through a lot."

"And you would like more?"

"Nah. I used to, but not now. It's much better this way." George wasn't sure if he'd convinced her. Then again, he wasn't that convinced himself.

"I think I'm going to have to go to the house and check everything's all right," Sophie said, sensing his discomfort and taking the chance to switch the subject back to what was most on her mind.

"OK. I'll give you my number," George said. "Call me if you need me."

Sophie offered up her phone, and he typed the number for his own into it. "Thanks. I really appreciate it." She took her phone back from him, stood up and zipped her jacket. "I must admit, I am a bit worried. I wonder what's happened?"

"It'll be nothing," George assured her hopefully.

They left the café together, heading for the campus exit and chatting about essays, placements and their plans for the Christmas break. At the gate, they parted company, with Sophie making her way to the bus stop to pick up the bus out of town, while George continued on, towards Josh's surgery, to see if there was any news. He and Josh hadn't properly spoken since their drink in the jazz club a few nights ago, and he was interested to see what Jess had made of James's statement.

Now he came to think on it, George had hardly spoken to anyone for a while. Since the whole saga with Dan and Andy, things had been more distant between them all, which George had always assumed was purely an age thing. But with the reading he'd undertaken since starting his course, it was like seeing his friends through prism lenses. Their personalities and relationships were all in a state of flux, and at times, it was bewildering taking it all in.

It was one of the reasons he and Josh were closer now than ever before, whilst his friendship with Kris had dwindled long ago. Kris's breakdown had made it even more difficult to communicate, which worried George tremendously, particularly in light of his change in career. Whenever he and Kris were alone, he was at a total loss for words, not knowing if what he said would hit a still-raw nerve. It was silly, because at one time they had shared everything with each other, been deeply intimate.

It was George that Kris had told when he concluded he was bisexual—a fact that remained in dispute in George's mind for many reasons. With all due respect to Shaunna, Kris had married a slut and turned her into a diva, his impressively creative imagination allowing others to invest in this belief also. Added to this was Shaunna's outstanding performance as a mother, and both elements combined to rebuild her in everyone's eyes. Krissi was a well-balanced, intelligent adult now, a manager of a successful restaurant. Even Ellie had said how good she was at her job, and it was one she herself had performed exceptionally for many years.

So yes, it was age and the passage of time, but it was much more besides. There were so many things going on in all of their lives. Dan and Adele's constant worry with the baby had kept them apart from the rest of the group for months. Now that had settled, George was busy at college; Eleanor was studying and working at the same time. Kris was on the road to recovery, but Shaunna was working full time to support them and pay for her dad's rest home. Jess was always busy, although she preferred it that way. Indeed, Josh had it easiest of all, and even he was up to his eyes in work, between lecturing, everything else he did for the university, and his private clients.

Then there was Andy, supervising an enormous building site, thousands of miles away, and all of a sudden, George realised he missed him more than anyone else. Funny, as in the past they had been the most distant of the friends, ironically, for the same reasons that he was missing him now. Andy was uncomplicated, always full of fun and with a childlike honesty and innocence sparkling away behind the masculinity.

These thoughts carried George all the way from the university and up the stairs to Josh's waiting room, vacant but for the little fibre-optic Christmas tree, a neat pile of magazines and an empty coffee cup. The slight murmur of conversation from behind a closed door indicated therapy was in session. George sat down and picked up the topmost magazine. It wasn't old and gossipy, like the ones in doctors' waiting rooms—a state of affairs that had seen Eleanor make it her top priority to ensure her magazines were always up to date—that and the fact that Jess was only half-joking when she told Eleanor she was banned from embellishing their rooms with five-year-old copies of *Woman's Own*. There again, the magazine wasn't very interesting, either; George put it down and took a textbook from his bag.

It was getting on for one o'clock before Josh opened the door and ushered out a rather cheery woman who didn't look much in need of counselling—testament to a job well done? Josh waited until he heard the door at the bottom of the stairs come to a close and then turned to George.

"Now what does he want me to do?"

"Who?"

"Sean. Who else?"

"Oh. It's not that. The lecture was cancelled. Well, it wasn't officially cancelled. He didn't turn up."

"Oh really!" Josh rubbed his chin thoughtfully. "That's not like him. He's not one to let people down."

"That's what we thought. Sophie's gone to his house to see if he's OK."

"Sophie?"

"The girl with the long brown hair?" Josh still looked puzzled. "Usually sits next to me?"

"No idea. A student?"

George frowned. He knew where this was going.

"How does she know where Tierney lives?"

"Don't start."

"It's professional misconduct."

"I know where you live."

"That's different."

"Actually, Josh, it's exactly the same. What have you got against Sean? I know you said it's because he's smarmy and offloads work onto you, but there's a bit more to it than that."

"There isn't."

"Come on, what gives?"

"Nothing."

"He must've done something to upset you."

"He hasn't."

"So what is it, then?"

"I don't like him, that's all. Now, would you please stop asking me bloody questions?"

George shrugged. There wasn't any point in pushing it further.

"So, what *are* you doing here?"

"I came to find out if there'd been any developments."

Josh considered for a few seconds and, having decided it was as it seemed, recounted the meeting he and Jess had had the previous evening with James, starting with his statement, which was almost an accidental confession, and concluding with his worries over the outcome of proposing to Eleanor.

George wasn't surprised by any of it, least of all that James planned to propose but was too frightened to do so. He'd been in some equally emotional dilemmas himself, where there was no right thing to do, and in the end whatever he did turned out to have been a bad choice. Going to America was probably the greatest example of this, closely followed by coming back. At the moment that was how he was feeling, although his sensible side told him it was little more than a mid-life crisis of some sort.

In the midst of this account, George's phone buzzed twice to signify two text messages had arrived. He didn't look to see who they were from until Josh had finished and was sitting writing up his notes from his last appointment, but correctly assumed that they were from Sophie. The first message told him that no-one was home at Sean's house; the second described Sean's cat with more expletives than an adult comedian used in an entire show. As he read it, he started to laugh.

"What's funny?" Josh asked without looking up from his notebook.

"A text from Sophie. Did you know Sean has a cat called Sphinx?"

"Hmm. Mind you, he never put much stock in old Siggy, so I imagine he wouldn't appreciate the joke himself."

"Well, it doesn't seem to be an especially friendly animal, by the sounds of it."

"I told you he was anal retentive, didn't I? You weren't having it, though." Josh pointed his pen accusingly at George to ward off any further defence of Sean. Just what Josh had against him, George couldn't figure out, but it clearly went way beyond professional rivalry.

"Anyway, I'm going," he said, putting his phone in his pocket and zipping his jacket right up to the neck. "I've got way too much reading to do to be sitting here, watching you write. D'you fancy going out this evening? Movie or something?"

"Sure," Josh said absently. "Ring me later, when you're done studying."

George nodded his acknowledgement and left Josh to his meticulous note-taking.

Josh still refused to trust technology to care for his work, even if it would make the whole process so much easier, and all this because his laptop had been stolen once. As it was, he was having to flick backwards and forwards through pages and pages of notes from previous sessions, all handwritten, to cross-reference specific comments, guidance, events of significance—anything which appeared especially relevant to where a particular case was heading.

In part, Josh recognised it was an excuse to emulate his hero: Freud had maintained in-depth case notes on all of his patients, and the published versions skipped back and forth between cases in much the same way as Josh's books, now numbering somewhere around forty-five, most of them stashed in the attic at home. It had to be one of the most securely locked loft hatches ever and would probably do more to arouse the suspicion of potential burglars than if it were just left open, like everyone else's.

Two more clients came and had their designated thirty minutes during the afternoon—a quiet and uneventful one otherwise. Typically for the time of year, by the time Josh was done with them and their notes, it was dark outside, a pleasant and mild evening emerging from the earlier rain, leaving shiny pavements, houses full of people and tree lights in windows. These evenings were the best for taking the walk home. Josh had already planned to have a bath and watch a bit of TV while he waited for George to call and only felt slightly guilty about not popping in on Jess and Eleanor before he left.

If he had stopped by, he'd have found Eleanor on her own, trying to come up with reasons not to return to her flat. James would be there, waiting and wondering why she was still at work when she had no appointments scheduled. He was going to ask, and she couldn't tell him why, not when it meant telling him she wanted him to leave. Especially because she actually didn't want him to leave.

Chapter Fifteen:
Unexpected

George 'sort of forgot' to ring Josh. That's what he told him, anyway, because the truth was he'd gone home, spent the afternoon reading and typing up an essay and then fallen asleep on the sofa, only waking up when the boiler started making that awful clanging noise again—either that or his phone ringing, or possibly both. Whichever, he'd been asleep for a while, because his arm had gone to sleep as well, making it almost impossible to lift it high enough to switch off the boiler, a situation made all the more frustrating by the fact that his phone was ringing again and he was, essentially, one-armed.

When the feeling finally returned, accompanied by brutal pins and needles, he noted that there were five missed calls: two from Sophie, two from Josh and one from a number he didn't recognise. There was also a text message from Sophie, explaining that she'd finally got past the cat, checked Sean's house for clues, found none, and decided to stay over. George called her back.

"Hi, Sophie. You OK?"

"No. This bloody cat is driving me insane."

Her explanation was unnecessary, because he could hear it yowling in the background, and it sounded pretty hoarse, like it had been doing it for a while.

"I've tried to feed it, but it won't let me in the kitchen."

"It's only a cat, Soph." George tried to sound gentle and consoling, but it came out exactly like a patronising parent.

"Ha. Only a cat! How about you come and deal with it then? I've no idea where Sean's gone—no note or anything—but I bet he's gone off on one of his bloody jollies and forgotten to tell his students. And me. And I've got none of that blasted essay done."

George empathised entirely, for his own effort was looking a bit thin on the ground. Now he had the feeling back in his arm, along with a full blood supply, and was entirely awake again, it was even possible he might get some more done. However, with a promise to one friend and a plea for help from another, he was finding it even more difficult to find the motivation to study than he had earlier on, when he'd fallen asleep in front of the TV. Regardless of his academic requirements, he was going out this evening; it was simply a case of deciding where and with whom.

He sighed and flipped over a page of scribbly quotations to reveal a clean one. "Give me the address."

Sophie gave him Sean's address, explained about the hole in the front garden and hung up.

Now to tell Josh.

There was no hiding the truth. When it came to Josh, George was a total pushover. All the things he needed to do, like call out the plumber *yet again* to fix the boiler, finish his essay, have a shower, sleep—any one of those would have made for a perfectly passable excuse. Instead, there he was apologising, and taking the flak on Sean Tierney's behalf, when a movie with Josh would have been the perfect way to spend the evening. Plus, he was going out unshowered, unshaven, hungry and exhausted in spite of his extended nap.

He liked Sophie, though, he justified to himself as he set off for the bus stop and hopefully not too long a wait in the cold. Sophie was his kind of person, and they'd hit it off right from the start. How strange that both of them had unconventional relationships with the course leaders—two people who could barely sit together long enough to plan how to deliver their own course, most of this accomplished via email or memos left with the faculty secretary—although Josh and Sean were very dominant personalities and alike in many respects. Sean seemed as fond of Rogerian theory as Josh was of Freud, which left little time to deal with all the cognitive behavioural stuff and much researching for the students, who had thus far gleaned that CBT was currently the 'prevailing discourse in the field but not a reason to expel an infant via the corporation drainage system' or other corny paraphrased cliché to the same effect. That was Sean: nice guy, but wincingly unwitty at times.

Why it took George forty-five minutes to realise that the buses out of town stopped at six o'clock escaped him for a while, until he also realised that he'd spent most of the day—when he'd been awake—thinking way too much about why he was feeling miserable, or if not miserable, then somewhat apathetic. It was a kind of hiatus to everything, a big teenaged 'So what?', which was most unlike him and entirely without reason. His next question to himself was what he was going to do about there being no buses, now that he'd promised to meet Sophie at Sean's house in some poky little village that was distant enough to make a taxi prohibitively expensive.

So, Josh explained, he'd been perfectly fine with not going out, or postponing the cinema to a late viewing, because he was in the bath, with a book and a carefully perched mug of creamy hot chocolate. Investing in one of those spa bubble baths was the best thing he'd ever done, he said for about the tenth time. Needless to say, he didn't appreciate the suggestion that he might like to shorten his extended period of relaxation to give George a lift, especially to Sean's house.

A couple of minutes later, George was heading, on foot, towards Josh's, by way of a compromise, giving him a little longer to soak in Blueberry Float, before being wrenched from the blissful warmth. George thought it sounded disgusting but quickly changed his mind when Josh opened the door and the fruity aroma wafted all the way down the stairs and out past him onto the street.

"Tell me again why I'm doing this?" Josh asked, keeping hold of the door to make it crystal clear that he wasn't going to let George in.

"Because you love me?" George beamed hopefully. Josh tutted, grabbed his keys and jacket and slammed the door behind him.

"There are occasions when you really know how to take the piss, George. This being one of them. I'm not going in, by the way." Josh said all of this as he unlocked the car and climbed into the driver's seat, and he continued to repeat it for the rest of the journey, followed by a reaffirmation in the form of, "I'll wait here," once they arrived at the house.

It really was a significant hole in the front garden, to the extent that the garden didn't actually exist around it, other than a narrow ledge of precariously muddy path leading directly to the front door. George stepped carefully over the larger patches of mud, still losing his footing a little, and half knocked, half fell against the door. The effect was the same, for a moment later, which he spent looking back at Josh sitting in the car and ignoring him, Sophie appeared, with several large scratches running the length of her left cheek and considerably more on her hands and forearms.

"I'm so very glad you came." She gave him a watery smile. "It's still in the kitchen—attached to the blinds, last time I looked." George nodded gravely and went inside, closing the door behind him.

***

After two nights of babysitting, both great successes, Alice was starting to take a real shine to little Shaunna, and she to her. The third was an overnight stay: Dan was taking Adele away for their anniversary.

He'd told Alice he and Adele weren't married, but he hoped they would be sometime soon, anticipating—as most did—that Alice would be a prude regarding such matters. On the contrary; she had moved in with Neil at the young and tender age of sixteen, ignoring her parents' warnings about keeping bad company. He hadn't been all bad, but there had been no-one to spend her time with since, other than Albert, and his predecessors, who were also called Albert, making him Albert the ninth, or something like that, and all because the first had been rescued by Neil from an apartment above Albert's Outfitters, an old-fashioned tailor long since closed.

Shaunna happily played away in her pen whilst Alice carefully re-read the instructions on feeding the fish. They were beautiful creatures, who bobbed to the surface each time she passed their pool. Dan had assured her they were very easy to care for, but she wanted to be sure she got it right. Plus, staying here allowed her to put off shopping a day more—an arduous task without a car, now it had completely given up. That was more unplanned expense; early retirement was starting to sound ever more attractive.

Once she'd fed the fish and put the baby to bed, Alice was at a bit of a loss as to how to spend her evening. Adele was terribly house-proud, so not a cushion was out of place. There was no crockery to wash, nor ironing to be done, and with all those channels on the television, the task of choosing something to watch was far too tall an order. Instead, she took off her slippers and curled up on the large, leather sofa, with a book she'd found in the nursery—a short romance novel—not her kind of thing, but it would pass some time.

***

George lifted the cat onto his knee and stroked its sleek coat. It purred loudly, and Sophie shook her head in even greater disbelief than when George had walked straight into the kitchen and talked the animal down from the blinds, where it had been clinging since she arrived.

"What the hell am I doing wrong, do you think? I don't dislike cats. We had one when I was little, so why does he hate me so much?"

"Maybe he's just a man's cat. I don't know much about them, to be honest. Or maybe he can sense you don't like him. Horses do that."

"Really? How do you know?"

"I had one when I was younger, and spent a lot of time with them in America, although mostly trying to avoid them, other than for getting from A to B on the ranch. I didn't mind the horses so much. It was the cows I didn't like. They're just so damn stupid."

"Well, you seem to have Sphinx onside, which is something. It's a shame he can't tell us what's happened to Sean. He wouldn't just leave him like this, and all his stuff—wallet, keys, coat—is still here."

George frowned. It was a very odd state of affairs, and he was coming around to the possibility that Sophie's suggestion of ringing the police wasn't an overreaction after all. Yet there was nothing suspicious about the place; no signs of a break-in, nor anything else indicating that a person might have needed to leave in a hurry. Maybe Sean had just gone to stay with a friend. After all, that was the kind of thing he, Josh and their friends often did—or used to—without telling the whole world where they would be for the next twenty-four hours. It didn't look like Sean had even been gone that long, and a cat could easily fend for itself for that amount of time.

"I'm going to have to go, Soph," George said, carefully setting the cat down at his feet. "Josh is waiting outside, and we're supposed to be going to the cinema. Do you want a lift back to town?"

"Oh, no—thanks—I'd best stay here with crazy cat. I'm sure me and he can learn to get along." She smiled ruefully.

George laughed. "Well, good luck. Call me if you hear anything."

"OK. Will do." Sophie walked him to the door, and he waited until he heard her lock it behind him before returning to the car and Josh.

"Sorry I was so long. She was having a spot of trouble with the cat."

Josh nodded to confirm he had heard but still said nothing.

"You're not still cross, are you?"

"No. Not cross at all," Josh replied sharply. And he honestly wasn't angry with George. How could he be angry with someone helping out a friend? That's what he did himself all the time.

"So, what's up?" George asked.

"I don't know." Josh flicked the indicator arm and pulled out into the flow of traffic. It was busy for the time of night and moving slowly, due to the speed bumps along the section of road through the village.

"It seems a nice place, this," George said, examining the rows of terraced housing, the little stone church and school next to it. It was an old village, with buildings a couple of hundred years older than those in town.

"Yes," Josh answered, after a fairly lengthy pause. He'd been thinking about his mood and trying to work out why he felt so aggravated by George's request for a lift. The only reason he could come up with was that it was, however indirectly, a favour for Sean Tierney.

***

Alice had dozed off, warm and comfortable, soothed to sleep by the bubbling of the pump in the carp pool and occasional gurgling noises from the baby monitor. The entire apartment had underfloor heating, set to maintain ambient temperature, so not even the creaks and groans of fittings expanding and contracting disturbed the peace. With no overly pungent aromas of air fresheners or anything else to upset Alice's senses, it was quite possibly the most restful place she'd ever been, other than her own home.

All of a sudden, there was the sound of a key in the lock, followed by several more attempts to open the door—which was deadlocked from the inside—and then a loud rap. Hesitantly, with heart still pounding from the shock of being woken, Alice went towards the door and squinted at the person behind the obscure glass. It was too dark to say anything more definite than that it was a man.

"Hello?" she called, through the closed door, as there was no safety chain and it was past ten o'clock.

"Hello?" a voice came back. "Can I come in, please?"

Alice recognised the voice as Dan's and unlocked the door, puzzled as to why he had returned on his own. She hoped nothing awful had happened.

"I locked up, because I wasn't expecting—oh!" Alice stopped and stared at the man before her. He looked very much like Dan, although he was darker skinned, with slightly longer hair and not so broad in the shoulders.

"I'm Andy, Dan's brother." Andy smiled.

"I—yes, I can see that. I'm Alice," she explained. "Dan's babysitter. I'm afraid they're not here."

"Oh. That puts a bit of a dampener on things. Serves me right for not phoning first, I suppose."

Alice frowned, unsure what to do. "Would you like to come in?" She indicated towards the living room with her free hand.

"Thanks, I will. I've come straight from the airport." Andy followed Alice inside, closing the door behind him.

"Yes, Dan told me you were working in the Middle East."

"I am. I was. I decided I wanted to come home for Christmas."

"Well, that's lovely. Would you like a drink of something? A cup of tea?"

"Oh, yes, please. But I'll make it. I've been sitting for a long time. Would you like one?"

"Really, I'll make one for both of us," Alice said, moving towards the kitchen and blocking Andy's path so that he had little choice. She was pleased to have something to do.

"OK, then, thank you." Andy sat down anyway, as Dan's sofa was more comfortable than virtually all soft furnishings, let alone economy airline seats. It had been a bit foolish to arrive unannounced, and it had seemed like such a good idea at the time. Admittedly, it was only a couple of weeks since he last saw his younger brother, but time stretched like a gaping yawn in Dubai. Work, shower, sleep. That had been his routine for months, and the sum total topics of conversation were two: the weather or the job. No drinking, not that it bothered him, although there were places to go where they could drink if they wanted to. No women—again, not much of an issue, because Jess would have his testicles hung out to dry if he so much as looked at anyone else. Even spending an evening with Alice, with whom he was fairly certain he had very little in common, other than a mutual and already apparent admiration for Dan, was a welcome break from the curious loneliness he'd felt. After trekking the remotest corners of the globe, that definitely wasn't something he'd anticipated.

"Here we are." Alice returned, carrying two steaming cups of tea, on saucers, complete with a pair of Rich Tea biscuits afoot. She hovered in front of Andy whilst he telepathically determined she was waiting for him to place a coaster in a suitable location and obliged.

"Thanks, Alice." He picked up the cup straight away and sipped carefully, a thirst too big to wait for the risk of scalding to pass.

"You said you *were* working in Dubai? What happened?" Alice asked the question with sympathetic inflection, but it was driven by sheer nosiness.

"I resigned."

"I must say, it does look rather impressive on the TV."

"Yeah, it does. What can I say? It's not all it's cracked up to be, although I'm sure it's heaven for some people. Not this English boy, though. Too hot and too many tourists."

Alice nodded her understanding and sipped at her tea, balancing the tiny china handle on a slightly crooked finger, the consequence of twenty-five-plus years of heavy typing. She didn't miss the old typewriters much these days.

After twelve hours of the constant drone of jet engines and air conditioning, Andy appreciated the silence. It had been quite a shock emerging from the airport into the cold evening air, mild for the time of year, but still thirty degrees cooler than where he had been. Once he'd caught his breath and the feeling returned to his fingers and toes, it felt just perfect, with all the wonderful Christmas decorations and real December weather. It made up for the impending stress, however positive it might be, of setting the ball rolling to make a living again. No more earning big bucks with nothing to spend them on, although he reckoned he had two or three months before the cash ran out, so no real urgency yet.

"So," he said after several minutes of this quiet contemplation, "where is my brother?"

"He's taken Adele for a lovely evening out, followed by a night at an expensive hotel."

"Has he indeed? Have I forgotten a special occasion?"

"No, no. Well, it is special for them, I suppose. Dan tells me it's their anniversary, I'm not sure what of, but I think he might be proposing tonight."

"Now there's an interesting thought. A tenner says she'll say no again."

Alice frowned, unimpressed by Andy's wager against his brother's success. She hoped very much that Adele would accept, but then, she was only speculating, and tonight may be nothing of the sort.

It was getting late, and both Andy and Alice were very tired, yet neither seemed eager to move from where they were, mostly because it was comfortable and warm, and each was appreciating the other's respect for the quietness of the evening, with little more than the sound of occasional tea-sipping, the gentle bubbling of water and a clock ticking somewhere.

Andy looked around the room but couldn't see a clock. Perhaps it was in the baby's room, or perhaps Alice was an impostor in his brother's house. *Yeah, right.* He slowly drifted away, letting his eyes rest. When he opened them again, all he could see was an orange glow across the room, the tiniest dot, blurred and out of focus. The duvet was so warm and soft he couldn't possibly get up to see what it was. It would wait until the morning.

Chapter Sixteen: Oh, Shoot

James picked up the small holdall and placed it on the bed, not entirely sure what to do for the best, seeing as Eleanor had just launched it across the room. He'd stepped aside, and it had landed a few feet away, taking most of the stuff off the bedside table with it. She was raging again. It was a temporary yet recurring state and hardly surprising, all things considered, but how he wished she would just calm down for a while, or keep her thoughts to herself until she was sure she meant what she was about to say. It would save her having to apologise afterwards. Of course, he didn't dare give voice to any of these notions, or he'd have got more than an empty holdall hurtling in his direction.

Now she was banging around in the kitchen, slamming cups into the sink as if they were unbreakable, or as if it didn't matter to her whether they were or not. James knew better than to approach and hoped that it would pass as quickly as the last time, which had been—he checked his watch—just under two hours ago. Worst of all, he wanted to be supportive, but even if he wasn't the cause of it, he wouldn't have known what to say or do to make it better. If he thought it would help, he'd have suggested she visit her mother, or Josh. Instead, he said nothing, for fear she would think he was trying to pass the problem on to someone else.

The tinkling of crockery hitting a hard surface signalled another casualty and also the likely cessation of current hostilities. *All this from a misunderstanding over a murdered man.*

Put like that, it seemed so trivial. Alistair was one of the most important people in his life, second only to his son, and the prospect of losing them both, as well as Eleanor, was too dreadful to contemplate. James waited a few minutes before he took a handful of socks and boxer shorts from his dresser, and placed them in the holdall—for effect, as Eleanor was standing in the doorway, with a dustpan in one hand and a brush in the other.

"I'm sorry," she mumbled, poking at the broken shards in the dustpan. "I just don't know how to deal with this."

James stayed where he was, waiting to see if there was more to follow what had become her mantra over the past few days, but there was nothing else.

"Nor do I, Eleanor. I believe most sincerely that we must struggle on together, however. This fighting is a terrible drain. Oliver is coming in two days, unless you have changed your mind, and he has heard enough shouting to last a lifetime."

"No, Oliver must come. Of course he must. He's looking forward to it and so am I. I guess I'm just trying to get it out of my system first."

"Well, I have an idea about that," James said carefully and edged around the bed in Eleanor's direction. He took the dustpan and brush from her and placed it on the corner of the bed, and then put his arms around her. "I propose we go out for the day and indulge ourselves with all kinds of Christmas fayre. Then we should lunch at The Pizza Place—I hear the manager is excellent—and later, I would like to spend some time sitting quietly beside you in evening prayer. I believe it will grant us both some tranquillity."

Eleanor considered for a moment and nodded her agreement. "I'd like that." She gently kissed him on the chin. And then, business as usual, she picked up the dustpan and returned to the kitchen. "You can put your underwear away again now," she called back.

She knew his ploy all too well, considering he'd done it at least three times yesterday. She was no better, throwing the bag at him, and his suggestion seemed the best idea all round. Even though he was a Buddhist, he said that one of the greatest aspects of his faith was that he could respect others and their beliefs. His ex-wife was bringing Oliver up to be a Christian, if anything, and James said he was satisfied with her plan to send their son to a Church of England school, which would ground him in the morals, values and beliefs that all good people shared, regardless of their named religion. James had, until the arrest, been as excited about Christmas as Oliver was, and if Eleanor could just get her head together, she would be, too.

***

George and Josh had stayed up late, drinking beer and playing a racing game, their performance getting progressively worse as the night went on. Thus, when his phone woke him before there was even daylight outside, George was far from impressed, and it took all his strength to lift it to his thumping head, by which point the blessed thing had stopped ringing. He squinted at the screen, painfully bright on four hours' sleep and six cans of lager, just able to make out the words:

Missed Call: 07:58
Sophie

He put his other hand on his forehead, in an attempt to muster up the will to call her back, but then decided against it and let the phone fall to the floor. *Surely it can wait a bit longer?* Thirty seconds later, he discovered it couldn't wait at all, because there it was again, ringing and now out of reach.

"Crap." He carefully swung down to pick it up, groaning as the blood rushed to his head. "Hi, Sophie."

"George. I'm so sorry to call at this time. I hope I didn't wake you up."

"You did, actually, but don't worry," he replied through gritted teeth, hoping she wouldn't hear the lack of sincerity. "What's up?"

"I've found out that Sean's in hospital. He said he's got food poisoning, but the doctors don't agree. They think he accidentally overdosed on painkillers."

"No way! Is he all right?"

"Yes. He's fine now. They had to give him an antidote of some sort, but he should be able to come home today, thank God. Sphinx is still giving me a hard time."

A loud meow in the background pushed the point home and made George laugh, which, in turn, made him groan and grab the side of his head.

"Well, thanks for letting me know. If there's anything I can do just give me a shout, OK?"

"Err, well, actually, there is. Would you mind coming over and sorting out the house while I go and pick him up at the hospital? I've ordered a taxi for ten o'clock, seeing as they're so busy."

"Sort out the house?"

"The thing is, the cat had…an accident. That's probably the best way to explain it for now. You'll see what I mean when you get here. I'm a bit squeamish about things like that. So, please, George, I'm really sorry. I know it's a lot to ask, and you've been great—"

"All right, all right. I'll be there in about an hour." George sighed, said goodbye and lay down on the bed again, but quickly changed his mind. Now he'd been upright, there was no going back. He'd just have to deal with the hangover and whatever this 'accident' of Sphinx's was.

Very carefully, he crept downstairs, filled the kettle, crept back up the stairs and went for a shower, the jets of water like needles on his scalp, although it was nowhere near as painful as the fuss Josh was going to make now he could hear he'd also disturbed him.

This whole business with Sophie was starting to get a bit much, not for George, but certainly for Josh. With limited options, George was going to have to ask for a lift, or a loan, given that he'd spent all the cash he could get hold of on boiler repairs. A fat lot of use that had been, as was evidenced by his staying with Josh yet again. He was beginning to wonder whether it would be as well to suggest they came to a more permanent arrangement, but then he remembered. When he first came back from the States, it had taken less than a month for them to reach the point of intolerance they were at now, so maybe it wasn't such a good idea, after all.

***

"You ready yet?" Dan shouted from outside the bathroom door. "The party's leaving in five minutes, and we'll miss them."

"Oh, stop going on, will you! I'm coming," Adele shouted back from just the other side of the door and emerged in the most intriguing outfit Dan had ever seen her wear: a mauve deerstalker hat with coordinating hunting jacket and jodhpurs, the whole look rounded off with riding boots and fluffy-cuffed suede gloves.

"Wow!" he said, not really sure what else he could say. She did look striking, but they were only going clay-pigeon shooting and she was all dressed for some kind of fox-hunters' fashion show, if there were such a thing. "Your beige boots might get a bit muddy, you know."

"Camel."

"Pardon?"

"They're camel, not beige, but I don't expect to be trudging through mud much today. I hear the clubhouse does a wonderful martini."

“It’s nine in the morning. Are you really going to drink martini at this time?”

“I most certainly am. I haven’t been away from the house for more than a few hours since the baby, and I fully intend to make the most of it.”

“Fair enough,” Dan said and started to move off. It was his idea, so he only had himself to blame. He opened the door to the suite and turned back to find that, once again, he was standing alone. “Now what are you doing?” he shouted. No response. “Adele?”

This time, he really was stunned to silence, for now she had a riding crop as well. Dan shook his head and ushered her out into the corridor before she remembered she’d forgotten her mauve saddle, or Lord only knew what else.

***

For some reason, which remained unfathomable to George, Josh agreed to take him to Sean’s again. It was entirely the opposite of what he’d anticipated, to the extent that he’d asked for a loan rather than a lift. Even more bizarre than that, Josh was in fine spirits: no hangover, hardly any sag under his eyes, even though they had both had the same amount of sleep. To cap it all, he talked incessantly all the way to the little terraced house in the village, parked up, switched off the engine, got out of the car and followed George up the path to Sean’s front door.

The trench was a bit tricky to negotiate today, on account of the rainy night. The amount of mud it had splashed up onto the concrete flags made for a serious hazard, and both men lost their footing, grabbed at each other in an attempt to steady themselves, laughed at the futility of it, and slid into the hole. Now they were covered up to the waist in mud, it wasn’t just the cat’s little accident that would need cleaning up.

Getting out was a far greater chore than falling in. The sides were steep and slippery, and there was nothing to grab hold of in order to lever oneself upwards, other than a bare and decidedly dead-looking plant further towards the house. George grabbed one of the outstretched limbs and pulled himself out just in time, the end of the branch now a twig in his hand. Reluctantly, and knowing the consequence before he even started, he leaned down and offered a hand to Josh, which he took and clung to whilst trying desperately to find a foothold. By then, they were both laughing so much they were crying, and still Josh was no closer to getting back to ground level.

Sophie had heard the commotion and appeared at the front door, where she remained, watching from a distance as they both finally scrambled up onto the path, and sat, dangling their feet in the trench, absolutely covered in mud.

"Good grief. You look like a pair of naughty schoolboys," she said with a grin and then remembered Josh was her lecturer and swiftly straightened her face. That made the situation even worse, and Josh was now helpless.

"You might want to…" he stuttered through hysterical giggling, "tell Tierney…he's got a…bit of an…uneven lawn." He doubled up again, and George joined him.

Sophie tried to maintain her serious expression, but it was no use. She started to giggle, too, and it was quite some time before the three of them made it into the house, their sides aching from laughing so much. However, it didn't take long for the smell of Sphinx's 'accident' to sober them up once and for all.

"Oh, shit," George said.

"Yes," Josh and Sophie replied in unison.

***

The shopping centre was very quiet, considering it was only two weeks until Christmas, which gave James plenty of time to mull over the vast number of objects Eleanor had coveted so far that morning. What he really wanted to give her was still just out of reach, and there was little he could do about it until he'd cleared his name. He hoped Josh and George were having better luck than he was, because, after speaking to Jess, he was starting to feel that the best he was going to get was an early release for good behaviour, by which point Eleanor would be married with her own family, and he would have long been forgotten about.

The path into melancholy was familiar and easy to take, and he shook himself out of it once more as Eleanor headed back to his location, armed with two more bags to return to the car, parked four storeys above. James smiled and held out his hands in readiness.

"Oh no you don't," Eleanor said, clutching the bag against her. "This one's not for your eyes."

"I promise I won't look," he beseeched.

"I don't believe you!" Eleanor replied, but then realised what an awful thing this was to say, given the situation. "I'm sorry. I didn't mean—"

"I know. It's all right." He kissed her on the head. "Now, shall I take those bags from you?"

"Nope. You're still not getting to look inside," Eleanor said and stepped away, all forgiven. They moved off, towards the escalator and the next floor down, James having made the decision in that split second that he was going to propose, whatever the outcome. He was strong enough to let her go if and when the time came. Right now, she was all he wanted.

***

Adele poked at the brambles in front of her with an expression of utter disgust on her face. True townies like her really weren't cut out for the countryside, but it was a beautiful day, with crisp clear air, and the sun was doing its best to be warm and bright, so low in the sky it was just visible over the trees at the other side of the clearing into which they were about to emerge. This was where the shoot would take place, and she had to admit she was so close to not caring about her appearance anymore that she might even start enjoying herself. It was only a few hours before they'd be leaving for home, so she needed to hurry up.

Dan seemed to have a lot on his mind, as if he wanted to talk to her about something but couldn't quite bring himself to do so. As a general rule, Adele wasn't the greatest at reading people, but she and Dan had known each other for so long she could tell exactly how he was feeling. Like that time he'd written on her coat with correction fluid: he'd felt so guilty about it and really wanted to confess, but instead let her walk around all day with *I wuz ere* emblazoned in white that shone out all the more starkly against the navy fabric.

When she'd finally discovered it, he'd lied and said it was Andy, but she'd known it was him the whole time. The next day, she'd found his shoes outside the gym, filled them with green poster paint and stolen his laces. He never did ask if it was her, either because he didn't think it was, or more likely, took his punishment on the chin, as always.

The instructor beckoned them all closer and handed each of the party a pair of large, black, protective headphones. Adele smoothed her hair down and placed them carefully over the top of her hat. They looked like giant panda ears, and there was no way they were going to stay put. She took them off again. The instructor gave her a warning glance and continued to load the gun with pellets, ready for the first of the twelve of them to take a shot.

Adele struggled away, took off her hat, put on the headphones and put her hat back on, which looked absurd, because now it was perched on top of her head like a policeman's helmet. Dan raised an eyebrow and smirked, but said nothing. As she was about to take them off a second time, the instructor yelled, a disc shot up in the air, and the man with the gun pulled the trigger. The loudest bang she had ever heard made her whole body vibrate and her heart pound. The disc continued momentarily on its trajectory and then fell out of the sky, still in one piece.

The man shrugged and handed the gun back to the instructor, who muttered something Adele couldn't make out on account of her earmuffs. He did something with the gun and returned it. This time, the man looked like he was much more focused on what he was doing. Once again, the instructor shouted, a disc shot up over the trees, and the man pulled the trigger. The disc sailed safely past and dropped to the floor. He gave the gun back and moved away to let his wife take her turn.

She was a very robust woman, probably about fifty, as was her husband. Both of them were in matching tweed jackets, although hers was more tailored to trace the curves of her well-rounded hips. The instructor mouthed some words, handed the gun to the woman and called out for the disc to be fired.

The woman pulled hard on the trigger and watched as her disc, like her husband's before her, made it back to earth in one piece. A look of determination on her face, she took aim again, and this time, the disc wasn't so safe. The shot just caught the tailing edge, sending a small chunk firing off in the opposite direction. All the women in the party applauded, including Adele, although her own clapping was somewhat muffled by her gloves.

The next two people, another twin set of tweeds, both hit one disc each and Adele started to get bored, wondering why they called it clay-pigeon shooting when it had nothing to do with birds, but then, she concluded, big fat clay models of pigeons probably wouldn't fly quite so well.

The next man hit both discs, little pieces fracturing, but leaving the main disc intact. His wife hit one disc full on, and it broke into two perfect semicircles, which kind of plopped out of the air.

It was finally Dan's turn. He'd never been shooting before, and he was feeling a little nervous, not entirely convinced he would have any more success than the first man, and his ego wouldn't withstand the strain of failure.

The instructor explained the same set of tips and safety points as he had for everyone else, waited for Dan to give the nod and called out for the disc. There was a second or two delay, and then out it flew, rising in a clear arc above the trees.

Dan followed it through the sight and pulled back on the trigger, focusing on that little round blob like his life depended on it. A split second later the disc shattered into a thousand tiny pieces, like a firework in negative. Dan fought the urge to punch the air and just grinned instead, although he wasn't satisfied yet. If he could hit the second shot, that would secure it. But with the tension building in his chest, his own stupid pride and competitive nature made it increasingly difficult to stay focused on the challenge ahead.

The disc fired upwards, and Dan tried to calculate how he had done it the last time, but it took him too long to think, and he missed his chance. His shot whistled well clear, and the target remained whole. He cursed to himself and handed the gun back, furious that he had spent so long thinking instead of just going with his gut instinct.

Next, Adele stepped up to take her shot. Again the same set of instructions, the same preparation of the rifle, and the instructor handed it over. It was much heavier than she'd anticipated, and she had to hoist it up with her left hand to get it against her shoulder. The sight was so small, and standing there, squinting with one eye, made her feel like a total idiot.

"Go on, love. Show him how it's done," said the tweedy woman who had taken the second shot. Her words made Adele feel a bit more confident. People on her side. What a strange thing that was.

Adele listened carefully for the shout indicating the disc was heading upwards. *Don't worry,* he'd said, *most people don't hit it the first time. Most of these people have been here lots of times before.* She had to beat Dan. She just had to. Just for that correction fluid all those years ago.

There it was, gliding through the air, almost in slow motion. She strained to see it through the sight and pulled the trigger, staggering backwards with the force of the blast. The rest of group cheered, and she regained her posture just in time to see the last fragments of the demolished disc fall out of the sky. She could hardly believe it. She'd hit it!

This was it. The second shot. Could she do it? The pain in her shoulder was quite something. The force of the rifle butt hitting it was bound to have left a bruise, but she didn't care. She was going to do this—for her, for all those other women and their smarmy, condescending husbands, for all women everywhere. The man yelled, the disc flew, and Adele, like she'd been doing it all her life, fired the pellet straight at it.

The shouts of absolute joy in celebration for this tiny woman in her totally over-the-top outfit, whose achievement by far surpassed that of all the big macho men in the party, could be heard all the way back to the clubhouse, and Adele was loving it. She'd never done anything that she felt so proud of and had been promised a double Scotch once they were back in the bar. She didn't like to say she didn't drink whisky, but there again, until half an hour ago she didn't shoot, either.

***

"I've never seen so much poo come out of such a small animal. How much did you feed him, Soph?"

"I told you, George. I swear I didn't give him anything else." Sophie sighed, glad to hear the sound of the taxi's horn outside to relieve her of all responsibility. She really hadn't done anything to give the cat diarrhoea, not that she knew of, anyway.

"Well, it's eaten something that doesn't agree with it. Poor thing," Josh said, carrying the rather dejected-looking creature through to the living room, where it curled up tightly on his lap and quietened its mewing to a slow purr.

"It just doesn't like me," Sophie said. "Thank you, both. I really mean it. I'll see you later." With that, she disappeared through the front door, closing it hard behind her.

George emptied the final bucket of water down the drain outside and then followed Josh into the living room.

"Sean's going to hit the roof when he sees the state of his house," he said. "At least the smell's gone now."

"Or we've got used to it," Josh said, stroking the cat. "Don't suppose a cup of coffee is out of the question, is it?"

George huffed but did as requested, seeing as Josh was sitting with the cat. He could still hear him from the kitchen, telling the cat how awful it was that he should be named after a body part, and the least flattering body part at that. Whether the cat was paying attention or not, it was an interesting monologue that revealed a little more about Josh and Sean's relationship. Finally, George realised how they knew each other. They must have been at uni together, which didn't explain why Josh hated Sean so much, but at least he'd figured out the connection, because Josh was now consoling Sphinx, with tales of the mess his owner used to make after late nights in the Students' Union.

George picked up the kettle, about to top up what was in there, but then changed his mind. It might have been there a while, after all. He removed the lid and tipped the half pint or so of water into the sink.

"Some people really need to learn how to descale their kettles," he muttered to himself, examining the pile of white powder slowly swirling away down the drain. On second thoughts, it didn't look much like limescale.

"Josh. Come and look at this."

"Can't. The cat's gone to sleep."

"No, really, I need you to come and look. Tell me what you think it is."

Josh grumped and lifted the cat onto the sofa beside him. "Sorry, Sphinx, his master calls."

"Look." George pointed at the remaining dregs he had saved by shoving the sink plug in quickly. "What do you think?"

"Limescale, you goon."

"No, there was too much of it. It looks like soluble aspirin or something—you know the way it never does quite dissolve? I bet you anything it's whatever painkiller Sean overdosed on. I'd even go so far as to say the cat got a dose, too. We'd better get it to a vet."

"It still looks like limescale to me. Don't you think you might be overreacting?"

"Maybe, but we should get Sphinx checked out anyway. What harm can it do?"

Josh still looked doubtful and was about to protest again, but George was right about one thing. That cat definitely needed to see a vet before it turned its insides out, for the noise coming from the living room sounded none too healthy.

"OK. I'll go get the cat."

Chapter Seventeen:
Pet Hates

Even cats that like cars aren't the best passengers when they have an extreme case of flatulence-powered diarrhoea and have psychically established they are on their way to the vet. Josh and George weren't enjoying the experience particularly either, although the prior state of Sean's kitchen was good evidence that most of what needed to be expelled had been so already.

In such circumstances, it was always true that the one and only bus, which ran every two hours at its greatest frequency, was directly in front, and its route coincided exactly with that required to reach their destination. Hence, Josh's language was choice, to say the least. All of the windows were fully open, it was zero degrees outside, and still the smell was making him bawk. And what was George doing in all of this? He was laughing. Josh concluded it was hysteria.

In spite of the bus, they made it to the vet's in good time, dumped the car in the closest parking bay and evacuated before the engine had stopped ticking over. They weren't even sure it was the surgery Sean used, but it was the closest, seemed logical and it didn't actually matter. The most important thing was to get the cat seen, and not just for Sphinx's benefit.

"Yes," the vet said, having poked a small thermometer up the cat's bottom, shoved the cat's eyelids in all directions, pulled at its lips to check its gums, and all other manner of things, each resulting in further injury to George, who was doing as he was told and holding on very tightly to whichever aspect of feline anatomy wasn't being subjected to invasive examination.

"Yes," the vet said again. George went to suck the newest wound on his finger but thought better of it, and waited with increasing impatience for further elaboration of this affirmation.

"Did you bring any of this mystery substance with you?"

"Damn. No, we didn't. Should I ask my friend to go back and get a sample?"

"It would be wise, yes." Every time he said the word he dragged it out, making it sound like it was so much more than just three letters. He took the cat from George, freeing him to go back to Josh in the waiting room.

"He needs a sample of the stuff from the kettle," George explained, ready to duck, knowing precisely how Josh would react to this news. Under that surface calm, there was something equivalent to Mount Etna, but it appeared to be saving itself for a time and place when only George would be privy to Josh's thoughts on the matter. Now was not that time or place. Instead, Josh strolled quietly out to the car, slammed it into reverse and pulled out onto the road with sufficient acceleration to create smoke.

George swallowed hard and went back to the consulting room. "He's just gone to get it."

"Good, good. We'll put this little chap in here for now." The vet opened a small cage on the floor, dropped Sphinx into it, ushered George out to the waiting room and called in the next patient, all in one swift, continuous motion. A little old lady and her hobbly, ancient Jack Russell went through, and George sat down to wait.

***

It probably wasn't hours since Josh left, because there had only been two more dogs, a rabbit and six kittens in a basket, and there were apparently two vets working. So, giving each appointment a generous fifteen-minute slot, George estimated he'd been waiting thirty-five minutes, at most, by the time he heard the car pull up outside. It seemed much longer without a watch, and he'd left his phone in the car, thus he'd had nothing to do but ponder over how the strange-looking farmer type was able to stop the deranged kittens escaping from their picnic-style wicker hamper, whilst a German shepherd did his very best to entice them out of it.

"Here," Josh said, throwing a small plastic bag of white paste into George's lap. "Your sample."

"Thanks. Traffic problems?"

"Sean was back and wanted to pass the time of day. He was all for coming back with me, but Sophie somehow talked him out of it. I must say, I do feel a little bit sorry for him. He looks terrible."

"Oh, dear." George could think of nothing else to say, because Josh's words were caring enough; it was the matter-of-fact delivery that made George wonder why Josh had bothered saying anything at all. Josh looked like he was still waiting for George to elaborate, so he held up the sample and said, "I'll take this to the vet when the kittens come out."

"Kittens?" Josh's question was immediately answered when the man with the basket appeared from a doorway on the right. He put the basket on the counter while he paid his bill, pausing every so often to push down the six tiny mewing things scrabbling to escape from their curious carrycot.

The man left, and George went over to the receptionist, who indicated that he could go in to the vet; a moment later he was back out and ready to leave.

"What next?" Josh asked, digging his keys out of his pocket for the fourth time that morning. It wasn't yet eleven o'clock.

"He's going to run some tests and call us."

"Us?"

"Me."

"What does he think?"

"Not a clue. He just hummed and said 'yes' a lot."

"Not much else we can do, then, is there? Other than go home," Josh said hopefully, but he knew they had to go back to Sean and tell him what was going on.

Compliance wasn't Josh's strong point—not without protest—and as they drove back, he told George everything he had been keeping in all morning, his driving a direct reflection of his mood. The car swung dangerously on a couple of sharp bends and came to a very abrupt halt outside Sean's house. Josh put on his best 'grin and bear it' face. Yet more interaction with that idiot Tierney. Just what he needed on an empty stomach and four hours' sleep.

George had to agree with Josh's earlier observation; Sean looked terrible, although it wasn't surprising. As he explained, at length and in true Sean Tierney style, he'd spent the past two days attached to drips, delivering an antidote and restoring his fluids, the prospect of food anywhere in the immediate future a very remote notion and not a good one at that.

In the absence of anything else to talk about, Josh listened to Sean's blow-by-blow account of every medical procedure he had endured. From what George had said, it didn't sound a whole lot different from the vet's examination of the cat.

"Thanks, George, by the way," Sean finished off. "I know old Sphinxy and Soph don't get on so well. It's very good of you to step in like that. You, too, Josh, mate."

"No worries…mate." The last word was accompanied by a scathing smile. *Mate? As if!*

"It was no trouble," George said quickly, trying to move things on before they got out of hand. Given his ear-bashing in the car, it could happen very quickly. "I think we've also figured out where the paracetamol overdose came from."

"God. Would you believe they had one of my own team come down and ask me to complete a depression inventory? I wrote the thing. So what's this you're saying, George? I don't even take the things for a headache."

"The stuff in your kettle. It looks like soluble painkillers. Any idea how they might've got there?"

"No idea at all. As I say, I've no need for them. Are you sure about this?"

"No, but the vet's running some tests to see if the cat also got some."

"See now, I made a drink the other night, and Sphinxy, well he always likes a drop himself. Terribly unhygienic, sharing a cup with the ole fella, but you know. He's like my son. But he wouldn't touch it. They say cats and dogs know, that incredible sense of smell of theirs. I should've taken heed."

"So if he didn't touch your drink, why did he have the shits," Josh asked bluntly.

Sean pulled himself up and hobbled through to his kitchen, looking much older than his forty years. Sophie, George and Josh followed at a distance, all equally intrigued as to what he was up to. He stopped at the bin, peered inside, nodded his head and bent down, with a grunt, to retrieve an empty cat food tin.

"This," he said, grinning. "It's not his usual brand, see, and I meant to take it to the rescue. I bought the two tins, on special offer, and after the first one, well, I wasn't sure if it was the food that set him off, but what a dreadful state we were in for a good few days!" He dropped the empty can back into the bin. "You've done a great job, though. I couldn't smell a thing when I came in."

That came as no surprise to Josh, for one of the many things that irritated him about Sean was the way he sounded as if he had a constant cold. Although the house smelled much better than it had earlier, there was still a markedly unpleasant odour in the air. It was as well for Sean his sense of smell was jiggered.

"Well, maybe it was only limescale then?" Josh suggested.

"Hmm. Maybe," George said thoughtfully. They'd know for sure in the next few hours.

After Josh and George left, Sophie rinsed all the remaining powder from the sink and filled the kettle with hot soapy water—not the best idea she'd had, she realised, when boiling it a fourth time still resulted in a stream of airy foam frothing from the spout. *Sean and his cups of tea!* She'd have thought he'd have learned his lesson by now. Well, he was just going to have to wait until the kettle stopped acting like a bubble machine.

***

It was lunchtime, but to Andy, it felt like the middle of the night, even though in Dubai it would only be early evening. He knew this because his watch was still in the wrong time zone. It sort of made things better to cope with, that he could justify how tired he was and avoid going to see Jess for a bit longer. Alice was upstairs settling Shaunna down for another nap, and he'd promised to have a sandwich ready for her return. The sound of the door gently being pulled to was just audible through the baby monitor, and he quickly got up and went to the kitchen to do as he'd said, or been told, he wasn't sure which.

Now that his brain was starting to catch up, he found he was far less surprised by his brother's choice of babysitter than by the fact that Dan had managed to get Adele away for the night, not least of all because she generally refused to go anywhere with him unless Kris and Shaunna went, too. It was like some kind of safety net for them both: left to their own devices, they generally ended up getting drunk and having terrific arguments, where every bad thing they'd ever done to each other was dragged up and scrutinised once again.

Andy was a frequent, and therefore, expert witness to their bickering. *How many years has it been now?* He absent-mindedly positioned sliced ham onto the bread as he tried to calculate. It had to be at least thirty since they first met, falling thereafter into a pattern of always 'happening' to be in the same place at the same time, and age had done little to mature their silly childish games.

All things considered, Andy decided, it was probably better being single, or single-ish, as he and Jess weren't actually free agents. There was some allusion to the possibility of dating other people and seeing where it took them, yet he couldn't bring himself to do it, partly out of fear, but mostly because he loved Jess. He wasn't interested in anyone else, not that he'd had the time or energy while he was away. Jess had assured him the same was true for her, so it appeared their busy lives had ensured their fidelity.

Andy added the top slice to the sandwiches and cut them diagonally, as it seemed a bit posher, and Alice came across as the sort of person to appreciate such gestures. On that count, he had read her perfectly, and she beamed at him as he placed the plate in her hands before returning to the kitchen to collect the tea, in matching cups and saucers. Jess would be very impressed with his multi-tasking. *And* he'd cleaned up the mess. All those months in Dubai, living as a bachelor, and he still hadn't forgotten his training.

"I was wondering…" Alice hedged, daintily wiping crumbs from the corners of her mouth with the tip of her little finger. "Would it be awfully rude of me to pop home and check on Albert? He's not used to being left uncovered overnight."

"Of course! You go right ahead. I'm not going anywhere. Yet."

"That's very good of you," she said and then, forgetting herself, shoved most of the remaining half of the sandwich in her mouth in one go, keen to check on her beloved Albert now she had permission to do so.

Andy was happy to have a reason to stay where he was. He'd barely seen his niece at all—certainly not since she'd been allowed home from hospital for good. So far today, he had warmed a bottle of milk and played Peek-a-boo for a record-breaking hour and a half, after which he'd fed her some kind of brown goo on a tiny plastic spoon only just concave enough to call itself that. He'd also got to change a nappy—not an especially pleasant uncle's responsibility, but essential to the process of proving to his brother that resigning was the right thing to do.

Alice finished her cup of tea and collected the assorted crockery, clanging the plates together and feeling guilty about it. She'd noticed the bone china set in the cupboard, of course, but felt it would be taking advantage to use them, when she'd only seen Adele take them out the once, on her first night of sitting.

"Leave those, Alice," Andy called after her. "I'll do them. You go and see Albert." He hadn't even asked who Albert was but assumed from the comment about him being left uncovered that he was some kind of bird. Alice didn't protest and returned a moment later, garbed in coat, hat and scarf, and pulling large woolly mittens onto her hands.

"I'll be back as soon as I can—before Dan and Adele return home, I would think."

"There's no rush. You take your time. See you later." Andy watched her struggle with the door handle for a few seconds but could take it no more. There was no way she was going to turn the catch on the front door in those mittens. She giggled giddily and waved back like a little cartoon character, from the end of the path, skidding slightly on the icy pavement, before she trotted off at speed in a homewards direction.

Andy laughed to himself and returned to the warmth of the living room, rubbing his hands together, largely for effect, even if there was no-one there to see it.

***

George pressed the button on the phone and turned to Josh, who was as eager to hear the result of the vet's tests as George had been a moment earlier, but Josh was doing an excellent job of concealing it by refusing to look up from his laptop—not that he was actually doing anything other than opening and closing documents for the sake of doing something.

"It was paracetamol, but Sean's right. The cat had an upset stomach. The vet says that if Sphinxy had ingested any, he'd be dead by now, so that's kind of good news."

"For the cat. But what the hell was all that paracetamol doing in the kettle?" Josh still didn't look up from his laptop. George knew what he was doing, so it was pointless. "Mind you," Josh continued, still without eye contact, "Sean has a shocking problem with sleepwalking, so he probably did it himself."

"Does he now?" George said, peering around the edge of the screen. Josh moved it away so he couldn't see. "And how do you know that?"

He'd known all along there was more to it than mere academic rivalry, but evidently, Josh hadn't intended to share, because now he was scanning the screen, like he was reading.

"Well?"

"What?"

"Sean. How do you know he's a sleepwalker? I mean—it's not exactly something people tell you when they introduce themselves, is it? 'Hi, I'm Sean and I'm a somnambulist!' You might as well just spit it out."

"We went to university together, but you knew that."

"Whoa. No, I didn't. You've not mentioned it at all."

"Yes, I have. Well, no, I might not have done, seeing as it's totally irrelevant to anything. We were on the same course, then he went off somewhere else to do his PhD."

"And you've despised him all these years?"

"Far too strong a word, George. I don't like him. I don't like his attitude, the arrogance, the smarmy fake humility, always playing on his good looks and local celeb status."

"Too strong a word. OK. Have it your way."

"I will," Josh said curtly and started typing.

Chapter Eighteen:
Comings and Goings

Dan took all of the bags out of the boot and piled them onto the gravel driveway a third time. They'd all fitted on the way there, and to his knowledge, Adele hadn't been anywhere she could have purchased more clothing or accessories. So there should only be what they had started with, but it just wouldn't go. Quite why she needed a case and an overnight bag for a one-night stay was a mystery he had given up trying to solve a long time ago.

Meanwhile, Adele sat in the passenger seat, with the sun visor turned down, squinting into the tiny, poorly lit mirror while she tried to add even more extra length to her already absurdly lengthened eyelashes. Every now and then, she peered over her shoulder to see what the delay was. In due course, she realised it was because of her luggage and thought better of asking if Dan needed any help. Whatever she did, it would be the wrong thing.

The car tilted, bounced up and down a couple of times, and the boot swung wide open again.

"Fuck!" Dan shouted, pulling out the topmost of the bags, for the fourth time. "What the hell's in this one, anyway?"

"Which one, sweetie?"

"The pink monstrosity with the airport tags on the handle."

"Oh. Not much. My clothes, washbag, hair straighteners. No, they're in the little mauve bag."

"I swear there wasn't this much stuff in here when we left home."

Adele blushed and said nothing. The foyer shop sold fabulous woven jackets, with coordinating jodhpurs, and various other hunter-esque attire. She hadn't spent much. Well, she hadn't *bought* much, and it was an exclusive range. The lady behind the reception desk had been most helpful in allowing her to store the items, whilst Dan went to get the rest of the luggage from their room.

One last try and then he was giving up. Anything that didn't fit could stay on the driveway for the hotel to deal with. Dan seriously considered it, but he was too competitive. He had to make it all fit and without further griping, or else Adele would be on at him about getting a car without a foldaway roof that took up half of the boot. Then, of course, he'd have more space into which he could stack the incredible expanding suitcases, although she would also have more space to fill, so it would make no difference in the end. Having said that, even he had to admit it was getting a bit difficult for all three of them to go anywhere these days. Maybe it was time he gave in and bought a four-by-four, then he could be just like all the other men departing the lodge, packed up in a jiffy and giving a courteous wave as they trundled away down the significant driveway, leaving him to struggle with the damned luggage.

It wasn't an especially long journey back home, but they were more than three hours delayed on their initial departure time. Dan called to let Alice know they were going to be late. She probably wouldn't mind, and he could give her a lift home, as it would be dark before they were back. Except it wasn't Alice who answered the phone, which made Dan think he'd called the wrong number. He apologised and hung up before double-checking and trying again. No; the last call was definitely listed as 'home'.

He called again, this time instantly recognising Andy's voice.

"What the hell are you doing in my house, answering my phone?" No 'hello', although the accusation was made in jest.

"And what the hell are you doing phoning your own house?" Andy retorted.

"I was calling to tell Alice we're on our way back. Put her on for me, will you, bro?"

"She's popped out to feed what's-his-name…Albert?"

"And left you in charge? Bloody hell! I'd better put my foot down, then."

"Ha ha. How long you gonna be?"

"About two hours. See you in a bit." With that, Dan hung up and climbed into the driver's seat beside Adele, who hadn't heard the conversation, because the doors were closed. Best not to tell her that his reckless lunatic of a brother was back in the country and looking after their one-year-old just now. The journey home would be insufferable.

***

Alice was convinced she'd locked the back door when she left. Indeed, she was so obsessive about such things that it was extremely unlikely she could have forgotten. Yet everything was exactly as it should be, including the money for the milkman under an empty pint bottle on the drainer—precisely where she always left it—and Albert wasn't agitated in any way. Still, she had an uneasy feeling that something wasn't right, and she couldn't put her finger on why.

She filled Albert's seed hopper and checked he had enough water, chatting away to him in a gentle voice. He chirruped back, a quiet, guttural sound, indicating his pleasure for her company. She promised to be back soon, made sure that the back door was definitely locked, and stepped out into the darkness that had descended completely in the short time she had been inside.

The walk back to Dan's house wasn't so bad, not wrapped up in hat and scarf and gloves as she was. She'd also thought to put on a pair of men's long johns, acquired at a jumble sale some years ago. They were very grey and not the sort of thing she hoped she'd be wearing should she ever require medical attention. But they were warm and comfortable and saved a fortune on the gas bill during the colder months.

As she marched along, her thoughts turned to Dan and his brother, Andy, who not only looked very similar, but gave off the same colours also. Andy's odour was slightly brighter than Dan's and had become increasingly so as he settled into being back in England. This, she had come to realise, was something that happened to people when they were happy, and it made sense to her: the darker their state of mind, the darker their aroma.

It had been her way of detecting when Mr. Campion was most in need of tender loving care, and she imagined a fellow synaesthete would find her to be all blacks and deepest purples since her wonderful employer had passed from this world to the next. They were not as close as they once were, but she missed him more than she could ever have anticipated. The rest of the workforce hardly seemed to notice.

There was now nothing about the job that she found enjoyable or challenging, and going in each day was becoming an awful chore. The coffee machine was much more than a sufferance; the typing of letters to previous clients to cancel their contracts was both tedious and tragic, considering all that Mr. Campion had achieved. And she appreciated now how well he knew his business, so often seeing his decisions as foolish when he was her employer. It was an injustice that they should take on his name and then turn his company into something so far removed from his life's work it simply wasn't Campion Holdings anymore.

The reality of it was that the money was no longer a necessity. Her parents had left her a house and a small, steady income, which, along with her pension, was more than enough. Added to that was the joy she had discovered in her newfound role of babysitter. Children had always been someone else's thing to want, and even now she had no interest in having her own. Not that she had much choice at fifty-four, long past the menopause and without nephews or nieces to appreciate her distant benevolence.

The decision had been right at the time, she had always known that. Still, it haunted her, in the odd dream here or there, or unchecked thoughts connected to the present. It was too late for a change of heart or career, but there was always the possibility that one day, she might find the courage to do something about it.

Fishing out a small key without first removing a mitten isn't an easy task, as Alice discovered when she was standing outside the front door, with her hand firmly wedged in her pocket, and she was there long enough for Andy to notice and come to her aid. Try as he might, he couldn't help but laugh, and she had to join in when it became clear she wasn't going to get it unwedged without his help.

Little Shaunna had slept all afternoon, so she was bound to be awake, and with a full nappy, right on time for her parents' return, leading Adele to question whether her babysitter was as efficient as she first seemed, and Dan to wonder just what she'd been thinking when she'd left Andy alone in the house when she didn't know him. Then again, even a total stranger would have instantly known they were brothers.

"I'll just bring in the bags, then get you home, Alice," Dan stated rather than offered, once he'd given the place a quick look over and could see all was as it should be. Alice nodded her approval, not that she had any choice in the matter. Andy spotted Adele's expression when she returned from the mammoth nappy change and decided helping Dan with the bags was far less dangerous than staying and facing her wrath. He quickly followed his younger brother out to the car.

"Good trip?" he asked, lifting the vast suitcase from the boot.

"Yeah. Excellent, in fact. It was good to get away. First time we've been anywhere on our own since—well, ever, now I come to think on it." Dan grabbed all of the other bags with one strong hand and yanked the boot shut with the other.

"You must've been away together at some point?" Andy already knew the answer.

"Only with everyone else. Not just the two of us. Mind you, it wasn't much of 'just the two of us'. Not with Adele's thing for gossiping with anyone and everyone. I even took her shooting this morning, and she still managed to bond with all those funny middle-class women."

"Just like Mum. You went to the lodge, I take it?"

"We did."

Now that the bags were safely inside, and Alice had put on her coat and all of the other garments she had just taken off, Dan took her home, leaving Andy at the mercy of Adele, who appeared to be in a better mood than earlier, although only slightly. He wasn't even sure he'd done anything wrong, but knew well enough that humility was his saviour at times like this. He went to the kitchen, made tea for the both of them and returned with the little gift he'd picked up on his way through Duty-Free: a new scent, not yet in the shops and one he knew she'd like. Quite how he knew was still screwing with his head.

"For me? Oh, how lovely," Adele gushed, passing Shaunna to her uncle and gently tugging the dark metallic pink ribbon from the box. "There were samples of this in the store the other week. It's very expensive. How thoughtful of you." She sprayed the little bottle at her wrist, waved her arm to diffuse the scent, and wafted it under Andy's nose. It smelled just as he thought it would on her and all danger of a ticking-off for crimes unknown passed in an instant. She kissed him on the cheek, took the baby back and nodded to cement her appreciation. Andy's heart skipped a beat, and he suddenly understood what was happening. How utterly stupid and what a crazy thing it was, too.

Adele. His brother's girlfriend for ever and a day, not even someone he considered especially attractive, or, at least, not someone he had ever been attracted to. She was a good-looking woman—she'd been a real looker as a teenager and was definitely improving with age and motherhood, but still not his type. For it to have even crossed his mind was punishable by death, no exaggeration.

Fortunately, it wasn't very long until Dan returned—just enough time for Andy to get the thought out of his head and hopefully bury all traces of it ever having been there. Now on with the explanation of his decision to return to England, instead of seeing out the two-year contract that would have given him enough money to live off for several years after that.

That was what he thought would happen. The moment Dan came back, he would leap straight in with a thorough quizzing on every aspect—why Andy was home, what his resignation meant in relation to the contract signed between the company and Campion Holdings—in itself a somewhat difficult feat, bearing in mind the situation with Alistair. But not a word was said, leaving Andy to wonder if Dan had sussed him already.

It was much worse this way, because at some point he was going to say something. It was a mind game. It had to be. His little brother had always been too interfering for his own good. Then again, he and Adele had been away for the night. Perhaps he had other things to think about. Had she finally agreed to marry him? Unlikely she'd have stayed quiet on that front.

Whatever, it was time Andy left. Dan might have nothing to say, but the same wouldn't be true of Jess. He wasn't sure which was the lesser of the two evils, and at some point, once this cup of tea was drained—about the twelfth he'd had today—the decision would make itself, because parents of very young children need their sleep and have a tendency to retire very early, not to mention that he felt a bit of a gooseberry. That was the second major revelation he'd had in the last ten minutes. Dan wasn't asking questions, because he still had to ask *the* question. Andy downed the rest of the tea in one go, scalding his throat in the process.

"Right. I'm out of here. I'll catch up with you tomorrow."

"Night, Andy," Adele said, "and thank you for the perfume."

"No problem," he replied. He thought about digging out Dan's gift but then decided against it, as Dan was already waiting by the door.

"Night, bro," Andy said and winked, to show he'd cottoned on to the plan. If he had it wrong, then Dan would've commented, but he didn't.

"Night," Dan said, returning the wink and closing the door in his brother's face. Andy chuckled and started the walk to Jess's house. If he was lucky, he might just catch one of the very occasional buses instead of freezing his extremities off along the way.

***

"Sean thanked us for taking the cat to the vet for him and also for the hundred and twenty quid bill," George said, putting the phone down.

"Ungrateful bastard. Would he rather we'd let it die? All right, I appreciate it wasn't that serious, but we didn't know that at the time. Never mind the state the house was in, or getting dragged out of bed to clean up sh…cat mess at nine o'clock in the morning." It was now evening and, almost out of spite, Josh was cooking eggs and bacon. In his annoyance, he accidentally broke a yolk.

"I don't think he meant it like that," George reasoned. "He did ask if you're OK to run the lectures next week, though. I'm guessing it's a 'no'?"

"No, or at least, yes. I'll do them, even though it'll mean moving several appointments." Josh affected a mock Irish accent and continued, "But let's not be worrying about that. We can't be letting the students down now, can we?" He flipped the second egg over, snarling at the telltale spread of gloopy yellow around the upturned white. He cursed and dumped it on the plate alongside the one holding his previous failure. The oil in the frying pan was spitting almost as viciously as he was.

"Are you at all interested in hearing what the police had to say?"

"Not really." He was lying.

"OK, fine," George said and decided however hard he was pushed, he wasn't going to surrender, just to teach Josh a lesson.

Josh shoved one of the plates at him and wandered past moodily with his own unappetising meal.

There was nothing on the TV, which made the mutual stubbornness even harder to uphold, because Josh was desperate to know what the police thought and George was equally desperate to tell him. Sitting there, in silence, watching the same old news go round and round, was doing neither of them any good. Eventually, one of them was going to have to give in. It was Josh.

"Go on then, please do tell me about the police."

"You said you didn't want to know."

"I was fibbing."

"Fair enough." George carried on eating.

"George! Just bloody tell me, will you?"

"Man, you're impatient. Let me eat my supper first." He continued to munch away without another word until his plate was empty and made a big deal of putting his knife and fork together. Josh watched on in aggravation and amusement.

"Done yet?"

"Yep," George said and grinned broadly. "So." Another pause. "Basically." And still another.

"I'm going to hit you in a minute, George."

"Go right ahead." George took a breath, held it, gauged Josh's growing impatience and quickly went on. "The police said there was no sign of disturbance, but they've asked the scene-of-crime team to take a look. We need to go to the station at some point so they can eliminate our prints from whatever they take."

"Oh, joy! How many more things do I have to do for that idiot? I should've just lent you the money for a taxi. It would've been far easier."

Josh had so much more he wanted to say on the matter, none of it very flattering to Sean Tierney, but in all honesty, there was no way he would have attempted suicide—certainly not with a paracetamol overdose. He knew the dire consequences, had seen them firsthand too many times. No, if Sean Tierney really was going to end it all, he'd do so in style—perhaps a public plunge from a bridge, or be found hanging in the lecture theatre—something that would get all the glory and attention of the press.

***

That night, Josh had a dream, not the recurring dream of being naked on a waterslide, thankfully. On this occasion, he and Sean were fencing, fully clothed and kitted out in all the gear. He'd taken a quick peek down to check, thus granting his erstwhile opponent the opportunity to lunge at his midriff, and poke him directly in the navel. Josh backed off and bowed, no clue what the general conventions of such duels were, yet in his dream this was apparently the correct thing to do, and Sean bowed back.

They were off on another round, Sean hopping from one foot to the other, driving forward, leaving less and less floor space for Josh to gain any momentum, denying him the opportunity to manoeuvre himself into a winning position. Then, inexplicably, Sean lost his balance, staggered slightly and checked himself. Now was the chance, the time to take him out with one final, defeating blow. Josh raised his foil and danced forward, bringing his arm down as he did so, in a perfectly choreographed move. Sean regained and was there at the ready, the imminent clash of steel on…

Banana. There was no resounding clang as Sean's sword came up against the ridiculous fruit, which naturally fell right in two. Both Sean and Josh stopped to watch as half of it tumbled to the floor in slow motion and landed with a pathetic splat. Game, set and match to Sean bloody Tierney. Again. Bastard.

***

Another night on another couch for Andy, whose return to England hadn't been the glorious homecoming he'd imagined when trying to justify leaving Dubai. Night one: Dan and Adele were away and he was left with Alice, who was very nice, but he'd hoped to get a bit of time with his brother—a chat, a few beers—and return to the normality they'd almost acquired prior to Andy's departure.

Night two: he quietly slid his key into the lock, putting gentle anticlockwise pressure on the fob—a pointless effort, he discovered, because Jess's key was in the other side. He was locked out, and the total absence of light inside meant he had two options, both far from ideal. He could hammer on the door until she woke up and let him in, in which case she would be livid and unlikely to be in a receptive state for his plea of innocence. Alternatively, he could go and call on someone else, appeal to their generosity and hope they had a sofa to spare.

First stop: Josh. His excursion did little more than disturb the dog next door, the barking interspersed with howling and shrieks of 'shut the hell up', the latter not emanating from the dog. Josh's house was in darkness; onwards to Eleanor's.

When Andy, Dan and Kris were little, one of their favourite games, not that they'd ever admit to it in company, was role-playing weddings in their living room. Fortunately for Andy, being the elder and therefore slightly taller of the three resulted in his part generally being that of the groom.

In any case, the net curtains would be down in seconds and swathed around whichever of them had drawn the short straw, and they'd parade up and down the aisle (the space between the sofa and coffee table), reciting their vows to the priest (more often than not Dan, wearing a back-to-front school jumper), until the wedding was rudely interrupted by person with 'just reason or impediment' (their mother, threatening to strangle them with the curtain wire).

His passion for both role-play and net curtains had long since diminished, although watching household objects fly across Eleanor's living room was potentially enough to rekindle his enthusiasm for window coverage, even of the white nylon variety. In fact, on this occasion, some decent blackout blinds might've been a wiser choice. Whatever, he couldn't possibly ask to stay there, not without risk to life and limb.

The only other people he could try, and whom he wanted to avoid only marginally less than Jess, were Kris and Shaunna. With no other choice, he reluctantly trudged the short distance to their house and knocked on the door.

Kris wasn't home, but Shaunna was still up, watching *The Wizard of Oz*—Andy's least favourite film of all time. She was so wrapped up in it that she let him in without comment, or offer of refreshment—not that he expected it as a matter of course. They were all too familiar with each other for him to be treated as a guest. No, he'd expected it because it was what Shaunna did. She was the queen of 'cup of tea crisis management'. It also took a while for her to realise that Andy wasn't supposed to be there, and when he explained, she didn't listen, more interested in voicing her thoughts on what breed of dog Toto was. Casper, who didn't care much for Toto or any other film star of his species, sat with his head on Andy's knee, poking a fat, wet nose against his hand each time he dared to stop stroking the soppy Labrador's silky-smooth head.

After the film was over, Shaunna provided the traditional beverage, without asking, and Andy thanked her wholeheartedly, even though he really didn't want any more tea right now. He was feeling extremely uncomfortable, being alone with her, as the last time they'd spoken properly had been when he'd told her that he was the one at The Party. After that, there had been a couple of brief exchanges regarding financial arrangements.

At first, Shaunna had been very resistant to him sending money, but she eventually agreed out of pure necessity. They'd otherwise evaded all discussion of the matter, and with Kris so unwell, it was virtually impossible to reach any kind of resolution.

"Where is Kris, by the way?" Andy asked after a short while. He hadn't intended to say anything, but his curiosity had taken control of his mouth.

"Staying at George's—your old place."

Andy frowned. He thought that was a bit strange, and Shaunna must have picked up on it.

"George moved there just after you left. Didn't you know?"

"No, I didn't. But why is Kris…" He trailed off. "Sorry. It's none of my business."

"It's what he does when he's starting to go downhill again. Just his way of coping," she explained, ignoring Andy's apology.

That only made him feel worse, and all of a sudden he realised he needed to get out of there as quickly as possible. He made his excuses and headed back to Josh's, urging him to be home, because, after that, there was only George left to try, but it was to no avail. All right, so if neither George nor his temporary lodger were there—which was almost his preference—then he still had a key to the shed, so he could at least get out of the wind. If he hadn't been so exhausted, it would probably have crossed his mind to give up seeking the hospitality of his friends and book into a hotel instead.

The house lights were on, and Andy rang the bell, holding his breath and listening for movement within. For a moment, he thought he was out of luck, but then the door opened a few inches and Kris peered around the edge, his face breaking into a smile.

"Hello, you! What a surprise. What are you doing here? Come in, come in." Kris opened the door and let Andy through.

It was nothing like the kind of welcome Andy had imagined. After all, he was the cause of Kris's breakdown—or a significant part of it—and it was only out of desperation that he was here at all.

"I'm sorry to land on you like this. I hope George won't mind."

"George isn't here. What's up?"

"I need somewhere to stay for the night. Would it be all right? Only I'm knackered, and Jess is in bed. I don't want to burden Ellie, and…" He was about to add that he'd already seen Shaunna and couldn't possibly stay there.

"Sure. I'll make up the bed in the other room."

"Oh, don't worry about that. If you've got a duvet that'll do just great."

Kris shrugged, went upstairs and returned with a duvet and some pillows, all of which were plump and downy and smelled of newness and fabric conditioner. Andy thanked him sincerely, and Kris left him in the living room to snuggle down on the tiny sofa under the massive mound of bedding, legs hanging over one arm and head precariously perched on the other. Being six foot two was no bonus when attempting to kip on a sofa, but it still beat the plush, Egyptian linen-covered mattress and air-conditioning-hum accompaniment he had left behind.

Chapter Nineteen: Loggerheads

Monday was one of those gloomy, wet days, slightly warmer than it had been over the weekend, but never quite reaching the status of full daylight. Even the starlings were quiet for a change, and the roads were nowhere near as busy as usual. It was the kind of day that Eleanor always wanted to spend in bed with a good book, on her own, ignoring the world's mad rush around her. Alas, it wasn't to be, and at some point soon, she was going to have to get up and get going with giving the flat a good clean, ready for James and Oliver.

She'd almost convinced herself that she was looking forward to it, *before* the murder investigation, although if she was honest, she'd been having some doubts even before that. She'd not really considered starting a family of her own, couldn't imagine herself under the constant bombardment of a troop of little people, created in her likeness or otherwise. It wasn't even that she'd made the decision to focus on a career and forego motherhood. It just hadn't occurred to her before now. Did that make her abnormal? After all, almost every woman she had welcomed onto her books had mentioned something about childbearing during their preliminary checkup, like it was a mandatory requirement of womanhood to have at least weighed up the options.

Interestingly, her mother had not even so much as hinted that Eleanor should settle down and start a family one day. The array of grandchildren her brothers and sisters were in the throes of delivering had perhaps shifted the burden away from her and eased pressure on her to perform her daughterly duties. As the eldest of the seven, she supposed she should have been the first to start a family. Yet it was her youngest sister who had beaten them all to it, giving birth to Ashleigh when she was eighteen. Of course, she'd married while the bump was small enough to disguise under a bouquet; miraculously, ten years on, she was still happily married and still blaming the whole thing on her mother's decision to call her Matilda, not that she had ever been known by anything other than Tilly.

Ashleigh's younger brother, Benjamin, was the spitting image of his dad and the most polite six-year-old Eleanor had ever met—nothing like his namesake, her own younger brother. Even as a toddler, young Benjamin was much more sensible than his cousin Louise—Ben's daughter—who had several months on him age-wise and a stay-at-home mum on account of Ben's insistence on traditional family life. He was the second eldest, a year younger than Eleanor but two years below her in school because of when their birthdays fell, and they'd always got along reasonably well.

However, it was almost time for their annual argument about how unfair it was of him to expect Jo to stay at home when he had spent most of his twenties travelling around Australia and Japan. Meanwhile, Jo had completed only two years' teaching after qualifying before she was married, caring for a baby and husband, and keeping a large house in the middle of nowhere. Even now, with the four of them, the house was well beyond their requirements.

Last Christmas, the entire Davenport clan had headed down to Ben's for the festive season: Eleanor's parents, her six siblings, their respective partners and the seven offspring they had so far produced between them, all piled into one place, together. Eleanor took Josh along for moral support and someone to talk to on Boxing Day, when the chaos of putting toys together and dealing with breakages always ensued. She'd hated looking after her brothers and sisters when she was at home and wasn't about to start playing Aunty to their children, either. Her nephew Benjamin was a bit different, though. He loved Josh and confided in him—his words—that he didn't much like his cousins because they were 'all so spoilt and childish'.

This Christmas was again to be spent at Ben's seven-bedroom cottage. The renovation had taken him no time at all, and since last year, he'd also converted the barn, so, Eleanor's mother had ruled, it was the perfect place for them to be. The little village church could barely accommodate them all for midnight mass, and it was Church of England, but 'it would do'. The vicar was still somewhat bemused by the whole affair, when Mrs. Davenport commandeered him after Morning Prayer and suggested that a few more candles wouldn't go amiss. If he knew what was good for him, he'd have sorted that out, ready for their arrival this year.

Eleanor was dreading it, right through from the drive down there for Christmas Eve in the kitchen with the other women—her sister Charlotte had much to say about this after a couple of cans of lager—organising the troops for the trip to church, back again, getting seven over-excited children—Ben junior would claim that he was just playing along—to go to sleep, and then staying up 'for Santa', followed by waking up at four in the morning to see if Santa had been.

Christmas Day with fifteen exhausted adults, seven impatient children and a heap of gifts more imposing than Everest. Boxing Day was supposed to be a time of joyful rest, but it was more like the aftermath of an explosion in a wrapping paper factory, where all the workers had been drinking for the previous seventy-two hours and couldn't remember where they'd left their beer.

Then there was Eleanor's brother, Luke. When he first introduced Kaz to his parents, he'd run it past Ellie first, being as she was his big sister and would know instinctively what their mother would truly think of his beautiful and undeniably Muslim girlfriend. Kaz's parents thought Luke was a gracious young man, and they were right. He was far less imposing than his older brother, more sensible than his younger brothers and genuinely wanted to make sure everyone was happy all of the time.

The reality was that Kaz was more conventional than her parents, and she didn't agree with their progressive attitude at all. Eleanor knew at once that this would go down a storm with her own mother, who might not have taken it upon herself to highlight the possibility that Eleanor may find herself too old to have children before she got round to thinking about it, but at every given opportunity sang the praises of Ben and Luke—how lovely their wives were, how polite their children were, how responsible and sensible, and so on and so forth. Luke hated the favouritism; Ben revelled in it.

Growing up in a strict Roman Catholic household, Eleanor had not imagined that her parents would be so tolerant or accepting. It seemed that as long as the prospective partner was as devout as they themselves were, then that was good enough. For the most part, Dad didn't care one way or the other. He'd struggled to find the right words, so didn't say much at all at Luke and Kaz's wedding, a combined ceremony in the church, where everyone wore traditional Muslim dress.

The reception was the best Eleanor had ever attended, with dancers and entertainment and no alcohol. Some of the men had gone off to the club later in the evening, to down a few pints, and then returned for the farewell of the bride and groom. It had been a colourful and fun celebration, far removed from the solemnity of Ben and Jo's wedding, in a church full of strangers wriggling uncomfortably in morning suits, or flowery dresses and overstated hats.

None of it helped Eleanor to feel any better about introducing James to her mother and father. True, he was conventional, traditional, devout—all of those qualities they respected and admired. His being a Buddhist would not matter. Nor would they care that he was black, although both would be met with her father's usual unease. However, the fact that he was a suspect in a murder case was a step too far. Eleanor wasn't about to volunteer the information, obviously, but as soon as anyone asked him about his job—her mother was very British, it was that or the weather—they would instantly recognise him as 'that man in the paper'. Two weeks until Christmas: it was unlikely that he would be in the clear by then.

Eleanor gave up on 'reading' and closed the book. If she stayed in bed any longer, the misery would completely engulf her, and there was too much snackable food in the kitchen. Time for a shower and to get on with the day.

***

Josh pulled up outside the main building, very pleased he'd found a parking space so close to the classroom, not so pleased at having to listen to George all the way to work. He hated sharing the car first thing in the morning, and to be fair, George hadn't said a lot. It was the combination of that and the session Josh was about to give on cognitive behavioural therapy. He'd only had cause to use it twice, and on both occasions, it had failed in demonstrating any enduring efficacy. The first time was on a client with a phobia of ice, with no trigger event that might have led to such an unusual fear. Josh had considered suggesting the client decline his job offer in a frozen food factory—it would have been far easier—but instead they set to work on a rationalisation programme, and it did work initially. Then the stupid man caught his arm on an unlagged pipe, saw it as a chance to make a quick buck in compensation and made such a big deal of it that, hey presto! Return of previously suppressed phobia.

The other occasion was Josh's second failed attempt to stay off cigarettes, which lasted a few years, although he'd spent so much time being sorely tempted that he couldn't honestly say the therapy had ever worked. He was doing much better this time around, with the avoidance and displacement strategy—fortunately—as that was tomorrow's lecture boxed off. Right now, he was more worried about his lack of planning for this session, which so far consisted of two hastily typed slides and a discussion of recently published studies, all contradicting each other.

The classroom was empty, which was normal for this group, who generally arrived five to ten minutes after they were supposed to. If this were Josh's course, he'd have done something about it, but it wasn't, so he put up with it. Still, it gave him the chance to get his laptop hooked up to the projector and to add a bit more to his patchy presentation.

"Don't you tell anyone how little effort I've put into this," he warned George, who had sat in his usual seat and was busy thumbing through his notepad in order to locate the first blank page.

"Why would I do that? In any case, you have an excuse, seeing as you only knew about it on Saturday evening."

"That gave me all of yesterday to prepare. I bloody hate CBT."

"You said already," George responded flatly as he delved inside his bag and pulled out a smaller, hardbacked notebook, bulging on account of the numerous pieces of paper sticking out of it, and held shut by a fat elastic band. "You need to check and sign off our logbooks too."

"Christ, anything else?"

"It'll kill an hour. Stop whining."

Josh huffed, switched on the projector, and then sat at the front desk and started typing frantically. Thirty seconds later, the door started to open and he stopped, mid-sentence. It was Sophie.

"Morning, Soph," George greeted her.

"Hi, George. Josh."

"How's Sean?" George asked.

"He's much better. I went home yesterday, left him and the sabre-toothed beast to it. I felt a bit of a spare part, anyway, with the pair of them snoring their heads off in front of the fire." Sophie sat next to George and replicated his earlier motions.

"Oh, well, that's good to know. Any more news from the police?"

"Nothing," she replied. "Are you OK to do our logbooks today, Josh? They normally get checked on a Monday."

"I know," Josh said gruffly, still frantically trying to finish his presentation before the rest of the class arrived. Sophie nodded and looked at George.

"He knows," he whispered, and they both giggled quietly.

"I heard that," Josh said sternly. He just finished typing the last slide as the rest of class arrived en masse, having all first met up in the coffee shop, by the looks of it, as one of them came in with a takeaway cup, headed straight for Josh, but then stopped.

"Oh. We have an arrangement to pick up a cappuccino for Sean on the way in. Of course, you're welcome to have it."

"Thanks. I will," Josh said with a smile. "And I won't hold it against you that you don't ever bring me a cup."

The student looked relieved and joined the rest of the group, who were sitting down and more or less all present and good to go. Josh sucked a little of the coffee through the hole in the lid and screwed up his face.

"For the record, I don't take sugar," he said to the class. Several students, including the guy who had given him the drink, made a quick note on their A4 pads, and then put their pens down expectantly. *Putty in my hands*, Josh thought. *I could tell them any old crap and they'd believe me.* As great a temptation as it might be, he was far too professional to contemplate it for real.

"Right, let us begin. Today we are looking at cognitive behavioural therapy, and, before anyone mentions it, I will check your logbooks after break, which will be in about—" checking his watch "—an hour and a half. OK?" Lots of nodding heads. "So..."

***

Andy was starting to think that he'd left it far too long to go and see Jess. It was now three days since he'd arrived back in the country, and she still didn't know. The longer he left it, the harder it was going to be to explain, and it had reached the point where he was deliberately putting it off. Now, he was sitting in Dan's again. Adele had gone to the gym, leaving the two brothers to catch up, with a warning not to forget to feed Shaunna in an hour, and also to check on the washing machine when it finished spinning.

It had finished spinning, and Andy kept thinking he should maybe remind Dan to go and deal with it. But then, that wasn't in keeping with the positive atmosphere he was trying to maintain, for fear that Dan would explode with rage when Andy explained that one day, he'd decided enough was enough and caught the next departing plane after the contract was signed.

Dan still wasn't asking any questions, because he'd known the minute he'd arrived at his brother's Dubai apartment that he was miserable as hell and homesick. He'd concluded that it was a simple matter of time before Andy jacked it in and came back. Being so close to Christmas, Dan thought it might have taken a bit longer for him to get out; one month's notice, or leave and lose a month's salary was usual, which meant Andy was probably skint. The absence of comment on his resignation was, Dan assumed, due to Andy needing a loan and not knowing how to ask. That was, after all, how it had been before he took the job.

So there they were, pondering over the *Daily Mail* cryptic crossword, both utterly useless when it came to anything vaguely intellectual, neither saying a word about Andy's prior employment, based on their own incorrect beliefs about what the other was thinking. On top of that, there was the possibility that Dan had proposed to Adele and been turned down, which Andy dared not ask about, and then the whole issue of Andy not contacting Jess, which Dan didn't like to mention.

"Alice drinks a lot of tea," Andy said, instead of anything else that he should have said.

"You're not wrong there." Dan laughed. "We had to buy another box of tea bags last week. Two boxes in six months. Unheard of in this house."

"She seems nice. She was Campion's PA?"

"Yeah. Can't see her sticking it out now Al's gone, though. She can't stand the job. It was only her unrequited love kept her there all those years."

"I only met the bloke once. I can't say I saw much to love about him. I mean, he was all right, but..."

"There's no accounting for taste. Fourteen across is 'recipe', by the way."

Andy scanned over the clues, shrugged and wrote the letters in. "So it is. Speaking of which, did you propose?"

"What? God, no. I tried that once. Twice. Look where it got me. Or didn't, as the case may be. What has that got to do with recipes?" Neither of them broke eye contact from the crossword.

"Nothing, other than recipe for disaster. I actually meant the 'no accounting for taste' bit." Dan play-punched his brother's arm—enough to knock most people over, but Andy barely felt it. "Actually, I thought that's what you were doing on Friday."

"To be honest, I did consider doing it while we were up there. In fact, when I booked, that was exactly what I had planned, but then, you know Adele. She got all carried away with planning out Shaunna's meals and writing detailed instructions on what needed to be done and when. By the time she'd given Alice her orders, it was so late we missed the reservation for dinner and had to eat in the dining room. Then all day Saturday, we were up on the range."

"You know what you need to do? Buy the ring first and have the box ready. Once she spies that, there'll be no resistance whatsoever."

Dan laughed. "I'm not sure what you're suggesting is ethical."

"Maybe not, but I guarantee it'll work a treat."

"I do have the ring. I bought it last year, when I asked her the second time. I appreciate that technically she was still married to Tom."

"Technically? She was still living with him, as I recall. Twelve down—isolation."

Dan watched him write in the letters, running out of space before the end of the word. "Try 'isolated' instead," he suggested. Andy wrote over the last two letters. It fitted.

"So, are you going to sell the ring and just carry on living over the brush?"

"Living over the brush? You sound like Ellie." Both of them started laughing this time.

"I think that's probably where I got it from. Seriously, though. You do still want to marry her?"

"Of course I do. I always have. And it's been great, you know? The baby's put a totally new light on things, given her something to think about other than herself."

"And you, too," Andy pointed out, because the problem had always been two-way. They were both vain and selfish, a reality which had brought their relationship to its knees many times before. Dan was about to protest, but didn't.

"Yes. That's true," he agreed. "I'll get round to it eventually."

"What're you waiting for, exactly? Only there's no such thing as a perfect moment, irrespective of what all those girly magazines said." Andy paused and rephrased. "Girls' magazines. You know what I mean, anyway."

"Yeah, I gathered. There is something to be said for making an occasion out of a marriage proposal, Andrew."

"Alternatively, you can make some bullshit excuse about arriving late for dinner and bottle it again. Just as well she'll wait forever, huh?"

"What's your problem exactly?" Dan felt the hairs on the back of his next start to rise. "After all, it's none of your damn business whether I marry Adele or not. It's not like she's up for grabs either way."

Dan glared at his brother, and Andy held his gaze, trying to work out what that last remark meant, neither of them consciously aware that they were now standing. Andy focused on letting his shoulders drop, having recently learned a lesson or two—the hard way—about how aggressive his body language was.

It had to be nothing. He couldn't have picked up on it. But then, why had Dan got all fired up like that? There was nothing threatening in what Andy had said. He was just trying to push his brother into having the balls to do what he had always wanted to do. It was a total overreaction, and it was also Dan who backed down first.

"I'll go and sort that washing." He left the room, and Andy sat down again, trying to focus on the crossword clues and block out the possibility that his brother had somehow detected that forbidden stray thought, that split second of desire for Adele.

By the time Dan returned, everything was once again back to normal, as was always the case. The pair of them had incredible tempers, short-fused and ferocious, but quick-burning and always over almost as soon as it began. There was just one missing element, and that was Dan's requirement to get the last jab in. Andy didn't have to wait long for it.

"Speaking of bullshit excuses, or in this case bollockless ones—when the hell are you going to go and see Jess?"

Andy snarled, but let it go.

***

Lecture over, all logbooks checked and signed. All students safely dispatched. It hadn't been anywhere near as bad as Josh had anticipated. In fact, he'd rather enjoyed it, because he had done it his way, instead of always thinking 'What would Tierney do?' Right now, Sean Tierney could do nothing about it, and that pleased Josh no end. Not that he wished any suffering on the man; just that whilst he was tied up at home, there was no chance of him coming and sticking his nose into anything, which was his usual wind-up strategy.

Josh packed up his laptop, picked up the papers he had brought with him and nodded to George.

"Coffee?"

"Sounds good to me. You coming, Soph?"

"I'll have a quick one, then get going," she said, and the three of them went off to the college café. Since their last visit, it had been done out in cheap and cheerful decorations, and they were playing Christmas music. It made George feel rather festive.

Secretly, it was starting to get that way for Josh too.

***

"We are home," James called from the hallway. He closed the door and carried Oliver into the kitchen. The whole place smelled of fresh baking, and the wire rack was loaded with Christmas-tree-shaped cookies, the chocolate chips poking out like little brown and white baubles.

"Hello, men," Eleanor greeted them with a smile. She kissed James on the cheek, leaving a floury impression of her lips and nose, and then kissed Oliver on the head with the same effect.

"You have been very busy, I can see," James said, reaching out to take one of the cookies. Eleanor pushed his hand away.

"Oh, no, you don't. Oliver and I have got to decorate these first, if you'd like to, Oliver?"

The child nodded eagerly and wriggled to be put down. James lowered him to the floor. "Shall we put on some better clothes for baking?"

"Oh, he'll wash, won't you, sweetheart," Eleanor suggested, realising a moment too late what she'd done. They'd been back less than two minutes, and already she was over-riding James's authority as a father.

James noticed, too, but found it endearing so said nothing and tucked a tea towel into the top of Oliver's trousers. He was wearing very smart, black cords and looked just like his father in miniature form. Eleanor showed him how to squeeze the tube of green icing so that it made an outline around the little trees, guiding his hand while he traced a wobbly border around the next cookie.

"Make star please, Enna," he said. He couldn't say 'Eleanor', although he might have stood more of a chance if it weren't for the way that James pronounced it.

James laughed—that deep, booming laugh he had when he was truly happy. "I will get the bags and return in a moment," he explained and went out to the car.

Eleanor glanced up briefly and smiled to herself. On the whole, things looked like they might not be so bad after all.

Chapter Twenty:
Left Hanging

It had been on Josh's mind throughout the whole weekend to ask George why he wasn't going home. It kept happening, and after a day or two, he would just up and off, not that Josh minded, as he was quite used to the company by now. They may as well share a house and save on the bills, because here they were once more, eating together, watching rubbish on the TV and fighting over whose turn it was to wash up. It was pleasantly comforting—so long as it didn't go as far as daily lifts to work, that is.

Pleasantly comforting and so middle-aged.

"George."

"Mmm?"

"What are we doing?"

"Mmm?"

"What the fuck are we doing, George?"

"Watching *Coronation Street*? Eating sausages and mash?"

"I didn't mean that." Josh sighed and put down his fork, an entire sausage still impaled on its prongs. "We're not past forty yet. Why are we sitting in, watching the telly? Shouldn't we be in the pub or something?"

"Well, I suppose we could be, but then we'd still be watching the telly, along with all the other middle-aged men."

"That's my point. We aren't middle-aged. Are we?"

"Nope. Just eat your tea, Joshua, and shut up."

Josh smiled ruefully and picked up his fork, bit one end off the sausage and put it down again.

"It's just—"

"Oh, man. Here we go."

"What are you doing here, George? Have you moved in? Only I was thinking."

"Hang on a mo..." George started, but reconsidered. "What were you thinking?"

"I was wondering if we should consider making this a permanent arrangement."

"Now, what was it you said? I couldn't stay here?"

"That was then. I wasn't used to having anyone...having *you* around."

George didn't know what to say to that, and, try as he might, he couldn't even put what was going around his head into words. It could be some kind of sick joke, which Josh would reveal any second. Or he was dreaming. No, it seemed real enough. All that was left, then, was for him to come up with an answer. Right at that moment, when anything could happen, there was a knock at the door.

"Crap." George moved to put down his plate.

"Eat. I'll get it," Josh commanded and went to answer the door. "Hello? Ah," he said, opening it to find two uniformed police officers standing in the porch. He recognised them both from the search of Eleanor's flat: the bossy, aggressive female officer and her rather apologetic colleague.

"Good evening, Mr. Sandison. May we come in?"

"By all means." Josh indicated towards the living room with an over-theatrical flourish. He was going to have to behave himself.

"Thank you," the female officer said and stepped past, turning down the volume on her jabbering radio as she did so. The other officer followed her, nodding politely. They waited for Josh to close the front door and followed him to the living room, where George had just finished his meal and was in the process of swallowing the last mouthful.

"And you are?"

"George Morley." He rose to his feet and held out a hand for it to be shaken. Neither officer accepted. "Please," he invited, "sit down." They did, leaving him to perch on the edge of the coffee table.

"Mr. Sandison, Doctor Tierney mentioned that you and Mr. Morley were at his house the day after someone gained access."

"Well, no, Officer. That's not quite accurate," George interjected. "I was there with Sophie, Doctor Tierney's girlfriend. Josh only dropped me off and picked me up."

"I see." She paused, took her notepad out of her breast pocket and jotted something down. "I think we need to take formal statements—from both of you. We also need you to provide your fingerprints. If you could come to the station tomorrow morning, we can deal with all of that in one go."

"Can you make that tomorrow afternoon?" Josh asked, and not politely. He didn't like this police officer one bit.

"Before one-thirty is fine," she said. It wasn't up for negotiation. Soon after, she and her colleague were gone, leaving Josh in a rage once more, and George completely confused by the whole affair.

Josh slammed the door shut behind them and stomped back into the living room. "Who do they think they are? Coming here in the middle of the night, demanding bloody statements." He snatched up the plate containing the cold remnants of his meal. "Before one-thirty is fine," he mimicked.

"They were all right, really."

"You didn't see her in action at Ellie's. She was brutal."

"Forceful, you mean."

"No. I mean bloody brutal. So, why are you here, George?" There was nothing friendly about it this time. It was more of an accusation.

"Do you want me to go?"

"I want you to tell me why you haven't." Josh scooped up George's empty plate and went to the kitchen.

"It's a bit complex," George shouted after him.

Josh stamped on the pedal of the bin and shoved the plates at the opening, losing the fork with the sausage attached into the bargain, which only made matters worse. Knowing George as he did, he was fully aware that when he said it was a 'bit complex' it was going to be some horrific mess of a situation that he wasn't going to like. He decided not to ask any further questions about it. After all, if George had wanted to tell him, he'd have already volunteered the information; given he hadn't, it could wait. When Josh went back to the living room, he could see that George was feeling very unhappy about being questioned and, like the good friend that he was deep down, Josh made a very obvious change in subject and mood.

"I wonder how Ellie's getting on with Oliver this time?"

George breathed a sigh of relief. He was off the hook. There was no way he was about to start explaining to Josh about Kris, and the problems he was having trying to get him out of the house. Kris was usually gone within a few days, and George could safely go back without having to face any hassle about where he'd been. This time, not even the lack of heating was deterring him. The same pattern over and again—he'd thought Kris would have got the message by now. Maybe the drugs were screwing with his logic circuits. Whatever, George was starting to feel like he was harbouring a criminal.

***

With Oliver safely tucked up in bed, James returned from storytelling to sit on the sofa with Eleanor.

"Thank you for today," he said. "You worked very hard to make Oliver feel welcome."

"Oh, don't be silly. I've enjoyed every minute of it. Well, every minute other than the three where he screamed and held his breath after you told him he was having a bath."

"Ah, yes. He was not happy about that." James laughed. "Do you know, Eleanor Davenport, I love you."

"I sort of assumed you did, but you haven't told me before."

"I know. It is hard for me to say those words when they are thrown about so carelessly by others."

"And they mean all the more for their well-measured execution, James Brown." She leaned over and kissed him—on the chin, because it was the only place she could reach without stretching. He bent his face down towards hers, and she aimed again, this time making contact with his lips.

"Just in case you didn't know, I love you, too."

For the time being, they were alone. Oliver was sound asleep, exhausted by a day spent travelling, baking and making paper chains. He had an astonishing concentration span, was as determined as his father and wanted to try everything Eleanor suggested. She'd even got a hug at bedtime.

James allowed himself to relax into the sofa, and Eleanor snuggled even closer, maintaining the contact of their lips, moving slowly so that she was against him. She turned with her body pressed to his. For the first time in weeks, she wanted him; typical when there was a small child in the room across the hallway, who could awaken at any time.

James sensed the tension, the urgent desire. "We should go to the bedroom first," he suggested. "We can position the ottoman against the door."

Eleanor exhaled shakily and pulled herself up from the sofa. James followed.

Moving a bedding-filled ottoman, whilst trying to maintain maximum body contact and not lose the heat of the moment, was not easy, and their attempt to do so was making Eleanor want to laugh, but she didn't dare. In the time she had known James, she had come to realise that he was a very serious individual when it came to intimate matters, so she struggled on, trying to simultaneously unzip her trousers, pull off her top and kick off her shoes, while he shoved the ottoman with one knee, unbuttoning his shirt as quickly as he could, all in the dark.

There was much to be said for the undressing of each other as part of the seductive foreplay process, but it was far easier to remove one's own clothes, and soon they were both naked. Eleanor perched on the edge of the bed, waiting for James to find a condom. She knew that was what he was doing, because she heard the clip on his wallet close.

"I do not have any protection." He sat down on the end of the bed defeatedly.

"It doesn't matter, James," she said and climbed onto her knees behind him, running her hands over his firm shoulders and down his chest. He caught hold of her arms before she ventured any further.

"You must be certain."

She kissed his neck, making her way across his cheek and moving to his side, from there lifting one leg and straddling him.

"I am," she said, slowly sliding downwards until their bodies locked together.

James took a deep breath in and held it, unsure whether he should allow her to do this. It was the heat of the moment. Not a doubt in his mind that whatever the consequence he would be happy, but for her, caught by desire, it may not be as reasoned.

"Let it go," she whispered, caressing his earlobe with her tongue. He did as she said, releasing a breath that cascaded down her breasts and across her nipples. He put his hands on her hips and went with the movement, slow, gyrating, abandoning of reality to this motion. There was no time as pure as this one, the sensation of being truly together, in perfect synchronisation, as if they had waited forever for it to arrive.

James felt Eleanor push closer into him and lifted her with his body, onto the bed, coming down on top of her, feeling her legs lift and press against his sides. There was nothing to be done now to change the course before them. With each thrust, he drove deeper, and she pushed harder against him, until the rhythm was perpetual, irrepressible.

It was too much to take, yet to end it so soon seemed a waste. There, caught in a second before the climax, Eleanor realised that her life after this could be very different, and the thought carried her over the searing sensation of blood coursing through her body, pumping into every organ, making her want to cry out at the intensity of those few seconds. She stifled the noise in her throat, felt James do the same, and then they were falling, falling, back to the bed, still in tandem motion, hearts pounding as one, her head a fuzzy mess of absolute bliss mingled with a certain amount of clarity that this was the best or worst decision she had ever made.

James lifted a little of his weight from her and kissed her gently on both cheeks, on the nose, and then slowly rolled sidewards so that they still remained connected but he was no longer on top. He ran a finger across her cheek and let it rest against her lips. She bit it playfully.

"Why did you do this?" he asked gently.

"Because I wanted to."

"And now?"

"Now I'm thinking rationally? I would do it again."

James took her in his arms and pulled her so tight to him that she almost lost her breath. Now was the time, and he loosened his grip.

"Will you forgive me if I do not see through the entire tradition?"

"You mean you aren't going to roll over and go to sleep?"

"Ah, yes." He chuckled. "That is not quite what I had in mind."

Eleanor was intrigued but knew better than to say so. These little mysterious things James said were always worth waiting for, so that's what she did. He rolled away from her, searching for his trousers, unceremoniously dumped on the floor at the side of the bed. He turned back to face her and found her hand.

"I do not know how—" hesitation seeped around the determination in his voice "—or even if I should ask this of you. I promised to wait until you were certain of my innocence, and this you have shown to be true. It was not how I had anticipated."

"I do believe you are innocent, James."

"You misunderstand me, sweet Eleanor." He shushed her gently and brought her hand up so he could kiss the tips of her fingers. "I would like you to become my wife. I cannot imagine my life without you. Will you please honour me, by accepting my proposal of marriage?"

Eleanor couldn't speak. She couldn't say yes; she couldn't say no. She didn't even have the words in her head at all to shape them and turn them into sound. She wanted to say yes. She wanted it more than anything she could ever remember wanting, but every part of her was pulling against it, like falling from a tower into oblivion and searching for that one last foothold.

The pain of trying to find something, a sound or a movement that would indicate she wanted him, needed him so desperately, grasped at her throat and made her retch. She struggled free, tugged her bathrobe from the door and flung the ottoman across the room, reaching the bathroom just in time.

***

Andy stared at the floor, in full naughty-schoolboy mode. He'd known what the outcome would be of staying away from Jess for so long, and if he hadn't been rumbled, he still wouldn't have had the guts to come round. He tried to explain. Friday, it was too late and he was tired. Saturday night, when he had tried to get in, the door was locked and he didn't want to disturb her. Sunday, he knew, she'd be at her parents' place. Today, he had been waiting for her to return from work. She was having none of it.

He'd arrived, armed with flowers and an extra special gift bought at Duty-Free. He'd picked up a huge bottle of her favourite scent, of course, but he'd also spotted a bottle of spiced spirit, which he remembered from their younger days that she loved. His gestures were fruitless. He was going to have to take whatever came his way, because however hard or convincingly he grovelled, it didn't change a thing. He'd given up the job he'd promised to keep, for her, for them. Perhaps, once she'd calmed down, she'd care about how miserable he'd been, but not right now.

Thirty minutes, she ranted, called him names, pausing every now and then to shake her head in total disbelief that he had done this. There was no way she could afford the house without his wages, not with the rent on the offices on top. Business was going well, but not well enough to support him, whilst he sat around wondering what to do with his life. Why had he bothered coming home at all? And, on that subject, what made him think he could hide at Dan's and not get found out?

True, she rarely phoned Dan, because he had been so vile to Andy in the past that she couldn't bring herself to talk to him most of the time, not without making some snide remark that he generally didn't even pick up on. When it happened in face-to-face situations, Adele caught the gist of what Jess said but didn't quite follow the exact meaning.

This time, Jess had phoned and, she'd believed initially, Dan had answered, but then he'd gone quiet and another voice had asked, "Who is it?" Now one of them had to be Dan, and therefore the other was Andy. There was no disguising it, and he'd tried. He'd actually lied and said he was Michael, and for a moment, it had almost worked. Then Dan, in the background, had said, "Andy? Who is it?" and that was that.

Ten minutes later, Dan's car had skidded to a halt outside Jess's house, and Andy had tumbled out, looking as if he'd already done three rounds with a heavyweight. He didn't know the half of it.

After hearing everything she had to say, then hearing it once more in a slightly different order, Andy thought he'd chance a comment in his defence.

"Jess. Can I explain to you now?"

"Explain what, exactly? I can't see there's any need really, can you? I'm going to have to get rid of the offices. Do you know that? I've only had the blasted place for fourteen months. So what can you possibly have to tell me that is going to make this whole stupid, selfish situation any better?"

Andy went quiet again, this time, because he had a winning ace and, having taken the full force of her attack, concluded that it would be worth waiting to deliver his news. It was a bit mean, because Jess would feel silly after all she'd just said, but it'd be fun anyway.

Chapter Twenty-One: Statements

Josh waited while George went back to the classroom for his phone, typically having left it when they had less than an hour to get to the police station before the formidable female officer went off duty. Josh's own phone was almost out of battery, which made it sound like a frog with a sore throat whenever a text message came through, so he'd set it to silent and stuffed it in the bottom of his laptop bag. However, his horn pipping had attracted the attention of half the student body, although seemingly not the half that included George, and he dug it out, all set to give George an earful.

He didn't get that far. George appeared from a doorway, mouthed 'be right back' and darted off in the opposite direction. Clearly, he wasn't as frightened of Constable Whiplash as Josh was.

Five minutes later, George returned with two takeaway cups, and Josh instantly forgave him. It had been a pretty rushed morning all round. Now, trying to drink the too hot liquid, turn the steering wheel and get over the speed bumps with maximum velocity, minimum injury, he was starting to panic that they would end up getting arrested if they didn't make it to the station in time.

He needn't have worried; PC Granger had given him the wrong shift time and even had the decency to apologise—after a fashion. She took them to a waiting room beyond the keypad-protected door of the reception area, sat George down and told him to 'stay', much as a dog owner does to a new puppy. He did as he was told and commenced reading the multitude of crime prevention leaflets on display.

PC Granger led Josh to a small interview room with a table, two chairs and an audio recorder, which was exactly the same as the one he used for recording therapy sessions. She didn't use it, though; she had with her an A4 printed pad with duplicate sheets, and filled in the first few boxes at the top with his name, address and date of birth, before the questioning began in earnest.

"Tell me, how long have you known Doctor Sean Tierney?"

"Nineteen years."

"A long time."

"Yes. We went to university together."

"And in what capacity do you know him? As classmates?"

"Originally, yes. We're colleagues now, obviously."

"In what sense? You're registered as self-employed. He works for the hospital."

"We both lecture on a counselling diploma course at the university."

"I should also note down your qualifications, Mr. Sandison."

"BSc Honours in Psychology, Diploma in Counselling, Master's in Counselling and Psychotherapy."

"You're not a doctor?"

"No."

"Is Doctor Tierney your superior?"

"Erm, no. Most certainly not. He is, however, the course leader for the diploma in counselling. How is this relevant?"

"I just need the background information. Now, please tell me what happened last week. From the beginning, if you could."

"Well, George went to his lecture. Sorry, George Morley, my friend, is a student on the diploma course and was attending a lecture due to be given by Sean—Sean Tierney. When he didn't arrive, Sophie Spyris—a student who is…a friend of Sean's—called his mobile phone and didn't get any response. She went to the house and found that it was empty, apart from his cat."

"One moment." PC Granger scribbled away furiously. "Are you saying Mr. Morley is one of your students, and Miss Spyris, also a student, is a 'friend' of Doctor Tierney's?"

"Yes."

"That seems a little—unconventional."

"They are pre-existing relationships, and neither of us assesses the work produced by our friends. That would be unprofessional."

"But you say you and Doctor Tierney have been friends a long time."

"Acquaintances. Not friends."

"And has this relationship ever been more than academic acquaintance?"

"Yes. Again, is this relevant?"

"Possibly."

Whether it was or it wasn't, she left it alone and allowed Josh to narrate the events at Sean's house, including the trip to the vet with the cat and the tests indicating that it was paracetamol in the kettle. Once he'd finished, she asked a few more questions about specific details, such as the address of the veterinary surgery that conducted the tests, where in the house he had been during the cleanup operation, how long he'd been there, how many times, and whether he saw anything out of place. It was all very well asking, but it was only the second time he'd been to the cottage—as Sean insisted on calling it—the first so long ago that he had no way of knowing if anything was out of place.

Finally satisfied with his responses, PC Granger brought the interview to a close. "Thank you, Mr. Sandison. You have been most cooperative. If you could just check through this for me and sign each page. We may need to call you back, once we've taken the fingerprints from Doctor Tierney's house."

"Look. What is this insistence on calling him Doctor bloody Tierney? How many times did you refer to Eleanor Davenport as 'Doctor'? Not once! And she's a general practitioner. Just because she's cohabiting with the number one suspect in your murder case does not mean *she* is guilty of anything. No, I'd say that was downright discriminatory, maybe even a little bit sexist. All Tierney's got is some nonsense doctorate for a state-the-bleeding-obvious paper about comorbid bereavement. He's not even a real doctor."

Josh stopped ranting, and PC Granger wondered if she was about to get an apology. But that wasn't why he'd stopped.

"Actually..." He'd just figured something out, a connection he hadn't seen before. He leaned in close and PC Granger, who felt herself being drawn into the story, leaned in too.

"Sean—Doctor Tierney—works with terminally ill patients and their relatives. I bet you anything he's treated Alistair Campion and his wife."

"Why do you think this is important, Mr. Sandison? I can't see how—"

"I think it is," Josh interrupted. "You have a murder and an attempted murder. Now, maybe it's nothing more than a curious coincidence that they're both connected to Alistair Campion. Who knows? It might be nothing. But if I were you, I'd follow it up."

"Well, thank you for the information. As I say, we'll be in touch if need be. I'll walk you back to the waiting area, where my colleague will take you through to provide fingerprints."

Josh signed the statement and passed it back. PC Granger separated the two copies, gave him the bottom one and moved towards the door, indicating that he follow. They returned to the waiting room, where George waved his blackened fingertips to show he had already been processed and exchanged places with Josh before undergoing the same process. He was finished long before Josh was done having his prints taken. There wasn't much he could say, beyond providing a more or less identical account to the one PC Granger had just heard.

On the journey home, Josh explained what he had realised during the interview.

"So? What does that mean?" George asked, not really seeing the connection.

"It means someone is trying to get at Alistair Campion. Or at his associates, at any rate. First, they set up James to look like he murdered Campion, then they go after his therapist—the two people he was most likely to confide in. Someone's trying to keep something quiet. That's what I think, anyway."

"You're such a conspiracy theorist."

"Me? Ha! That's usually your job."

"This early criminal career James told us about. Surely that precludes him from being someone Campion would share classified information with? I know if it were me, I wouldn't be telling some jumped-up little yob anything important."

"But he isn't a jumped-up little yob anymore. He said Campion turned him around, became like a father to him. If Campion was that important to James, it stands to reason he also meant a lot to Campion. He had no children of his own, did he?"

"No. I can see where you're coming from, but it's not as if Campion's firm was involved in top secret defence work or anything like that."

"To our knowledge. Anyway, what do you think? Are they connected—the Tierney thing and Campion's murder—or am I doing really bad maths again?"

"You? Do bad maths. Ha! I'd say it's worth asking James if he can think of anything that would lead to him being fitted up."

Josh nodded in agreement. He pulled into the next side road, turned the car around and headed for Eleanor's apartment block.

As soon as they arrived, they could tell there was something very wrong—not dead bodies and planted paracetamol wrong—as Eleanor was in the living room, wrapping presents, with a child they correctly assumed to be James's son, whilst James was sitting on a stool in the kitchen, doing nothing at all. Anywhere else, that might be considered a state of normality. But James, sitting, staring into space? It wasn't like him, on top of which neither he nor Eleanor had even noticed Josh and George were standing there. A silent arrangement was made via jerks of the head for George to go and talk to James; meanwhile, Josh approached Eleanor. It was going to be tricky with the boy there.

She finally acknowledged him and waited until Oliver was absorbed in 'writing' out a label before she shuffled back across the floor on her knees.

"Hey," she whispered, "how's things?"

"Fine. I may have some interesting news. How are things with you?"

"Great. Oliver has been so good, and we've made cookies, wrapped presents—we're going to the park this afternoon, after we've—"

"Ellie, stop it."

"There's so much to do before he goes home. I'm really glad I said he could come now. It's been lovely to have—"

"Eleanor. Stop it now," Josh ordered. This time, she stopped and bowed her head.

"Oh, Josh. I did an awful thing."

"What?" he asked gently, for the first time in a long time unsure of what he was about to hear. Maybe he'd got it all wrong, believing James was innocent, that she knew nothing of what he had done. "What did you do?"

Eleanor burst into tears, and he put his arm around her, which made her sob uncontrollably and drew Oliver's attention.

"It's OK," Josh said kindly. Oliver smiled and held up the little gift with its newly written label. "That's very good writing. What a clever boy!"

Eleanor laughed through the tears, making a noise not dissimilar to choking. Josh turned his attention back to her.

"So, then, what have you done that is so bad you can't even put it into words?"

"That's typical of you, reading my mind, as usual. It was…embarrassing. I don't even know what happened. Never had anything like it before."

"Do you think you could be a little more specific? It might just be me, but I have no idea what you're talking about."

Eleanor plucked a tissue from a little square box on the table next to the sofa, wiped her eyes, blew her nose, and took a deep breath.

"James and I, what I mean to say is, we, no, he…oh, Jesus." She started sobbing again. Josh waited patiently for her to get herself together. She started over. "What I'm trying to tell you is James proposed to me last night."

"He did? Wow!"

"You might well say 'wow'. It blew me away."

"What did you say? Yes, I hope?"

"I wanted to, Josh, I really did."

"But? You didn't turn him down, did you?"

"If only! That wouldn't have been anywhere near as bad." Eleanor handed Oliver another small gift, ready wrapped with a label attached and the words 'To Daddy, love from Oliver' lightly sketched for him to follow with his pen. She continued, "I couldn't breathe. I couldn't speak. I felt like my throat was closing up. My heart was pounding, my head was about to explode. And then I threw up."

"Hmm," Josh said, trying desperately to conceal his amusement, because it wasn't funny. He coughed to stifle it, pleased she was too preoccupied with watching Oliver and sniffling into her soggy tissue to notice. "I can see your problem. However—" he passed her another tissue "—it was only a stress response, and it has happened before, although I can understand why you've blocked the memory. Didn't you talk to him about it afterwards?"

"No. He left the room and slept in here. And now I think he's started packing all his stuff, ready to leave when he takes Oliver home at the end of the week." She started crying again.

"Oh, Ellie. You've got to talk to him. This is silly."

"I know." She sniffed and steadied herself. "That's one good thing about having a child around—got to keep it together, for Oliver's sake."

In the kitchen, James was repeating the same story from his own perspective, which involved Eleanor running away from him and failing to return. He'd frightened her, misread the signals she'd sent his way, and now it was time for him to accept her feelings on the matter. The only decent thing to do was to leave as soon as he could and try to get back to how life was before. Which, he added, was empty and devoid of meaning, but he would survive, because Browns were fighters. It mattered not if he cleared his name.

From one extreme to the other, life without Eleanor was the common theme, and George had no idea where all of this had come from. He hoped Josh was having more success in getting to the bottom of it.

"George. We have a job to do." Josh was standing in the kitchen doorway and had been for a while. "We're going to the park with Oliver, while these two sit and talk to each other."

"Righteo," George replied. He climbed down from the very uncomfortable stool and gave his legs a good rub in an attempt to get the blood circulating again. Josh had already instructed Eleanor on what she had to do, and she was fighting with Oliver's tiny coat and gloves, trying to get him to comply with the sudden change of activity. He'd only just met Josh and George and was confused by what she was saying, but he trusted 'Enna', because Daddy said she was kind.

Josh held out his hand to the bewildered little boy, and he took it but then halted in the hallway, looking to his father for reassurance. James noticed him, and his face changed immediately.

"Josh and George want to go to play in the park with you. They're my friends, so it is all right, Oliver," he said, aware that everything he and Oliver's mother had instilled in their son so far about strangers was being undone in an instant.

"Come on then, little man," Josh said warmly, "shall we go and play on the swings and leave Daddy to talk to Eleanor?"

Oliver looked up from inside his hood, examining Josh with a very serious expression, still not convinced.

"And afterwards, we can go to one of Daddy's shops and eat ice cream. Would you like that?"

Oliver nodded solemnly.

"See you in a couple of hours," Josh called back.

Eleanor closed the door behind them and turned to face James. She didn't see how she was going to follow through, but she had to try and explain what had happened last night, before he walked away forever.

Chapter Twenty-Two: Pure…Bliss

They hadn't even reached the corner of the street, before somebody passed comment.

"You want to watch out, you know." The woman scurried past, dragging a tartan shopping trolley behind her. George and Josh looked at each other, frowning in confusion.

"Was she talking to us?" George asked.

"I don't know." Josh shrugged. They carried on walking towards the park. Next was a glazier in a transit van, who didn't say anything, but slowed and wound down his window, staring at them as he passed by. Surely these people didn't recognise Oliver Brown? He could have been anyone's son.

"When this is over, James should see Jess about suing that ridiculous rag mag. It's a disgrace," Josh said angrily. It wasn't the first time he'd seen someone's life torn to shreds by a supposedly 'in the public interest' hyped-up headline in the local paper. Their top reporter had designs on a career with one of the nationals and was precisely the sort of lowlife who'd get it. Nor did he care who he destroyed in the process.

They crossed the road and went through the park gates. At least on a damp, dreary day like today, it was virtually empty, so there would be less likelihood of them having people stare or remark for a while.

There was just one other adult—a mother, with her son—on the part of the park where the swings and slide were. The other little boy appeared to be about the same age as Oliver, and George found it quite amusing; they looked like little clones in their coats, hats and mittens. He lifted Oliver onto the swing next to the other child's and pushed gently. The boy's mother peered around the edge of her hood at George and smiled.

"Cold, isn't it?" she said.

"Sure is," George replied, pushing the swing a little bit harder.

"They don't care." She waved her arm towards the two children. "When they're out playing, it doesn't matter if it's five below. Just as long as they're having fun. And here we are, freezing to death!"

"Very true," George agreed.

"More, please." Oliver giggled, kicking his legs so that the swing wobbled. George obliged, pushing him as hard as he dared, absolutely terrified that he'd fall off. He could remember his own dad taking him to the park when he was little—although quite a bit older than Oliver—and begging to be pushed higher and higher. His father, being more of a risk taker than he was himself, always did as requested. Then one day, George forgot to hold on, or thought he'd try and be clever, he couldn't recall which, but he slipped off the swing from quite a height and hit his head on the way down. Eight stitches in the back of the head and scarred to this day—it was no wonder he was being so cautious. Not long after, his father left to live in the States and he never saw him again.

Children were very fickle when it came to these things, and soon Oliver was bored with the swings, inspired by the other little boy's change to the slide, so they moved over. George watched on with his heart in his mouth as Oliver climbed the steps to the top and then came down the other side, not hurtling exactly, as the slide was wet and his jacket was sticking to it. The children's coats soon dried it off, and they started to glide down more easily, giggling at each other, one at the top, the other arriving at the bottom before sliding off the end and onto the floor.

George glanced around and spotted Josh, still over the other side of the park, talking on his phone, his expression intense, body language animated. It looked serious, so George let him off for literally leaving him holding the baby.

"Is he adopted?" the mother of the other child asked.

"Sorry?"

"Oliver, is it? Is he adopted?"

"Oh. No. He's my friend's...son." He was going to explain the whole chain of relationships, which went something like 'my friend's friend's partner's son', and in the time it took him to shorten this, he discovered that in his mind he had referred to Eleanor as Josh's friend, not his.

"Ah, OK. I don't wish to be rude, but I wondered if the guy over there was a social worker or a probation officer or something. I heard that sometimes fathers only get access to their children under supervision, but obviously, you're not his biological father."

"I hadn't thought of it like that. It must look pretty odd, us two and Oliver."

So that's why people keep staring. To the rest of the world, two men with a little boy didn't fit, particularly when the adults and child did not share the same ethnicity, and the comments were nothing to do with the newspaper or James. People made dreadful assumptions.

George felt that he should explain.

"My friend, Eleanor—" he emphasised this in his own mind, still beating himself up over the way he'd constructed it before "—she's with Oliver's dad. He proposed to her last night and they had a bit of a misunderstanding, so me and Josh—over there—offered to bring Oliver to the park to give them time to sort it out."

"Oh, that's very nice of you. It's hard work occupying a three-year-old. I'm on my own, and I don't get a minute. His dad's supposed to have him today. Eleanor is very lucky, to have good friends like you."

George blushed slightly. He wasn't feeling very much like a good friend just at that moment. The jealousy he'd been experiencing over the past few months had to stop. They were all friends, always had been. When he went to live on the ranch, it was Eleanor who had helped him keep it together, and there he was, trying to steal Josh away from her. It was selfish and unnecessary, and for all that Kris was a very significant part of his reason for not going home, he was becoming increasingly aware of the fact that his obsession with Josh hadn't diminished any. If anything, it was stronger than ever; he'd merely adjusted it in his head to make it acceptable, pushing for placement at his surgery, staying at his house for days at a time. He was ashamed to admit it, but he was even a little bit pleased that Sean Tierney was sick; it meant they got to spend more time together. Then, right at the moment when he'd thought it was heading somewhere, that damned policewoman had arrived.

George pushed all of this to the back of his mind for now, as Josh was walking towards him, something evidently preoccupying him. He was about to ask, but Oliver started crying, and everything else was momentarily forgotten, to rescue their charge from the bottom of the steps to the slide, where he had fallen a fortuitously short distance. George scooped him up and gave him a tight hug, which made him wriggle and cry more. George put him down again.

"Let's have a look at your knees," he said and lifted Oliver's trouser legs to check for injury. A couple of minor grazes, nothing more. George gave Oliver's knees a quick rub, and then the little boy was off again, chasing after his temporary new friend, back up the steps and down the slide.

"They bounce back quickly at that age," the woman said, watching her son come down the slide, followed by Oliver, around again and again, until the adults were exhausted from watching.

It was so cold, yet the children still wanted to play, and they'd been at it for nearly an hour. Josh checked his watch, and it triggered the woman to look at hers as well.

"Time to head off?" George asked.

"Yes. I'm bloody freezing." Josh shoved his hands deep in his jacket pockets. If he'd known he was going to be wandering out in the open air, he'd have brought his coat. As it was, he was only wearing a blazer, jumper and lightweight trousers—perfectly suited to the over-warm environment of the university, but not ideal for standing in the park on a winter's day.

"Come on, then, Oliver. Let's go and get some ice cream," George called.

"Ice cream? Are you mad?" The woman laughed, but she knew as well as they did that the playing-out rule extended to ice cream.

"Nice talking to you," George said, taking Oliver's soggy-gloved hand.

"And you. I hope it works out for your friend," she replied. She watched as the three of them walked away and back out onto the street.

"She seemed nice," George said to Josh and Oliver, and then quietly addressed Josh. "That looked like an intense phone call."

"It was. I'll tell you later," Josh cut him off, and the silence it created was a little uneasy, but they were only around the corner from Krissi's restaurant, so it wasn't so long to endure it.

The door opened, and the waft of heat was immense and welcoming. The place was buzzing, with lots of families, a birthday party and Christmas music. It was noisy, but in a good way, and as soon as they stepped inside, Krissi spotted them and came straight over.

"To what do I owe this pleasure?" She beamed. It was the first time Josh had been to this branch of The Pizza Place; it was bigger and far busier than the one Eleanor used to run.

"We've brought young Oliver for some of your extra special ice cream," George said.

"Oh, well, in that case, I'd better make sure it is extra, *extra* special," she said, smiling at Oliver and then, as an aside to Josh and George, "especially as he's the MD's son."

"Because the MD is obviously in a fit state to do anything about it right now," Josh remarked. Krissi looked at him, questioning for more. He shook his head and thumbed in Oliver's direction. "Later."

Krissi ushered them over to a table in the corner and found a bumper cushion for Oliver, who was too big for a high chair but too small to sit directly on the padded bench seating and still see over the top of the table. It felt cosy and festive, and George could sense the excitement starting to build inside him, in spite of all that was going on.

"It's beginning to look a lot like Christmas," he said and then laughed at himself.

Josh shook his head in dismay, although he was already giggling. "I can't believe you just said that."

"Neither can I."

Krissi returned for their order. They were both in fits of laughter and couldn't even begin to explain why, knowing that it wouldn't sound anywhere near as funny in replay. They pulled themselves together and managed to glean from Oliver that he wanted chocolate and strawberry ice cream, with sprinkles, marshmallows and sauce. George ordered exactly the same thing for himself and sat back and waited—

not so patiently—while Josh scanned the menu, trying to make a decision.

"I have the perfect thing for you," Krissi said.

"Which is?"

"Wait and see."

She moved away from the table, disappearing through the swinging doors into the kitchen. Josh caught a glimpse of a familiar hat through the gap as the doors swung back and forth. It was Wotto, Eleanor's old chef, boogie-ing across the kitchen, with a circle of dough spinning above his head. Josh smiled to himself.

Whatever James Brown was, he certainly remained true to his word. All of Eleanor's staff had been offered their old jobs here, and he recognised Karen as well—the assistant manager. Both she and Krissi had originally applied for the position of manager, neither succeeding, but with Krissi unofficially promoted to acting manager, Eleanor had worried they would struggle to work together. In the end, Karen had been absolutely fine about it, agreeing that Krissi was the best woman for the job. It was a far more demanding post than running the other branch, which was now a popular Thai restaurant.

Josh was so deep in thought that he temporarily forgot his surroundings, until a floury hand suddenly appeared in front of him. He followed it up, to the vast, white-toothed grin.

"Hello, Wotto. Great to see you."

"Alright?" Wotto shook Josh's hand enthusiastically. "Ain't seen you since they closed the other place. How's it going?"

"Not bad at all. How're you?"

"Yeah. I'm good. Been promoted to head chef, as well. Listen—" Wotto leaned in close "—I heard all that stuff about Mr. Brown and Eleanor. Are they doing all right? She was good to me, you know? Stuck up for me, gave me the job when she shouldn't have because of the money thing, and all that."

"They're coping. That's all I can say, really. You should give her a call sometime. She'd love to hear from you, I'm sure."

"Yeah, might do that. Anyway, better get back to it. Krissi—she's a great boss, too, but she's a bit stricter than Eleanor. Told me off for dancing in the fridge the other week." Wotto tutted, gave Josh's hand a final good shake, patted George on the back and reached into his apron pocket.

"And for the big man in the hood," he said, handing Oliver the most enormous red and white swirly lollipop. Oliver's eyes grew to almost the same size.

"Thank you," he said politely. He took the sweet from Wotto and then sat there staring at it, as if the swirls had sent him into a trance.

"My pleasure, Mr. Brown," Wotto said, winking at Oliver, before heading back to his kitchen in a kind of street dance sliding step.

"What money thing?" George asked.

"I was wondering myself." Before Josh got any further in puzzling, Krissi was at the table, with a tray containing two bowls loaded with ice cream and a whole array of toppings, and a tall, stemmed glass, topped with chocolate flake and some sort of orange syrup.

"This is awesome," she said, placing it in front of Josh, whose expression matched Oliver's a moment before, when he was handed the lollipop—something he wasn't letting go of, not even for his ice cream.

"What on Earth is it?"

"Just try it and see," she said and left them with their assorted desserts.

Josh cautiously poked the long-handled spoon into the top of the glass, the chocolate crunching and cracking under the pressure. He lifted a small amount with the tip of the spoon, allowed the residual syrup to drizzle away, and placed it in his mouth, carefully holding on to the contents with his teeth and withdrawing the spoon through closed lips. He let it all melt on his tongue. He was in heaven.

"Well?" George asked, searching Josh's face for clues.

"Oh my word. That is absolute joy. In a glass. Who'd have thought it?" Josh dug the spoon in deeper this time, removing a much larger scoop. He placed it on his tongue and let it slide down his throat. This had to be the best dessert ever.

"Can I try a bit?" George ventured.

"No."

"Meanie."

"Yes."

For the next five minutes, the three of them were totally silent, the only sound from their table the clang of spoons on ceramic and glass.

"How about now?" George tried again.

"Still no." Josh grinned.

"Please?"

"Oh, go on then." He moved his spoon out of the way to let George take some of what he had now worked out was orange sorbet, white chocolate ice cream, an orange liqueur-based syrup and flaked dark chocolate. George put his spoon in his mouth.

"Mmm, I see what you mean. That is pure…" he was about to say 'sex' but checked himself just in time. "Pure bliss." He aimed for another scoop, and Josh blocked him with his hand.

"No way! That's your lot."

***

Eleanor and James hadn't got very far. Every time she tried to explain, he placated her by saying he understood that she wasn't ready, but he was, and if it meant they must go their separate ways, if she didn't want to be with him, then that was perfectly fine. That wasn't what she was trying to say at all, but the more she said, the worse she seemed to be making it. It had reached the point where she was locked in the bathroom, sitting on the edge of the bath, staring at her socks, and rehearsing. Saying it to herself made perfect sense, so why, when he was in the same room, did it come out in some kind of garbled 'English is my second language' form?

She tried again.

"James. I told you yesterday that I love you, and I do. I'm sorry I reacted the way I did. I don't know why, but what I wanted to say, what I meant to say, was that I would love to…I accept your…oh, fuck. The answer is yes, woman, just say 'Yes, I will marry you' and be done with it. Stop trying to qualify."

She stamped her feet in anger at herself, a fairly useless vent in socks, on a bathmat.

"James. I love you, as I said, and so I would be honoured to become your—why is this so hard?" She raked her hair with her fingers and held on.

"James. I love you and would love to be your wife. Of course I will marry you. See? Now, why couldn't you just say that to begin with?"

And that was the problem, because now James was so focused on her initial reaction that whatever she said it made no difference. He didn't believe her. One way or another, she had to convince him, because Josh and George would be back with Oliver soon, and this was the only chance she had.

"That would be right, wouldn't it? I lose the only man that I am absolutely one hundred percent sure I love to an involuntary stress response." She smoothed her hair, straightened her top, and prepared to go back outside.

***

Josh and George rounded the corner into Eleanor's road, Oliver holding Josh's hand with one of his own, the other keeping a firm grasp on the red and white lollipop, which was very sticky and made his face shine. They'd stayed out for as long as they could—more than two hours—and now they were really cold. George felt sick from the amount of ice cream he'd just consumed.

Josh felt a bit tipsy and was thinking that the car was going to have to stay where it was until tomorrow. More importantly, he was hoping that when they arrived back at Eleanor's flat, she would be showing off a glitzy new engagement ring, and there would be smiles and joy all round. Having seen her backed into a corner in the past, he wasn't so naïve. Her reaction had always been the same; that urge to run as fast as she could. He knew it well, for it was the one thing they had completely in common.

"Fingers crossed," George said optimistically as he turned the door handle to let them in, but then changed his mind and knocked instead. Eleanor came and opened the door. One look at her face told Josh all he needed to know and also what he needed to do. She'd probably kill him later, but he couldn't let her lose this.

"We won't come in, Ellie," he said gently. "Oliver's been very good, incidentally, but he will need a bit of a wash." Eleanor looked down tearfully at the little boy, who was sucking the top of the big round lollipop.

"Where did he get that from? I haven't seen those since Wotto…ah!"

"Yes. The very same fellow. He sends his love. I told him to give you a call. OK. We're going. See you soon, Oliver."

"Bye bye," Oliver said and waved at George and Josh.

"See you later." George embraced her and held on, hoping she would read the remorse in his actions. She patted him on the back and let go. "See you later, Ollie," he said.

"Bye, Dorge," the little boy replied, and George's heart melted.

"Can you ask James to give me a ring later?" Josh realised how insensitive his phrasing had been after he'd said it. Eleanor didn't notice. "I told you I found out something? I think that it might help him to clear his name, but I need to ask him about it first."

Eleanor nodded to confirm she would and watched on as they walked back down the path and onto the street.

"I'm leaving the car here," Josh called back and fell in step beside George.

Eleanor stayed where she was, waiting until they were out of view and she could delay no longer.

They heard the door close from far behind them.

Chapter Twenty-Three:
In the Air

Jess looked at the clock again and double-checked the time against her mobile phone. It was definitely gone six o'clock. Lois had left half an hour ago, and Andy was late. He'd promised to pick her up on time, for once; she imagined that he'd only want to endear himself, given the circumstances, but apparently not. Sometimes she wondered why she even bothered. It was like trying to parent an enormous child.

She'd brought her make-up with her, as well as jeans and a t-shirt, as advised. She'd even talked herself into believing that, after a day of court and appointments, the best thing in the world would be a game of ten-pin bowling, although if she had to wait much longer, it wouldn't just be the pins she knocked down.

Finally, at a quarter past six, the door downstairs slammed shut, followed by the sound of someone leaping two stairs at a time. It was undeniably Andy, and he appeared in her office doorway, grinning and slightly out of breath.

"Sorry. Had to run here, and I'm a bit out of shape."

"I was going to leave and go to the pub instead," Jess said brusquely, picking up her bag and her keys. "Perhaps you should consider getting another car? Oh, no, sorry, you can't, seeing as you don't have a job anymore." She stormed past him and down the stairs. "You coming, or shall I go play on my own?"

Andy shrugged and followed at a safe distance. Sooner or later, he was going to have to tell her the truth. It was far too dangerous not to.

***

Josh didn't ask George to leave; he decided of his own accord, after his epiphany in the park that afternoon. In a way, he felt responsible for what was happening with Eleanor, because Josh would have been far more effective on his own. Josh had done some relationship counselling in the past, and much as he'd complained about how complicated it was and how much he hated being caught in the crossfire, he was, surprisingly, very good at it. He'd have had this mess sorted long ago, without George's interference, of that he was quite sure. In any event, he didn't live there and it would be nice to sleep in his own bed for a night. It had been about a week, this time around, and Josh's spare bed was comfortable enough, but George was craving his own space, with his own things.

Aside from that, Josh had hinted—not very subtly—at his relief that things were finally returning to normal. He was back in his surgery tomorrow, with a whole day of cancelled appointments to get through, and he needed to try to fit Eleanor and James in somewhere. An early night was on the cards, he said, and George decided to leave him to it. Rejecting Josh's reluctant offer of a lift, George set off for home on foot.

George could tell from afar that he still wasn't alone, because all the lights were on, and there was now a Christmas tree erected in the living room window. That in itself didn't bother him, although talk about making yourself at home! He cursed his inability to stand up to Kris. It wasn't as if he was domineering in the way Dan was and Andy could be. Nor did he frighten George the way Joe had, before he'd come home last year. That was a stupid situation, which had escalated totally out of his control, with him losing more and more of his authority on the ranch with every passing day. Since he'd agreed to give Joe half—supposedly his biological entitlement—and sold the rest to him and the other ranchers, not one of them had been in touch to tell him what they were up to, and he liked it that way.

George was sick of feeling like the house was no longer his 'home'. He'd paid eighteen months' rent up front, so he was stuck with it, which would be all right, if only he could find a way to say what needed to be said. He went inside, picked up the pile of mail from the plant stand inside the door and started to thumb through it, all the while aware of the sound of the TV coming from the living room. Kris was on his own. *Good.*

"Alright?" George acknowledged him but didn't make eye contact.

"Hi. Where've you been?"

"At Josh's."

"All this time?"

"Yeah. We had to sort out a problem."

"It took a whole week?"

"It did, actually. Listen, I need to talk to you about this…thing."

"George, please don't start on about Shaunna again. She's OK with it. I went home yesterday, and I promised I'd be back before the weekend."

"Yeah, but she's not OK with it at all, though, is she, Kris? Because she doesn't know what 'it' is."

Kris didn't reply, and George could understand why. It would have been out of character for Kris to not feel guilty about sleeping with someone behind Shaunna's back, but she'd always known he liked men. It wasn't like he was cheating, as such. He was trying not to hurt anyone, even though George could see how much Kris was hurting himself. Whether forcing him to leave was the right thing to do, George didn't know, but he couldn't stand by any longer, not when it was making them both miserable.

Kris returned to the living room and flopped onto the sofa. George followed him in.

"So, I think," George continued hesitantly, "the best thing really is for me to ask you to leave. That's not to say I'm going to throw you out in the cold and never have anything to do with you again. But you have to tell Shaunna how you feel. It isn't going to be easy, I know, but you owe it to her."

"Right. I understand."

"I'm not sure you do," George said, more gently this time. He took off his coat and sat down. "I care for you, Kris. You've been one of my closest friends for such a long time. But Shaunna's my friend as well. And so is Josh."

"I suppose he knows now, does he?"

"No. I promised I wouldn't tell him, and I haven't. But I almost had to lie to avoid doing so, and I'm not doing it again."

"I wouldn't expect it of you, George. And I appreciate everything you've done. Really, I do."

"Where is Jack, anyway?"

"He went home yesterday. He's at the same point as me in all of this, but he has children. How's he going to tell her?"

"That's not for you to worry about, not at the moment. You have to tell Shaunna, because if you don't..."

Kris didn't need to hear the rest. He patted George's knee and took his hand. "You're a wonderful friend. Thank you."

George brushed the back of his hand across Kris's cheek. Over the years, he had loved and hated him with the same intensity. To have watched from the sidelines, whilst Kris fought his self-conjured demons, was one of the most painful and helpless experiences he'd ever endured. Instinctively, George reached over and hugged him.

"Just don't ever try telling me you're straight again," he said, looking him in the eyes.

"I didn't. I said I was bi, and I am. I just find men more attractive. But I promise you, I didn't go looking for this. I love Shaunna and would never deliberately hurt her. Deep down, I think she knew this was coming."

George let go. Kris held on a little longer and then released his grip, too.

"I'll go tomorrow, if that's all right with you?"

George nodded, unable to trust his voice with the burbling mix of guilt and relief currently playing havoc with his insides.

"But if she kicks me out, will you let me stay till I find somewhere else?"

"Of course." George stretched and stood up. "Right. I'm making cocoa. Want one?"

"I'd love one."

***

Jess was winning and taking every opportunity to gloat. It wasn't even a close match, although Andy insisted that he was losing on purpose to make her feel better. He deserved to lose, he agreed. So this was the final bowl of the last game, and she was already up two games. It was still a battle to see who won this one. Four to one was a clear win; three to two wasn't. There was everything to play for.

The first bowl took out eight pins, one remaining on either side of the lane. Jess measured carefully, took her time, did a run up and released the ball, intending to curve it from left to right—something she could usually control to perfection. This time, it started to curl, but then it straightened out, pelting right down the middle and leaving the two pins standing.

Andy stepped up and tried a few different balls until he was happy that he had the right one, and took a couple of practice runs before launching it down the lane. It hit the centre pin, taking out all but two on the left. His arm was aching. Most people played a couple of games, maybe three if they were very competitive. Five was ridiculous, but Jess had insisted—when it was two to one—that they went on.

He waited for the ball to return, stretching his hand and extending his fingers, clicking each one in turn. The noise made Jess wince. She could see it was part of the play, drawing it out to the bitter end. He picked up the ball, walked up to the line and released it with hardly any force at all. Jess looked horrified. For a moment, it looked like he'd done it deliberately, to lose the last game, which was even worse than him winning. She wanted the victory fair and square.

"*You* are taking the piss. What the hell was that?"

Still, the ball kept going, slowly rolling towards its target, yet looking as if it might stop or fall into the gutter at any second. Jess watched on, by now hoping that it would slow to a halt before it got there. He wasn't trying to lose at all. He was showing her he could have won if he'd wanted to, with a final play not dissimilar to being slowly and painfully tortured to death.

The ball collided head-on with the front-most pin, knocking it into the other. If a bowling ball could look smug, then this one did, as it slowly rolled away and out of view. Jess slumped onto the seat behind her.

Andy punched the air. *Now* he was going to tell her why coming home from Dubai was a good thing—not proof that he was the massive failure she thought him to be, but the first thing he'd got right in his entire life.

"Shall we walk?" he said, zipping up his coat and extending an arm for her to take.

"I suppose," she said sulkily, looping her arm through the gap he presented to her.

"Then I'll explain why I'm back so soon."

"Yes, that's right, Andy. Kick a woman while she's down."

"That's exactly my intention." He grinned.

Stepping outside onto the street, the silence and cool air were almost like free falling. It was a very strange sensation. The wind was gusting, but the pavements were so wet that all the fallen leaves were stuck to the edges, forming a slippery carpet. Andy stepped out onto the road so that Jess could walk on the clear parts, rather than either risk slipping and lose face.

Andy wasn't sure where to begin. It had all come out of the blue—a freak set of circumstances, leading to a great opportunity to set up in real partnership, rather than doing all the running on his brother's behalf and getting paid for the privilege. That was why it had been so important to have the contract in place before he returned to the UK.

When Dan had flown out to visit, it had been for pleasure, not business, but a meeting at an evening gala with the chief executive of the company Andy worked for had led to a discussion about installing a new cable system on the development, and the CEO wasn't happy with the company who'd completed the work on his previous project. Dan said he could easily do the job, and well before the completion date he'd been quoted by the original company. The guy took Dan at his word, and once he'd spoken to Campion Holdings, everything was in place. Signing on the dotted line was a formality.

In the meantime, Andy had arranged to meet up with the board of directors and put a proposal to them, which meant he would be working for them instead of the subcontractors and could return to the UK to liaise with Dan and other suppliers, making arrangements that were cheaper, more efficient and ultimately controlled by the company instead of the subcontractor—a decent firm, but with the old tea-break-labour mentality.

Of course, it meant Andy would still have to fly out to Dubai and other locations occasionally, but he could be based anywhere in the world and do the job of managing contracts, checking supplies arrived, and so on. Even better than that, he could do it from home, if Jess would let him. That was the only bit he wasn't sure of.

So, he drew in a deep breath and started to explain what he had done. Jess listened, without interjection, interruption or criticism, until the very end.

"Do you get paid the same?"

"More."

"How long for?"

"Permanent."

She nodded. "Sounds all right."

"Sounds all right?" he echoed, trying to gauge her response. Jess hadn't wanted him to go in the first place. He thought she'd be ecstatic that he was back, but the way she was treating him was like he was an irritation, a cold sore that had almost dried up then come back and brought its mates along for the ride.

"Can I ask you something, Jess? I don't want you to bite my head off, but I need to know."

"OK."

"Are you seeing someone?"

"That's a really odd thing to ask."

That wasn't the response he'd anticipated. A furious denial was more in keeping with how she usually dealt with questions she perceived to be pointless because the answer was obvious.

"It's not," he argued. "I've been gone for over twelve months. You've emailed me, and we've chatted online. I came home whenever I could, but not once did you come out to see me, when you said you would."

"Because I've been busy. I couldn't really justify the expense for the airfare, either."

"That's bollocks. You've spent that much on shoes before now."

"But that's for shoes, which I can wear again. A return flight to Dubai isn't exactly something you can enjoy more than once. Twelve hours is a long time on a plane on your own, you know."

"Yeah, I do, thanks." They were both getting angry, which wasn't how this was supposed to be. He'd missed her while he was away and assumed she was feeling the same. He tried again. "Just tell me. If you are seeing someone, I'll be gutted, but I need to know. I only want you to be happy."

Jess didn't reply. She couldn't think what to say, because she had been seeing someone, or, at least, she'd been out on a couple of dates and really liked him, but it was a while back now, and they hadn't stayed in touch. That wasn't the point, though. In the past, she'd have always told Andy about things like this. They were best friends, not lovers. He, too, had had his fair share of girlfriends over the years, yet somehow, everything seemed to have changed. He was acting as if they were an item, even though he had been thousands of miles away.

"There was someone," she said finally. "No-one special. We went out a couple of times, so the answer is no, I'm not seeing anyone."

They walked the rest of the way home in silence, Jess not knowing how to make what she'd told him any better, Andy regretting asking, but he had known. He'd had that feeling—that she didn't want him around. Sure, she was used to having her own space, but no sex had been the real giveaway. Best friends and more. Perhaps the intimacy they'd always shared wasn't healthy, but after they'd both been without for so long, he'd expected it. The realisation sent shudders down his spine; it felt too much like the accusation that had been levelled at him by Dan, and the way Jess had responded to him then. It wasn't like that, though.

When they reached the house, he took hold of her shoulders and turned her to face him.

"Do you want me to leave?"

"Don't be silly."

"Are you sure?"

"Of course I'm sure. A couple of dates, Andy. That's all it was, I promise. I don't know why I didn't tell you. It was stupid, really. But I'm so pleased you're home, and I *have* missed you." She ran her hand up inside his jacket and tickled his back with the tips of her nails. "Can we go in? I'm freezing here, and I really could do with one of your massages. My shoulders are killing me after all that bowling."

Andy sighed in submission. Using his body to steer her towards the doorway, he found his key and unlocked the door, with his weight against her and she pinned to the door. She fell into the hallway, and he descended on top of her, kicking the door behind him. It didn't close properly, but he stayed exactly where he was, pulling her shirt open with the hand that wasn't trapped under her back. This time, she didn't fight him.

***

Josh had booked James in for a 'formal' appointment, and he arrived precisely two minutes before the time they had arranged, on his own.

"No Oliver?" Josh asked, welcoming James into the consulting room and indicating to him to sit down.

"Oliver chose to stay with Eleanor," he explained—a very sad state of affairs, from his current viewpoint.

"They've really taken to each other, haven't they?" Josh remarked with intentional lightness. He was trying to shift the quality of the interaction before he attempted anything as intricate as explaining his best friend's psyche and her ludicrous response to James's proposal, or indeed anything else that caused her discomfort.

"They have. It makes it all the more difficult for me to say goodbye tomorrow, but I must no longer impose my presence on any of you."

"All right, James. I need you to listen to what I'm about to say, but I'd prefer it if you didn't tell Ellie that I've said anything. She will no doubt tell you herself in her own good time. But I cannot stand by and watch you walk out of my best friend's life, when she loves you as much as she does." He checked to make sure James was listening before he continued. He needn't have worried on that score. The attentiveness in those eyes was incredible.

"When we were at school, Ellie developed bulimia—an eating disorder—and kept it very well hidden. Her parents still don't know about it, because we promised never to tell them, not even if it got so bad that she needed hospital treatment. Ultimately, it was the reason I became a therapist, and, it would seem, George has followed the same route.

"We read everything we could find on eating disorders, although at the time, the majority of information was about anorexia, and Eleanor was far from starving herself. She ate massive amounts of food, in secret. The only way we got her to admit it was by following her home one day and taking photos through her bedroom window.

"She was devastated by what we'd done, although we assured her that we had known all along, and spying on her was the only way we could force her to admit it to herself.

Now, with the benefit of all my experience and training, I appreciate it was cruel and not exactly the right way to handle it, but it worked. She agreed to let us help her and, well…it's been quite a battle.

"Her idea to take up the job at The Pizza Place seemed like the worst one she'd ever had, and at that time, she was only just starting to recover. All the way through university she did it, spent her entire grant, borrowed more and more money, got into enormous debt and then, just before the end of her general practice, ended up in hospital with a ruptured stomach. She saw a psychiatrist for a while before she came home and took the waitressing job. She's been pretty stable since.

"There was no lasting damage—a few capped teeth and some scarring on her throat and stomach—but she has this stress response. We all get it—the heart pounding, stomach doing somersaults sensation? With Ellie, it makes her vomit. And the thing is, it doesn't matter if it's a good thing or a bad thing. The result is always the same."

Josh stopped to allow James a chance to take in what he had told him so far, and watched him reason it through, his facial expressions changing of their own accord. Several minutes passed while he worked through the information, no doubt rebuilding explanations for what he had seen.

"On our first date, she told me she had a problem with food. I did not imagine it to be so severe. Poor Eleanor. How awful that must be." He became silent again; pain registered in his eyes. He opened his mouth to speak a couple of times, but once more came to conclusions without needing Josh to clarify. However, there was just one thing he needed to know for certain.

"When I proposed, her reaction was one of these stress responses?"

"Correct."

"So it does not mean she is repulsed by me."

"Far from it, James. She loves you. Look. The words won't sound anything like the same coming from me, but what she told me was that she wanted to say yes. She could hardly believe you were asking her. When we brought Oliver back yesterday, and she still hadn't been able to talk to you, she genuinely looked like someone had pulled her world away from beneath her."

James pondered for a moment. "How do I support her with this?"

"First, you need to find a way to allow her to give you her answer. Then you take each day as it comes. It won't be easy. She isn't coping with the murder case too well. I imagine you're struggling yourself. But for Ellie, this is about control, and whenever she thinks she hasn't got any, that's when it all starts to go wrong for her."

James nodded resolutely. "I will talk to her today," he said. "No, I will listen to her today. She must know that I love her with all my heart and soul, and I do not want to lose her." He nodded again, this time to convey his gratitude, and moved towards the door, already beginning to plan his approach.

"Just one more thing," Josh said. "Do you know if Alistair Campion ever received counselling from Sean Tierney?"

"Sean Tierney?" James thought for a moment. "Yes, he did. He works at the hospice where Mrs. Campion is a patient. I believe they were both his patients at one time. Why?"

"Someone tried to kill him last week, and I think it might be the same person who killed Alistair."

"For what reason?"

"Is there anything he told you that could be valuable to anyone else?"

"I don't believe so. Mostly we spoke about the boys he worked with and how they made him proud. We didn't talk about business much."

"Well, if you think of anything, can you let me know? You don't have to tell me exactly what it is. I have a feeling that this has a lot more to do with keeping people quiet than it has to do with setting you up."

Josh's next appointment was due, so James agreed to do as requested and left, no longer feeling as if the weight of the world was crushing him. He was going to make things right with Eleanor and do the best he could to ensure she never suffered again.

***

Alice had her resignation letter all typed up and ready to print, but each time she tried to send it to the printer, someone would come over to ask a question, or give her something else to do, or simply stand there, waiting for their own printing to spew from the machine. She'd had it ready last night, before Mr. Meyer had told her to go home, which was very thoughtful of him, as she had the most dreadful headache. Her computer was always logged off, so she knew that no-one would have seen the letter, and she had to do it today. If she didn't, she'd miss the deadline and still be here two months from now.

She'd noticed them outside, arriving in Dan's car, the bassy music thumping across the car park and into the building, in spite of the double glazing. *They must be here to meet with the board.* Both boys together had the potential to transform her headache into a full-blown migraine. She watched as Dan pointed his hand at the car, the lights blinked twice, and then they walked towards the building, talking to each other jovially.

Neither was dressed suitably for a business meeting, in their jeans and casual shirts and jackets. Dan's was a flying jacket affair, in black, with a logo emblazoned on the right arm, whereas Andy's was blue denim, with buttons down both sides of the front. They looked much happier and far more comfortable with each other than they had been over the weekend. Things were clearly going well for them, and Alice was glad.

Now they were out of view, close to the building, and the smell of them had worked its way through the air-conditioning vent, drifting across the topmost strata of the typing pool. One of them was wearing a different aftershave—Dan, it seemed—not enough to hide him from Alice, though. The lift was visible from where she sat, and she could just make out the number displayed above the doors. They were coming to her floor.

The lift opened, and they strolled out, still engaged in the lighthearted conversation they had been having when they arrived. The aroma was overpowering. Alice searched for her handkerchief and found it just in time.

"Hey, Alice. How's things?" Dan smiled, slowing to a stop by her booth.

"Good morning, Dan, Andy," she replied without removing the white cotton square from her face.

"Do you have a cold?" Andy asked innocently. Dan nudged him with his elbow, and he turned slightly pink.

"We're here to meet with Meyer and the others. Are they upstairs?" Dan asked. Alice nodded. "Are you in the meeting?" Alice shook her head. "Are you making the tea?" Alice nodded again. "Would you like some help?" She shrugged and turned on her screen, open on her resignation letter, and pointed at it with her free hand. Dan moved closer to read it.

To Whom It May Concern:

It is with great sorrow that I write this, my letter of resignation. I have worked for this company for thirty-four years and have very much enjoyed the experience, until recently, when I have begun to feel that my services are no longer required.

Mr. Campion was always a courteous and respectful employer, and I am pleased to say that those who continue to manage the company have been as good to me as he was. However, I am nearing the age of retirement and want to spend some time engaged in pursuits of a personally rewarding nature.

I would like to take this opportunity to thank Campion Holdings PLC and to wish you all the very best with your future ventures.

Yours faithfully,
Alice Friar

Dan finished reading and nodded his head.

"Alice, that is one of the saddest things I've ever read. I'm so sorry you're leaving, and yet so happy, too."

Andy was completely confused, but before he could say anything, Dan pushed him back towards the lift.

"I'll tell you in a minute," he muttered and waved goodbye to Alice. "You sure you're OK with the tea trolley?" She nodded and shooed him away. The brothers returned to the lift, and Dan pushed the button for the next floor.

"What the fuck was that about?" Andy asked.

"In a minute!"

The lift arrived, and they both stepped in. Dan waited for the doors to close before he spoke, the pair of them turning in perfect tandem to face the opposite direction.

"Alice is coming to work for us as an au pair. That was her letter of resignation."

"Oh, OK. And the hanky?"

"That's a bit more complicated to explain. She has synaesthesia."

"Sin-az...what?"

"I dunno. Something to do with all the senses getting mixed together. She sees colours when she smells things. Sometimes it all gets a bit much, so she has to cover her nose."

"Was that because of us?"

"Looks like it." The lift bell pinged to indicate they had reached their floor, and they stepped out, heading straight for the boardroom. Time to kick some ass.

This would be over in no time at all. All they needed to do was deliver the news. The project was going ahead and Campion's would still supply the cable, but from now on, all communication was going to be handled by Jeffries and Associates. The associates were to be confirmed and probably wouldn't ever exist for real, but it sounded good, so that's what they'd agreed to register with Company House.

Bill Meyer was pleased to see Dan, and, like everyone else, easily recognised the man accompanying him as his brother.

"This is Andy. Andy—Bill Meyer." The men shook hands and exchanged the usual pleasantries, before Dan and Andy assumed the two empty seats, conveniently nearest to them.

"Thanks for agreeing to meet with us, Bill. I've just been filling Andy in on the details. As you know, he's been dealing with things at the Dubai end. He'll continue to work with you in the same capacity on this and future projects."

It had to be the worst timing ever, or the best, depending on whose point of view was taken, because, as Dan was about to elaborate and explain how they were taking over the provision of supplies to the east, the fire alarm sounded, and the sprinklers automatically opened on the entire boardroom—a clear signal that this was no drill.

Dan and Andy made for the stairs immediately, grabbing their papers on the way. Several of the other men contemplated chancing the lifts, before someone reminded them that they automatically opened at the nearest floor then powered down.

On the way down the stairs, Dan stopped at the administrators' floor.

"Let me just check Alice has left," he said and dodged between the people streaming through the door in the opposite direction. He scanned the room, satisfied that she wasn't there, and returned the way he had come. Andy was still waiting in the stairwell, pinned as flat as could be against the wall so he didn't block anyone else's passage.

"She must've gone already." Dan joined his brother in the procession down the stairs and out to the car park. The smell of smoke filled their nostrils as they exited the building, and looking behind them, it was no wonder. The entire front of the first floor was ablaze, flames licking up the exterior walls, windows cracking and then shattering with the heat.

For a moment, everyone assumed that the lightweight pieces falling on them were clumps of ash and smut being propelled outwards as the windows blew, but that was not the case. It had started to snow. It was bitterly cold, and the wind swirled the flakes in all directions, yet everyone stayed exactly where they were, watching the building burn more furiously with every passing second.

Two fire engines arrived and drew to a halt close to the reception area. The crews piled out of the open doors and unloaded the hoses. This was a big job.

A vicar suddenly appeared in the car park, fighting to open a bright-pink floral umbrella and searching the crowd for someone who looked like they were in a position of authority.

"Now there's something you don't see every day," Andy remarked, as the reverend neared their location.

"Thank Christ," Dan muttered under his breath. That was one step too far, because, it would seem they were the most official-looking evacuees, and now they had to try and be sensible, when the vision before them made it almost impossible.

"Gentlemen," the vicar called and gave up on the umbrella. "Would you let your staff know that the church is open for you all to take refuge?"

"Thank you, Reverend. That's very kind of you."

"Oh, no trouble at all. Mr. Campion was always very generous. And the Mothers' Union have just finished their meeting, so the urn is still full of hot water. I'll ask Mrs. Stevens to make up another pot of tea." He leaned forward and talked into Dan's ear directly. "We may even have a few mince pies left over."

Dan watched the vicar jog back across the road, the heavy flow of cars stopping to let him across. "Only a man of God could get the Christmas shopping traffic to part like that."

"Ha, yeah. They must have a direct line or something." Andy followed his brother to the front of the crowd to inform them about the offer of the church. Like little sheep, they all turned on their heels and scampered, the women shielding their heads with handbags, trying to stop their carefully straightened hair frizzing in the increasingly blizzardous conditions.

"Have you seen Alice anywhere?" Dan asked, scanning the herd as they moved away and disappeared from view.

"No, can't say I have."

"Best tell the fire brigade. She might still be inside." He was trying not to worry; after all, he'd checked before they left, and she was nowhere to be found. But then it hit him.

She wouldn't have been at her desk at the time. She'd have been making tea and coffee for the meeting.

"Excuse me," Dan said, approaching the nearest firefighter. "I think one of the administrators is still inside. On the first floor. There's a coffee room just on the left, second exit off the main corridor. That's where she said she was going."

"Thank you, sir," the firefighter responded and shouted across to one of the others, "There may be someone on the first floor in the coffee room." The other firefighter nodded and they both went to the engine to unload breathing apparatus from the back. Within less than a minute, they were entering the building, where the flames had now spread to all floors, virtually engulfing the entire left side.

"The coffee room is about—" Dan counted the windows "—there." He pointed at the fourth window from the left. It was one of the first to blow, and if Alice was in there, it was unlikely she was still alive.

Andy started to shiver, not used to the cold at all. "Shall we go over to the church?" he suggested.

"You go. Let me know if Alice is in there. Maybe we just missed her. I'll wait here and see what's happening."

"All right, bro." Andy patted Dan's shoulder and left him in the cold to wait for news.

Inside the church wasn't much better, but it was out of the wind and the snow, and that was enough to make it feel warmer in of itself. A woman in a tea-cosy hat brought a polystyrene cup over and handed it to him.

"There you are, love." She smiled kindly. Andy thanked her, his breath joining the steam rising from the hot, pale liquid in the cup. He looked all around him and was certain Alice wasn't there.

***

James opened the door and took a deep breath. Oliver came running to greet him.

"Daddy. I made a card. Look." He was absolutely covered in red and green paint, but he was so happy and excited about what he had done that James laughed as he took the wet card from him.

"Oliver. It's lovely. Thank you very much."

"Look, Daddy. Writing. It says Oliver."

"Oh, yes. So it does."

James rubbed his son's head tenderly, trying to balance the paint on the card whilst it did its best to run off the sides and onto his hand.

Eleanor was standing in the doorway to the living room, holding a tray with pots of paint, a tumbler of greyish-black water, and several paintbrushes.

"You've been having fun again, I can see. Without me. We will have to do something about that."

"We've had lots of fun, haven't we, Oliver?" Eleanor said, glancing up at the snow stuck in James's hair and glistening like stars in the night sky. She met his gaze, sensing that something was different; he wasn't going to leave her. She didn't know how she knew; she just did.

"Let's go and get cleaned up for dinner," James commanded his son and received total obedience. On the way past the living room, he paused and leaned over the tray, kissing Eleanor slowly on the lips.

"I love you, Eleanor Davenport. Just say the word. One word, that's all."

"Yes," she said. She waited for the usual reaction, but it didn't come. "Yes," she said again, laughing, "I will marry you."

James closed his eyes and opened them again. "You are still here. I am so pleased. I had to check I wasn't dreaming. I can't imagine you not being here."

"Nor I, you. Your son is still waiting."

James looked down at Oliver, who was standing right next to him, peering up into his face and grinning from ear to ear.

"Did you hear that, Oliver?"

"Enna is like a mummy now," Oliver said, and Eleanor's heart did a flip in her chest. She felt the tears start to fall and watched through the glittery droplets as her two men went, hand in painty hand, to the bathroom.

Chapter Twenty-Four: Out

When they found Alice, she was lying unconscious under a table on the ground floor. Later, she explained that she had climbed through a hatch into the air-conditioning system and followed it along the wall, down to an opening in the basement. She'd hit the floor with force but somehow crawled back up the stairs, to the offices on the ground floor. At that point, she had become so disorientated by the smoke and fumes, she could go no further. She had fallen, unconscious and on her knees, and rolled under a table, overpowered by the fumes—more on a synaesthetic level than through smoke inhalation, although she had inhaled some smoke, of course. However, it looked like a bang on the head had knocked her out, rather than anything else being responsible for her predicament.

The loss of consciousness may well have saved her life; had she tried to go any further, she'd have crawled right into the path of a stream of flames, which tore through the stairwells and destroyed the top staircase. She was so lucky, in fact, that she didn't even need hospitalising; a couple of hours on oxygen and she was ready to go home, with a head X-ray booked for the following morning just to be sure there was no skeletal damage from roller-coastering her way through air vents.

Dan insisted on driving Alice home. He wouldn't let her get a cab, and he was very reluctant to leave her at home alone—or alone apart from Albert—but she wanted to be there. Now that her place of employment had been destroyed, she only had her house, and in a way, she was pleased about that, for it meant she officially no longer worked for Campion Holdings PLC. Yet it had been a such a significant part of her life for so long that the thought of never going there again was almost too much—harder to comprehend, even, than Mr. Campion's death.

Now she had to get through a double bereavement and move on with her life, and it was time to start trying new things, the first of which was caring for baby Shaunna for three afternoons a week, while Adele worked in the fitness centre's beauty clinic. On occasion, Alice might be needed during the evening, but the rest of her time was her own. She'd always fancied taking up pottery, and the college ran classes on a Monday. Then there was the operatic society on a Tuesday. True, she'd never worked evenings. But getting involved in anything like that had proved impossible, even when she was younger and had more energy. That said, she had a feeling her lethargy related more to doing a job she hadn't enjoyed for many years than it did her age.

They arrived back at the house, and Dan carried Alice's bag inside for her. It contained the smoke-fumed clothes she had been wearing at work. He had already collected a velour top and pants for her, or a 'leisure suit', as she'd referred to it when he offered to get her a change of clothes. He'd been about to ring Adele to ask what one was, when he was suddenly struck by the memory of one particular occasion when his mum had referred to his favourite tracksuit as a 'leisure suit' in front of his friends from sixth form. It took a long time to live that one down.

"Now, Alice. You have my number, and the number at the flat."

"Yes, Dan. Thank you. And Adele's number and Andy's, too, but I'm sure I will be perfectly fine. The hospital gave me their number, as well, so in the event that I should find myself in need of conversation, I have plenty of people to choose from."

"OK. Point taken. But we're just down the road, so ring if you need us. Really."

"I will," Alice assured him. She allowed him to see her inside and settled on the couch; just as soon as he was gone, she was going to make a nice cup of tea and go to bed.

It had been quite a day, what with the fire, and having accidentally sent her resignation to the entire office on the internal mail system. She'd always thought she was above that sort of silly mistake, and wondered if a small part of her hadn't done it intentionally. It was lucky she had really, otherwise it would have burned with the rest of the documents on her computer. At the time, she was so overwhelmed by the colourful arrival of the Jeffries brothers that she couldn't quite see what she was doing, and the 'bulletin' button was right next to the 'private mail' button.

Albert was quiet tonight, as if he knew his mistress did not have the patience to put up with his chattering. Still, she wouldn't have minded a quick conversation about the day before she changed his water, topped up his seed and covered his cage for the night.

The peace was glorious; not even a noise from the snow-muffled street outside. Alice took her cup to the bedroom, closed the curtains and snuggled down between the covers. Her head was very sore, though not sufficiently so to keep her awake. It was, she considered, the third time she had almost been fatally injured since Mr. Campion's death. Maybe she should tell someone in authority. She'd ask Dan what he thought, when he came to take her to the hospital in the morning. He would know just what to do. The thought faded out of consciousness, and she drifted off to sleep, leaving the tea on the side to go cold.

***

Dan drove home very slowly, with the radio on low. The fire had made him think long and hard about how lucky he was. First the stabbing, and then to have nearly lost Adele and the baby—even before that, they had wasted too much time apart. The thought that he could have left them both today made him realise just how important they were to him.

As soon as Oliver was in bed, James tidied the remaining strips of paper and stray paint splashes from the living room and waited for Eleanor to return from the bedroom. She'd had a shower and smelled of lilies, her hair twisted up into a towel to allow it to dry. She came in and sat next to him on the sofa. He couldn't help but pull the towel from her head; her aromatic, wet hair fell against his shirt and soaked it.

"Ratbag," she said and scooped it back into the towel again. James didn't care. He delved into his pocket and found the ring he had been carrying for over a week, desperate for the time when he could slide it onto her finger. Finally, it had arrived.

"I wanted to ask you properly last weekend, when we were at the lodge," Dan explained, taking Adele's tiny, slender hand in his own.

"I'm sorry I put you through such a terrible ordeal the other day. I was wrong to think that it was the right time."

"It *was* the right time, James. My fault not yours."

"We were so late arriving, and then we missed the booking in the restaurant. All my plans—well, they didn't go according to plan."

"Are you blaming me for that, Dan?"

"No, of course not. I was just trying to explain why I'm doing this now."

"Eleanor, I wanted to do this the right way, on one knee as is tradition, so here goes."

"It's not the most romantic setting in the world, but you know what it's like. Between looking after Shaunna, and work, and all this with Alice today. Beggars can't be choosers."

Down on bended knee, small children sleeping nearby, one of the most important events in someone's life, passing like a normal night in front of the TV.

"Will you marry me?"

Eleanor held her hand as steadily as she could, and James slowly, gently pushed the ring up her finger and into place. The stones reflected the lights from the tree, making them dance in their eyes.

"No. I can't. I'm sorry."

"Yes. I said yes already. Didn't I? I was so sure I…"

"I don't understand. You said it was all you wanted."

"When I was like twelve, maybe."

"But we're together already. What's the problem? You were keen enough to marry Tom."

Dan stood up again and rubbed his hand through his hair, embarrassed and confused.

James stood up and pulled Eleanor to her feet, taking her in his arms. A jazz ballad began to play, and they danced slowly around the room, the music filling the moment and transporting them to another place.

***

Kris had been dreading telling Shaunna, unsure whether it would have been better to tell her how he was feeling generally, or to come clean about the affair.

She reacted the way she did to everything: she filled the kettle. Otherwise, she had no idea how to respond, what to say, or how she was supposed to feel. If he hadn't been distant while he'd been ill, it might have been different, but she was used to being on her own, and she didn't feel anything at all.

Their relationship had worked so well for so long—was she at fault for allowing Kris to create the illusion in the first place? When Krissi decided she needed to know who her biological father was, Shaunna's reluctance to encourage her was for precisely this reason. It was never about not wanting to know. It was what knowing would do to their marriage. Kris had been what she wanted and needed him to be, not who he was. In time, it had become an impossible illusion to maintain, and he had cracked, the real him emerging, blind and startled, from his broken shell. That was when it happened. Not now, when he was talking about this other person.

She wanted to ask about Jack. She wanted to know who he was, whether he was being good to her Kris. Her Kris? No more. The game was over, and the best thing she could do was let him go.

There were times, when Shaunna looked back and really thought about it, that she could see Kris had struggled to be her husband. He'd played the part, like he played the other parts in his work, but every so often, the mask slipped. She'd catch him watching George with such intensity, and she'd tried to pretend it wasn't desire. But there was looking, and there was acting on it. Had Kris and George done anything since school? Just the thought of it made her angry. It was one thing for Kris to be telling her about his secret life with Jack—in George's house. She could hold herself partly responsible for that. But if it had been happening even before he met Jack, then that was very different.

Had she ever wanted to ask him? If so, she couldn't understand why she hadn't acted upon it. Maybe it was because she didn't want to know. Living a lie for the past fourteen months she could handle; for the past twenty-two years not so much. So she chose to believe that he was telling the truth—that this thing with Jack was new.

Unthinking, she stirred several spoonfuls of sugar into both cups of tea. She needed chocolate. And she needed it now. There was usually a bar in the cupboard where she stored the teabags, but the cupboard was bare, and it was freezing outside. At any other time, she might have tried to turn on the feminine charm and persuade Kris, but that wasn't going to work anymore. And then it came to her that perhaps it had never worked. It had all been part of the act, and it made her cry.

Kris didn't know what he should do. This was his fault, and nothing he could say was going to make it better. He wanted to hug her, to hold her close and tell her it would all be OK, like he had when she found out she was pregnant...when he made the decision to become the man he had been for all this time. It wasn't an act. Not entirely. He loved Shaunna and he desired her. She was a very beautiful woman, but if he didn't let her go, she would be wasted on him and his pathetic fling.

Was Jack going through the exact same thing right now with his wife? Was he watching as her world was shredded to tatters around her, powerless to do anything that could take back who he was, who he needed to be? Or was Jack still living the lie in cowardice, leaving Kris to risk a life alone and making him break Shaunna for nothing?

Whether Jack told his wife was irrelevant. The deed had been done. He couldn't go on with the deception, and that was all there was to it. He'd had to tell her, he'd always known.

She rejoined him at the table and placed a cup in front of him. "I think I put a lot of sugar in these. I don't know. I wanted chocolate, but there isn't any. I can't remember which cup is yours, and I've lost my bracelet in the teabags…" She talked until she ran out of breath.

"It's OK. Would you like me to go and get some chocolate?"

"No." She burst into tears again. "I don't really need chocolate. And it's cold outside."

Kris lifted his hand to smooth the stray strands of red hair from her face, where they were sticking to her tears. He had always loved to lift her hair from her neck, but that was before. He dropped his hand to the table and swallowed back his own tears. This was so awful, and he wished he were dead. Right now, that was the only thing he believed would take away the dreadful ache inside.

***

Alas, Jack was back at home, living the dream, or the lie, that was his life, with little intention of bringing it to an end. It wasn't that he didn't care for Kris; he did. It was just that to tell her was to make it public for the first time. He knew the radio station wouldn't care one way or the other. But he'd seen—and been a part of—far too many media seek-and-destroy missions. He would not survive such an ordeal himself and could only hope Kris would understand.

Chapter Twenty-Five:
By the Fire

There was no fracture in Alice's skull, she was pleased to hear, although her eyes were so swollen and black that she thought she'd rather enjoy a fractured skull instead if it meant she looked a little more normal.

Dan waited outside the X-ray department until she was finished and drove her home once again. There was something that troubled him about all of this. First, there was the car, which he'd originally put down to mechanical failure. The garage hadn't noticed anything out of the ordinary, although they weren't really going to be looking for it. Even when it broke down a third time—with a leaky brake cylinder—he still accepted it was just an old car nearing the end of its life. But now, on top of the car, there was the fire.

According to his contacts, the fire had been traced back to a bin in the coffee room, and it had been started intentionally. It was remarkable that Alice had escaped, and for all the world it was starting to look like she wasn't meant to; that in fact, the whole point of the fire was to make sure that she, of all people, didn't.

Now, why would that be? Sure, Alice could be annoying sometimes—obsessive, picky, overly curious—but she was harmless. There was a lot about this that didn't add up, but Dan didn't like to say in case he frightened her, so he dropped her back at home without a word, and then went to meet up with Andy at the shopping mall, where their first job as partners was nicely taking shape.

***

Josh had long since finished reading the news report about the Campion Holdings fire, but it was continuing to preoccupy him to such an extent that he couldn't have said what was on the pages that followed even if his life depended on it. He wondered who the target was—not that the paper had mentioned arson—but that was how Josh's mind worked. If George had been around, he'd have shared his thoughts on the matter, but George had stayed away, and that got Josh thinking, too. Hadn't he said something about it being complicated? At the time, Josh hadn't asked, because the police had arrived shortly afterwards, and he'd totally forgotten about it until now.

He contemplated giving George a call, to see if he fancied meeting up for a coffee, but quickly changed his mind. It was only two days since he'd seen him, and it would send out entirely the wrong signal. *Oh, balls to that.* They'd known each other long enough to be past accidentally misinterpreting each other's intentions.

However, it was the first day he'd been on his own for ages. He had no appointments, no lectures and nowhere to be. As far as he could tell, everything was well with Ellie, simply because she hadn't phoned to say otherwise. He could even go into town and do the rest of his Christmas shopping. *Yes, a trip to Gadget Heaven is definitely on the cards.* He folded up the newspaper, finished his coffee and grabbed his keys and jacket, swapping the jacket for a coat as an afterthought.

It was ridiculously busy at the shopping mall, with a queue of about twenty cars waiting to go into the multistorey car park. Had he planned in advance, he'd have parked at his surgery and walked the rest of the way. The gifts he bought tended not to be bulky, but now it was too late, because he was stuck in the queue and wouldn't have been able turn around in the narrow road even if he'd been the only one trying to do so. There was nothing for it but to wait it out.

He turned on the radio and tuned in to the first station he found playing Christmas music, hoping to get himself in the mood. Each time another car passed by, the radio signal faded out and in again, and he was picking up the local taxi transmissions, which started to get a bit irritating after ten minutes of sitting with the engine idling, having only moved forward by about the length of three cars. It was a stupid idea, but he was here now, and it had to be done.

Finally, after a further ten minutes, he started to climb the spiral ramp through the levels of the car park and knew from past experience that the fourth level, far right corner, always had a spot that didn't look like a space, so he headed straight for it. He wasn't disappointed. He parked up and walked diagonally back across to the lifts and stairs.

People everywhere: families out in full, now many of the schools had broken up; old people tottering along with bags dangling from arms and trolleys. It wasn't going to be a whole lot of fun getting through the hordes. In the middle of the main floor, there was a cordoned-off area, with workmen in hard hats, taking measurements but otherwise doing very little. He did a double-take. The man closest to him looked like Dan, and on second glance, Josh was certain it was. But he was determined; however much he loathed shopping, he was doing it today, so he left saying hello for after he'd done his shopping.

Gadget Heaven was one of the shops closest to the lifts Josh had taken. He knew because he spent so much time in there and always made for the quickest in-browse-purchase-out procedure. Even so, it took much longer than usual to reach the shop, as Santa's grotto was between him and where he needed to be, and hundreds of shoppers had stopped to admire the full festive montage designed precisely to attract their attention. Children only needed to see the words 'Santa's Grotto'—even those who couldn't read could pick out the letters from a mile away—but adults needed mechanical elves, fake snow, fairy lights and as much other tat as it was possible to dump in fifty square feet of walkway.

The new owners of the shopping mall were spending a great deal of money on renovation work and security, but as far as Josh could tell, most of the decorations were recycled from previous displays. There were still the mechanical elves—those were mandatory—and there was still fake snow—also mandatory—and various other gaudy accoutrements, but it had been organised with a little more thought for aesthetics, which weren't mandatory, not at Christmas. It was the only time when the tasteless and tacky became the pinnacle of style.

"I take it you're not queueing to see Santa?" a female voice asked from just behind Josh's left shoulder, and he turned around to see who the enquirer was. A tired-looking woman with two small children in a double buggy looked at him hopefully.

"No. I was just admiring the display, if admiring is the word for it. I'll get out of your way. Sorry." He smiled apologetically and sidestepped to his right, squeezing through all the other childrenless adults blocking the route, doing exactly what he had been doing. He felt tremendously guilty, as if his and their lack of consideration was stealing Christmas from babes. To Gadget Heaven, then.

It wasn't a lot less crowded inside the shop, and Josh made a quick analysis of the types of people he was competing with for the sales assistants' attention. If it were not the truth, he'd have felt bad for judging, but the place was full of women trying to find gifts for men, and men buying gifts for themselves or their other male relatives. Of course, there were always going to be exceptions to the rule, but generally, even women who liked gadgets were much easier to buy for and tended to get the usual battery of confectionery and toiletries in their stockings. Men, in spite of their collective claim that a monogrammed handkerchief would do nicely, thank you, liked to get things they could play with, if only for the duration of the festive season.

Josh always liked to theme his gifts in some way, and he'd been having a real problem this year, which was why he'd left the shopping excursion to the last week before Christmas and ignored his stomach lurching every time someone on the TV or elsewhere struck another day off the Shopping Days 'til Christmas countdown calendar. Now, wandering up and down the shop, examining the contents of each cabinet, interrogating his memory for clues of what each of his friends liked, he had to decide, because there was no way he was coming back again, not in this madness. It was today, or not at all. *Gift vouchers?* No, they were a cop-out.

He moved on to a display in the corner, consisting of the types of toys that could well have been manufactured by Santa and his automated assistants before they departed from the North Pole. *Not very gadget-like*, he thought, picking up a small, wooden helicopter, which looked like a bunch of ice-lolly sticks bound together with rubber bands. On closer inspection, he concluded that it was exactly that; he glanced up at the sign over the display. *Eco Toys.*

That's it! That's my theme!

Now on with the shopping.

Josh started at the beginning of the maze around the shop again, this time looking for anything that could be construed as eco-friendly, soon realising it was going to be easier than he'd expected, because there was a full range of solar-powered gadgets on display across the back wall, so it was simply a matter of finding them in the shop. He looked to see what the sales assistants were up to, but none of them were free, so he soldiered on alone.

A solar-powered talking bible: that was Ellie sorted in record time and first to cross off his mental list.

A solar reading lamp that clipped onto the edge of books and could be adjusted for even the thinnest of volumes—he wouldn't have minded one of those himself, so he knew Jess would love it, and it would be great for Kris, too, for reading his scripts on the journey home from work, once he was ready to return to it.

Solar wind chimes. Now, personally, he hated wind chimes, although Shaunna's garden was filled with them—wooden ones, metal tubed ones, even a set of little coloured birds designed to clang together harmoniously, whatever the weather. The solar-powered edition was nothing special, other than with solar power they tweeted too, but they would suit Adele, who had started her own collection during the summer and didn't have anywhere near as many as Shaunna.

A slight variation: wind chimes that projected rainbow colours onto nearby surfaces. And there, on the shelf above, was a solar-powered Ferris wheel, with little carriages lit in different colours. Krissi's fascination with fairgrounds made that absolutely the best choice for her. Other than baby Shaunna, that was the girls sorted.

The sensible people who owned the shop had thought to arrange everything in handy gender-biased sections, Josh realised, as he moved along the shelves, peering into the large, cylindrical baskets filled with smaller items, such as a car, and an amphibious vehicle—for Dan and Andy—and a pair of solar racers—he could see Oliver and James, and even Ellie, having hours of fun with those. With just George and the baby to buy for, it was starting to look like Josh could be out of there in less than an hour.

George was always difficult, because he didn't really like anything. He had no hobbies, no interesting collections. He didn't have a games console, because Josh had a collection, and the only time he played was when they were together. His phone was a recent purchase, although the number of times the battery was flat and he'd left the charger at home made Josh wonder whether he should just buy him a spare battery or…

"A solar-powered gadget charger. Excellent."

Back to the workshop toys, then, all of them as unimpressive as the lolly-stick helicopter, although it was admirable how the toy manufacturers had almost convincingly recycled rubbish to make them. Josh blew air out of his nose and moved his shopping basket to the other arm; it was becoming too heavy to hold. He stared into space, trying to think of what a one-year-old could possibly want that was recycled, solar-powered or constructed from managed forests. *What do one-year-olds even think about?* But then he spied it. A clockwork 'My First Radio' at the bottom of the basket. *Perfect.*

Into the cordoned queueing area for the final stretch, other purchasers were delayed while assistants searched for the right size of batteries for the gifts. Josh felt smug, with his impossibly heavy basket of batteryless buys now resting at his feet, allowing him to nudge it forward each time someone else made it to the tills. Other than wrapping paper, he had all he needed. He hated the wrapping even more than the shopping but felt he hadn't put as much effort as he ought into choosing the gifts, so reluctantly rejected the assistant's offer to gift-wrap his purchases for him.

Ten minutes later, armed with three full bags, Josh pushed his way through Santa's congregation, made a beeline for the nearest shop that sold wrapping paper and bought a pack of five rolls. His fingers were turning blue with the weight of the bags, and the workmen were still in the mini construction site—still doing nothing that looked like construction—so he made a quick detour, seeing as there was a coffee shop just by where they were.

"I thought it was you," Josh called across to Dan.

"Hey, Josh. Ah. I can see what you've been up to. Had fun?"

"Oh, without a doubt," he said wryly. "So, what's happening here?"

"Cabling in the new security system after Christmas. We're checking the existing power supplies and whatnot."

"Good stuff. Is that… It is! I didn't know you were back home!" Josh had spotted Andy amongst the other men.

"Alright, mate? How are you?"

"I'm fine, thanks. I don't know. You come home for Christmas and he's got you working."

"Ha, yeah. That would be par for the course, but Dan and I are working together on this one, aren't we, bro?"

"Sure are. You're looking at Jeffries and Associates."

"Oh!" Josh was stunned and didn't know what else to say. "Congratulations."

"Cheers. By the way—" Dan took off his hard hat and gave his head a quick scratch "—did you see the news about Campion's?"

"I did. It looked nasty."

"We were in a meeting when the alarm went off. Something very dodgy going on there."

"Really?"

"I reckon. Anyway, must get on."

"Me, too. See you later, guys." Josh waved the lightest of his bag-laden arms as he moved away in the direction of the coffee shop. Andy and Dan simultaneously raised a hand in acknowledgement and then returned to instructing their crew.

As he meandered his way through the crowds and back to the car park, Josh pondered the new development. *When did Andy get home? Is it for good? And where has this Jeffries and Associates nonsense suddenly come from?* The idea of Dan and Andy working together as partners wasn't something Josh could see succeeding in the long term, not with them both vying for the role of alpha male. God knew, it had caused enough trouble in the past.

With immense relief, Josh pushed through the doors to the car park and started the trek across the darkened level, with its square concrete columns, fuel-fumed through-draught and the constant hum of engines. *How does one go about laying cable in a construction like this?* He wouldn't even know where to begin. Dan had always said he admired Josh for his intellect, but he was only book-clever, and it was typical of Dan to understate his own talents. That had always been a part of the problem with him and Andy. Maybe he was finally starting to believe in his own worth for real, instead of putting on an act.

Josh loaded his shopping into the boot and gave his hands a rub. It was freezing in the car park, although the change of weather had more or less turned any remaining snow to grey slush. Even so, apart from his hands, he was quite warm, from the physical effort of walking so far with heavy bags. He got in the car, and allowed himself a moment to relax with his takeaway coffee, before putting on his seat belt and starting the engine for the slow-stop journey home again.

***

It was Oliver's last day before returning to Birmingham, and James and Eleanor wanted to make it special. She also needed to introduce James to her parents and had been trying to pluck up the courage to suggest a visit at the weekend. At the same time, she had an inkling that taking Oliver with them would work in her favour, because her mother loved children. It might just distract her sufficiently for Eleanor to quickly slip in, 'This is James, we're engaged, and he's coming for Christmas.' There was no need to mention that they'd been together for a year already.

She also didn't really understand why she hadn't told her mother before now. It would have been far less of a shock, not to mention avoiding the entirely predictable lecture about jumping into a relationship. Because she hadn't jumped into a relationship, ever—not since her ex, anyway. That was the turning point for Eleanor on that score; it had fallen apart so easily and so amicably, but they'd gone straight from their training into wedding plans and mortgages, and it was easier to go along with it than call off the wedding.

With Oliver having already wrapped presents, made cookies and painted Christmas cards, it was proving far harder than they imagined to come up with something special to do. The only thing left was visiting Santa's grotto, and Eleanor had just received a text message from Josh, lamenting his trip to the mall. There was always the department store; the grotto there was a lot more tasteful and generally less busy. It was also close to her parents' house and would kill two birds with one stone.

"James. I was thinking. We could go up to see you-know-who at the department store."

"That sounds like a wonderful idea. I think that someone would like to see you-know-who." James was playing with Oliver's building blocks and replied without looking up. Between them, they had made an impressive city of skyscrapers.

"And then we could go and see my mum and dad and tell them about us," she added, as if James wouldn't notice if she did it quickly. He stopped mid-build, with a little blue brick in his hand, and turned to face her.

"That is what we shall do today." He said it so seriously that even Oliver stopped to see what the matter under discussion was.

Eleanor had already been introduced to James's parents, who were very polite and welcoming. His father was an older, more distinguished version of his son, with hair greying at the temples and a stronger Afro-Caribbean accent, but otherwise, they were alike in every way. He, too, referred to her as 'El-e-a-nor' and it sounded equally as charming, but she couldn't get past the distance between him and his wife and son; even now—retired and at home—he spent so much time in quiet solitude that she could see exactly why James would have gone off the rails.

Mrs. Brown was lovely. She was taller than Eleanor, with her hair braided in long, thin plaits scooped back in a loosely tied headscarf and weighted with black beads that jangled musically against each other whenever she moved. She adored James and was a very tactile person, which Eleanor eventually got used to, but initially it had made her feel uncomfortable.

James didn't notice how much his mother did it—smoothing an arm as she passed, taking hold of a hand at the dinner table, kissing the tops of heads if they were sitting and she was standing. It was only later, when Eleanor pointed it out, that he had to agree that his mother was, on occasion, embarrassingly open with affection. It made the pairing of the Browns a very strange one indeed.

That introduction was some time ago, when Eleanor and James had first got together, and there wasn't even the slightest hint that it was a long-term relationship, although James's mother had been certain from the start, because her son did not 'date' women. He was faithful and steady, and chose his companions with great care. Therefore, if he was bringing a woman to her house, then it was the beginning of an enduring partnership.

So, just Eleanor's parents to deal with, and there was no time like the present, seeing as James hadn't protested, which she was slightly disappointed about. Still, it was preferable to do it now, rather than delay until Christmas Eve, when it wouldn't just be her mother she had to contend with, but Ben and the others as well. It was only really Ben who mattered, because it was only he who was likely to be upfront enough to say exactly what he thought, and that was before the alcohol started flowing. After a few drinks, it could go either way.

Oliver, being a very perceptive child, had caught the gist of the conversation and tidied his bricks into their box without prompting. James helped him finish up, and Eleanor went to get their coats. It was a horrible day and too far to walk to her parents', so they were going in the car.

A quick check that she looked reasonably presentable—James and Oliver were *always* presentable—and they were on their way. Her stomach churned over and over, and a couple of times, she thought she might need to ask to stop the car. But then she twisted the ring on her finger, and the thought that it was all worth it helped to calm her down. At some point, she would need to tell James about her self-inflicted health problems, but for now, it could wait.

The department store was also packed, although with consumers of a very different breed to those Josh had encountered in the mall. Here, middle-class women and older people sprayed perfumes, tested out facial products and carted little nylon baskets of gloves and other small, stereotypical gifts for the relative strangers who made up their families. That was how many of Eleanor's friends had been brought up, Josh in particular—raised by his grandmother after his parents died, hence his traditional, even old-fashioned dress sense and attitude to life in general. George's mother, as far as she could tell, was very much of this type, too; Dan and Andy had aspired to it but didn't quite make the grade. Their mother was on her fourth husband, the last one having been dispatched by Jess right at the start of her solo career. It wasn't the mother's fault, really. She just kept picking the lying, cheating bastards who wanted her for her perpetual good looks and figure.

Visits to The Grotto were technically by appointment only, but seeing as this was Tom's store and he held no grudge against Adele's friends—who had all been very supportive during the break-up—he let Eleanor, James and Oliver through at the next available slot.

And what a grotto it was! They entered through a large wooden door with a significant brass door knob and letterbox, behind which was a sack spilling carefully prepared letters from children onto the floor. On the wall was a chalkboard divided into two halves, with 'Naughty' and 'Nice' at the top of each section. The naughty column was empty.

Moving on, they followed a winding pathway that glistened and crunched under foot, like real snow, and it was chilly enough to be the real deal, making magical mist of their breath. On each side of the path were little workshops staffed by elves, some fixing toys together, others wrapping up small square boxes in plain paper, like brown parcel paper, but in red or green.

Further on still, they came to the reindeer stables, where the sound of animals moving around and grunting could be heard, each door carrying a reindeer's name on a small brass plate decorated with mistletoe and holly. Over the top of the last stable door, a pair of antlers were visible, slowly lifting as the head turned to face the people passing by. It was Rudolph, with his distinctive nose and a mouthful of hay.

They reached the inner sanctum: a small enclosure that looked a lot like the downstairs floor of George's old house on the ranch, except that here, there was a roaring log fire; next to it was a small, round bucket of logs and a pile of open letters. In front of the fire was a rocking chair, in which sat a large man dressed all in red. He picked up a letter opener, carefully slit the top of an envelope, and took out the paper contained within, laughing jollily as he read. Even for adults, it was absolutely enthralling. Santa turned slowly to greet his newest visitors.

Having been through this with her younger siblings, nephews and nieces, Eleanor knew that for as much as it was an amazing, unmissable experience, Santa had the capacity to terrify the life out of small children. But not this one. Oliver stood, silent and observant, his mouth wide open in awe.

"Hello, there," Santa said kindly. "Now who do we have here? Is this little Oliver Brown?"

James and Eleanor nodded slowly. Oliver didn't move a muscle.

"How nice it is to see you, young Oliver. Why don't you come over and have a warm by the fire."

Eleanor and James stepped forward. Oliver didn't. They pushed him gently, enough for him to understand that it was all right to do as requested. He went towards the outstretched arms of Santa, his eyes flitting between the fire and the round, kindly face of the man in the rocking chair.

"There. That's much better, isn't it? It's so cold outside. Now then, Oliver, my chief elf tells me that you've been a very good boy this year. Is that correct?" Oliver looked to his father, who nodded. Oliver mimicked the movement.

"Santa," Oliver uttered.

"Ho ho. That's right," Santa replied warmly.

Eleanor and James watched on while Santa talked quietly to Oliver about what he wanted for Christmas, and the importance of making sure his mummy and daddy had a lovely time. It was captivating, and they themselves were tingling with excitement. James squeezed Eleanor's hand, and she fell against him, the worries of the imminent visit to her parents temporarily suspended, along with the rest of reality.

Santa reached inside a sack to the left of his chair and found a small, neatly wrapped gift, which he handed to Oliver.

"Thank you," Oliver said.

"My pleasure," Santa replied. "Now you have a wonderful Christmas, all four of you." He smiled at Eleanor and James, and then carefully returned to his letters so that they knew it was time to go without feeling they had been pushed out. They turned back the way they had come and left Santa to his work.

Chapter Twenty-Six: Just a Man in a Suit

Josh phoned Dan in advance to check he was in, which he was, and arranged to pick up George on the way. The slush at the edges of the road was turning to ice, making corners a bit hairy to navigate, but Dan's remark about the fire at Campion's had caught Josh's attention. If it had been started deliberately, they needed to know, for Eleanor's, and James's sake.

George was ready and waiting, watching through his living room window, from which he disappeared as Josh pulled up outside. The lights went out, and he emerged from the house, looking ready for a trek through the Andes.

"I know it's cold, George, but bloody hell! Do you think you might be overdoing it a bit there?"

"Oh, it's all right for you, with your lovely warm car. Some of us have to walk everywhere!"

"Good point. We never did get around to those driving lessons, did we?"

"No. *You* didn't. Now, what's this about a fire at Campion's?"

"Dan thinks it was started on purpose."

George looked puzzled.

"Don't you read the papers? Obviously not. Right. There was a fire at Campion's yesterday. Dan and Andy were there—"

"Andy? Since when has he been home?"

"A few days, I think. That's another story. Anyway, they were at Campion's when the alarm went off. No-one was seriously hurt, but someone's told Dan it was arson."

"Ooh. How exciting!" George settled into the passenger seat to play out a few scenarios in his head on the way.

***

It had taken a while, but Adele had at last decided on a colour scheme for her Christmas decorations. She paused from hanging crystal tree ornaments to answer the door, still with several tiny shimmering balls dangling from her fingers.

"Come in," she said. "They're in there." She nodded towards the dining area, where Dan and Andy were leaning over the table, absorbed in whatever it was that they were doing. Josh and George went through, and Adele returned to her metallic lilac tree.

A blueprint was spread the entire length and breadth of the table, which wasn't small. Dan pointed at one corner of the paper. Andy took the pencil he had clenched between his teeth and marked where indicated.

"That looks like fun. Are they the plans for the mall?" Josh asked, taking his jacket off and hanging it on the back of a dining chair.

"They certainly are," Andy said. "We didn't think we'd get them until after Christmas, but now we can make a head start." His expansive enthusiasm was the kind he generally reserved for extreme sports.

"Time for a beer break?" Dan suggested. George nodded.

"Coffee for me, thanks," Josh said.

"Tea for me," Adele called from across the room. Dan went off to the kitchen and returned with three bottles, handed one each to Andy and George, put his own down on a window ledge, and left again to make the coffee and tea.

"So, this Jeffries and Associates malarkey," Josh said.

"Yeah. My idea actually," Andy admitted. "And we've already got two contracts—a third on the way."

"You don't waste any time."

"Ha. No. I'd had enough, and it was this or the dole."

"So long as you don't think you're going to spend every evening filling my dining table with drawings," Adele muttered, passing them on her way to the kitchen. She closed the door behind her, and the three men immediately launched into meaningless conversation so they couldn't hear what was taking place.

A short while later, Adele returned, carrying a box of lights and another bag of decorations; Dan followed her in with two mugs. He handed one to Josh and placed the other on a coaster on the nearest surface to Adele.

"There you go, *sweetie*," he hissed.

"Thank you." She gave him a false smile.

"They've been at it all day," Andy whispered to George and Josh, "and I think I know why. I'll tell you later."

Dan came back within earshot, huffed and snatched up his beer. "Bloody women. I've never figured out what they want. Especially *her*." He swigged half the bottle's contents in one go. "Right. The fire at Campion's…"

The fact that Dan blew so hot and cold probably had a lot to do with it, but as none of them wanted to get involved in a domestic just now—nor at any other time—they let him continue on this theme instead.

"If I mention the name 'Alice Friar', does it ring any bells?"

Josh and George looked at each other and shook their heads.

"Should it?" Josh asked.

"She was Campion's PA, a lovely woman, but—"

"Mad as a stick," Andy interjected.

"No, she's not. A little eccentric, maybe. If I thought she was insane, I wouldn't have suggested her as our new nanny. Adele's going back to work in the new year. Anyway, that's by the by. Anyone who's ever visited Campion Holdings or had any dealings with Alistair would have met Alice. They'd have also known that she spent a large part of her day in the coffee room. She'll tell you it's because the coffee machine always needed refilling, but actually, it's the hub of activity, gossip central.

"Needless to say, that was where she was when the fire started. More than that, the fire started in the bin, an accelerant was used, and whoever planted it had to know she was in there."

George and Josh exchanged knowing looks.

"You were right, then," George said.

"Looks that way."

Dan frowned. "Right about?"

"First, there was Alistair's murder. After James was released from custody, he came and told us he thought he was being set up by one of the young offenders Campion used to employ. But then Sean Tierney—a psychologist at the hospice—was poisoned with paracetamol.

"I didn't connect the two things at first, but I spoke to Sean, and after going on and on about confidentiality and a whole load of other pompous bollocks, he confirmed that Alistair and his wife were both his patients."

"Oh. I get you," Andy said. "You think someone's trying to shut them up."

"Precisely."

"But why? What d'you think they know?" Dan asked, running his fingers over his chin and subconsciously thinking he might need to shave again before he went to bed.

"That's the bit we haven't figured out yet," George said.

"No." Josh continued. "And Sean couldn't think of anything that Alistair had said that might be some kind of industrial secret, not that he was giving anything away."

"Is that who you were talking to?" George asked. "In the park?"

"Yes. Arsehole, he is." Josh could feel himself snarling just thinking about it.

The four of them fell silent for a few minutes, the only sound the perpetual bubbling of the carp pool, interspersed with the jangling of little silver bells being placed here and there on the branches of the tree.

George thought the decorations were beautiful. He made a mental note to tell Adele so, when the opportunity presented itself.

"See. I can't honestly think of anything Campion had been working on that could be this valuable," Dan said thoughtfully. "The cable industry isn't exactly at the forefront of innovation these days. It's all pretty boring, run-of-the-mill stuff. Like this shopping mall job. Old technology. Back in the early days, Campion was working on new products, but that was a long time ago, well before I had any dealings with the company, which is what? Going on for ten years."

"So maybe it's something more personal than that," George suggested.

Josh nodded. "Whatever it is, I think it's the key to what's going on, and I'm hoping the police have realised that, too."

"I can ask Aitch about it, if you like," Dan suggested. "I'll give him a call tomorrow and see what I can get out of him."

"Aitch?" Josh asked.

"Henry Hartley," George reminded him. He'd been the mystery guest at The Party.

"That's Detective Inspector Hartley these days," Dan corrected. "I can't guarantee he'll tell me anything, mind."

"Well it's worth a try," Josh said. "Right. Are you ready, George? Only I'm at the university at nine in the morning, and I'm knackered."

"Give me a minute." George quickly finished his beer and put the bottle down on the table. Andy glared at him and snatched it up again.

"Andy's very precious about his plans," Dan said with a wink.

"It takes a long time to draw them up," Andy retorted, turning his glare on his brother, who raised his hands in a way that implied surrender, but not quite—exactly the kind of gesture that generally leads to bar-room brawls.

Josh picked up his jacket and started moving towards the door. "See you later. Give us a call if you find out anything."

That was the only trouble with visiting Dan. Between Adele, Dan and Andy, there was always bound to be some kind of disagreement going on and it was best to get out of the way as quickly as possible.

"Night," Dan called after them. Andy had already moved to let them out.

George stopped on the way to admire Adele's work. "That looks stunning," he said, and it really did. She'd just turned on the lights, which were pale yellow, rather than white, and placed behind the crystal ornaments, projecting little spectrums between the branches and cascading out across the room.

"Thanks, George." Adele climbed down from the stepladder and moved back to take a good look. She clapped her hands together excitedly.

Josh pushed George gently to move him on.

"Bye, then," he called back over his shoulder.

Andy followed them out and pulled the door to behind him, leaving his foot in the gap so he could get back in. "I'm pretty sure Dan proposed again last night, and Adele said no. He's been miserable as sin all day."

"Ah. That would explain it," Josh said. "I think James has proposed to Eleanor, too." He crossed his fingers.

"About time! I thought those two would never get it together."

"Yeah, they nearly didn't. See you later." Josh and George turned and walked out to the car, which had iced up again.

Andy waved and waited a moment, rubbing his arms. "I'm going back in. It's too damn cold out here."

"Tell me about it!" George said, scraping the windscreen, whilst Josh started the engine and turned on the blowers. The door closed and Andy disappeared from view. George gave the back window a very quick once-over and climbed in beside Josh.

"Tell me again how I'm overdoing it on the staying warm bit," he said through chattering teeth. He put his ice-cold hand against Josh's cheek.

"George!" Josh shouted and jerked away. He put the car in gear and moved off, very, very slowly.

***

Shaunna came back from visiting her dad in the rest home, which always sounded far worse in her head than it was in reality. It was a well-furnished, modern building, with large bedrooms, en-suite bathrooms, lounge, games room and self-catering facilities. It was very expensive, and the sale of her parents' house had covered most of the bills, but there were still other services—such as the in-house laundry and other housekeeping—that she was having to pay for from her own income. Her dad couldn't cook, either, and spent most of his pension on accompanying the female residents to bingo, pub lunches and indoor crown green bowling. She was pleased he was so active, but with Kris being sick, it had been a real stretch on the finances.

Now she was going to have to find a way of making up for the loss of all of his income, especially with Krissi making plans to move out. It would mean selling their own house, and that was just the start of it. She wasn't even sure she was entitled to half, seeing as Kris had paid the deposit and all of the mortgage for most of their 'married' life. She needed to talk to him, and it seemed so petty. He was taking the break-up hard enough already—not helped by the gradual withdrawal from his antidepressants—and trying to hold a practical conversation was going to be tricky.

They had yet to decide on other matters, such as who was going to sleep where. Last night, they had stayed together in their bed, holding on to each other until they both finally fell asleep. It wasn't anything like any other break-up, because it was so final and inevitable, and they still loved each other. That was what made it all so much worse.

Shaunna's feelings were swinging from hating him and wanting him to suffer, to wanting him to be happy, even if it cost her the house she had worked so hard to turn into a home. With each cycle around these thoughts, the tears would start again, and then she'd pull herself back together. It had to end somewhere.

When she arrived home, she found him sitting in the kitchen, poring over the local paper, looking for accommodation to rent. He had already made her a cup of tea, and there was a meal waiting in the oven, but she wasn't hungry. She sat in the chair opposite and unbuttoned her coat.

"How's Dad?" Kris asked, circling another ad.

"He's smashing. He's been to a Christmas dance this afternoon and had way too many sherries, but you know what he's like. That Florence, or whatever her name is, she's a dreadful flirt. I didn't know where to put my face. So what've you been up to?" It was a stupid question.

"I had no idea how expensive houses are. Flats aren't much better, so now I'm going through the bedsit section."

"Bedsits? Kris! You can't live in a bedsit."

"Why not?"

"I won't let you, for one."

"I don't have much choice, really, do I?"

"You do. I want you to stay."

Kris glanced up from the paper, briefly, and carried on. "Don't be silly. You know that's not going to work."

"Not like it is now, no. But I was thinking."

Kris exchanged the pencil for his tea and sat back so Shaunna could see she had his attention.

"All right. I wasn't thinking. It just came to me then, when I saw you circling that bedsit. Do you even know what Drummond Street is like? One of the customers lives down there and the stories she tells! You can't possibly live there, especially with—Jack."

"I won't be living anywhere with Jack. He's staying with his wife."

Shaunna instinctively reached out and took his hand.

"It's fine," he said. "Really. I don't love him. I have never loved anyone but you, but I can't be who I've tried to be any longer."

"Which is exactly my point. We've got two bedrooms, haven't we?"

"Yes."

"So we can still share the house and be friends. I know that sounds gooey, but I think we could actually make it work. On a selfish note, I can't afford to live here on my own, and I can't bear the thought of moving out."

"No. Neither can I. Do you really think we can do it? What about if we start dating other people?"

"We can cross that bridge later. What do you say? Do we have a deal?"

Kris thought for a moment and closed the newspaper.

"We have a deal."

***

It was an awful thing to say, but true. Oliver was the perfect excuse for escaping from her mother, and Eleanor was grateful. It was only the second time he'd decided to act up all week, because he was tired and it was late. He was asleep before the ice on the car had thawed and didn't even wake up when James carried him back into the house, only stirring slightly when his shoes were removed. James left him in his clothes and pulled the covers over him.

Eleanor delved inside her bag and quickly located her engagement ring, shoving it back onto her finger before James came back from putting Oliver to bed. She'd lost her nerve on the way to her parents' but didn't know how to tell James—she'd spent the entire visit hoping he didn't drop her in it.

James had noticed immediately what she had done and played along impeccably. So he was the new boyfriend, the implication being that they'd not been together very long, but Eleanor had at least conveyed that this was a serious relationship with a future, and her mother had been courteous, if not a little over-inquisitive.

There were no questions about the newspaper article to fend off, which was what surprised Eleanor the most. It was the one thing she'd been dreading from the outset, although there was still time for it to come up in conversation, which it undoubtedly would over the Christmas holiday. On that score, her mother assumed that she—and James—would be joining them all at Ben's. Eleanor confirmed that this was their plan and managed to cleverly steer the conversation in that direction, which kept her mother occupied for the rest of the evening.

The youngest of the Davenports, Peter, was still living at home, although as a typical twenty-one-year-old, he was somewhere around the point of finding his own place whilst at the same time delaying for as long as possible, fully aware of the benefits of living with his parents, even if it curtailed his freedom somewhat. Even as far as Eleanor was concerned, David was his 'roommate' from university, which was likely to remain the cover story until their parents had 'shuffled off this mortal coil'. Tolerance of difference was one thing. A life of what they saw as debauchery and sin was an entirely different matter.

"That wasn't so bad," Eleanor said, leaning gratefully against James's warm and delicious-smelling body.

"Indeed. It went exceptionally well, aside from Oliver's tantrum."

"Oh. He's been so good. And he was very tired."

"Yes, he was. I have left him in his clothes. His mother would not approve."

"He has clean ones for the morning, so what does it matter?"

"My thoughts also. Incidentally, I stand by your judgement."

"My judgement on what?"

"On not informing your parents of our engagement just yet. I would very much like to have been declared innocent beyond all reasonable doubt before they discover I am to be their son-in-law."

"I didn't know you... Sorry. I just couldn't stand her interrogation. It was bad enough as it was. And I'm sorry about that, too."

"She cares about you, Eleanor. Do not fret so." James stroked her hair. "I wanted to ask you something else, though."

"What?"

"Santa Claus."

"Oh, yes. That."

"What do you make of it?"

"He's just a man in a suit. What does he know?"

“Just a man in a suit. Yes, you are right.” James laughed.

But there was something so enchanting, so magical, about their visit to the department store’s grotto, that both of them couldn’t help but wonder if Santa Claus was more than just a man in a suit.

Chapter Twenty-Seven: Bubbling Past

Alice was waiting for the police to call and take her statement. She'd offered to go to the station, but the lovely policewoman had said that after the terrible ordeal she'd been through, she should stay home in the warm. Albert was happily chirruping away at his reflection, bobbing up and down and flirting, as he usually did, in time to the music playing quietly in the background. Alice had put on her favourite CD for this time of year: a selection of carols sung by a cathedral choir. She was feeling relaxed and content, and she had just started to doze when the police knocked at the door.

"Good morning, Miss Friar." PC Granger smiled. "May we come in?"

"Certainly," Alice said and carefully stepped aside. She had woken with quite a stiff neck, well, generally aching all over, but it was her neck that was troubling her the most. "Please, go through."

The two officers went into the living room and waited to be instructed on where to sit. They took their seats and PC Granger brought out a statement pad.

"Before we begin, Miss Friar, can you confirm for me that you feel well enough to provide your statement today. If not, we can arrange another day."

"No, no. That's very kind of you, Officer, but I am perfectly well, apart from being a tad stiff from the fall."

"All right. Can you please give me your full name?"

And so it began. Nothing out of the ordinary: Alice had gone to replenish the coffee and to prepare the trolley for the board meeting. She'd had her back to the doorway, so hadn't seen anyone or anything suspicious. Next thing she knew, the bin was ablaze and, being plastic, it melted before it started to burn.

Her exit was blocked, the fire alarms were sounding, and no-one could hear her over the commotion. She stayed low on the floor, crawled across to the external wall, and waited by the window, hoping to see someone look her way. No-one did, and the ceiling was on fire, the flames spreading towards her. She waited as long as she could, but then the window exploded, and the cover on an air vent came off with the force of the blast. She felt herself being sucked into it, so let it happen. Next thing she knew, she was lying on the basement floor and somehow got as far as the ground floor, but not quite to the exit. She passed out and came round sometime later on a stretcher in the car park.

It was straightforward enough. She couldn't tell them anything more than they already knew. Even if she had gone to the trouble of explaining about her synaesthesia and her ability to see people's body odours, it wouldn't have been a lot of use, not with her nose still firmly stuffed in a handkerchief. That was the only part she was annoyed about. If she didn't find Dan and his brother so overpowering, she might have picked up on the person who had done this, and she was certain it was the scoundrel who had murdered Mr. Campion.

At the end of Alice's account, PC Granger read back what she had written.

"Does that sound right?" she asked Alice to confirm.

"Yes, dear."

"If you could sign here, then I will leave you with a copy and my card. If you think of anything else, you phone me at the station, anytime. All right, Miss Friar?"

"Of course." Alice smiled. The police officers let themselves out. Alice made herself a cup of tea and settled down for a read.

***

James called Eleanor a little after one o'clock to say that he'd only just got Oliver home. It had taken four hours to make a journey—on account of Christmas travellers and shoppers and exacerbated by the icy conditions—that normally took less than half that time. He was going to stop in at the office and then head straight back.

Eleanor was missing him already and hoped that he wouldn't do what he usually did when he 'just popped to the office', or she'd be lucky to see him again before tomorrow evening. To think that only a couple of weeks ago, she was considering calling off the whole relationship and asking him to move out. *How things change.* She didn't even have a sense of foreboding about the wedding, although that was a long way off, and they had yet to talk to the priest about whether they could marry in the church, with her being a divorcee and James not being Catholic. If they couldn't, then it wasn't a major problem—for her, anyway. No doubt her mother would have much to say on the matter.

At Eleanor's first wedding, her mother hadn't said much at all, because it had been quick and quiet, in a church up near Newcastle, with Kevin's family present, because they lived nearby. Only Eleanor's immediate family and her closest friends had attended, and even then not all of them. George had stayed away because of Josh, with her approval. Jess was in the middle of her first major court case. Luke was away at university and couldn't make it. Tilly was in hospital, having given birth to Ashleigh the night before. Unfortunately, Ben was there, and for some inexplicable reason had expected to be the one to give Eleanor away. Dad said he didn't mind if it would keep the peace, but she didn't want Ben to do it. In the end, and only to stop an all-out tantrum from her brother, she agreed, and so it was Ben who had walked her down the aisle to marry Doctor Kevin Callaghan.

Not exactly Mr. Perfect, but he was a decent guy. Kev was very quiet and studious—an only child and a bit spoilt, but not a brat, like a lot of the others studying medicine. It was nobody's fault. It wasn't meant to be. They had fallen into the relationship, fell out of it and went their separate ways. They still kept in touch, with Kev offering her lots of advice when she decided to return to medicine. In fact, she hadn't spoken to him since then and thought maybe she ought to give him a call to see how he was doing.

The problem was that his number was on her old mobile phone, which had stopped working a while ago, so getting in touch might be a bit tricky. She wasn't even sure where Kev was working, as he, too, had only given her his mobile number. All she knew was he'd said it was a general practice somewhere in the town where they had bought their house—a dwelling now occupied by a family whom he had the constant misfortune to have to treat and who were well aware that he had lived in the house before them. Ten years on, there was still mail being delivered in both their names.

Eleanor looked at the pile of Christmas cards ready for the post, including one to Kev, and mused over whether she should send it to their old address. It seemed a very funny thing to do, so she decided against it and instead went in search of her old phone, just in case she could get it working long enough to extract his number.

***

Judging by the long list of missed calls, Dan had been trying to call Josh all morning, but the university was a bit of a dead zone, certainly the part where his office was located. In any case, it didn't matter, because, by quirk of coincidence, Sean Tierney had come to tell him the exact same thing Dan had discovered: Alistair Campion and his PA, Alice Friar, had an affair twenty-three years ago.

Sean had been trying to decide all week whether he should share the information, as, by rights, it was covered by 'doctor-patient' confidentiality, and it may well be totally irrelevant. However, he and Josh had this hold over each other, always needing to go one better, and to tell him what he knew was, in part, a play in their ongoing game of one-upmanship. The other reason was that Sean was a nice guy, and he cared what Josh thought.

Having listened to Josh's explanation about the innocent people involved in this horrible mess, Sean concluded there was little point withholding the information any longer. If they could sort it out between them, Alice Friar and Jenny Campion wouldn't need to know anything about it. Unless Alice had something to do with it, which was possible, but unlikely.

Josh stayed silent throughout Sean's rambling justification of why he hadn't said anything sooner and why he'd decided to tell him now, all the while thinking that it was utter drivel. On this occasion, he believed what Sean was telling him, although when it came to the truth, Sean Tierney was decidedly economical. It was what pissed him off so much at university.

"And that's the bottom line, Josh. I don't think it will help anyone to know about this, unless the police indicate it's vital to their investigation. I'm sure you can see where I'm coming from."

"Oh, absolutely. This is the only information you can think of? It still doesn't seem motive enough for murder, attempted murder and arson."

"I grant you that. Really, though, I can't think of anything else. Alistair was a good man."

"So people keep telling me."

"You've not lost your cynical edge after all these years, no?"

"If anything I'm more cynical than ever. Although I take exception to that. Sceptical, maybe."

"I miss being a student sometimes, don't you?"

"*Sometimes.* It was fun. Too much beer and not enough time to drink it."

"I remember you drinking quite a bit of whiskey, as well," Sean remarked with a wink.

"Not half as much as you did. Do you remember that party in the new halls? The one where you dropped the bottle?"

"All down the stairs. Oh, God, yes, I do." Sean laughed. "And it didn't smash until it got to the very bottom. Jesus, what a terrible waste."

Josh laughed, too. They had been good friends when they first started out as undergraduates, with similar attitudes and values, and they were equally serious about their studies. Many of the other students were there purely because psychology 'sounded interesting', but none of them had a clue what it was about and quickly settled into the usual scrape through on minimum effort, maximum fun approach. In contrast, Sean and Josh worked unbelievably hard, most often to be found in the library together, researching assignments long into the evening, or until the staff evicted the pair of them, complete with their precarious hardback skyscrapers and maxed-out library cards.

It was only in their last year that their relationship went awry. They were both heavily involved in working on their dissertations, under the supervision of the same professor, who was living his own academic career through his students and steered them towards research in areas they had no interest in. When Josh had first proposed researching friendship from a psychodynamic perspective, their professor had tried very persuasively to make him change it to something he said was more 'contemporary'. Josh refused, knowing that his lack of cooperation may well cost him his first class.

Sean was much easier to convince, because he wanted it badly enough and knew, like Josh did, that if going against the advice of professors was likely to end with work being downgraded, then the opposite was also true. In short, he sold out. The professor told him what to research, and he followed that lead, not that it was a bad one, because he was still making a career out of it to this day.

"Josh, I know what you think of me," Sean said. Clearly, they had both been engaged in the same thought process, sitting either side of Josh's desk in silence, for heaven knows how long.

"What's that, then, Sean?"

"You think I took the easy option. And I did, I won't lie to you. But you were always more certain to make the grade than I was. I couldn't risk it."

"For the sake of professional integrity?"

"We were undergraduates. What professional integrity?"

"Rubbish! You start your academic life as you mean to go on. And as for me being more likely to make it than you—that's a load of crap, and you know it. You sold out, Sean. I thought you and I were on the same wavelength, had the same values."

"And we do, or else you'd be laying into me for not telling you about Alice Friar."

"That may be so."

"It is so. I'm sorry if I disappointed you, but we got there in the end, didn't we? We have the careers we wanted, even if we did have to slog our guts out and make a few sacrifices along the way. We deserve it and should be proud of each other, not still fighting like this. I was so proud of you. And I admit it, I felt I'd let myself down at the end. I admired you for sticking to your guns. There. I said it."

Josh had no comeback to that. Sean admired him? Was proud of him? After he walked out of the house and never came back? That was why he stopped at Master's level, couldn't stay friends with Sean, who was a bit of a rebound from George, not that he understood that at the time. The further Sean progressed with his studies, the more mercenary he became, to the point where Josh didn't want to start hating him, so he walked away.

"Sean," Josh said eventually. "Would you like to go for a drink? For old times' sake?"

"There's nothing I'd like more," Sean replied with a smile. They both got to their feet, embraced swiftly, and left for the Students' Union. It was the last day of term. That's where everyone else would be.

***

Dan wanted to run the information by Alice before he went anywhere else with it, and he wasn't sure how to broach the subject, which was why he'd tried to get hold of Josh. Still no answer, he was just going to have to try a little tact and diplomacy, neither of which were Dan's strong point. This was a very delicate matter, and if he screwed up, he was going to upset a lot of people, including Adele, who was now so excited about going back to work that he was beginning to think aliens had swapped his girlfriend. It was only a few weeks since he'd had to bribe her to leave the house for the night.

And still she wouldn't marry him. She had her reasons, and they sort of made sense. After the big ceremony and expense of her wedding with Tom—which had been a farce from the outset—she didn't want to go through that again. At the same time, she didn't feel it was right to settle for less, and there was no way her father could afford to pay out twice. Nor should he; Dan had plenty of money to give Adele a huge fancy wedding, but that she would let him.

Adele was completely transparent, and Dan didn't need to be a genius to understand. Even if he hadn't figured it out for himself, she'd confided in Shaunna, who had told Kris, who had told Dan. It was no mystery why she kept turning him down. And it wasn't because she didn't love him. Their commitment to each other was made long before baby Shaunna was born. It was something they'd both tried to leave behind, but it was like they were joined by invisible elastic. Since the day they started school, they'd sat next to each other in every class where boy-girl seating was imposed and most of those where it wasn't.

Thirty years of tried and failed relationships, living apart, always to spring back together. All the baby had done was shorten the elastic. But it didn't ease the bruising Dan's ego took each time she rejected his proposal. Of course, the sensible thing would be to stop asking.

And so, on to Alice. It was good to have friends who were 'in the know', and Aitch had been more than glad to help out, reiterating that if anyone asked, Dan hadn't got it from him. Accordingly, twenty-three years ago, Alice Friar had left Campion's employment for six months and then returned. Her old job as his secretary had become the role of PA, and she wasn't up to it. That was no secret, as in the time she'd been away, Campion Cables had become Campion Holdings PLC and was a far greater entity, making Campion's loyalty to Friar the source of much gossip over the years.

A brief search through the registry uncovered the reason for Alice's leave of absence; she gave birth to a son, twenty-two last birthday and adopted by a local family. On the register, the father was listed as 'unknown', and Dan had a reasonable idea why. There was no other man in Alice's life but Alistair Campion, and it would have destroyed his wife to know that he had fathered another woman's child. By all accounts, it looked like Alice had done the decent thing and given up the baby to save Alistair and spare his wife. Now Dan had to ask her if that was so.

He stopped outside her door and raised his fist, hesitating to practise the questions under his breath once more, to make sure they sounded right. He didn't want to accuse Alice, or her son, of anything. He knocked, and waited.

He knocked again, a little louder. The sound of Christmas carols was just audible from inside, so he knew she was home. She was likely taking a nap, given that she was probably still quite shaken by the fire. He tried one more time, counted to sixty and gave up.

Chapter Twenty-Eight: Amends

It was Sean's round, their third so far, because he'd insisted on buying the first. The second had got them through a very heated discussion about how much Josh owed him for the year's lease on the house. By way of an apology, Josh had accepted the offer of a whiskey chaser, followed by a pint of Guinness—something he'd completely avoided since the last time Sean had insisted; in other words, for a very long time.

"There y'are, Sandison. Get that one down yer," Sean said, putting the two glasses down hard in front of Josh. The more he drank, the more his accent came out. A few students had spotted them in the corner of the bar and noticed that they were both much louder than normal, not to mention the unusualness of them being together. Those on the counselling course had realised long ago that their two lecturers didn't much like each other and had concocted all sorts of stories about why, none of them even remotely accurate.

"So, you were telling me about George," Sean said, even though Josh hadn't even mentioned George.

"I was not!"

"You were so. I remember his name coming up a few times when we were at uni. The same George I take it?"

"It will be. We've been friends since school."

"Just friends?"

"That's a bit forward, Sean. After fifteen years of not talking, I'm hardly about to start sharing my private life with you."

"Ah, that answers that question then."

"It bloody well doesn't. Can we talk about Sophie instead?"

"Sophie? If you like. It'll get you off the hook for now, so. You can tell me about George when you've loosened up a little."

"Maybe. We should ask them to join us later."

"That's a great idea. They won't believe their ears."

Sean went on to talk at great length about Sophie, although any eavesdropper would have thought she was his little sister, not his girlfriend, the way he described her as 'a lovely girl' but a 'pain in the neck', a 'bit of a torment' and someone who he 'gets along with mostly'. By the time he was done, Josh realised that with a change of pronoun, the exact same description would apply to George, and he said as much.

"So you are together, then?"

"No, Sean, we're not, and I wish people would stop asking that." Josh slurped at his beer, wiped the foam from his mouth and belched. "By people I mean psychologists," he explained, gesticulating widely across the table. If he hadn't still had hold of his glass, he'd have knocked it over.

"Are we not people?" Sean sang. "Do we not bleed when you cut us?"

"Yes, you can stop that. What I mean is last year I was at the airport waiting for George. He was in America, you see. Some psychology postgrad asked if I was waiting for my girlfriend."

"See, now that's what it looks like, not that George is a girl. He's definitely all man, and if he wasn't so obviously gay I'd be a little more worried about him and my Soph. They're very close. Did you know that?"

"I did."

Sean finished his pint and pushed the empty glass across to Josh. This was quite possibly the worst idea he'd had since the last time he suggested that he and Sean went drinking. He walked to the bar in what still approximated to a straight line, ordered two pints, and went off to the toilets, knowing that as soon as he took a pee that would be all he'd be doing for the rest of the night, until he fell into a drunken stupor and either wet himself or choked in a pool of his own vomit. Or blood, if he fell in the street. Yes, he was well on the way to being very drunk.

"George? I'm in the Students' Union having a drink," he shouted down the phone, on account of both alcohol and Slade's 'Merry Christmas Everybody' blasting in the background, accompanied by about thirty students.

"I can hear that," George shouted back. "Me and Sophie are in the library. We'll be there in about ten minutes." George hung up quickly; the few remaining students and the librarian were glaring at him, having heard Josh perfectly. Sophie laughed. George blushed.

"He hung up on me!" Josh said, a little offended.

"What now?" Sean shouted over the din.

"I said, George hung up on me."

"Oh." Sean drummed on the table in perfect time with the drum fills in the music. Josh joined in, and they played their way through the next three songs, Sean taking the break in between the last two as an opportunity to get in his round and visit the Gents'.

***

Just before six o'clock, James arrived home and sauntered into the living room, where Eleanor was wrapping the last of the presents for her nephews and nieces.

"Good evening, my lovely Eleanor. I believe we are alone now." James grinned broadly, no concealing his intentions for the rest of the night.

"I can see you're in a good mood," Eleanor remarked, placing the gifts under the tree with all of the others. "What's that behind your back, Mr. Brown?"

"Oh, just a little celebratory drink, Miss Davenport." Eleanor moved towards him.

"Miss Davenport?"

"Doctor Davenport."

"Try again."

"Doctor Brown?"

"That will do nicely," she said, kissing him and at the same time trying to see behind him. He swapped the bottle to his other hand, but she'd already spotted it. It was expensive champagne.

"I will put this on ice and run a bath," he said, trying to pull himself away, but failing. Eleanor ran her hands down his chest, and he closed his eyes, focusing on the thrill of the sensation and the bliss of being there, alone with the woman he loved. Reluctantly, he stepped backwards and she followed, so that they moved together all the way to the kitchen, where they deposited the bottle in the refrigerator, then on to the bathroom.

James held Eleanor at arm's length while he plugged the bath and turned on the taps, and allowed her close again.

She pulled off his jacket and unbuttoned his shirt. He had followed her lead and removed her blouse, unfastening her bra with expert precision, even though he was not well-practised in these matters. Somewhere in the distance, they could hear the phone ringing, but it was too far from this moment to be anything more than a vague awareness. Eleanor pressed her breasts against his chest and started to nibble his neck.

"I suppose we can bathe afterwards," James said, caressing her bare back with his palms. He glanced at the slowly rising water level in the bath; there was no way either of them would last that long.

Eleanor, meanwhile, had unbuckled his belt and was in the process of unzipping his trousers. She let them fall to the floor, and he stepped out of them, along with his shoes.

He raised an eyebrow. "I cannot possibly allow this to continue, when I am standing here in my socks and you are still half-dressed."

She looked down at his feet and laughed. "That's a very good look for you." Once he'd taken off his socks, she stepped out of her trousers and let him remove her knickers. She'd surreptitiously shoved off her own woolly and wholly unsexy socks already.

The bath was now at a sensible level, although not deep enough for what they had in mind, so they waited, teasing each other, kissing nipples, running fingertips across bodies and lips, licking, squeezing and pulling apart just in time. James checked the temperature of the water, turned off the tap and added some bubble bath. He bent over, trying to mix up a bit of lather, an action made all the more difficult by Eleanor running her hand up and down between his thighs.

Slowly, he lowered himself into the bath, and Eleanor knelt in front of him. He cupped the scented water in his hands, tipping it over her breasts, where it fell in tiny waterfalls back into the pool below. She threw her head back, so that her hair hung down behind her, and James caught hold of it, using it to move her towards him. He kissed her hard on the lips, then harder, probing deeper with his tongue, exploring every part of her mouth, her lips, her neck, her breasts, her navel and down. She gasped and thrust against him, barely able to contain it. He drew away and came back again, this time pushing against her, deep inside her, and they moved together as one, soon after climaxing and falling back into the water, panting and satisfied.

"I will get us champagne in a little while," James suggested.

"When it's had more than five minutes to chill?"

"My thoughts exactly," he said, and they both decided that they'd been there long enough already. Eleanor got out first, leaving James to wash, before they arrived at the living room at the same time, he in his dressing gown and she in her flannel pyjamas.

"How sexy," she said.

"You always are," James replied and pulled her down on top of him so that they were face-to-face. The phone started to ring again, but it was just out of reach. James stretched his arm as far as it would go, only succeeding in pushing it further away. It stopped, and he shrugged. "I shall fetch the champagne."

***

The evening in the Students' Union was going marvellously well. Josh had convinced Sean that he was actually allergic to the ingredients in stout and got away with a couple of orange juices by telling him they contained vodka. By the ninth round, Sean was too unsteady to go to the bar himself and sent Sophie and George instead.

"See. Told you," he slurred. "Thick as thieves. Look at the pair of 'em."

Josh squinted in the direction indicated by Sean's swaying arm. He had to agree. They looked like they were together, and if he didn't know George the way he did, he wouldn't have trusted him in the same set of circumstances. Sophie was laughing at something George had said with far too much enthusiasm, but then stopped abruptly, putting her hand to her eye, as if she had something in it. He lifted her chin to get a closer look in the eye and tweaked her nose. She pushed him away, they paid for the drinks and returned to the table and the undisguised jealousy therein.

"What?" George asked innocently.

"Nothing." Josh took his drink from the tray. "'What is it?"

"Bacardi and Coke." George gave him a wink. Josh nodded his appreciation for continuing the deception.

"On the shorts again I see, Joshy," Sean said, raising his glass and clanging it against Josh's with such force that he nearly knocked it out of his hand. "You shouldn't mix them up so, terrible sickness and hangovers from that, you know."

"Don't you worry about me," Josh assured him. "I'll be just fine. Cheers."

"I was saying before to Josh here that you two have got to be close all of a sudden," Sean more or less accused Sophie.

"Not that sudden. We've been doing this course for three months, and we sit next to each other. You'd remember that if you weren't so pissed. Didn't the doctor tell you to lay off alcohol for a week or so?"

"It's been a week. Or so. It's Christmas, balls to doctors. What do they know?"

"That policewoman liked that you were a doctor," Josh said. George nudged him, knowing where this was heading. "She kept going on about it. 'Doctor Tierney' this and 'Doctor Tierney' that. Oh, he's so charming, that 'Doctor Tierney', with his Irish brogue and his lovely hair."

"I don't imagine she said all that, now."

"She may as well've done!"

"You're just a bit envious of the girlies there, are you?" Sean winked with nothing that resembled subtlety. Josh rolled his eyes.

"Well, I'm glad the term's over," George said, trying to change the subject.

"And me," Sophie agreed. "Far too much work. Can't you two make it a bit easier next year?"

"Me? Nothing to do with me," Josh said pompously. "All *Doctor* Tierney's doing. I only teach the damn thing. With great skill and intellect, I might add."

This time, Sean didn't take the bait. "So you do, Josh, so you do. Let's drink to next year," he said and raised his glass again. The four of them clanged together and pulled hard on their glasses. It was a fun night, but a little too close to going off on the wrong track; it looked like George and Sophie had got there just in time.

***

Dan had been phoning Alice all day, but she wasn't answering, and he was worried. A couple of hours would have been fine, but it was a lot longer than that since he'd called round. With all that was going on, he was starting to think there could only be a bad reason for it. It seemed he had no choice but to go round again and check everything was all right.

As he pulled up outside, he noticed that the lights were on, so she had to be home and conscious. Someone was in there; he could see a silhouette moving across the curtains in the living room. He decided that calling through the letterbox was probably the safest way to attract her attention without startling her. He was wrong.

"Alice. It's Dan. Are you all right?"

She almost jumped out of her skin and came scurrying to the door, cautiously lifted the flap of the letterbox and peered through.

"Hello, Dan. What are you doing calling at this late hour?"

"It's only just nine o'clock. I've been trying to get hold of you all afternoon."

"Have you, dear? I haven't been anywhere."

"Is your phone working?" Dan stopped, suddenly realising how ridiculous this was. "Would you let me in so we can stop shouting through the letterbox?"

"Oh, yes, of course." She unlocked the door and opened it to let him into the house.

"That's better."

"Yes. Do come in. I've just made some tea. Would you like a cup?"

"No, thanks. I need to talk to you about something. It's a sensitive matter, but I won't stay long."

"All right, then. Sit down. Sit down." Alice plumped the cushions for Dan, and he sat down. It was a very upright, yet surprisingly comfortable sofa.

"I hate to ask about this, Alice, but I'm sure you can understand that there's something very strange going on, and I think that you and quite a few other people are in danger."

"Oh, I quite agree."

"Good. Well. How do I put this?" Dan ran his fingers through his hair and tried to think back to his earlier rehearsal. *Yes, that's it.* "Now then, Alice, I understand if you don't want to confirm any of what I am about to say. It's entirely up to you. Whatever happens, Adele and I still want you to come and be Shaunna's nanny."

"Adele is still returning to work in January, isn't she?"

"Yes, she is. The thing is…" Dan stumbled again, almost tempted to bottle it and make up some change of subject, but it had to be done, so he forged on. "My friend, he's a police officer, and he's following up on some possible lines of inquiry. Now, he's found out something about your past." Alice became pale and serious. "Don't worry. Only my friend Josh and I know this."

"Is he the police officer?"

"What? Oh. No. But Josh is a counsellor, so he is very good at keeping secrets. Anyway, where was I? Ah, yes. The information from my friend—the police officer, that is—shows you registered the birth of a child, father unknown. Is that correct?"

"A child? Me? I'm not married, dear!"

"If you can tell me anything, it will help a great deal. You see, Josh is in touch with the psychologist at the hospice who used to treat Mr. and Mrs. Campion. He told Josh that Mr.

Campion had an affair." Dan bit his lip. This was awful. "With you."

Silence. Or at least regarding the conversation. Albert was chirping, and the carollers were still carolling, but Alice remained tacit, because she didn't know what to say, and Dan said nothing, because he felt like he was assaulting her. This very private woman, who had tried so hard to keep her past to herself, and here he was trying to rip it from her.

"Your information is reliable," she said quietly, staring into the tea she had been holding in her lap the entire time. "I did have a son, and Alistair is his father. He was adopted, because if Mrs. Campion had ever..." She stopped and sniffed, the tears dribbling down her nose and caught by the cup below, subsumed and mixed with the tea so that they almost never existed, just like her son.

"I understand how hard this is for you, and I'm so sorry," Dan said, taking her hand. She pulled it away.

"Don't. Please." He retracted it. "The colours." He mouthed an 'oh'.

Alice went on. "He hasn't tried to find me. He's twenty-two now. A good-looking young man, just like his father."

That was as much as she could give him, and all he needed to know. Even if she didn't have any idea who or where her son was, Aitch seemed to think they'd tracked him down.

"I'm going now," Dan said, feeling utterly wretched about everything he had put her through. "You make sure you lock your doors tonight, Alice. I promise we'll get to the bottom of this soon."

***

Josh's legs were completely numb from sitting so still with them crossed, in the hope that it would reduce the frequency of his visits to the toilet. In fact, they were so numb that he could feel the blood vessels in his thighs protesting at the cut-off of blood supply, almost as if they were vibrating from the pressure.

"Is that your mobile?" George shouted across the table.

"What?" Josh couldn't hear a thing, with the whole bar singing along to whatever Christmas song happened to be playing.

"I SAID, IS THAT YOUR MOBILE?" George shouted so loudly that half the people around them took out their phones to check for a missed call.

"Oh." Josh giggled. *Damn.* He was going to have to move to get it out of his pocket, and that would be it again. Floodgates open. He looked at the phone and saw five missed calls, all from Eleanor, and then another, coming in. He pressed the button to answer, knowing that somehow he was going to have to get outside to hear her without falling over or wetting himself. He wasn't quite sure that was possible.

"HELLO?" he shouted. "HANG ON A MINUTE!" Slowly, he pushed his way through the crowds, staggering and falling against people, apologising continuously as he made his way towards the doors. It wasn't much quieter outside, and he stuffed a finger in his other ear so he stood some chance of understanding what she was saying. Except it wasn't Eleanor. It was James.

"Hello, Josh? I…we need your help. Come quickly."

"Erm. Yes. OK. I'll be there as soon as I can."

"And please call the police on your way. I think Eleanor might be in great danger."

Chapter Twenty-Nine: Shunt

Josh was cursing under his breath. It was like some inversely proportionate law of the universe: the more urgent one's need for a taxi, the longer it took for it to arrive. And all the while the thoughts were racing around his head. *Ellie in danger? Why isn't she with James? Why didn't I go for a piss before I left the Students' Union?*

He knew the reason James had called him was not for his physical strength. There was a talking job needed doing, and on any other night of the year, he'd have been fully up to the task. Tonight, with four pints of Guinness, two pints of lager—he'd lost count of the whiskeys, and they were doubles—well, he wasn't exactly on top of his game.

For all he had said or thought about Sean Tierney over the years, if they had been sober, Josh would have trusted him to deputise, just as Sean had trusted him with the counselling course. Academia was as important to Sean as Josh's friends were to him—a silent spouse, empowered and sustained by his research.

Yes, those four years of living, working—spending every single minute together—had bestowed an understanding far beyond the comprehension of mere mortals. Desires could not be hidden, lies were an impossible feat. In the time that had lapsed since, each had perfected their own psychic shield to keep out unwanted trespassers, but when they were young, they were open and unafraid, enthralled by their mutual superpower of stripping a mind naked in seconds.

Back, back further in this drunken reminiscence, Josh felt an uneasy twinge, for there had been just one other to make it past the gatekeeper; no tricks of diversion, no sneaking through when he wasn't looking. They just walked right in and set up camp. *Set up camp? Ha!* They brought the bricks and built a castle. But it wasn't Ellie mocking him from across the moat, forever consumed by her own consuming and incapable of knowing his doors were open.

George glanced back from his vantage point on the edge of the kerb. "Have you got your umbrella?"

"When did it start raining?"

A smile teased the outermost creases of his lips. "Taxi won't be long now," he said and returned to his roadside vigil. Sophie shivered, and he pulled her close, inside his coat. *Why is she here again? Ah, yes, that's right. She's Sean's girlfriend, poor thing.*

Earlier, when Josh had returned after James's phone call, it had been his intention to keep his current concerns private, but with the alcohol, his ability to explain was so far from discreet as to almost be a public announcement. Under the circumstances, George suggested they should all go, because they didn't know what they were facing. Josh wasn't entirely happy with the idea, but as always, he would do whatever was necessary to get to Eleanor. *What if we're too late? I'll never forgive myself—*

"Joshua." The voice was like a fist, smashing through the wall of terror. The taxi had finally arrived, and all four of them piled in, heading off at good speed towards Eleanor's apartment block.

"How many therapists does it take to change a light bulb?" Sean joked from the back seat. Sophie shouldered that one, literally. There were no more tasteless gags for the rest of the journey, undertaken in silence other than directions from George on where to turn left, right, then pulling up, opposite Eleanor's building. They immediately saw James standing inside, watching through the window.

George paid the cab driver and climbed out second after Josh, who was already standing, swaying, on the pavement, trying to weigh up the situation. He hadn't called the police, as James had advised. He'd called Dan, who arrived with Andy half a minute later.

"What's going on?" Dan asked, marching straight up to Josh. His eyes were fixed on the car parked directly outside Eleanor's building.

"Not sure, but she's in the car. I can see her, lying down on the back seat."

Dan squinted and saw Josh was right.

"Who's she with?"

"I don't know. Did you get anything more from Alice?"

"Not really. She confirmed what we knew already—about the affair and that she had a son. Aitch came up trumps on that one."

Design or coincidence, Dan didn't know, but Bill Meyer—the new CEO of the defunct Campion Holdings PLC—and his wife had adopted Alice's baby all those years ago. Whether that was sufficient motive to attempt to murder three people, thankfully succeeding only once, was yet to be seen. Dan hoped with all his heart that the body count would stay as it was.

"So do you think that's Alice's son? In the car, I mean?" Josh asked.

"Looks too old to me. He might not even know he was adopted."

"Someone else, then. Fucking hell, this is complicated. Why in God's name did she get in the blasted car? She must know who he is, although…I need to try and get to James, find out if he knows anything more."

"I'll ring Aitch and see if he can get down here with some of the troops," Dan said. He pulled out his mobile phone.

Josh weaved across the road and past the car without looking, although if the man in the front had been paying any attention, he would have spotted the six of them by now. However, James *had* seen Josh and went to the door.

"Come in," he whispered and pulled Josh inside, closing the door quietly behind him.

"What happened?"

"The phone kept ringing, but every time I answered it, there was no-one there, or they hung up. Eleanor answered it and heard someone playing music, she said. She thought she recognised the song, but she wasn't sure."

"That wasn't me, was it? Ringing by accident? My phone's been in my pocket all night, and it's happened before."

"No, it was quiet, other than the music. Then that car pulled up outside, and he knocked at the door. She said she knew who he was. She didn't seem worried. She followed him outside, and they've been in there ever since." James nodded gravely at the dark saloon, its driver still preoccupied with something below the level of the window. Josh squinted in his direction.

"It has to be someone she knows, but I can't see him, it's too dark. Did you hear any of their conversation?"

"Nothing."

"I see. Well, don't worry, James. It will all sort itself out. Believe it or not, there're four therapists here tonight. I'd be amazed if none of us succeed in talking him down, if, indeed, that's what is needed." Josh patted James on the arm and opened the door.

"Thank you. There's just one more thing you need to know." Josh turned back. "He has a knife."

That put a slightly different light on things.

"Can I just use your loo?" Josh asked, and staggered past without waiting for the answer. He got there just in time and threw up, instantly feeling a hundred times better. He swilled water around his mouth and went for the long-awaited pee. On the way to the bathroom, he'd noticed the half-filled champagne glasses in the living room. It was sufficient pause for him to find some new resolve. No lunatic with a knife was going to take his best friend from him. And not from James. He flushed the toilet and walked back outside, across the road to the others.

"OK. Here's the situation. James doesn't know who the man in the car is. I can't tell, either, but Ellie went with him willingly, so she must know him. He's got a knife. James has been calling me since seven-thirty, so she's been in there for almost two hours. Is that copper friend of yours on his way yet, Dan?"

Dan nodded. "About ten minutes away, he said. They were in the middle of an arrest when I called."

"OK." Josh rubbed his hands together.

"What do we do?" Sean asked.

"We wait?" Sophie suggested. Josh nodded.

"No. We can't just wait," George said. "He could turn on her any minute. He's already killed one person. It's not like he's frightened to use a knife, now, is it?"

George had a very valid point. If this was the man who had killed Alistair Campion, he could turn on Eleanor just as easily. However, the likelihood that it was the same man was only slightly less ridiculous than the whole series of events having been isolated attacks that just happened to involve people they were all connected to.

"I think we should wait for the police," Sean said. "We don't know what we're dealing with here."

"Sean's right," Josh agreed.

"That's fucking typical, isn't it?" George snapped. "The first time you speak to each other in years, and what do you do? Cop out, like the pair of bookworms you are."

"All right then, smartarse. What do you suggest?" Josh was glaring at George, something that would usually have resulted in him backing off, but not this time.

"I'll go and talk to him. Dan, you drive round the block. When you get back, make sure you hit his car—a rear shunt should do the trick. Then Andy can open the door and pull him out, and Sophie—you grab Ellie."

They all looked at him as if he were insane.

"Alternatively," he continued, "we can wait till the police get here, he spots them and slashes her throat. It's up to you."

"Hit his car?" Dan repeated incredulously. "Jesus wept, George! That baby cost me a fortune."

"It's just a car!" George said it as loudly as he could without drawing attention to their already conspicuous group. So far, the man in the driver's seat hadn't even looked up.

"I think you've lost it," Josh said.

"You would. You seem to think that all you need to do in these situations is talk your way out with some cleverly measured bullshit. Well, sometimes it requires a bit of brute force. That's Ellie in there. Your best friend."

"Really?" Josh could feel the colour rising in his cheeks, but now was not the time for this. Because it was Eleanor that mattered now, not his feelings for George, nor George's for him. "All right," he relented. "I'll go along with it, but I'm coming to talk to him with you."

"As you like," George replied tersely.

Dan shrugged, returned to his car and started the engine—quietly, for once. He drove off with the lights dipped and disappeared from view at the corner.

"Are you ready?" George asked everyone.

"As we'll ever be," Andy said. He and Sophie crossed the road and stepped back behind the hedge of the building next door to Eleanor's.

"George?" Josh paused to make sure George was paying attention, and to get the words in the right order. "I still think this is crazy, but just in case we don't get stabbed to death in the next five minutes, I'd like us to share a house. I've got used to having you around."

"Thanks. I accept. Now stop being a soft pisshead, and let's get on with it."

They crossed the road, assertively, Josh following George's lead. It was a very alien thing to do, but he was in no fit state for reason or complaint. Sean had wandered off down the street; with no job to perform, he'd decided it was better to keep out of the way.

George walked around to the driver's side of the car and peered through the window. The man in the front was peeling the edges off his mobile phone with a knife, and judging by the precision of his work, it had a very sharp blade. George gulped and tapped on the glass. The man shoved the knife under his seat and looked up. He wound his window down a couple of inches and stared with empty, dark-ringed eyes.

"Hi." George smiled. "Sorry to disturb you. This is our parking space, and I don't wish to be obnoxious or anything, but there're plenty of other spaces, so I wondered if you wouldn't mind moving before my friend returns with the car?"

The man jabbed soundlessly at the top of the dashboard. George peered at what he was pointing at.

"Doctor on call," he read aloud. He couldn't think of a response to that, but he was going to have to. Dan was still nowhere in sight.

Alarm bells rang in Josh's head. He moved closer and looked through the small gap. "Hello, Kev. Fancy seeing you here!"

"Err…h…hello," the man stuttered, taken aback at having been recognised.

"How've you been?" Josh asked, sounding so genuine that George wondered if he'd forgotten Eleanor was lying in the back seat, with her head down and her arms across the top of it, exactly as Kevin had told her to stay until he said otherwise. She was only wearing pyjamas and socks, and she was shivering violently.

"Not too bad," the man replied, bewildered and unsure of what he should do. He was starting to become agitated, and just as George was thinking that now would be a good time for Dan to get back, the screech of tyres sounded at the top end of the road, and Dan's black convertible came tearing down, closely followed by a police car. Dan slammed into the back of Kevin's car.

Kevin lurched forward, smashing his head on the windscreen with such force that it cracked the glass and knocked him unconscious. Andy sprinted over and yanked open the driver's door, pulling Kevin onto the pavement and pinning him face down to the tarmac. Sophie climbed through the front to release the back door and helped Eleanor to sit up. Josh opened the door, took off his coat and wrapped it around Eleanor's shoulders, almost carrying her back to the building, from which James ran, his expression one of both anxiety and relief. Eleanor fell sobbing into his arms, and he steered her inside.

"Nice job, Dan." Detective Inspector Hartley came over and shook Dan's hand. "On this occasion, I'll let you off on the driving without due care and attention."

"Cheers, Aitch," Dan said with a grin. The detective inspector patted him on the shoulder and went inside to speak to Eleanor. Dan looked back to the street, where Andy was still holding Kevin, now conscious again and fighting to get free. Dan went to assist, arriving at the same time as two officers, who cuffed Kevin and pulled him to his feet.

"Kevin Callaghan, you are arrested for murder, two counts of attempted murder and abduction. You do not have to say..." The words faded away as they moved towards the car.

"You OK, bro?"

"Sure am," Andy said, cracking his knuckles.

"That was fun, huh?"

"Fucking awesome. We should do it again sometime." Andy laughed and held up his hand for Dan to high-five.

Chapter Thirty: Minute

Josh didn't have a hangover when he woke up the next day, because he still felt intoxicated and a little bit fuzzy. He hadn't even drunk that much—compared to Sean—although his tolerance of alcohol was very low. Sean had always been able to drink past him and still keep plying him with more, until, as a general rule, he'd end up spending most of the night with his head resting on the toilet seat. Sean insisted it was because he mixed his drinks. Josh didn't believe him, in part because he didn't. He *pretended* to mix his drinks and, in spite of feeling rough as hell, took some comfort from the fact that after all these years, Sean still hadn't figured it out. No, Josh was laying the blame squarely on the Guinness. Well, that, and the whole thing of saving Eleanor from her ex-husband.

Kevin Callaghan. Josh was still having a problem with that one. In all his years as a counsellor, he'd never come across anything quite like it. Stalkers, yes. He'd had to deal with a few of those—students with crushes on their tutors—and they were always quite a challenge, although none had gone so far as to attempt kidnapping at knifepoint. But Kevin? He was well-educated, came from a good, stable family and had a respectable career. What could possibly have happened to turn him into a crazed killer?

To think, Eleanor might have been at risk all those years ago—Josh shuddered and quickly pushed it from his mind. He was sure it would make more sense once his head cleared, but for now, he was content knowing that Alistair Campion's murderer was safely locked away and awaiting a psychiatric consultation.

George was already up and moving around downstairs, which wasn't helping at all. He'd stayed over, because now he lived there it was the thing to do, but also because they needed the company. Once their adrenaline levels returned to normal, they were both shaken, and when he realised he'd put his friends at risk, George had cried. It was the George that Josh knew of old—tough in a crisis, doing what needed to be done—even if most people only got to see his soft side. Josh joked that he should consider training to work in the prison service and in the cold morning light, George was starting to think that it might not be such a bad idea.

***

James and Eleanor stayed in bed until lunchtime, eating toast and sharing stories of Christmas from when they were little. James was trying to distract Eleanor from thinking about the night before, and neither had achieved sleep, disturbing each other as soon as one of them started to drift off because the other was wide awake. In the car, Kevin had kept saying he couldn't believe she'd left him after so long, and try as she might to blot it out, that phrase kept echoing around her head. It was ten years since their divorce finalised. It had been a mutual agreement. They'd stayed on friendly terms. So what was he talking about? Why had he done this? This wasn't the Kevin Callaghan she went through medical school with. It was some deranged psychopath who'd taken over his body.

What worried her more was that he had been watching her every move. He'd talked about the day she put up the tree and the lights packed up, repeated whole conversations she'd had with James, and with Jess and Josh. He said he could have had her back, but for the people who kept getting in the way, stopping her from being where she ought to be: with him.

James lifted her hand and placed it in his own larger, warmer hand. "Stop thinking about him. He is a very sick man," he said gently.

"Clearly. What I don't understand is—"

James shushed her. "We should get up soon and visit Josh and George, to thank them for what they did last night."

"You're right. I didn't know George had it in him, but he saved my life. I'm sure of it."

***

"Krissi?" Jason called through the open door of The Pizza Place. There was no-one in sight, just the sound of stuff being banged around in the kitchen. "Are you there?" he called out again.

Wotto put down the flour, wiped his hands on his apron and turned off his MP3 player. There was someone in the restaurant, and they weren't due to open for a while. Maybe it was another delivery. He went out to see.

"Hello, sir. I'm afraid we're closed."

"I was looking for Krissi Johansson. Is she in yet?"

"Not for another half an hour. Can I help you with anything?"

"Oh, no. Thank you. Can you tell her Jason Meyer called and that…" Jason stopped talking, and the colour faded from his face.

Wotto caught him before his head hit the table. As he fell, he started to convulse, and Wotto had to fight to stay between him and the table pedestal. A few seconds later, it was over. Wotto's mother used to have seizures, caused by the tumour that killed her when he was twelve. Before that, he had stayed up every night to sit with her, to make sure she didn't choke or bang her head. If Mr. Campion hadn't come to the rescue, he'd never have recovered. Then to get this job, after doing time for robbery. It was against company policy, Mr. Campion had told him, but he had a friend who would make sure he was all right.

A few minutes passed before Jason came round, confused and unsure of where he was.

"It's all right, mate," Wotto said gently. "You just had a little fit there."

"Did I? Oh, dear. I didn't take my tablets yesterday. Plus, I've had no sleep." Jason looked down and was pleased to find that he hadn't done anything else embarrassing. He tried to get up.

"No, you stay there. I'll find something you can rest your head on and call Krissi. All right?"

"Thank you," Jason said and relaxed again.

Wotto returned with a pile of chef's aprons and placed them under his head.

"The last twenty-four hours have been shit," Jason said, not really knowing why. After all, he'd never met the guy before; he didn't even know his name. "I got some really bad news last night, then I got arrested. They let me out at two this morning, and I've just been wandering around since, trying to work out what's going on. They didn't even tell me why I was a suspect. Funny, really. Just as you think your life is going in the right direction, it all falls to pieces right on top of you."

"I know what you mean." Wotto hadn't got as far as calling Krissi, but she was there now, so it didn't matter.

"Wotto? Jason? Oh." She took one look at the scene before her and knew immediately what had happened. "You OK, Jay?"

"Yeah. Your chef's been looking after me. He's a star."

"You don't have to tell me that. You want to see him dance. He's brilliant." She smiled at Wotto, who looked bashful.

"Right, well. Now you're here I'll get back to the dough mix. The delivery's come, by the way."

"Cheers," Krissi called, as Wotto disappeared into the kitchen. She sat on the floor next to Jason, her best friend, the goth her mother loved to pretend to hate. She stroked his black hair back from his face.

"You've lost your earring."

"Yeah," Jason said apologetically. Krissi started to scan the floor for the tiny piece of silver jewellery. "I lost it ages ago. I'm sorry."

"It's all right. I've got the other one at home still. You might as well have it, especially if it'll stop you putting one of those stupid tunnels in this ear, too. So, what's up?"

"Oh, you know. Everything. Found out I was adopted, got arrested for murder. The usual."

Krissi sighed and bent down to kiss him on the forehead. It was going to be another crazy day.

***

Dan put the phone down and turned to Andy and Adele. She was nursing Shaunna, simply because Alice had gone to make tea. It was the only chance she got to hold her daughter, although these opportunities did come quite frequently; somehow Adele thought Alice might get on rather well with baby Shaunna's namesake. They could sit for hours and drink tea, just the two of them.

"Right. That explains all that, then," Dan said informatively, even though his end of the conversation didn't explain anything at all.

Andy frowned at his younger brother. "Care to enlighten us?"

"Kevin Callaghan. Ex-husband of Eleanor Davenport?"

"Yes?" Andy and Adele queried in unison. Dan was clearly enjoying spinning it out.

He waited a few seconds longer before continuing. "According to Aitch, Callaghan's got a list of outstanding convictions from Newcastle, Hull, Durham and Lincoln. He thinks he's the next Harold Shipman."

"What? You mean he's a serial killer?" Adele gasped.

"Well, not exactly."

"So, what then?" Andy asked, starting to become impatient.

"He only actually killed Alistair, and by all accounts, he didn't mean to. But he's failed to turn up for trial six times for practising without a licence. That's not including his short spell at the hospice."

"Blimey."

"And it would seem he's been stalking Ellie for the past year."

"Oh, God. That's awful," Adele said. "But why?"

"Since she started seeing James."

"I thought things were all right between Ellie and her ex. She said they both felt the same way."

"Ah, well, she stopped calling him, and she was the only friend he had, so he upped sticks and moved here."

"What a freak."

"Yeah," Dan agreed. "He was trying to take out all of her friends by setting them up. First Jess, then James himself, with Alistair—"

"Jess?" Andy spluttered—a reaction Dan completely misread, although attempting to bluff his way out of it wasn't an option.

"Apparently, Jess went out with him a couple of times, but she called it off."

"Good God." Andy was stunned beyond further comment. After interrogating her about whether she was seeing someone else, he felt awful.

"So. Then he—"

"Surely Jess must've known who he was," Adele thought aloud, ignoring Dan's effort to move on with the explanation.

"She didn't go to Ellie's wedding," he said quickly. "Then he—"

"Why not?" Adele persisted.

"I don't bloody know, do I?" Dan snapped. "Then he—"

"She was on her first big case," Andy said. Adele mouthed an 'oh'.

Dan took a deep breath and made a third, somewhat more forceful attempt to finish what he was saying.

"*Then he* had a go at Josh—with that Sean Tierney bloke from the university—then you and me." He pointed to Andy.

That brought him back to his senses. "Alice. Of course. And we were there on the day of the fire."

"Yeah. Anyway, I'd best let Josh know so he can tell Ellie."

"Bloody hell. I suppose at least it keeps us on our toes."

"It certainly does. Oh. And just one more thing." Dan moved in close to tell them in a quiet voice. "You know Krissi's weird emo mate? Jonathan, is it?"

"Jason," Adele corrected.

"Yeah, him. He's Alice's son."

***

James checked Eleanor's list again. If he hadn't been the same way himself, it would have been a real irritation, but he could see the logic in checking that everything was packed and ready to go. They were only going for three days, not that anyone would think it to look in the boot and the back seat. Poor little Oliver was stuck in the middle of piles of presents, although he didn't seem to mind one bit. He was pretending to read all of the labels and poking little holes in the wrapping paper.

"Oliver. Stop it!" James said sternly through the open window, and Oliver did so immediately.

They had their clothes in the big suitcase, Oliver's clothes in the little suitcase, which his mother had thrown out the door when James went to pick him up. James had been set to ask if she'd mind Oliver coming for Christmas, but she'd beaten him to it by ordaining that that was what would happen. It worked out well all round, and still the woman hated the sight of him.

The gifts were all in the car. Josh had the spare key so he could keep an eye on the place. There was just this one last item on the list that James couldn't make sense of, so he couldn't check whether it had been done or not.

"Eleanor. Are you ready yet?"

"One minute," she called from inside the hallway. That's all she needed. Just one more minute, and she'd be there.

"It's getting late. Have we got everything?"

"Have you checked the list?"

"Yes. It's all done, but for this last item. What is PT, please?"

"Hang on. I'll be out in a second."

"All right. I'll wait in the car." James walked around to the driver's side and climbed in. "Are you happy there, young man?" he called over his shoulder to Oliver.

"Where's Enna?" he asked, as she came running down the front steps.

"Here I am, Oliver." She climbed into the car, breathless. "All set?"

"Yes, if you have dealt with this PT thing."

"Oh, you can cross that off."

James ran his pen across the letters. "What is it?" he asked, his expression one of puzzlement.

"Pregnancy test," Eleanor replied breezily. "I guess Santa was right, after all."

***

Alice arrived home, went straight up the stairs to her bedroom and to her bedside table, her hands shaking as she fumbled around in the dark for the tiny object she had lifted from the boardroom floor and concealed all this time. Its shape made it difficult to lift from the lining of the drawer, smooth and flat, yet not so flat that she could possibly have missed it. Finally, she grasped it, carefully, between her thumb and forefinger, and dropped it onto the palm of her other hand: a minuscule, hooped, silver earring.

The story continues in…

The Harder They Fall
(Hiding Behind The Couch Season Three)

A fatal plane crash in Kathmandu, a fateful high school reunion, the wedding of the year and a honeymoon that eight best friends will never forget…

* * * * *

Dan touched his brother's arm, simultaneously envious and amazed at Andy's ability to sleep so soundly while travelling. He'd slumbered his way through the vast majority of the twelve hours they had spent in the air, not to mention most of the seven endured waiting for their onward flight from Istanbul, and now, with the noise of the engines once again rising to a scream, he barely stirred. Dan poked him in the side and he jumped.

"What you do that for?" Andy slurred with a stretch and a yawn.

"We're about to land." Dan lifted the blind with the intention of demonstrating how close to ground level they were, only to be met by an impenetrable haze of greyish-white. "Or not," he said dubiously. The engines continued to screech as the plane banked left and upwards.

"Whoa. Has it been like this the whole way?" Andy was now fully awake and in need of a pee, but it would have to wait. There was no way he'd be allowed out of his seat.

"Only for the last half hour or so." Dan closed his eyes. The turbulence was giving him nausea, and he was desperate to get off the plane. He wasn't about to tell his brother that though, for it would be an admission of weakness: something else Andy was better at than he was. It hadn't gone unnoticed, but Andy did the decent thing and didn't say a word.

"Good, err, afternoon." The voice of the pilot came through the speakers again, not sounding quite so confident as he had a few minutes previously. "Unfortunately we have had to abort the landing, due to poor visibility. We have five minutes' worth of fuel, so we will not be diverting, but we will be taking a different approach within the next couple of minutes. Please remain in your seats. Thank you."

* * * * *

"Sorry. Was there something else?" Lois removed the earphone again.

"Lovely earrings."

"Thanks. They were a twenty-first birthday present. Aquamarine is my birthstone—oh, that reminds me. I meant to give you this earlier." She lifted a stack of files and retrieved a small, white envelope from underneath, handing it across. Jess read the names on the front and frowned.

"Andrew and Jessica Jeffries?"

"It's from—"

"Your Uncle Rob. I know! It's a very old and not funny joke. He's getting married again, is he?"

"Not that I'm aware of."

"Oh." Jess had been convinced it was a wedding invitation. "I guess I'd better open it and see what's inside, then."

***

Eleanor arrived home to find an empty house, other than the white envelope addressed to 'Ms. Eleanor Davenport' and propped against the coffee jar. She frowned and set down the shopping bags, too curious to leave it until everything was put away.

"Oh, good Lord," she said, as she pulled the card from the envelope and realised what it was.

***

Adele was vacuuming the hall when the post arrived and didn't notice until the pitch of the vacuum cleaner changed. She tugged the envelope away from the nozzle and squinted at the writing on the front.

"Mr. Daniel Jeffries and Miss Adele Reeves. Hmm." She placed it on the telephone table—she had always wanted one, even though the phone was in the living room—and continued on her way, little Shaunna tottering along behind her with her own mini pink version of an upright Hoover, complete with the 'H' logo on the front, but with the batteries removed so it didn't play that dreadful music all the time.

***

Kris pushed the envelope across the table to Shaunna and raised an eyebrow.

"What's this?" she asked, reading the front. It was addressed to the pair of them.

"You'll never guess," was all he said. She eyed him suspiciously.

"It best not be money from Andy again."

"Can't be, with both our names on it," he pointed out.

Shaunna shrugged and put it down on the table, picking up her cup of tea instead. Kris tutted and continued folding the washing.

***

George and Sophie were idly 'chatting' away, when all of a sudden a message appeared from Joe, whom he hadn't spoken to since he signed over the ranch and was almost certain he'd removed from his 'friends'.

Hey, G. How's it going?
Great, thanks. How're you?
I'm good. Just came on to say there's a fax come for you.
Who from?
It's back in the office. I was going to send it on, but don't have a number.

George pondered for a moment. They didn't have a fax machine, so that wasn't an option.

Can you scan it and email it?
Sure thing. It'll be a couple of hours. OK?
OK. Thanks.

And then Joe was gone again. George sat back and rubbed his chin. It was the first time he'd ever received a fax and a bit of a mystery all round.

***

It was bound to be a bit of a challenge, sharing a house after living alone for so long, Josh reasoned, as he noted the sound of the running shower and observed the laptop strewn across the sofa, stupid little email icon blinking in the corner of the screen. He took a deep breath and continued through to the kitchen to make coffee, trying to reason away his annoyance. The thing was, George knew it irritated him, which made him wonder if he'd done it deliberately, but then he did it every time he was studying at home, so it was probably an innocent, but nonetheless infuriating, oversight.

Josh filled the kettle and thumbed through the post, sifting out the obvious junk mail and restacking the rest for later perusal, stopping when he came to the white, handwritten envelope and examining it in an attempt to establish whether it was by a hand he recognised. He kept it in view as he spooned coffee into two cups—an assumption on his part—concluding that it was from someone male with a manual job—scrawled, angular, block capitals, it wasn't difficult—but otherwise he didn't have the faintest idea. The kettle came to the boil just as the bathroom door opened and closed, George bounding down the stairs a couple of seconds later, with a towel around his waist.

"You want a coffee?" Josh called.

"Please," came the reply.

Josh poured the water into the cups and carried them, envelope dangling from his teeth, through to the living room, catching a glimpse of his housemate slow-stepping up the stairs whilst he tried to read his computer screen, hold up the towel and coordinate his legs, all at the same time. Josh tutted and put down the coffees, carefully peeling the envelope away from where it had stuck to his lip. He opened it and pulled out the card inside.

"What on Earth?" George stopped dead and almost dropped his towel.

"Oh no," Josh said, re-reading to confirm that his eyes weren't deceiving him.

"You're not going to believe this, but I've just received—"

About the Author

Debbie McGowan is an author and publisher based in a semi-rural corner of Lancashire, England. She writes character-driven, realist fiction, celebrating life, love and relationships. A working class girl, she 'ran away' to London at seventeen, was homeless, unemployed and then homeless again, interspersed with animal rights activism (all legal, honest ;)) and volunteer work as a mental health advocate. At twenty-five, she went back to college to study social science—tough with two toddlers, but they had a 'stay at home' dad, so it worked itself out. These days, the toddlers are young women (much to their chagrin), and Debbie teaches undergraduate students, writes novels and runs an independent publishing company, occasionally grabbing an hour of sleep where she can.

Social Media Links

Twitter: www.twitter.com/writerdebmcg
Facebook: www.facebook.com/DebbieMcGowanAuthor
and www.facebook.com/beatentrackpublishing
YouTube: www.youtube.com/deb248211
Tumblr: writerdebmcg.tumblr.com
LinkedIn: uk.linkedin.com/in/writerdebmcg
Google+: google.com/+DebbieMcGowan
Goodreads: www.goodreads.com/DebbieMcGowan
Website: www.debbiemcgowan.co.uk

By the Author

Stand-Alone Stories

Champagne

Sugar and Sawdust

Cherry Pop Valentine

When Skies Have Fallen

Coming Up ~ co-written with Al Stewart

Checking Him Out Series

Checking Him Out (Book One)

Checking Him Out For the Holidays (Novella)

Hiding Out (Novella - Noah and Matty)

Taking Him On (Book Two - Noah and Matty)

Checking In (Book Three)

The Making of Us (Book Four - Jesse and Leigh - exp. 2016)

Seeds of Tyrone Series

~ co-written with Raine O'Tierney

Leaving Flowers (Book One)

Where the Grass is Greener (Book Two)

Christmas Craic and Mistletoe (Book Three)

Sci-fi/Fantasy Light

And The Walls Came Tumbling Down

No Dice

Double Six

General

'Time to Go' in *Story Salon Big Book of Stories*

Hiding Behind The Couch Series

The ongoing story of 'The Circle'…
Nine friends from high school;
Nine friends for life.

The Story So Far…

in chronological order:
novellas and short novels are 'stand-alone' stories, but tie in with the series. Think Middle Earth—well, more Middle England, but with a social conscience!

Beginnings (Novella)
Ruminations (Novel)
Class-A (Short Story - exp. 2016)
Hiding Behind The Couch (Season One)
No Time Like The Present (Season Two)
The Harder They Fall (Season Three)
Crying in the Rain (Novel)
First Christmas (Novella)
In The Stars Part I: Capricorn–Gemini (Season Four)
Breaking Waves (Novella)
In The Stars Part II: Cancer–Sagittarius (Season Five)
A Midnight Clear (Novella)
Red Hot Christmas (Novella)
Two By Two (Season Six)
Hiding Out (Novella)
Breakfast at Cordelia's Aquarium (Short Story)
Chain of Secrets (Novella)
Those Jeffries Boys (Novel)
The WAG and The Scoundrel (Gray Fisher #1)
Reunions (Season Seven - exp. 2016)

www.hidingbehindthecouch.com
www.debbiemcgowan.co.uk

Beaten Track Publishing

Lightning Source UK Ltd.
Milton Keynes UK
UKOW01f0841090916

282597UK00002B/30/P